METROPOLITAN GRAND THEATRE

Under the direction of
Hermann Gorelocke, Marvin Tyler

GEORGE GIBSON DORIS STEIN
present

HAROLD WHITNEY

ZIGGY BRONOWSKY TARA MARTIN

in

GALILEO

with DEE BRUNEL
ELIZABETH STROMAN THOMAS PAUL
LEYDON JOHNSTONE KEN IRVING

and ADRIENNE FEUER

Music and Lyrics by JERRY TRIMLOCK
Book and Original Conception by MICHAEL KERSHON

Set and costume design	Lighting design by
KARL-HEINZ ZEISS	SAM MOLE

Musical Direction by	Orchestration and Dance Arrangements by
STAN WARBURG	PETER LOMBARDY

Sound design by	Press Representative	General Manager
SAM LEE	NORMAN NAFF	GENE LANDAU

Assistant Director	Casting	Production Stage Manager
FLY GOLD	CATHY NEWMAN	CHARLIE BRODSKY

Choreography by
TAM TOPP

Directed by
ROSS BOARDMAN

RUNNING
DOWN
BROADWAY

Mike Ockrent

RUNNING DOWN BROADWAY

A Novel

NICK HERN BOOKS

London

A Nick Hern Book

Running Down Broadway first published in 1992
by Nick Hern Books
A Random Century Company, 20 Vauxhall Bridge Road
London SW1V 2SA

Copyright © 1992 by Mike Ockrent

British Library Cataloguing-in-Publication Data

Ockrent, Mike
Running down Broadway
I. Title
823.914[F]

ISBN 1 85459 131 2

Typeset by ⊼ Tek Art Ltd, Addiscombe, Croydon, Surrey
Printed and bound in Great Britain by
Mackays of Chatham PLC, Chatham, Kent

For Tash, Ben and my Mother.
And for Susie – without whose determined opposition
this book would never have been written.

Acknowledgements

To Stephen Sondheim for the use of lines from 'Being Alive', © 1970, Range Road Music Inc., Quartet Music Inc. and Rilting Music Inc. And to Ted Chapin and the Estate of Rodgers and Hammerstein for lines from 'June Is Bustin' Out All Over'. Copyright © 1945 by Williamson Music. Copyright Renewed. International Copyright Secured. All Rights Reserved. Used by Permission.

For their help, encouragement and advice,
many thanks to Jane Price, Ken Ludwig,
Sara Randall and Nick Hern.

The Two Rules of Showbusiness:
1. Every Show has a victim.
2. Don't be that victim.
(Boris Aronson)

PROLOGUE

'This is musical comedy! You gotta be deaf *an'* blind, Ross! The ending doesn't work an' you know it!'

November 5th 1969, 45th Street, New York. Outside the stage door of Irving Berlin's old theatre, the Music Box, two men are arguing. At the end of their fight they will not talk to each other for twenty-two years.

'You're becoming repetitious, George . . .'

George Gibson is carrying a walking stick. He is waving it threateningly at Ross Boardman. 'Well, I'm gonna tell you it again . . . Change that finale! It's killing the show!'

Ross is smiling. 'Calm down George. Waving your stick's not going to get me to change anything.'

George calms down. 'You're a smart man, Ross. I don't have to tell you how to direct . . .'

'And I don't tell you how to produce . . .'

'You know what you have to do! Any waiter, any barman in this street, any garbage collector will tell you . . .' and he begins to get excited again – Ross watches his face turn red, beads of sweat appear at his temples. '. . . You gotta finish this show on a laugh! You need a button! This is *The Love Boat*, for Chrissake Ross, not some fucking Shakespeare crap in the Park!'

The director puts his face close to the producer's. 'Forget it, George. This is the night before we open. We've frozen the show. The ending's staying as it is. That's how you're going to see it when we open tomorrow!'

The director walks away up 45th Street towards Broadway.

The producer stares at his receding back. Tears well in his eyes. His frustrated shout echoes along the empty street: 'You're finished! Through! You hear me, you schmuck! You'll never work on Broadway again!'

1

1

There was only one appointment listed in John Lewis's filofax for Monday March 30th, 1992. Carefully underlined in red he had written next to the time 9.45 a.m.: – *Kill myself*. Lewis sat at his desk staring at what he had written three weeks earlier. It was now Friday. He had two full days of his life left.

He opened a drawer in his desk and extracted his calculator from the jumble of jottings, stationery, stamps, elastic bands and show leaflets. He wrote:

$$\begin{aligned}
\text{(years)} \quad 42 \times 365 &= 15,330 \\
\text{(months)} \quad 9 \times 4 \times 7 &= 252 \\
\text{(days)} &= \underline{12} \\
\text{TOTAL DAYS OF MY LIFE} \quad & 15,594
\end{aligned}$$

And added: 'Survived the eighties (just about). The Ninja nineties offer little. I have lived 15,594 days (not counting leap years) and the last 7,500 days have been crap . . .'

Later in the morning, still not dressed, eyes closed, he was lying in his bed. Willesden High Road, normally busy and noisy, was unnaturally quiet below him. From his bedside radio cassette player Barbra Streisand was softly singing:

> Someone to hold you too close
> Someone to hurt you too deep
> Someone to sit in your chair
> And ruin your sleep
> And make you aware of being alive . . .

'Jesus, I love musicals,' he said aloud but there was no-one to hear him.

The afternoon was clear and surprisingly warm. Lewis, driving through Hampstead with the sun roof of his Peugeot 205 open, had to a certain extent cheered up. He was off to play tennis with his old schoolboy chum, now a doctor, Jason Moore.

'As frightened as you,' sang Barbra over the car speakers, 'of being alive . . .'

Jason was already on the court practising his serves.

'Wotcha,' Jason said by way of a greeting.

'Sorry I'm late. Had to drop by and see my dad.'

'How is he?' Jason asked as they began to knock up.

'Pretty frail – then what would you expect? He's lived through thirty thousand days.' He gave the ball too hard a swipe and it sailed out into the road. 'He's 80. I've been working it all out.'

'Be careful,' said Jason. 'They cost a quid each!'

Lewis lost the first set 6–1. Taking a breather, they sat on the clubhouse steps sipping Coke and soaking up weak rays of London sun.

'How's the newspaper business?' Jason asked as if he was really interested. 'Did you get that job you went after?'

Christ, how'd he remember that?! Lewis was aghast. *Lie? No point. Jason reads the Guardian.* 'No,' he said weakly.

'Oh, sorry to hear that,' Jason said studying the strings of his racket.

Then, unbidden, the loathsome, grinning face of Clive North popped into Lewis's mind. Clive North had just been appointed Senior Arts Correspondent and Feature writer on the Guardian – a job Lewis had wanted desperately. But North was the Son of God and God, who hated Lewis, had organised this appointment to hammer the final nail into Lewis's coffin. At least this was what Lewis had figured out. On the face of it, both he and North were equal in every way: the same age, the same qualifications, seven years working together on the Arts page of the Independent and in the business the same amount of time. But Lewis knew such a list was merely superficial, not getting at the real contrast between Son of God and Lewis of Willesden. North was a strikingly handsome 6'2" and Lewis a mean 5'5". North had independent means, was married to a leading Harley Street paediatrician, had two beautiful children and lived in a large detached house with a carriage drive in Swiss Cottage. Lewis lived alone in a one room bed-sit in the dull greyness of North London suburbia . . .

'Are you okay about it?' Jason asked.

Or was it simply that North was a better journalist? The facts unfortunately, spoke for themselves. North knew the *right* people. The *right* people were his friends. Therefore it wasn't surprising, for heaven's sake, he heard the gossip first, knew the backgrounds . . .

No mistake, Clive North was largely responsible for Monday's date with death.

Lewis took a sip of Coke. 'No. Actually I'm not okay about it.' Lewis had a sudden desire to tell Jason everything, cry on his shoulder, beg for help. 'I've been feeling bloody. Want to hear about it?' After all Jason was his oldest friend and a doctor.

Jason didn't. 'Tell me later,' he said. 'I'm getting cold. Let's play.'

But later the moment had passed. Lewis was soundly beaten 6–1, 6–0, 6–1 and as he sat dejectedly watching Jason devouring a Mars Bar he was forced to listen to his friend complaining about the bad deal the doctors were getting under the Government's new health plan. Lewis watched an attractive young mother being coached whilst her baby was screaming from its carrycot on the sidelines. 'Well, whatever you say,' Lewis heard himself say, 'Margaret Thatcher was a true radical. She's shaken up the system.'

The mother missed a volley. *I could go for her*, Lewis thought.

'You don't really believe that, d'you?' Jason was horrified. 'Aren't you a member of the Labour Party?'

'I was,' Lewis replied. 'Then three years ago I joined the SDP. Now I suppose I should support the Liberal Democrats but I don't think I really believe in anything. I'm viewless in Gaza. Washed up. Finished.'

Jason looked at his watch. 'Well, sorry old chap. Got to be off. On duty. How you fixed on Monday? It's my half day.'

'Sorry,' said Lewis. 'I've got important business on Monday.'

Lewis had ordered a '75 Margaux. He had wanted to impress but he had wanted to enjoy it too. Even under sentence of death there was little point in not having the best wine with dinner. Tennis had given him a healthy appetite.

'It's very sweet of you to do this,' Diana said as she took her first sip.

'Well, you can't beat a Margaux.' Lewis took a sip too.

'No, I meant phoning me up, asking me out – after . . . I mean after everything that happened.'

Diana was unfinished business. Maybe if this evening turned out well and Diana could be persuaded to come back to the flat, Monday might be postponable. Lewis gazed at her, wanting her. Her perfect, pellucid blue eyes gazed back almost into his but just missed. She seemed to be looking at his right ear. Instinctively he felt for his lobe – a pimple? – or his usual give-away burning ears? She leant forward and scooped away a handful of long blonde hair that fell across her face.

She whispered, 'Isn't that Clive North over there?'

Lewis quickly glanced over his right shoulder. Clive North was sitting a few tables away animatedly telling a story to an attentive group. Lewis noted how easily he held their attention. They only had eyes for him. North came to the end of his story and his whole table laughed so loudly that other diners looked towards them. 'Don't you think he looks like a young Robert Redford?' Diana whispered. Then as an afterthought: 'But perhaps better looking?'

Lewis turned back and looked past her into the mirror behind her head. The restaurant, appropriately called Le Miroir, was decorated entirely in mirrors – floor to ceiling reflections. There, interestingly framed, was his own small head: short-cut dark hair, dull pool-green eyes, too large nose, turned-down mouth – his whole expression, he noted with alarm, a reflection of his inner despair. And just behind his head in the mirror, Clive North sitting back enjoying his moment of approbation. Fleetingly their eyes met, but nothing was communicated.

'Isn't that Jack Nicholson with him?' Diana whispered again, a hint of suppressed excitement in her voice. 'I read he was in town. Filming. God, the people Clive knows!'

'I've been wanting to talk to you properly for months,' Lewis said in an attempt to regain control of the evening, 'ever since that wonderful weekend in Dover.'

'Wasn't it Bournemouth?' Diana was picking at her melon and Parma ham.

'Dover. I was doing a piece on the influence of Europe on the culture of the Channel ports. You came down on the Friday evening.'

'I could've sworn it was Bournemouth or Eastbourne. Still it was a year or so ago.'

'Actually it was two years ago, almost. The point is, Diana, and I know this sounds really naff but . . .', he stopped as the waiter cleared their dishes, 'there hasn't been a day when I haven't thought about you. I wanted you to know that and remember it . . . and I hoped that tonight, for old times' sake . . .'

'You had my number, Johnny, you could have called. When you didn't, I assumed you weren't interested.'

'That's not true! Of course I was interested. I think I loved you.'

'Funny way of showing it. A sexy weekend then not another word for two years.'

'I did try but either your son or your husband picked up the phone. I'd panic and hang up.'

'Silly boy. You could have been more imaginative. I thought you were mad at me because I'd picked up that photographer in the pub.'

'I meant to ask you about that . . .'

'He drove me back to London.'

'And . . .?'

'And what?' she opened her eyes wide with mock innocence and smiled saucily.

Lewis couldn't let it go. 'It's just that we'd had those two wonderful nights – I'd thought I was going to drive you back . . . You did rather abandon me . . .'

'He was an old friend. We'd done assignments for the paper together. I had to be careful. Besides he knew Simon. Not that *that* mattered when he discovered Simon was away till the Monday.' She smiled and blinked a few times. 'It took me 45 minutes to get him out of the house.'

'Oh, so you didn't . . . er?' Lewis clutched at straws.

'They're going.' Diana was looking past him again. 'Isn't that what's-his-name with them . . . er . . .?'

Lewis looked in the mirror. 'Steven Spielberg. I tried to interview him once.'

'Oh?' she looked interested.

'He was too busy.'

'Clive North did a piece on him in the Guardian last week. Did you see it? Smashing. I do miss journalism. I've got the kids though – and that's a full-time job – and Simon's home all the time – writing. We've never been happier. By the way, I hope you don't mind but I told Simon we were having dinner together and he said he'd join us for coffee.'

2

As he went up in the lift, Lewis rechecked the memo from his editor.

> Saturday 28th March, 11.00 a.m. Savoy Hotel, Room 323.
> Ross Boardman will be waiting for you.

But the celebrated Broadway director wasn't. Instead a Japanese chambermaid was making the bed. 'Currin, currin,' she waved him in.

'I'm looking for Mr Boardman,' Lewis explained politely.

'Nobuddy ear. Sit please.'

Lewis did and pulled out the notes he had prepared for the interview. He began to absorb the details. 'R.B. born March 28th, 1932 Washington, DC . . .'

'You Lonnon?' the maid enquired obscurely as she tucked a pillow into a starched pillowslip.

'I'm sorry?'

"O'Amelican?' she smiled and pointed to him.

'No, no I'm English.'

'Japanese,' she pointed to herself.

'Oh good,' said Lewis . . . and he read on: 'Began his career as an actor in 1951 . . .'

'Me hubband die in Japan ten year ago. Ah come 'ere stay me blest flend. You like Lonnon?'

Lewis nodded and read on. 'In 1953 R.B. turns to directing. *The Three Musketeers*, at the newly opened Arena Stage in Washington, is his auspicious début.'

'You like musical teata? He like musical teata.' She pointed to a half-opened suitcase. 'I like musical teata. I see *Cats*. You see *Cats*?'

'Mmmm.'

'You like *Cats*? *Phanto o' Opela*?' She laughed. 'S'velly good – no? Me, ah plefer wok of Stephen Sondhei'. Yer know?'

Lewis grunted. 'Boardman directed his first Broadway musical: *Owen's Valley* October 1954 at age 22. At the time the youngest director working on Broadway . . .'

'Into Woods, Tweeny Todd.'

'Sorry I kept you.' A rich clear voice.

Startled, Lewis shot to his feet. 'I made myself at home. Hope you don't mind?'

'Relax,' Ross Boardman tossed his fur-trimmed coat on to a chair. 'Coffee?'

As Ross telephoned room service Lewis composed himself and observed the director. About 5'11" . . . A surprisingly soft face, jowly, a kind of Walter Matthau look. Is there a twinkle in the eyes? Lewis considered this. He had learned from bitter experience that twinklers were dangerous to interview. The shock of red hair shot through with grey was the most significant feature . . .

'You didn't bring the champagne?'

Lewis's fears materialised. He felt himself blushing. *I was supposed to bring champagne? No-one told me!*

'Champagne? No, was I supposed to?'

'It's my 60th birthday – and I've no-one to celebrate with, 'cept you.'

Lewis glanced at his memo. 'R.B. born March 28th 1932 . . .' *Oh, shit! North wouldn't have made this mistake. He'd have at least said, 'Happy Birthday . . .'*

He mumbled apologies.

'Never mind! We're in luck!' Ross seemed in high spirits. Was he, Lewis wondered, a little high? 'My gallant producer would never allow me to forget I'm 60. Nearer death, you see! Besides which,' he added confidentially, 'he's trying to be nice to me for once. Look what he sent!'

He bounded across the room and threw open the mini-fridge to reveal a dozen bottles of Bollinger crammed inside.

'He's always sending me liquor. I guess he's hoping to destroy my liver.'

'Ah finish da loom, good luck wid da show, Meesta Baldman. Ah off now tull next wick. Bye na,' and she swept out.

'Grab those glasses!' Ross ordered. Lewis obliged.

'Not too much for me,' Lewis said, as Ross filled two tumblers. 'It's a little early.'

'Champagne lifts a veil. It makes you see the world as it is. It's never too early for that. The coffee will keep you sober.' He placed himself in a chair and nursed his drink. 'Shoot.'

They settled into the interview. Ross Boardman was relaxed, confident. The champagne temporarily liberated Lewis from gloom. On form he was encyclopaedic about musical theatre. His wide knowledge impressed the American, who chatted freely about his youth in Washington, his early influences: O'Neill, Synge, Shaw.

'Did you get to much musical theatre?' Lewis accepted his second glassful.

'No. I wasn't interested at the time. I thought it a lower form of theatre art.'

'*Oklahoma* made no impression on you?'

'Sure. I saw it. I enjoyed it. But I enjoyed productions of O'Neill more. It seemed to me that musical theatre skirted emotion, tended inevitably to sentimentality. I still associated it with Viennese Operetta – a form I detested.'

Lewis made copious notes. The second glass of champagne had gone straight to his head. He cursed his missed breakfast. No coffee arrived.

'What changed your mind?'

Ross poured himself a third glass and topped up Lewis's.

'Heard of the Arena Stage in Washington?'

Lewis nodded.

'It was inaugurated in 1950. I joined the acting company in early 1951. I was in at the beginning so to speak. Guess you could say I didn't keep my mouth shut. Had opinions about everything. Still do. So the company pushed me to direct. Maybe they reckoned I'd be a better director than an actor. After that I never wanted to act again.'

'You directed *The Three Musk*-hic-*teers* first. Wasn't that a strange de-hic-cision?' The champagne had given him hiccups. He apologised. 'I mean why didn't you start with a Shaw or one of your favourites?'

'The project was suggested to me and it seemed a challenge. They gave me a long rehearsal period and although I had adapted it, I improvised with the actors around the text within the given situations.'

'Hick!' *Oh, shit.*

'I brought in a local composer and we added some tunes. All the rehearsal techniques that I still use I developed for that show.'

'Such as . . .?'

'Such as getting the actors to research the period, improvisation, that kinda thing.'

Lewis hiccupped again. 'Sorry.'

'You want me to give you a fright or anything . . .?'

'No, I'll be fine. *Musketeers* was very successful, right?'

'Sure. We got a great notice in Variety. A lot of folks flew in to see what we'd done. Specially the Broadway guys.' He sniffed his champagne thoughtfully. Then he looked up. 'Where's that coffee?'

'Is that when you first met George Gibson?' Lewis noted the shadow that seemed to cross Ross's face at the mention of the celebrated producer's name. He decided to tread warily. The clashes between Boardman and Gibson were legendary; two Titans struggling for sovereignty of the Broadway stage.

'Yeah,' Ross said, suddenly getting up and disappearing into the bathroom.

Lewis sat there finishing his third glass, musing. Write this up tomorrow, he thought. *Last thing before oblivion.* He tried not to listen to the fanfare of sneezes and farts emanating from behind the closed bathroom door. *Boardman is a do-er. I'm an observer. If I had been a do-er, would I be in the mess I'm in? Those who do, do; those who can't, write about it.* He poured himself another glass of champagne.

We're all inextricably linked together . . .

Sounds of flushing before Ross emerged sniffing. He seemed calmer, more ethereal. He stood for a moment at the window staring at a police boat racing down the Thames.

'George saw the show and without a word went back to New York the same night. Next day there was a case of champagne waiting for me at the stage door. The note with it read "Congratulations. Call me." It was signed "Gibs". I called and he sent me the first draft of *Owen's Valley*.'

'And nothing was the same again.' Lewis heard himself slur slightly. The champagne wasn't lifting his veils.

'*Owen's Valley* changed my life completely. After Broadway, I directed it in London, Paris, Sydney and Munich. The New York Times, hailed me "the leading director of his generation". This was echoed by The Times in London, le Monde in Paris and the Süddeutsche Zeitung in Bavaria. Only the Australian Times was less effusive! I was under thirty and damned successful. There were girls to be had in every town, in every company . . . Where the hell are they now!' He laughed uproariously.

'I've read that you revolutionised the Broadway rehearsal progress . . . *process.*' Lewis was now having to make a determined effort to hold himself together. His head was spinning and the words were jumbling up. All the suppressed emotion welled up inside. Ross was smiling. *God, can he tell the state of me*? Where was that coffee?

'Putting into practice everything I'd tried on *Musketeers*. See, I had only directed one piece. I had never ever been in a musical. I had to invent my own rules. I simply decided that if the

11

methodology worked once there was a good chance it would work again.'

Suddenly Lewis felt unbearably claustrophobic. He loosened his collar. Then those unmistakable signs of nausea . . . Bravely, he carried on.

'Can we move on to the project you're working on now? It's with Mr Gibson again, right . . . ?'

'*Galileo* . . . We open in Washington in December, on Broadway in February next year.'

'Right. This musical will be your third collaboration in 35 years. You must have a very special relationship. Can you talk about it?'

But even as he finished the question the tears came, streaming down his face. A curious phenomenon. His body, he realised, was out of control. 'Kind of an allergy, I reckon,' he managed to gasp.

'Can I get you something?' Ross towered above him solicitously. 'More champagne . . . ?'

A spasm gripped Lewis's stomach; he tasted champagne bile . . . In this weakened state he was no match for alcohol. *Is this the way to leave the world? Is there no alternative?* At that moment, he felt nothing but self-hatred. The weeks of despair had left him drained of energy as well as hope.

And then, just as the bottomless, black pit opened before him, the germ of an idea popped into his befuddled brain.

Ross watched as Lewis tried to make it to the bathroom . . .

3

The following morning, Julie Page, a newcomer and one of the younger sub-editors on the Independent, perching on the edge of Lewis's desk, was doubled up with laughter. She was part of a small group listening to Lewis's tale of woe.

'What happened then?' she gasped. 'I mean, after you threw up on his floor.'

'I felt better,' Lewis told the assembly, 'sort of purged.' He toyed with his computer terminal not looking up. Why tell them everything? He hadn't meant to tell the whole office, only Julie. The rest had wandered over. It was too personal. Too revealing.

'What did Boardman do?' Julie asked. She was a breezy, attractive girl-next-door type – a fresh complexion, hair pulled back from her face, held in place with what looked like a giant red paperclip. She occupied the adjacent desk.

'Not a lot. Picked up the phone and asked for housekeeping. Then he called room service to find out what happened to the coffee. The Japanese lady came back and cleaned up. End of story.'

Disappointed, the crowd dispersed back to their blinking computer terminals and work-in-progress. Julie went back to her desk. For a while, both of them returned to work, Lewis finishing his Boardman article with the help of a pile of reference books, Julie cutting and re-arranging a book review. Presently Lewis pushed back his chair bringing him close to Julie's desk. He looked at her over the top of her VDU. She smiled at him.

He said, 'Actually, there is a bit more to tell. Want to hear?'

'About what?'

'About the couple of seconds it took between my being sick and passing out.'

'You want to tell me, right?' Julie smiled and crossed her legs.

'Yes, actually. You see my life was changed in that moment. Completely. Utterly . . .'

As he talked he watched for any sign of contempt. But there was none

13

'. . . Just before I hit the deck I *knew* what I had to do. When I revived I was a different person.'

Julie looked doubtful. 'How different?'

The phone rang on his desk. It was the Arts Editor responding to his request for a brief meeting. He had to go now.

'How about a drink at lunchtime?' Julie asked. 'Then you can finish your story.'

'Okay. Great! I got to see the Boss. Meet you at one?'

He smiled at her and hurried off. It occurred to Julie that that was the first time she had seen Lewis smile.

The Angel on the City Road was jammed with Sunday drinkers. Julie and Lewis were crowded into one corner clutching gin and tonics, their ploughman's lunch squeezed on to a shelf beside them. Lewis had asked her if she was enjoying her new job.

'Enjoy isn't the word. Ecstasy would be closer.' She radiated vitality. The crowd pressed in and their bodies touched. 'You look a lot happier. More relaxed. Has something happened?'

Lewis sipped his drink, then said, 'I've just handed in my notice.'

'Oh dear,' said Julie. 'And I was just getting to like you.'

He paused for a moment. 'I've been through a bit of a crisis you see. Everything was going wrong . . . work, personal relation-ships. I felt . . . well, I just felt I could see the future and I didn't like it. Do you need a refill?'

'No, I'm fine, go on.' Her eyes shone brightly.

'I was even contemplating fairly drastic solutions.'

'Like what?'

Uncomfortable with specifics, Lewis avoided a direct answer. 'Then yesterday, in the Savoy, coming to, staring at the mess I'd made, I suddenly felt exhilarated. It was extraordinary.' Julie's body was hot, pressed against him. 'It was as if a veil lifted. I went back to interviewing Boardman somehow cleansed.'

'Your Road to Damascus?'

'Sort of. Well, we carried on talking and I was much more relaxed. Eventually we got to talking about the musical he's starting in August. Whilst he was describing it to me I realised I wasn't listening to a word. I'd gone into a kind of trance – a transcendental moment. Time stood still, and suddenly I under-stood what had happened before I'd blacked out . . . I knew what I had to do. This was quite . . . well, for me, you know . . . I mean I just don't get transcendental moments. I spend most of my time contemplating where I went wrong in the past – never what I should do in the future. Anyway, to cut a long story short my flash was – pack up the job, pack up the flat, pack up London and everything here – go to New York and be a part of it – New York, New York.'

'Emigrate you mean?'

'No. I don't think so. Just be a fly on the wall of Boardman and Gibson's next show. I want it to be like those old movies about Broadway I've watched all my life. If I leave it any longer it might not be there. Boardman said he'd only give it 20 more years. It's the end of an era – he thinks.'

'Well, he's 60,' Julie said. 'He would.'

'Perhaps. I've never been to New York.'

'Nor me.'

'Want to come?'

'Don't be daft. I've only just started here.'

'You could come and visit me.'

'Possibly. I've two weeks in the summer. Maybe. So what did Boardman say when you asked him?'

'I didn't.'

'What?'

'Ask him. I couldn't. Not in the interview. Not ethical somehow. I'm going to try to phone him this afternoon. But I can't imagine he would mind. No, it's George Gibson who might prove harder to persuade.'

Lewis tried all afternoon to reach Boardman. He left messages at the Savoy, at the National Theatre where he knew he had gone for some meetings. He'd even tried the Garrick Club (Boardman had spoken proudly of his reciprocal membership through the Players Club in New York). Nothing. Sitting at home, 7.30 in the evening, his calls still not returned, he decided to try the producer instead. International telephone enquiries gave him the telephone number of George Gibson Productions on the 39th floor of 1515 Broadway.

Somewhat surprised to find anyone answering on Sunday, Lewis lied and introduced himself as the deputy Arts Editor of the Independent from London. But the lady on the other end told him (in a tone measured, polite, but uninterested) Mr Gibson was away for the weekend and could he please get in touch with Mr Gibson's press representative, Norman Naff. Lewis wasn't sure he heard right.

'Naff, did you say?'

'Sure,' she affirmed and offered his home number.

'I rather wanted to speak to Mr Gibson personally,' Lewis explained. 'You see it's rather more personal than that.'

The woman was firm, said she could take Lewis's number but if she could offer a bit of advice, Norman Naff was the best person to talk to . . .

Lewis dialled Naff's number.

'And what can I do for you, Jaahn?' Norman Naff breathed down the phone as if he was talking to a lover. Lewis explained that he was taking leave of absence from his paper to write a book about the forthcoming Boardman/Gibson production of the new musical *Galileo*.

'You see, Mr Naff, I'd like to get Mr Gibson and Mr Boardman's permission to be a fly on the wall right through the production. I interviewed Mr Boardman in London yesterday and I understand from him that when he goes back to New York he'll be starting the whole process – meeting the writers, designers, etcetera. Can you please talk to Mr Gibson for me . . .?'

Naff interrupted, 'He's in France.'

'Oh.'

Did Naff at that point put his hand over the telephone and mutter to someone, 'Pick up the extension, get a load of this'? Lewis thought so.

'Anyway,' Lewis bravely continued, 'if you can either contact him in France or give me his number . . .'

'Gotcha, Jaahn,' Naff said. 'Here's what you gotta do. Put all this down on paper and include your résumé, list all your publications . . .books . . .'

Lewis interrupted. 'Thing is, Mr Naff, I can send you copies of my recent articles but I've not written any books. This would be my first. I'm good though and I'd be no trouble I assure you.'

'Okay,' Naff laughed, 'I believe you Jaahn. Now I'm gonna give you my fax number. You got access to a machine?'

'Yes.'

'Then send me your best material an' if I like it, I'll talk to Gibs for you. You gotta get Ross's permission too, you know.'

'I got on very well with him. I've left messages, I'll keep trying.'

They exchanged telephone and fax numbers.

Lewis dialled the Savoy again. The operator informed him that there was a 'Do not disturb' block on Ross Boardman's extension. When he tried again half-an-hour later the extension rang but there was no reply. He left another message.

It took Lewis until midnight to choose which articles to send to Norman Naff. He eliminated those that were too provocative and favoured those that were wide-ranging, descriptive and chatty. Populist stuff. The kind of thing press representatives like. At 2.00 a.m., happy with his selection, he went to the office and faxed it to Naff.

Later, back in Willesden, in his pyjamas, ready for bed, with white Tipp-Ex, Lewis blanked out Monday's appointment with annihilation.

16

4

'I really am very sorry about all this,' Michael Kershon whispered as he led Ross Boardman up the aisle of the Piccadilly Theatre. Michael was the bookwriter for *Galileo*. The auditorium was dark and they had to pick their way carefully. In fact there were two sources of light that partly illuminated their journey to the deserted stalls bar: the working lights on the stage and a light set up on a makeshift desk that straddled several rows of seats approximately at the centre of the auditorium. Ross and Michael had left two people sitting at the desk.

'It's okay,' Ross said politely. He was carrying a bulky script with 'GALILEO' embossed on the front. 'I know how it is.'

In fact he was distressed by the whole situation. He had arrived in London late on Easter Monday still exhausted after opening Dekker's *The Shoemaker's Holiday* at the Long Wharf Theatre in New Haven. He used to be able to shake off the tiredness in three or four days after opening a show. Now it took a week. With jet lag considerably longer. The plan was to phone Michael on arrival to arrange when and where they would meet to start discussions on the third draft of the script.

Ross had phoned Michael's home from the Savoy. Michael's wife, Heather, answered. Heather, who knew Ross slightly, was most apologetic on Michael's behalf. She explained that Michael had tried several times to reach Ross in New Haven to tell him of an unexpected conflict in dates. Because the wife of the producer was expecting a baby, the audition dates for Michael's new play, to be produced in London in June, had been re-scheduled for the same days that Ross was to be in London. Could they, therefore, make a start in the bar of the Piccadilly Theatre? Ross had been left with no choice.

The stalls bar was a dreary place of faded crimson wallpaper, more suitable for a crush of playgoers than for a script conference. The men found two high bar stools. Ross, hunched up, tense and eager to start work, put his feet up on a low bar table. Michael, nine years Ross's junior, dapper in a well-cut Italian grey suit, bright red tie, Stephane Kélian high black boots, resembling an accountant rather than one of England's most respected and successful playwrights, perched daintily, and rubbed his thighs.

Ross asked: 'Who've you cast so far?'

Michael glanced back through the open double doors and in the distance, on the stage, a young actress was auditioning, reading with a deputy stage manager. 'We think we've got Alec Guinness and Julie Walters. Did I send you a copy of it, Ross?' The director shook his head. 'Would you be interested?'

'Sure. I'd love to read it. Did you get the latest tape from Jerry?'

'"Play for Love" and "Anna's Song"? If my lad's reaction is anything to go by, we have two hits. I like them, too. What about you?'

'Writing love songs comes easy to Jerry. Most other composers find that the hardest.' Ross stretched out his legs. 'The struggle for originality is not something that troubles him.'

Michael sighed.

Ross continued. 'He has yet to tackle the difficult stuff – the conflict material . . . you know. Old Galileo versus the papal court . . . the Cardinal's number . . . that kinda thing.'

Michael rocked backward and forward. 'I spoke to Jerry on Monday. We've set aside the week after next to work together in New York. Will you be there?'

'Sure,' Ross said. 'Can I set an agenda for this week?'

'Go ahead.'

'One. We have to make some basic decisions about the shape of the whole piece. The arc of it. We have to . . .'

Michael interrupted. 'You still have problems with that in this draft? Didn't I do what you wanted?'

'I still wanna work on it,' Ross said. 'We've all got different views on the balance between the two sides of the story. George is pushing, as you know, for still more emphasis on the young ones. You and I are going for the meat – for Old Galileo's religious and political problems. Which should be the key storyline? We have to figure this out.'

Michael sniffed. 'What's going on here, Ross? I can't work like this. You and George had better get your acts together. You're pushing for more politics and philosophy, he doesn't give a toss about all that. At the meeting last week he . . .'

Now Ross interrupted him. 'Meeting? What meeting?'

'George was passing through London on his way to Nice and he asked me to have lunch with him.'

'And you discussed the script in detail?' Ross was surprised and angry. The director should have been the conduit to the writer.

'In detail yes. In between asides about anything and everything else we got through a lot of detail.'

Ross went silent. Michael, of course, wanted to satisfy both his director and producer. But they were pulling separate ways and he was becoming confused. I have a right to be angry, Ross thought. The writer must be protected. George's way of operating leads to chaos. Yeah, George is behaving true to character. No surprise.

Michael Kershon correctly read the moment and diffused the tension with a smile. 'Don't worry Ross, I understand the situation. I look upon this whole show as an interesting exercise in balance – poetic imagination and truth balanced against popular culture. I'm not against that – like Shaw, I despise idealists. Besides, this is my first musical – it would be nice if it worked.'

'I have specifics,' Ross said. 'We'll go through what we have line-by-line. I want us to be in complete agreement by the time we next sit down with Jerry.'

5

The Mercedes maintained a stately pace as it proceeded along RN 98 between Nice and Antibes. In the back seat the two passengers were gazing silently out of the left-hand window at the magnificent view. It was a crystal clear late spring afternoon with just a hint of northerly wind. The chauffeur had suggested his passengers keep the tartan blanket handy: the Mistral was forecast to blow later in the evening. Antibes was lighting up – it was a twinkling carpet of stars on the floor of the valley – visible intermittently through the pines as the car climbed towards Valbonne. The land, the sea and the sky seemed to be as one – a pale, grey-blue sheet.

The chauffeur, a goodlooking young Frenchman, immaculate in grey double-breasted suit and peaked cap, drove carefully but glanced into his mirror at every opportunity. Only recently recruited to the Compagnie des Voitures Executives (Côte d'Azur), François was still fascinated by his passengers, especially those typified by Dee. He'd put her age at 30-ish, that of her companion 70 or more. She was enveloped in fur worth thousands of dollars while the dense blue smoke from the old man's cigar created a miasma in the rear so noxious François thought one breath might be sufficient to induce terminal lung disease. He watched as Dee delved into her bag and produced a Marlboro which she lit with a disposable Bic lighter. Not my type, he thought, despite those long legs. Dancer's legs. Très sexy. He'd seen many like them in the presentation copies of Vogue and Paris Match placed in the limousine for clients. Blonde, yes, he liked American blondes, but a bad skin. And thin lips. He glanced again. Dee was studying her face in a tiny mirror. From her bag she pulled out a tub of Clinique face lotion and dabbed at her cheeks, took a drag from her cigarette, exhaled then dabbed some more.

She saw him in the mirror watching her. *I like the look of you too, Mr Driver.*

He smiled and understood. Well, maybe . . .

The old man began to cough. Dee Gibson delved inside her purse and found a pastille – he sucked, coughed, breathed heavily – then opened the window to let out smoke and let in cool evening air.

François turned off the main road. They were now travelling uphill through dense woodland. Dee saw lights through the trees. 'Hey, Gibsy, I think I see it.'

George Gibson grunted affirmatively and tossed the cigar butt out of the window careless of the danger to the forest.

They stopped outside grand iron gates which slowly, automatically, began to open. Quickly Dee finished her face – primped up her hair – and tidied away her implements. The car bumped along a rough, unmade road, turned a corner and there, set on a promontory overlooking a vast valley was a meticulously restored 12th-century monastery.

'Holy shit!!' Dee said, awestruck at the beauty of Doris Stein's property. They swept past a Romanesque bell tower, subtly lit from spotlights concealed in olive trees.

'Cost two million. Got pictures an' other stuff worth twenty,' George said. But he wasn't impressed. Art collectors mystified him. Why pay millions for something you need only look at once?

The road stopped some way from the house. To the right the ground fell away sharply, rock strewn and wild, then levelling out in a tangle of undergrowth, pine and wild herb bushes. Concealed in this verdant mass, the remains of early dwellings – broken stone bories.

A fox, startled, darted away. Dee, first out of the car, pulled up the collar of her coat against the chilling wind blowing hard. She stood, open-mouthed, her tongue moistening those too thin lips, her senses ravished by the sweet perfume of the herbs, the eerie howl of the Mistral, the magnificence of the vista.

George, climbing out of the other side, cast not one look at the view. Before him was a substantial tiered terrace leading, by way of ancient stone steps, ramps and paths, up to the house. Lights hidden in manicured clumps of thyme and lavender signalled the way. Circular stone tables and benches were arranged at strategic spots to allow tranquil summer picnics, some artfully placed close to medieval stone sinks and small fountains. From above, as George cleaned the corners of his mouth with the thumb and index finger of his right hand, a figure silhouetted against a bright chandelier was emerging from the house. A small dog skipped out from behind this figure and yapped wildly at the guests.

'Hiya, Doris!' George shouted over the wind.

The shout caused Dee to turn. François was directly behind her closing the car door she had left open. As she turned, they came face-to-face, unexpectedly close. The French boy's look was now unmistakably frank and sexual, suddenly aroused by the accidental proximity of the American girl. Flattered, Dee, for a brief moment, gazed at him.

'Merci,' she said and moved off round the car to join her husband.

'Merci, Madame,' François muttered politely.

Doris Stein awaited her guests on the top terrace. 'Quiet, Roget!' The dog settled on to his stomach, paws out in front. She watched the slow ascent of her old friend, his arm linked with his young wife. 'C'mon George, you can make it, or is Dee still sapping all your strength?' she shouted and laughed. But the wind blew the remark away. Only Roget heard it.

After the hugs and kisses, Doris slipped her arm through George's and briskly escorted her guests past the pool towards the house. 'You can float and take in the view – see it's a mirror pool – the water comes to the top. It's solar heated. I'll show you round. The house was once a monastery . . .'

The interior of the house was palatial, furnished with impeccable taste. Its heart was the Old Monks' Refectory, high and galleried, now part library, part sitting room. Standing in front of an enormous Provençale fireplace, logs blazing, Paul Etienne, arms folded, casually dressed, a long grey scarf draped about him, waited to be introduced to Doris's guests.

'All you see I owe to Paul,' Doris explained as they sipped Kir Royale prepared and served by Doris's housekeeper. 'He has designed and chosen everything. Even those Monets and Pisarros. Exquisite, don't you think?'

'Adorable,' said Dee, studying them closely.

Doris came and stood beside her. 'When Daddy died I phoned Paul in Paris from the Hamptons. I said 'Get on Concorde, Paul, get your butt over here fast.' We went through Daddy's house and chose the best of the art, had it crated and shipped here before the rest of the family knew what was happening. When they complained I paid them off!' She laughed gaily then caught Dee's eye. 'They never appreciated Daddy's collection. Art was something only he and I shared. I think his collection somehow made him feel less guilty about being a merchant, an industrialist.'

She sat on a Napoleon III couch and watched the logs crackle and pop. 'When he finally retired from plastic mouldings he would spend hours with these paintings. They were his number one love. I miss him, but when I look at the collection a bit of him's here, enjoying them with me. I like that.'

22

'It's a great place, Doris,' George Gibson said, bored already. He lolled restlessly in an armchair. A self-professed man of action he needed to make deals not chit-chat. Besides, he knew all about Doris and her father. Six years ago Doris went from rich to seriously rich. With the death of Sam Stein she became one of the world's richest women. 'Sure beats that other joint you had over here. That apartment in Nice.'

Doris nursed her drink and sniffed. 'Sure does. D'you want to talk before dinner, George?'

'Yeah. Let's get the business over. Then relax.'

Doris reached over to a straw basket and tossed another log on to the fire. George looked at Dee and she got the message.

'I'm gonna explore outside while you guys talk,' she said, smiling at her hostess. Paul offered to show her round but Doris insisted he stay with her. Dee stepped out through the double glass doors separating the refectory from the lengthy booklined corridor that led to other rooms and staff quarters.

'Paul, sit by me.' Doris patted the seat of the couch and Paul dutifully sat beside her. George hadn't met the man before but he'd heard plenty. For example, how Doris had come to rely on him not just for interior design. Thing was, Doris was more than George's principal investor, over the years she had become a partner and a friend. He treasured this and resented the third party.

'You're looking too thin, Doris,' George said. 'You still dieting?' She looks anaemic, George thought. Not healthy. Older too. At any rate older than the 51 years he knew her to be. 'We'll have to walk round you twice to see you once, Doris. I'm gonna have to fatten you up! When you're next back in the city I'll take you to Deli Delite on 45th. We've redone the whole place. You're gonna love it. Cheesecake like Lindy's was! It'll give you a backside, Doris.'

'Enough already,' she flapped her hand. 'I want to talk *Galileo*.' Paul handed her a Gauloise which he had already lit. He's too fucking familiar, George thought. Gays always liked Doris. They swarmed around her – the Queen Bee.

'I read the what-is-it, third draft.' Doris exhaled through her nose as she spoke. Paul was already fetching the script that had been carefully placed on a side-table under the lamp. Ready and waiting.

'Voilà!' he said with a flourish.

'It still stinks, George. C'mon doesn't it?'

'Sure, it still needs work. But you gotta give 'em some credit, Doris. It's a hundred per cent better than it was.'

'A hundred per cent of drek, George, is still drek. What you

23

gonna do about it?' She crossed her bony legs and leaned forward somewhat defiantly. Paul whispered something and she swiftly replied: 'Merde, darling. Shit.'

'Shit! Shit . . .!'

Coincidentally, outside on the terrace, Dee, on a mission of discovery in the dark had just broken her heel on a medieval paving stone. She peered around. The wind had dropped, the night air was now warm and sweet smelling. Twenty feet away she saw several dim lights concealed in bushes of wild thyme. Clutching the damaged shoe and broken heel she gamely hopped towards the illumination soon finding herself beside the swimming pool and its dark, still water. She knelt by the light to examine the breakage. Clearly there was nothing to be done. The shoe was damaged beyond repair.

She sat on the stone terrace and gazed into the water. *I wonder how warm it is?* She tested it with her finger. It was, as Doris had said, heated. And inviting.

Then her heart missed a beat. Suddenly she was aware that someone was close by in the shadows, watching.

The chauffeur? That's a nice thought . . .

Perhaps it was her imagination? She let her finger remain in the pool for a while longer as she thought about this situation.

A twig snapped close by. Now she was sure. *I know . . .* She smiled to herself. *If he's going to play Peeping Tom, I'll give him something to peep at . . .*

'Doris,' George was saying sharply. 'I'm not about to fire anyone. Ross is in London this week working on the next draft of the book with Kershon.'

Paul was whispering to Doris again – eager to learn and be loved, irritating George.

'Le livre, darling,' Doris explained patiently. 'In a musical, the book is the words, the scenes between the songs. Michael Kershon is writing the book.'

'He's done more than that, Doris – he structures the goddamn thing. It's his idea, Paul – the whole michagasse an' it's gonna be brilliant. I've brought a couple more songs Jerry's composed. He's just recorded a demo of the love duet between Young Galileo an' Marina Gamba. Where's your stereo, Doris?'

24

He held out a cassette.

'Donnez-moi,' Paul said merrily. 'I do it!'

'Picture the scene, Doris!' George got up and paced the room excitedly, the stage set of a square in Padua, circa 1593, vivid in his mind. Doris, kicking off her shoes, curled up on the couch. 'Galileo, young, handsome, just been appointed some kinda associate professor at the University of Padua. He's got all this suppressed energy, right . . .'

The opening chords of the song suddenly blasted out into the room.

'HOLD IT!! GODDAMNIT!' George shouted, glaring angrily at Paul.

The Frenchman apologised and switched off the stereo.

'He's in love with Marina, okay?' George continued crossly. 'She's beautiful, right, in that dark Italian way, but she ain't bright. She's the daughter of the guy who makes pannetto . . .'

'I know the background, George . . .'

George pulled out a cigar. 'Sure, sure but you gotta see the picture to get the song, okay? Wassis? Rodin right?'

'Iss an erlee Rodin. Le Poing Serré.' Paul had joined him at an exquisite small statue on a pedestal. 'Ze Clenched Fist, I zink you call it.'

'S'political? Or what?'

'Non, non, pas de tout . . . iss poetical not political.' Paul laughed.

George didn't get the joke and looked at the Frenchman suspiciously before continuing. 'Galileo's ambitious, see and he's been having an affair with Guido Ubaldi's wife – Anna. Guido's been his patron, supported him, helped him – and now Galileo's been pulling a fast one on him. Guido doesn't know about his wife's affair. So Galileo has these two women who both love him – but one's married, okay. Marina and Galileo have this big bust-up in the main square, Galileo's angry. He's about to go off then Marina starts to sing this song to him. She's sitting on the steps of the Basilica de Sumptin' . . .'

'Basilica de Santo,' Paul said helpfully.

'Okay, okay . . !' George said testily, lighting his cigar. 'Play the tape for Chrissakes!'

> Precious moments that I live
> Each hour that you give
> Gives me strength,
> Makes me whole . . .

25

The warm water supported and caressed Dee as she floated naked on the surface. *Is he there? Watching?* She closed her eyes, her heart beat faster as her imagination took over. *I come out of the pool, wet, dripping wet. I look around for a towel and he's there, standing, watching me, motionless. I look at him, he at me. He smiles. No words. We both know what we want. I look down, shyly, embarrassed at my nakedness . . . He takes a step toward me. Suddenly he's kissing me. I tear at his jacket, his shirt until he too is naked. He takes me in his arms, his maleness hard against me . . .* She opened her eyes. *Jesus Christ, 'his maleness hard against me'? What is this? I'm a married woman and this is romantic fiction! What's happening to me? Okay! I'm at Doris Stein's for dinner . . ! I gotta take control here . . .* Staring up at the canopy of stars, she quietly hummed along as her friend, Jerry, and his girlfriend, Debbie, sang 'Play for Love'. It was her favourite track and she could just hear it coming from the house. She'd told George that it would make a sensational single . . . *We hit the deck . . . The stones are cold but I don't give a shit . . . I open to him . . . He tears into me . . . His face above me, contorted with effort as he possesses me completely, totally. Stop it! Sonofabitch! Control, control . . .* She rolled over, excited and disturbed, and slowly swam across the pool. *Are you watching and wanting me, Mr Frenchman with the tight ass? Jesus . . ! Think about the music!* The music was important to her: Jerry Trimlock, the composer, had been her lover before she married George. It had been her idea that George hire Jerry to write the score for *Galileo*. George had wanted someone new and young. *George always wants someone new and young. I'm young . . . An' I wanna be fucked . . .* Now he treated Jerry like his son, which was fine by her.

She reached the side of the pool. The water lapped at the edge and there she rested, her head on her arms.

Again the movement in the darkness.

'Is anyone there?' she whispered.

After a moment's hesitation, out of the dark, François came to her.

'C'est moi, Madame,' he said gently.

'Well, hello,' said Dee looking up at him, his head silhouetted against the stars. 'Are you real?'

'Excusez-moi?'

'If you're real, you wanna get me a towel?'

26

. . . with me,
Play with me,
Play for me
Play for Loooove.

Big chords on the synthesised track and Debbie's powerful voice
finished off the 'v' and 'e' with a flourish that made Love into
Lover. Then two final chords.

Doris, who had been tapping in time to the number with a
pencil, was nodding appreciatively by the end. 'Jerry's good. The
music's great.'

'Jerry's a genius, Doris,' George agreed.

'Sure. The music's gonna be okay. Tu l'aimes, Paul?' Her accent
was recognisably American but nevertheless surprisingly good.

'C'est formidable. Very, 'ow you say, 'ummable.'

Doris looked at her watch. 'No, the problem's the book. See,
what I think is happening is that Ross is pushing Michael to
concentrate too much on Old Galileo's story. The Inquisition. All
that political stuff.'

'Yeah, I know.' George was retrieving his tape from the stereo
system. 'I'm gettin' Michael to fix that. Fact is, Jerry's best at
writing songs for the kids in the show – that's what the audience
wants anyway. They wanna see how Galileo makes it with the
girls. If Ross angles the whole thing to Galileo screwing with the
Church, Jerry won't be able to write that. See, I know his
limitations.'

'Well, for a start,' Doris said, 'Ross never wanted Jerry, did he?
He wanted Sondheim or one of the other older guys. He's resistant
to him.' She was leaning forward again, waving her spectacles at
George. 'I'm tellin' ya George, if it comes to it we need Jerry more
than Ross. Directors are two-a-penny. There's a coupla good
English directors . . . We don't want another *Love Boat* for
heaven's sake.'

That was a cruel dig. Muscular spasms tightened the skin on
George's face and he ground his teeth. *Love Boat,* the last show
Boardman and Gibson had produced together in 1959 had run five
performances on Broadway. It was Gibson's biggest disaster. They
had all suffered. Boardman didn't work on Broadway for five
years. And George's luck didn't turn again till the mid-eighties. It
said a lot for Doris's character that despite vast losses she'd stuck
by him.

'We ain't gonna have another *Love Boat,* Doris,' George said
firmly. 'You can be sure of that. *Love Boat* was crap. Albert
Schweitzer couldn't have cured that garbage. But there's not a

director on Broadway with a better track record, for Chrissakes. Name me one American director who over the past decade's done better work? Believe me, only Boardman can bring this off. He's got the experience and the style. Okay, so he's a pain in the butt! That's my problem. I know how to deal with him. How to get the work out of him . . . But we got the A-Team, Doris!'

He sat down next to her on the couch and held her hand. Paul, sensitive to the situation, announced he was going to check the progress of the crêpes with Chef. 'Quelque chose de spéciale,' he said, kissing his fingers as he left the room.

After a moment George said: '*Galileo*'s gonna be the most important show of my life, Doris. It's not gonna fail. Whatever it takes to make it work I'm gonna do. It's going to bring musical production back to America, Doris . . .'

Doris sat admiring the passion and determination. This was the old George speaking, the George of 30 years ago, the George with fire in his guts, who was afraid of nothing and no-one. The George who took on the unions and the theatre owners in the fifties and cleaned up Broadway. The George who fearlessly fed the press any story, good or bad, about himself or others, but did it for the show – to make the show, that wonderful show, work, run, survive, give pleasure and happiness to millions, make Broadway History. She loved this man sitting next to her, old, wrinkled, grey-haired but so alive!

'. . . Believe me, Doris,' she heard him say, 'this is gonna be it. The last one, the biggest but the last. After this, I'm gonna retire to San Diego with Dee.'

The kitchen was busy. Paul, with Chef watching, was testing a crêpe that was to be the highlight of the meal. Two local helpers were arranging the hors d'oeuvres on decorative Dutch serving plates.

Dee and François warmed themselves up next to the large country stove. Communication between them was minimal – Dee spoke no French and François no English. Their common language was their youth and their mutual attraction. Outside, despite the language barrier, he had understood her need for a towel. He had instantly run into the house and procured one from the house-keeper. He delivered it whilst modestly averting his eyes, and had returned to the kitchen for a glass of champagne. Dee had quickly dressed.

Half-an-hour later, in the candlelit dining room, George and Dee

Gibson, together with their hosts, sat chatting optimistically about the show whilst enjoying Foie Gras followed by Crêpes Valbonne, the Specialité de la Maison, washed down with a vintage Château Petrus.

6

The night porter pretended to be busy when he saw the two Americans come through the revolving door. François had dropped George and Dee back at the Negresco in Nice at about 2.00 a.m. The foyer was almost silent and deserted, except for two cleaners polishing the marble floor. Dee asked for their messages and she was given a large brown envelope addressed to George Gibson and a sheaf of telephone calls . . . In the elevator she opened the envelope and glanced at its contents, George flicked through the messages. The envelope contained faxes from Norman Naff in New York: British newspaper cuttings all written by the same person, John Lewis. But there was nothing about their shows, so Dee wasn't interested.

'I'm wrecked,' Dee said, tossing her coat on to a chair in their suite. She ran her fingers through her hair. 'You wanna drink, George?'

Already George was pressing numbers on the telephone. 'Gimme a Rémy, Dee,' he cleared his throat (a nasty grating sound) and sniffed a bit. He rarely seemed tired. Dee continually marvelled at George's capacity for work. He was happy at any time of the day or night to talk contracts, harangue colleagues, gossip to Sam Cohn at ICM, attempt to persuade some star to do a show. Dee needed her eight hours. Meanwhile she gave him his cognac.

George returned three phone calls in quick succession. The first to Gino Bernstein of Bernstein, Kraus and Dubitsky, his East Coast lawyer. It was nine o'clock in the evening Eastern Standard Time. Someone at the Bernstein residence took a message. The second was to Charlie Brodsky (George's Stage Manager for the past 25 years) at the Imperial where Charlie was stage managing a show for another producer. Although George had a version of his last moderately successful Broadway play *Birdsong* on the road, he had nothing currently in New York. So his teams worked for others (if they didn't want to go on the road, and most didn't). But

George demanded and got loyalty; he expected his guys to drop whatever they were doing for anyone else when he needed them. Night or day.

Dee was saying 'I'm gonna take a bath' as Charlie came on the line from the Imperial's tiny production office. She slipped out of her clothes and tidied them away listening to George ask Charlie to call Betty, his secretary, in the morning and get her to arrange a meeting of the *Galileo* writers for the afternoon of April 10th. As she emptied a sachet of Givenchy Bubble Bath into the steaming water, George was dialling again, calling his Press Agent.

Dee lay back in the bath, muscles relaxing in the heat, legs floating, wiggling her toes, eyes half-closed, pleasantly sleepy. Half awake, half asleep she replayed the events of earlier in the evening, imagining what might have been as the provocative sensuality of François permeated her again, evoking tantalising, dream-like erotic images. Her fingers fluttered lightly on her body, barely disturbing the bubbles.

Later, as they lay together in the large bed with its crispy white Egyptian cotton sheets, she nuzzling into his back, before sleep enveloped her, he staring at the chink of light coming through the window, she muttered: 'George, can I be in *Galileo*?'

But the request went unanswered as George was deep in thought. He had glanced through Lewis's articles before he'd switched out the lights. Naff had told him of Lewis's wish to attend rehearsals, to write a book. Hitherto George would not have entertained the idea. Theatre, George believed, had to have mystique, magic. Explain the tricks, discuss the process and what's left to believe in? Religion was dying, he would say, because people asked too many questions and were given too many answers. Besides, books weren't good marketing tools. By the time they were published the show was off.

However, for the past month or two, George had become increasingly preoccupied with hazy and (it must be said) largely unformulated conceptions about eternity and immortality. Two contiguous factors were chiefly responsible. Firstly, *Galileo* was likely to be his last major show and there is, after all, nothing like the completion of your life's work to inspire metaphysical meditation. Secondly, there had recently been published a number of autobiographies by George's contemporaries in the theatre. He hadn't actually read any but plenty of people had told him about them. In fact, it seemed to George, that people *relished* telling him.

31

Have you read, George, they'd say, Elia Kazan on Harry Clurman? *Harold Clurman*, for God's sake! That schlemiel! Artie Miller on Kermit Bloomgarten. Even Jed Harris had written his memoirs! They were all writing. Writing about themselves. About each other. They had achieved immortality, alive on bookshelves, in libraries; studied in colleges across the land, their lives meaningful, packaged, made sense of. Their productions gone, probably forgotten, but their place in the history of Broadway assured.

Recently George had snuck into Scribners and flipped through the indexes of some of these books. He was shocked to find barely a mention of 'Gibson, George: producer'. George had never produced a Miller play, never hired Elia Kazan, never co-produced with Jed Harris. He didn't like Alan Jay Lerner's lyrics so he wasn't in *On the Street Where I Live*. Even Eric Bentley, who mentions everyone, only mentioned George in passing and then only in an appreciation of Ross Boardman's contribution to post-war American theatre production techniques. 'Oh for Chrissake . . .' he'd muttered to himself.

Yet George was aware that on Broadway, the street where *he* lived, he was a legend. There, he had respect. He had worked for that. He had paid plenty for that. Liked – hell no – but respected . . . and feared. He knew you don't get respect without a little fear. But all of it, he knew, would die with him. He wanted more than a few lines in *Who's Who in the Theatre*. He, too, wanted a book – a guarantee of a place on the shelf, an everlasting theatrical life – that magic word, the ultimate accolade – a biography.

As Dee slept quietly at his back (he could feel her warm breath and smell her perfumed, lotioned body) – he recognised this might be his last chance. A biography! Lewis worked for a respectable British newspaper . . . He could string two words together. If Lewis wanted to do it, why not?

7

It took several rings before Lewis fully awoke and understood that it was the telephone. He switched on the light and looked at his watch. Christ! 3.47 a.m. His immediate thought – his father. The police have found him dead. A massive attack of guilt overwhelmed him: DEAD FATHER BLAMES SON – screamed a headline in his brain.

In fact it was George Gibson. 'Hi, Jaahn, this is George Gibson. Were you having breakfast?'

'No, no,' said Lewis politely but truthfully, trying to wake himself up.

'I've read your cuttings, Jaahn. And it's good. It's readable. So much you get in the papers is unreadable, pretentious crap. There are elections here. You follow French politics, Jaahn?'

'Er . . .,' Lewis tried to focus.

"I've just been to dinner with this friend of mine. She's a . . . Listen I wanna tell you about this place . . . Gaad, the cook makes the greatest crêpes . . . order any filling in the world . . . you name it, he'll make it. You like crêpes?'

'Well, sometimes.'

'What time is it in England, Jaahn? See I get very confused. It's a quarter to five in the morning here. What is it – a quarter to eight or nine?'

'No, it's about quarter to four in the morning.'

'Jesus, sorry, Jaahn, I'll call you later . . .' And he hung up.

Lewis reviewed the conversation: he had said he liked the material, it was readable. That business about French politics though. What was that about? Lewis made a mental note to do some research into that tomorrow. Obviously Gibson was interested in politics . . . and crêpes.

Eventually Lewis managed to get back to sleep. He dreamed that he was diving for prizes, representing his country. In mid-air, half way down, a phone was ringing. George Gibson again, he dream-thought. I'll answer when I've completed the dive . . . Then he woke. Daylight streamed through a gap in the curtains. The watch said 7.38 a.m. and the phone was ringing.

'Lewis?' A familiar voice but an unfamiliar tone. 'You're an asshole!'

'Sorry?' Then Lewis realised it was Ross Boardman and he hoped he'd misheard.

'I've just read that stuff you've written about me . . . "Boardman, who has had as many wives as hit musicals." What kinda vulgar crap is that? You drink my champagne, vomit on my floor. Then fire cheap shots.'

Help! Lewis tried to gather his wits. 'Mr Boardman. I'm ever so sorry you're upset.'

'I'm not upset. I'm mad as hell . . .'

Why am I always having to retrieve the initiative? 'You're right it was a cheap shot. It was only a miserable attempt at a joke – please don't be offended. The whole tenor of my piece is basically very complimentary isn't it? Look, I'm glad you've called. I've been trying to reach you to ask you if . . .' But he heard the dial tone. Boardman was gone. In vain he dialled the Savoy – the switchboard had instructions not to disturb Mr Boardman.

Lewis disconsolately sat on the edge of his bed. All his dreams of being a part of *Galileo* had been dashed, his life was in tatters again. He was back to square one. His heart pounding, he lay back on his bed. Panic gripped him. Suddenly, he found it hard to catch his breath. Heart attack! Call the doctor! No pain, however. Try to control heart, breathe gently, *gently* . . .

The phone rang again.

'I loved your piece on Boardman in the paper today, Jaahn!' George Gibson shouted down the phone at him. 'You've caught him to a T.'

Life on the roller coaster. Boardman casts him down, Gibson pulls him up. Lewis managed to say: 'Thank you. How'd you get the paper so early?'

'Friend in London faxed it first thing. Knew I'd be tickled. That bit about more wives than hits. Golly, Dee an' I had to laugh at that one.'

Lewis, looking into the mirror near his bed, saw himself blush.

'What was the other bit? Hey, Dee,' Lewis could hear, 'Dee, pass that fax, will ya. Okay. Here it is . . . This bit, er . . . pick it up, sweetheart . . . Okay . . . Er . . . Quote "I have been campaigning for American theatre to achieve a unique character that is rooted in its multi-racial, classless heritage and, in particular, divergent from the general thrust of the European cultural tradition",

34

unquote. See what I mean, Jaahn!' Gibson gleefully continued. 'That's Boardman! I can jus' hear him. Gaad, he's a pompous ass.'

Lewis had thought Boardman had his finger on the cultural pulse. Evidently Gibson didn't think so.

'I wouldn't say that, Mr Gibson. I thought . . .'

'Now what was it you told Norman you want to do . . . some kinda book or what?'

'Yes, a book, a diary of how *Galileo* is put together.' Lewis was disconcerted by Gibson's heavy, almost asthmatic breathing on the other end. 'I'd like it to be chatty, accessible, a book for the general public. You know, you could sell it in the foyer with the other marketing material – the cassettes, the brochures.' Lewis warmed to his theme. His heart had returned to normal, his breathing easy. He felt excited but good – the roller coaster was moving up. Please God keep it coming up towards you. 'There have been memoirs and biographies but never, I think . . .'

'Yeah, yeah. Sure. Sure. Okay, okay. This is gonna be a biography, right?'

'Well, no actually, I see it more as an account of a specific production rather than of any one person . . .'

'I wanna biography, Jaahn.'

'Oh, okay.'

'A biography . . .'

'Yes. It could be a sort of biography, I suppose.'

Anything to get this going. Silence. Gibson had not hung up. Lewis could still hear him breathing. Then a series of cough-like, rasping ejaculations. What did they mean? The options were: I've heard enough: drop dead. Or it's a great idea: go ahead. Or, I've got bronchitis: I smoke too much.

Cautiously, Lewis tried, 'You approve?'

Gibson said, 'I got this wonnerful view here, Jaahn. The sea, the Mediterranean sea is . . . What colour did you say it was, Dee? . . . yeah . . . azure . . . it's azure the sea. There are little fluffy puffy clouds skidding overhead . . . the South of France is somethin' else. You ever bin here?'

Lewis was getting the measure of Mr Gibson. 'You bet,' he cried. 'I love it.'

'You and I could work together, Jaahn. Any guy who loves the South of France has taste, you know what I mean. I gotta be surrounded by guys with real taste.'

'Anyway the book . . . No clichés, Mr Gibson! A truthful picture of the putting together of a show. The general public thinks the musical theatre's peopled by stereotypes – you know, drunken actresses having multiple affairs. The understudy going on and

35

saving the show – the *42nd Street* syndrome etcetera, etcetera. I'd
like them to read the honest truth. Show it for the hard grind that
it is. I'm eminently suited to the task – I'm in love with the genre
and yet I've never worked professionally in the theatre – so I can
see it from the layman's point of view.' He paused. Heavy
breathing still on the other end . . . 'What d'you think?'

'I'll help you all I can.'

'Oh, that's great! There might be one problem though,' Lewis
said.

'Whassat?'

'I'm not sure Mr Boardman will approve. I don't think he liked
my piece.'

'Fuck him. He'll do what I tell him. You need any money? I'll
pay you a per diem of $50 a day. It won't get you far but you'll eat.'

'Oh – I don't think I could accept . . .' Lewis tried to protest but
Gibson interrupted.

'Auditions start first week in May. I'll have my office deal with
your tickets . . . Welcome on board.'

8

The 6.00 p.m. flight to New York was already two hours late and still counting. Lewis, his fourth cup of overbrewed tea going cold, was sitting in a TEMPORARY CAFETERIA in the Heathrow Terminal. Everything about the building was temporary due to MAJOR IMPROVEMENT WORKS IN PROGRESS. In fact, more than half of the place was closed off so all the passengers were squeezed into one small area. Lewis had already used the TEMPORARY DUTY FREE, the WE APOLOGISE FOR THE TEMPORARY TOILET FACILITIES IN THIS LOUNGE, the TEMPORARY SEATING IN THIS AREA. A family of three was sharing his table and their plates, trays, cutlery and half-touched food were lying deep all over the table. Lewis had nowhere to rest his Economist, so he sat hunched up, magazine on his lap, sweaty and uncomfortable. (A sign above his head read SORRY OUR AIR CONDITIONING IS TEMPORARILY OUT OF SERVICE.)

'Mom, This is Yucko City! I can't drink this.' The child of the family whined over his orange squash.

'Cut it out, Ken!' his father said, mouth filled with apple pie from a box. 'We ain't gonna get fed on this flight for hours. So quit goofing around and get some more down yah.'

'Do as your Pop says, son,' said Mom.

Lewis, restlessly shifting his feet, toppled his attaché case and bent down to pick it up. With perfect timing, Ken accidentally knocked over his plastic glass and the sticky liquid flowed along the table and cascaded on to the back of Lewis's neck, trickling down his back to be absorbed by his shirt.

'Oh heck!' said Ken.

'Not to worry,' said Lewis, as brightly as he could manage. 'No damage done.'

Nevertheless, Lewis regretted that he had not packed a change of clothes into his hand luggage. That this was overlooked was hardly surprising given the speed with which Lewis's life had changed. George Gibson's office had moved quickly: by the end of the day on which his Boardman article had appeared, Lewis was in possession of a one-way airline ticket to New York delivered by a messenger on a motorbike. An incredible measure of trust, he had thought, shown by a man he had never met.

Packing hurriedly, Lewis couldn't wait to get out of a London that held nothing for him. He worried about leaving his father. Will he cope all on his own? Lewis had asked himself. Aunt Mary had promised to look in occasionally – but she and the old man didn't get on. 'I never want to get old and helpless,' Lewis had told Julie as he packed up his desk. Julie often seemed to pop into his mind; he would miss her, no-one else.

Someone brushed past him, a tall looming figure with a bulging black shoulder bag. Lewis glanced up and immediately recognised the back of Ross Boardman. The director was holding a tray and searching for somewhere to sit. Lewis buried himself in his magazine, his mind racing, his heart pounding, his damp shirt sticking to his back. Ross turned and was heading back towards him. It seemed to Lewis that Boardman looked straight at him – but no flicker of recognition or interest was discernible in the American's eyes.

As it happened, Ross Boardman *had* noticed John Lewis. Phrases from his appalling article sprang to mind. '. . . Boardman seems admirably suited to the *abrasive* nature of the Broadway business'; '. . . the decline in the American musical has, on occasion, been ascribed to the power wielded by star choreographers but also to the over–intellectual approach to musical comedy as exemplified by Boardman.' Complete garbage, Ross thought. The man is an arrogant fool, ignorant of the realities of American musical theatre. He dreaded the possibility of being cornered by Lewis in the confines of the terminal. *Or in the plane?* No, impossible! That would be too much of a coincidence . . . Lewis travelling on the same plane to New York? He was surely bound elsewhere. Ross was travelling first class (courtesy of Gibson's travel agent who was a friend of a director of the airline and got his 'clients' upgraded from business class to first). If, by an unhappy coincidence, they were booked on the same flight, Lewis, he assumed was in coach. Avoidance was possible.

Unable to find a seat, Ross dispensed with his tray and drank his coffee leaning against a wall under a notice which read: WE

REGRET THAT DUE TO BUILDING WORKS THE FIRST
CLASS LOUNGES ARE TEMPORARILY CLOSED.
He closed his eyes and wished he could sleep standing up. Was
it Stanislavsky who could do that? Ross had never been able to
catnap. The acute tiredness he felt at this moment seemed to
envelop him completely and for a moment he thought he might
faint. Next week he must see Lipschitz. Dr Leventhal, Lipschitz's
partner in the same practice had given him a thorough check-up
four months ago – given him a clean bill of health. 'I'll die before
you, Ross,' Leventhal had said jokingly. It was a remarkably
accurate prophecy as the doctor had a fatal stroke a week later.

'We regret to announce a further one-hour delay on flight 715 to
New York . . .' Ross opened his eyes. He felt somewhat better,
the extreme tiredness was passing, the coffee was helping. John
Lewis, he noticed, was reading and awkwardly scratching his back.

Ross was in transit having arrived back at Heathrow from
Munich just before 5.00 p.m. After four days of intense, wide-
ranging discussions with Michael Kershon (textual and general,
including a detailed analysis of Renaissance politics), Ross had
travelled to Munich for a meeting with the set designer, Karl-Heinz
Zeiss.

Karl-Heinz had designed the German version of *Owen's Valley*
and Ross had been impressed. Now Ross wanted him to design
Galileo even though they hadn't met for over thirty years. George
had readily agreed. Even he had heard of Karl-Heinz. In the
intervening period, Karl-Heinz had achieved world-wide recognition for the brilliant originality of his designs and for his
idiosyncratic behaviour.

He had always been unconventional. In the sixties, plump and
greatly in demand as *the* graphic designer for record covers, he was
joyfully eccentric. Typically he would conduct business meetings
in bed nude, wearing only sunglasses. People asked: 'Why the
sunglasses?' – his reply, invariably: 'Because my universe is too
bright'. (Jean-Luc Godard used to say the same thing – the French
and German avant-garde have much in common.)

Karl-Heinz, five years younger than Ross, was no longer plump,
in fact he was thinner than Gandhi. Almost bald, he nevertheless
grew the remaining hair to his shoulders and bleached it white.
Although still wearing the famous sunglasses, Karl-Heinz had
metamorphosed again: he no longer spoke. Ten years ago, Ross
discovered, he had taken a vow of silence and would only
communicate in writing. Ross had enquired about the origins of
the vow and had received an enigmatic note across the dining table
at the Bayerischer Hof, where they dined on the first night, which

read: THE SILENT SOW SUPS ALL THE BROTH.

Ross had talked, Karl-Heinz had listened. It was Ross's habit in preliminary discussions with designers to talk around the subject of the show. Often by coming at the thing obliquely, images presented themselves. And so it was with *Galileo*. Admittedly, working with Karl-Heinz presented unique problems. Usually there was an exchange of views, a debate, but with the German it was a one-sided affair. As Ross talked, Karl-Heinz sketched, his face unreadable behind the pitch-black shades. The world of Galileo: Copernican systems, revolving globes, solar systems, planes versus spheres, macrocosmic universality juxtaposed against a simple human feeling, Ptolemaic systems, art, music, food, Catholicism, crowds and symbols of power: the potency of ceremony and its significance to the individual – this and more featured in Ross's monologue to his designer over dinner.

Over the next two days, in Karl-Heinz's apartment they worked in detail. Ross set one major rule: no scene changes in blackout. Ross liked sets changing in view with underscore, the feel of a cinematic mix, transporting the audience from one visual situation to the next. Ross described it by comparing it to a river-raft ride in Disneyland through a series of magic kingdoms presented sequentially – continually surprising and developing as the show progresses.

They had pored over books of paintings. They studied Michelangelo, Da Vinci, Bernini; the pictures gave them a visual reference point. It helped with the costumes – the look of the era. They suggested design motifs and lighting. Michelangelo, in particular, suggested a colour palette for the overall design.

By the end of the two days, Ross was convinced Karl-Heinz's genius was undiminished. In addition, gratifyingly, he displayed much enthusiasm for the project. Before Ross left for the flight to New York via London, Karl-Heinz presented him with a portfolio of deftly executed sketches of hands clapping, portly gentlemen ho-ho-ing whilst slapping their bellies and dollar bills raining down on the famous municipal clock on the Munich Town Hall.

'Excuse me, it's Ross Boardman, isn't it?'

Lost in his reverie it took Ross several seconds to focus on his interlocutor. *Christ, the little shit, Lewis.* However, this was not Lewis. Lewis was still sitting at the table, mouth wide, eyes staring madly at Ross.

'I'm Clive North from the Guardian newspaper, Mr Boardman.

You might remember we met last year at Paul Newman's house in Connecticut.'

Lewis cursed his bad timing. Worried that Gibson might not have told Boardman he was coming to New York, Lewis had been on the point of getting up and going over to the director to make his peace. And then, from nowhere, that ingratiating smile materialising first, Clive North appeared on the scene. *CLIVE NORTH!* The name screamed through his head. There was now nothing to do but sit there and watch. Spontaneity was alien to his nature – he could no more saunter up and join them, act on impulse, than fly the 747. Lewis could only hear snatches of their conversation, but Ross looked as if he found Clive North stimulating; laughing and exchanging gossip. His earlier tiredness seemed now to have passed. Lewis watched with growing envy as they chatted happily until Clive's flight was called.

'Hello, old chap.' Clive North had stopped on his way to the gate. 'Where are you off to then?'

'New York,' Lewis said, dredging up a thin smile. 'I'm hoping to write a book. And you?'

'Japan. Series of articles on modern Japanese plays . . .'

'Are there any?' Lewis couldn't resist a dig.

'Cultural attaché invited me and fixed it all up. A month's tour all round the country – first class all the way. Have a good time! Good luck with the book! Cheerybye!'

Then he was gone, heading off for the Land of the Rising Sun.

At 8.45 p.m. Flight 715 to New York was ready finally for boarding. Separately Boardman and Lewis made their way to Gate 11 passing under a sign which read: TEMPORARY NOTICE: THANK YOU FOR YOUR PATIENCE. They sat waiting to board at opposite ends of the lounge, Boardman browsing through Braudel's *Civilisation in the 15th-18th Century: The Perspective of the World, Volume 3*, a present from Michael Kershon, Lewis just sitting staring at the nose of the Jumbo that filled the window opposite him.

An announcement: 'Would Mr John Lewis, Business Class passenger to New York, please step up to the desk.'

Somewhat apprehensively, he did so. Was his visa not in order? Had Boardman somehow got Gibson to withdraw the ticket at the

41

last moment? Out of the corner of his eye he saw Boardman glance at him. It wasn't a friendly look.

'Mr Lewis? Can I see your ticket please?' *Did she say this a little too aggressively?* Lewis sensed trouble as he handed it over to the stewardess. The girl punched buttons on her computer terminal and stared impassively at the screen.

'Right, Mr Lewis,' she said after some moments. 'You're on our VIP list and we've got availability in first class.'

Lewis's heart missed a beat. 'VIP? Are you sure? Me?'

She checked her screen again. 'You are the John Lewis of the Independent?'

'I suppose I am,' Lewis said feeling himself blush.

'Well we're upgrading you. Still no smoking?'

'Er . . . yes, please.' Then a thought struck him. 'How much extra is that?'

The girl smiled. 'It's a free upgrade, Mr Lewis.'

Lewis tried to sound casual and classy. 'Oh fine. Thank you.'

'Here you are.' She handed him a new boarding card. '2A, that's a window. Not that you'll be able to see much at this time of night. Sorry for the delay.' And she turned her smile to someone else.

Another announcement: 'We are now ready to board flight 715 to John F. Kennedy Airport. We will be boarding passengers at the rear of the plane first. Please have your boarding passes ready. First Class passengers may board when they wish. Please may we have passengers seated in Rows 30 to 55.'

There was a surge to the door. Lewis, eager to experience First Class and his surprising elevation to VERY IMPORTANT PERSON (even though, like the terminal, it would be TEMPOR-ARY) was in the second batch to be passed out of the lounge. Lewis sat down in the spacious seat. He stretched out his legs to test the leg room. He graciously accepted the champagne and orange juice presented to him. This is not so bad, he thought.

Ross was almost the last to board. Years of travelling had taught him that the less time on the plane the better. As he entered the plane he glanced into Business Class to see where Lewis was sitting. The compartment was full. He couldn't see him. At least they were a class apart. Lewis had been wise enough to stay clear of him in the terminal, presumably he would show similar sense on the plane. The stewardess looked at his boarding pass and showed him to his seat – 2B.

Trapped! Boxed in. It took Ross much self-control to avoid displaying the anger and irritation he felt. Glancing around the cabin, he could see there were no other empty seats.

If there was any pleasure to be found in long haul aircraft travel it was, for Ross, hours of reading and sleeping. Hobnobbing for seven hours with a second-rate Arts journalist was like being pitched into hell.

'Are you feeling better?' Ross enquired charmingly as he sat down and organised his luggage. He was good at charm even with nonentities. He figured, give him five minutes then withdraw.

'Oh much, thank you.' Lewis was greatly relieved at this friendly opening. The shock and surprise had been mutual.

The stewardess brought around menus and headsets. Lewis plugged himself into the audio system to gain time to work out a strategy for the next few minutes – the rest of the seven hours would have to wait. Luckily, Ross seemed engrossed in a book. Lewis pretended to study the menu but found the tension too much. In order to break the ice he said: 'I've never been in First Class before. It's very comfortable. Lots of leg room. Menu looks good too. Caviare, Filet de Boeuf Alsacienne . . .'

'You in New York for long?' Ross asked. Get the chattering over, a light meal then sleep.

Lewis was aghast. Clearly the director had no idea about the book or the purpose of the visit. 'Er . . . oh . . . um I tried to phone you last week . . . left messages all over town . . . didn't you get any of them . . . ?'

'No.' Ross seemed to lose interest.

'Have you spoken to George Gibson during the last week?' Lewis asked anxiously.

A curious question, Ross thought, and taken together with Lewis's shifty manner, he came to suspect something was afoot. 'I've spoken to him several times.' Once before leaving London for Munich to report on progress made with Michael Kershon and twice from Munich to fix dates for production conferences.

'Did he mention me at all?'

'Not that I can recall,' Ross said drily and accepted a champagne refill. The doors of the aircraft had been closed and the crew were going through their pre-flight checks. A profound sense of gloom and doom descended on Ross.

Lewis took the plunge. 'He obviously didn't tell you about the book then?'

Ross eyed him suspiciously. 'Book?'

'Yes . . . a book about how *Galileo* makes it to the stage. Work-in-progress, that kind of thing.'

'No. He did not . . .'

'That's why I have been trying to reach you. Of course it must have your approval . . . Mr Gibson . . .'

'He approved it, did he?'

43

'Oh yes.' Lewis was becoming rather more enthusiastic. 'He even arranged this flight. That's how happy he is.'

Now Ross understood. It was no coincidence then that they were both on this flight, sitting together in seats 2A and 2B. George had pitched them together on purpose. Why? Simply to antagonise and provoke Ross? Was George ever that obvious?

Lewis, on the other hand, had decided that the best option was to proceed as if all approvals had been given. He would not wait for Ross to say either yes or no. 'There's so much I want to ask you, Mr Boardman. Can I call you Ross?'

Ross nodded bleakly.

'Background, you know. Stuff I didn't ask in that other interview . . . you know. Sorry about some of that by the way but . . .'

Helplessly trapped, Ross listened to Lewis's voice talking at him. As the plane sped down the runway, he felt the ground slipping away from under him . . .

9

The cabin lights had been dimmed, supper taken and too much claret drunk. A film flickered noiselessly on the screen at the front of the cabin. Lewis, headphones clamped firmly on, was the only one watching.

Ross, eyes closed, reclined blanket-wrapped, flitting uneasily in and out of sleep, wanting the journey to be over. He lay gripped with the terror of being *not in control*, of being *manipulated*. Manipulated by George Gibson. This episode with John Lewis was only the last in a long line stretching back to 1954 . . .

It's after 10.00 p.m. on a hot night in the Village in September 1969. There's a small, lowlit, discreet Sicilian restaurant called Il Lampedusa on West 3rd Street (now a flower shop). Ross is sitting with Ellen in a dark corner. It's a favourite place for Ross because it's totally unfrequented by show people – the clientele are mostly midtown business executives. Ross has just finished a day's rehearsal for *Love Boat*, a musical produced by George Gibson, set on a Caribbean cruise ship. It's a romantic merry-go-round in which the couples spend a week wife-swapping, visiting islands peopled by dancing natives, ending up restored to their original mates.

It's a hard show for Ross because he agreed to direct it for the wrong reason – money. It has been 15 years since the triumph of *Owen's Valley*. The royalties from the show had virtually dried up by 1959 and there followed ten financially lean years. Artistically the work had been good and acclaimed but Ross's lifestyle was expensive. He had separated from – and later divorced – his first wife, Eve, in 1956 during the second Broadway season of *Owen's Valley*, a time when he was at the peak of his success. They had two kids, Miki and Betsy. In 1960 he had met and married Mary-

Anne Hody, a dancer/singer, and in 1962 Mary-Anne gave birth to Chloe and Chrissy, 'the twins'.

Now, in 1969, whilst still living with Mary-Anne and the twins in a duplex penthouse on Fifth Avenue overlooking the park and the Metropolitan Museum, he is in the middle of an affair with Ellen Frazier, a bright young Englishwoman who teaches dialect at the Juilliard. They had met nine months earlier during Ross's production of Shaw's *St Joan* back at the Arena Stage in Washington DC. (A theatre that Ross liked to consider his spiritual home and whose invitations to 'direct anything you like' he always accepted.) Ellen was employed as dialect coach and she paid several visits to Washington during that rehearsal period. They became lovers in a hotel bedroom after a boozy party celebrating the first night. Back in New York they continued seeing each other whenever possible. Ross found Ellen intellectually stimulating and her very Englishness charming. He was hooked. Whenever she could find an excuse to get away from her husband for an evening she would spend it with Ross. Luckily, Edward Frazier was a celebrated Professor of Economics at Columbia and was nearly always away, either at conferences or at faculty meetings, or else locked in his study writing a textbook on accountancy for Simon and Schuster.

Ross and Mary-Anne had drifted apart and now tended to live largely separate lives. Neither asked the other how they'd spent the evening – neither cared to know – yet somehow one of them was always there to kiss the twins goodnight.

The combined effect of alimony to Eve (who still lived in their Sutton Place apartment), the cost of putting Miki and Betsy through school, the sustenance and demands of his present family (in their rented Fifth Avenue penthouse), taken with a demand for back taxes from the Internal Revenue, made George Gibson's *Love Boat* on Broadway too tempting an offer to turn down. He told himself *maybe* it will work. I can make something of this trivial story. Maybe it isn't so trivial, maybe a tale of our times – infidelity directly related to a paucity of modern philosophy – maybe . . . with the right cast this could be made to work . . . and, after all, as he tells Ellen over dinner in Il Lampedusa – 'the music's okay . . .Elliott and Kreuze . . . they're not Rodgers and Hammerstein . . . but the tunes are hummable . . . and the lyrics clever and witty . . .'

'You sure you're not deluding yourself, Ross?'

[That wasn't a question you asked someone already deeply committed to a project. Of course he had been deluding himself, Ross thought, wrapped in the stifling embrace of the airliner. But it was easy to smile more than twenty years later . . .]

Suddenly there's a flash that momentarily blinds both Ellen and Ross. Waiters, led by the Maitre D', frogmarch a photojournalist past fascinated diners out of the restaurant and dump him with little ceremony in the street. Ross and Ellen, puzzled and shocked, continue their meal. Have they been mistaken for someone else? What's the big idea?

The next day the incident's forgotten. Early the following morning, however, Ross receives an urgent call from Norman Naff, the show's press representative. 'Don't buy the Daily News,' Naff warns. 'You're not gonna like what you see, Ross.'

'What is it? C'mon, you gotta tell me, Norman.'

'They gotta picture of you an' Ellen in some Village dinner place. Nasty caption Ross. Gee, I'm sorry.'

'Is this you, Norman?' Ross was getting angry.

'I swear to you, Ross, cross my heart – we wouldn't want this kinda crap. George wouldn't stoop to this – we've gotta great show – we don't need the coverage. Apologise to Ellen for me, will ya. Jesus, I dunno what the professor's gonna say . . . !'

Later, Ross buys the paper. Inside, under Showtime Gossip, there is a large headline and a picture of a startled Ellen and Ross:

PROF'S WIFE BOFFED

LOVE ROCKS THE *LOVE BOAT*

George Gibson's new musical *LOVE BOAT* in rehearsal for a slated Broadway opening later this Fall is the talk of the smart set. Why? Oh, boy! Because life mirrors art! Rumours that celebrated Broadway director, ROSS BOARDMAN and dancer wife Mary-Anne are about to split are confirmed TRUE by our quickwitted photographer. And who's the lovely companion Ross is dating? An English Rose and wife of PROFESSOR FRAZIER up at COLUMBIA. Gibson says the show's about a swapping party on a yacht – seems like swapping's the order of the day. Keep pumping Ross!

Is this George's work? Up in the office at the end of an unsatisfactory day's rehearsal Ross confronts George but the producer is full of commiserations and blames it on a disaffected cast member who perhaps bears Ross a grudge.

'Sure know how you must feel, Ross, but hell you know this is a small town – you can't keep a secret here. Man looks at a woman in a bar and two ticks later they're talking about it at Sardi's. Watcha expect? Say 'Hi' to Mary-Anne for me willya . . . How's rehearsals?' George doesn't wait to find out – he is already answering the phone . . .

Ross awoke with a start. He never had found out who had primed the News. Had to be George. Everything was always George.
George, George, George . . .
His head ached and his mouth was dry. His watch said 10.58 p.m. This was New York time – he had reset to EST after take-off. One and a half hours to go. He tried to stay awake. *I'm sixty. Too many memories. Too much past.*
And Lewis was still glued to that damned movie . . .

Drifting . . . drifting back to 1954 to a traumatic fourth perform-ance of *Owen's Valley* in New Haven. Ross is leaning on a pillar at the back of the auditorium jotting down notes about the perform-ance. The audience is larger and more responsive than at the first three performances. Nevertheless, Ross senses that the actors are tired and lacking in spontaneity. Ranged around him, in the rear of the house, some sitting some standing, are the rest of the team: the writers are sitting on aisle seats, the orchestrator, totally exhausted by five nights of almost no sleep, is slumped on carpeted stairs, his head resting on a mountain of programmes. Close to Ross the choreographer is whispering to his assistant, twisting his hands and fingers to demonstrate some new idea.
'Hey, Ross, you seen Gibs this evening?' The choreographer, Howard de Vroome, has come over. Ross shakes his head. 'I got idea for de arrival at de camp scene that's gonna blow your mind but it needs a coupla extra guys, Ross. It's dynamite! You'll love it. Talk to you at the intermission?' Ross nods. 'If you buy it, will ya speak to Gibs wid me?' He has a curious Dutch-American accent that Ross finds grating.
'Sure,' Ross says, attempting to concentrate on what is happen-ing on the stage. The end of the first act is approaching and on stage Ross is watching a crowd of Japanese Americans crouching before a hut; they are bathed in the warm rosy glow of a desert sunset and singing very low, very tenderly. Perfectly on cue, with great sensitivity combined with meticulous timing, Junji Fukuda, the young lead of the musical, rises up from the crowd and sings the song that is to become the great hit of the show – his voice, powered by an intense passion and great dignity, sends an electric

charge through the audience. Ross is mesmerised; Junji has been getting better and better but tonight he is supreme.

'Dat boy, Ross, he's gonna be a big star,' Howard whispered. 'They seem to like him tonight.'

Much relieved, Ross nodded. The content of *Owen's Valley* was proving to be controversial. It was hard to take, so soon after the war, a musical that was implicitly critical of the treatment of Japanese Americans in Los Angeles after Pearl Harbor.

In the penultimate scene of Act One, the Japanese families arrive at the Manzanar Internee camp and are made to lay out their meagre possessions on the concrete where they are inspected by a US army officer. It's not a cruel scene – the officer is curt, but relatively sensitive to the situation – nevertheless the first few audiences were clearly troubled by the implications. The principal narrative deals with the relationship between Junji's character and a working-class white girl from North Hollywood, played by Corinne Marlow. Despite the intense opposition of their families, and set against the war hysteria, they mature and survive.

The curtain's coming down for the interval. The applause whilst enthusiastic is not wild but Ross is much cheered by this. At the half way point on the last three nights there has been a discernible chill to the proceedings – listening to the audience going out for drinks and smokes, he overheard someone say: 'Well, I sure didn't like that act, but I never really know what I think till I read the critics.' And one large gentleman said loudly: 'A total waste of time!' Not quotes Ross or George would like to have outside the theatres on the billboards.

George Gibson in 1954 is a highly charged, restless bundle of energy. For the past three nights he has been nervously pacing the aisle at the back – occasionally brushing past Ross pausing to mutter notes that Ross could never hear. He too heard the interval comments. Tonight, when things are definitely better he is nowhere to be seen.

Ross goes backstage through the pass door, and makes his way across the stage avoiding the crew who are noisily changing the set for the second act. He walks along a corridor and knocks at Corinne Marlow's dressing room door.

'Wait a minute!' calls a muffled voice from within. Corinne's dresser, a diminutive black lady with a winning smile, opens the door an inch or two.

'Oh, it's you, Mr Boardman. Corinne's just doin' her change. D'you wanna wait outside or come in wid yer eyes closed?'

'I'll come in with my eyes closed.'

Corinne was sitting back down at her dressing table tying up her dressing gown as Ross entered.

'Going better, huh?' she drawls as she peers closely at herself in the mirror. With her wig off and her hair trapped tightly in a flesh coloured nylon net she somewhat resembles a creature from another planet – not the beautiful creature that had just fallen in love in Act One. 'You wanna drink, Ross? There's some white wine somewhere – the Coke machine's all fucked up. Nothing's cold.'

'I'll pass,' says Ross. 'I want to get in to see Junji before the curtain goes up . . .'

'Ain't he doin' fine . . . ?' she puts on her glasses and beams at Ross. 'Now ah can see you!' Ross likes her Texas growl. 'He's just growin' before ma very eyes.'

'You're doing good too, Corinne,' says Ross. 'But you're dropping cues.'

'Am I? La-di-da! If I can find 'em, I'll pick 'em up in Act Two!' She laughs gaily and starts to get ready.

Ross goes on: '. . . and you've gotta get out of that habit of dropping the ends of your sentences. It reads like a lack of confidence. Otherwise it's getting terrific.'

'Gotcha . . .' A last dab of powder and a hitch at the bra and Corinne from Houston is transformed back to Janie Jones from North Hollywood. As Ross turns to go, she says: 'By-the-by, what's Josh Logan doing out there sitting next to Gibsy?'

Ross's mind races. Logan sitting with George! Joshua Logan directed the legendary *South Pacific* that ran almost five years on Broadway. Logan's in his late forties and has been directing on Broadway since 1935. Ross is 25 and this is his first New York assignment. Ross knows Logan's hungry for a new show. His appearance here tonight can only mean one thing: George wants him to take over the production. On Broadway no-one is indispensable. It's a hard lesson to learn.

Betraying nothing, Ross shrugs. 'Enjoying the show, I hope.'

'You dropped the end of your sentence, Ross!' Corinne calls after him.

Down the corridor comes a Stage Manager shouting 'Places – ACT TWO!' A couple of chorus girls say hello to Ross on their way to the stage.

Instead of going to see Junji, Ross heads for the stage door and out into the street. He passes the last few remaining members of the audience going back in for the second half. A little way past the theatre he stops – the second act is starting, he should be there but his feet won't take him back. Instead he leans against a hoarding and lights a cigarette.

So the show's a turkey. Well, well. It looked and felt good in rehearsal. Yet, as he thinks back to tonight's first act, there can be no mistaking the quality of the work that is beginning to emerge. Junji was transcendental in that last number. The cool night air and the cigarette have a calming effect.

If I get fired after the show it won't be heartbreaking to go home. The guys at Arena Stage still love me . . .

The lights came on in the cabin and the first officer announced that they were one hour out of Kennedy, passing over Boston. Next to Ross, John Lewis was waking up.

'Sticky back,' Lewis said.

'I'm sorry?'

'Got a glass of orange juice down my back at Heathrow and it's gone all sticky. My shirt's stuck to my back. Can't you smell it?' He scratched at it as if to prove the point.

'You seem to have . . . bad luck,' Ross said icily.

'Did you sleep?'

'Dozed.'

Ross was little inclined towards conversation. He was happy in the past. He closed his eyes and returned to that night in New Haven 35 years ago.

He returns to see the end of the show. Junji and Corinne sing for the final time the reiterated motif and the curtain crashes down. In the centre of the stalls, a group of perhaps a dozen people rise and give the show and the performers a standing ovation – more join and soon the whole house is standing. This is thrilling. The Stage Manager finds him to get the rehearsal calls for the next day. Ross says he wants the whole company at 11.30 a.m. – there would be no notes tonight – the company can be dismissed.

'You okay?' the Stage Manager enquires.

'Sure,' says Ross.

'Good show tonight.'

'Yup.'

'What d'ya wanna do about the writers an' the rest of the team?'

'Tell 'em to be in my room at 10.00 a.m.' He could have added: to say goodbye.

There is still no sign of George. The previous nights during the curtain call, George would appear and lean over the brass rail at the back to watch the audience file out.

Ross goes back to the hotel alone. If George fires him tonight, Josh Logan could take over tomorrow's calls. There are no messages at the reception and, with a sudden sense of loneliness, he decides to have a champagne cocktail in the bar before going up to bed.

'Can I join you?' a voice asks.

Ross had been sitting in a corner staring listlessly at his notes.

'Sure, Corinne,' he says and Corinne sits down.

'Call me Cory, for Chrissakes. My ma used to call me Corinne when she was mad at me. I've hated it ever since.'

'What'll it be?'

'Pink Flamingo,' she says to the waiter then laughs at Ross's questioning look. 'My, oh my, wherever were you brought up Ross? Surely on the wrong side of the tracks! Pinkoes we used to call them in Houston. Two ounces of Plymouth gin, one and a half ounces of dry Vermouth, one and a half ounces of sweet Vermouth, juice of half an orange and a dash of angostura bitters.'

'That sure sounds like a Pinko,' said Ross.

'Ask me another.'

Cory passes Ross the cocktail menu. He studies it a moment. 'Maiden's Blush?'

'Not very appropriate but, let me see . . .' She closes her eyes and thinks hard. 'Three ounces gin, one ounce Pernod . . . dash of Grenadine . . . twister . . . stirred, not shaken . . . with crushed ice . . . glass from the freezer.'

'You sure? Wanna bet?' Ross is feeling comfortable with this girl.

'Two ounces of gin! Okay, okay! Never bet cocktail recipes with a number-one hostess.'

'I wouldn't dream of it, but I'll stick to champagne.'

'Then you'll go far, young man.'

He smiles, relaxes. The waiter brings the drinks.

'My daddy, God rest his soul, well he died four years ago, he used to have cute Louisiana expressions – that's where his folks came from, Louisiana – suffered all his life from pellagra. You ever been there Ross? Nor me neither. Well, he'd say to me, Cory, look out for Champagne Charlie – he'll surely rattle your cage.'

She looks at him through the top of her frosted glass. 'You've done well, Ross. This show I mean. It's been a pleasure, however it turns out. You've been a real gentleman an' I can tell you that's rare in this business, believe me. You can rattle my cage any time you want. Just whistle.'

Later, at around 2.15 a.m., up in his bedroom suite on the fifteenth floor, she is underneath him sipping cognac from his mouth, softly murmuring when the phone rings.

'Ross?'

'Yeah. George?'

Cory doesn't move, just holds him tightly.

'Am I disturbing you?'

'Yeah, George.'

'Good show tonight. It's sure coming together.'

'Just like us,' Cory listening, whispers. Ross gives her a look.

'Wassat? You say something?'

'No, George.' Ross is quite canned. At this moment he cares only for this hot, adorable creature wrapped around him.

'Okay, I'll let you sleep. You gotta load of notes from tonight?'

'George, what was Josh Logan doing here tonight?'

Then he bitterly regrets asking the question. Mixing drinks is bad.

[Was there a beat before the answer? Maybe yes, maybe no. Directing the scene in his mind, years later as the plane began its descent into JFK, he thought it played best with a small beat.]

'He's a friend of mine, Ross. I wanted to know what he thought.'

'And what did he think?' Ross is genuinely interested. Josh Logan is someone to respect.

'He loved it, Ross. Said it will run four to five years. You get some sleep now.' And he rings off.

Neither Ross nor Cory feel inclined to follow his advice.

Staring out at the lights of Long Island as the plane began its final approach, Ross was struck by his own ingenuousness. Years later it happened that Ross and Josh Logan were sitting on a panel together. They fell into discussing play-doctoring.

'Not something I would ever do,' Ross had said. 'Success or failure is determined long before rehearsals start. Coming in after the show's up and running is largely a waste of effort.'

Logan had said: 'You don't think you can unpick and scotch-tape a show together and improve it? It's happened.'

'Maybe,' said Ross. 'I suspect that it's only marginal. Great shows are there, on the page, in the writing from day one of rehearsals; great productions spring from discussions and home-work done before rehearsals. Have you been called in much, Josh?'

'Sure. On one of your shows once upon a time.'

Ross had remembered immediately.

'*Owen's Valley*. Tryout at the Shubert in New Haven, right? I heard you were in.'

'George begged me to come down. Said you were in a heap of trouble. Nothing was working. I can tell you all this now because it's what – 25 years ago – and you'll never have a bigger hit than that show. I saw it that night and loved it. Even then Gibsy wouldn't let it rest. He practically begged me to take over. Two days later I told him categorically, finally, unequivocally, no. He's your friend but he's an asshole.'

'With friends like mine I don't need enemies,' Ross had said.

'I think I can see Manhattan through the clouds,' Lewis said excitedly.

'That's Long Island,' Ross said. 'First time here?'

Lewis nodded.

'You say George was enthusiastic about your writing this book . . .'

'He seemed so.'

'And he's paid for your ticket?'

'Yes. And he's booked me into the Grand Lexington Palace Hotel for a couple of days till I find my feet. That sounds a grand place! He's been terribly generous.' Lewis chuckled. 'Even going to pay me a per diem! It's all the more amazing as he's never even met me. Just read my article about you.'

Ross thought about this for a moment. Then he said: 'You have to understand something about George Gibson, Lewis. He's only interested in himself and his own power. He's the last of the great manipulators. If he wants you to write this book you have to work out what's in it for him. It'll be a game.' Pausing briefly for a moment, Ross watched the lights of the runway rushing up towards them. 'The book has to be truthful, Lewis. It has to be an honest attempt to capture the essence of what'll happen. No newspaper sensationalism. If that's your intention, you'll find I'll support you.'

There was a bump and Lewis made contact with the New World.

10

Jerry Trimlock, the composer of *Galileo*, sat hunched up on a stool in one corner of the recording studio control rooms listening intently to a rough mix. His hands were clasped firmly over his head and his elbows rested on his knees. His concentration on the music was total.

The sound level was unbearably high and had given Lewis a low-grade headache. Lewis, seated on a swivel chair next to the sound engineer, watched the young man dexterously manipulate the vast array of knobs and sliders, imperceptibly changing the sound. To Lewis's right, Dee and Jerry's girlfriend (Lewis had been introduced but had missed the name) leant against racks getting into the number. The track came to an end.

Jerry looked up, his handsome black face broke into a grin and he wiped perspiration from his forehead with a Kleenex.

'Well!' said Dee appreciatively, 'Ain't that hot shit! Debs, you sound just great! I love it! Wow!'

'I tell you, Dee, nobody can sing my stuff better than Debbie. She's gotta be cast as Marina. You gotta back me up with George on that one?'

'Sure, you're gonna tell George aren't you, Deedee?' Debbie smiled sweetly at her best friend but Lewis detected ice in the smile.

Dee looked doubtful. 'He knows what a hot shot you are but it isn't just up to George, is it. I dunno how Ross feels . . .'

'Ross'll do what George tells him. Won't he?' Debbie turned her heavily made-up eyes towards Jerry. She's a toughie, Lewis thought. Strong bone structure. Arrogant. *Christ, whopping tits!* She made him nervous. He tried to concentrate on the conversation.

'I dunno, Debs . . .' Dee said 'But George'll flip out over this new stuff. He played the last demo to Doris in France and she was knocked out.'

'I think it's great too,' Lewis volunteered. 'I liked the one that sounded like a Bruce Springsteen number.'

'Oh, you think it's derivative and dated, huh?' Jerry said coldly, fiddling with the ribbon that kept his hair in a bunch.

'No, no! Not at all.' He had meant to pay Jerry a compliment but the composer seemed edgy with him. 'I love Bruce Springsteen. Who exactly sings that one in the show?'

The engineer lit a cigarette and the smoke drifted towards Lewis.

'It's a duet,' Jerry said, happy to get into detail. 'In the plot this guy steals the designs of one of Galileo's telescopes. Galileo gets mad an' gives him the business.' He turned his attentions to Dee. 'That's what I wanna call the number.'

'What'?' Dee asked.

'Givin' the Business'.

'S'cool.'

'Run the next one, Buzz.'

Lewis only half listened. His mind wandered. This was only his first day in New York and despite the adrenalin generated by the excitement of Manhattan he was conscious of jet lag. He had slept badly in the poorly ventilated room in the Grand Lexington Palace. The hotel was a dump. Opening a drawer in the room, on his arrival, he had been horrified to see a swarm of cockroaches scurrying for safety. The traffic had roared ceaselessly through the night. He was wide awake at 10.00 a.m.: 10.00 a.m. London time, 5.00 a.m. in New York. Exhausted, but giving up the notion of sleeping more, Lewis dressed and went out into a glorious fresh spring morning. A few fluffy clouds leisurely drifted through the brightening dawn. The grandness and sheer scale of the city was overwhelming, breathtaking. This was the stuff of Lewis's dreams and now, actually there, he found it almost impossible to believe that this was going to be home for a year.

He breakfasted at a coffee shop on the corner of Lexington and 53rd Street. Over his third cup of tasteless coffee he jotted down on the back of the ticket wallet he still carried, his first thoughts: *Restarting life in the New World: Credit side: no enemies (yet), eager to start work, unusually happy. Debit side: hate hotel but nowhere else to live, limited cash resources (haven't picked up my per diems from Mr Gibson), don't know anyone. Conclusion: just about in credit!!*

It was nearly 11.00 a.m. New York time when Lewis turned left and found himself, at last, strolling down Broadway towards Times Square. Both were an enormous disappointment to him: Broadway was lined with porno movie houses and Times Square wasn't square at all. Where were all the old theatres? Buried, he found, within towering hotels or hidden by scaffolding down side streets. He explored 44th and 45th Streets off Times Square. At least this *felt* like Theatreland – as he had imagined it. These were streets filled with theatres. This was Broadway . . .

George Gibson Productions had its office on the 42nd floor of a fifty-six floor all glass and steel block on Times Square. Lewis arrived without an appointment on the off-chance that the producer might be free for a chat.

'Deli or showbiz?' Betty suspiciously eyed the Englishman from behind a desk piled high with scripts and files.

Lewis looked round and saw the white-haired old lady. 'Oh, I'm not hungry, thanks.'

'Huh?' The lady, Lewis noticed, was chewing gum, and idly turning the wheel of an enormous card index file. 'Who d'ya wanna see?' Her nails, Lewis noted, were half chewed away.

'I wondered if I might have a word with George Gibson?' He gave his name. The office reeked of cigars.

She sighed heavily. It was going to be a tough day. 'What side of the business? Deli or theatre?'

The penny dropped. 'Oh, you mean there are two businesses?'

'Sure,' said a voice from behind Lewis. 'I gotta interest in three delicatessens. You like Jewish food, Jaahn?'

'Well, I've not eaten it that much . . . chopped liver . . . that kind of thing you mean?' Lewis said, highly flattered to be recognised.

'I'm sorry, Mr Gibson,' Betty said, 'I didn't . . .'

But the Producer was already firmly pumping Lewis's hand and slapping him on the back. 'How're ya doin' Jaahn? Nice flight? Hotel okay? Settled in?' Without awaiting a reply, he ushered him into a small, neat, functional office decorated with playbills. Lewis's attention was immediately drawn to the fax machine, with its blinking lights and its mechanical hum, spewing out pages of dense contract into a wire tray. A jumbo-sized IBM computer filled a corner of the room, the keyboard strategically placed on the glass-topped desk. Everything had its place . . .

Gibson moved to his desk and was immediately reduced to a silhouette by the intensity of the light from a floor-to-ceiling, plate glass window, with an awesome panorama over the roof-tops of Manhattan, the docks, the Hudson River and to New Jersey beyond. At that moment the QE2, far away, in miniature, was docking at a pier. From Lewis's point of view it appeared to be docking into George Gibson's thigh. The young Englishman had not been asked to sit. He felt 14 years old and hauled once more

57

before the headmaster.

'The hotel's okay for the next day or two till I can find my feet. An apartment or a room . . . it's . . .'

But Gibson interrupted. 'You heard any of Jerry's music, Jaahn? HEY, BETTY!!! Bring in one of Jerry's compilation tapes will ya!!!'

Whilst Betty noisily rooted through her drawers and cupboards for a tape, Lewis asked Gibson about the schedule for the next week or so.

'Okay. Casting's number one priority at the moment. We're going to start principal auditions on Monday. We've offered the leads – that's young Galileo and Old Galileo, Marina and Anna – and we're waiting for their agents to come back to us . . .'

'Can I ask who . . .

'No . . . I'll tell you later. Problem is Jerry and Michael are still working on the book and the score. We're going to get a complete score and script in two weeks . . . The actors will be waiting for this. Jerry is a . . . HEY, BETTY! WHERE'S THAT GOD-DAMNED CASSETTE!?' George screamed.

'It's here somewhere, Mr Gibson.'

'Betty's been with me 32 years,' he leant over the desk and whispered hoarsely. 'I haven't the heart to fire her *yet*. I'll fire actors, directors, designers, anybody, but I can't fire Betty. Peculiar, huh? I guess one day I'll do it. Fire her jus' before she retires, then I won't have to pay her a pension, yeah?' He laughed uproariously and pulled a cigar from a monogrammed humidifier on a filing cabinet.

Lewis wasn't sure whether he was joking.

'I got compassion. I mean where's she gonna get another job at her age? 'Sides she knows all my secrets.'

He lit up and coughed nastily. 'Now, let's talk about your book . . . You're gonna have to start with my early life . . . I came over on a ship from Lithuania in '29, aged 12 . . . nightmare journey shut in an airless hold . . . five days of storms . . . old women throwin' up . . . kids screamin' . . . you writing this down . . .?'

Not expecting to plunge in this quickly, Lewis wasn't prepared. 'Hold on a sec, Mr Gibson . . . er, d'you think you can lend me some . . . er . . . paper. I'm afraid I've only got this . . .' He brandished the ticket wallet, already covered with scrawled notes. Lewis didn't feel this was getting off to a good start.

'BETTY, BRING IN SOME PAPER! WHERE THE HELL ARE YOU?'

'I know the tape's here somewhere, Mr Gibson . . .'

'. . . Plan was, I was goin' to get a job here in America, earn enough dough to send back to my family who were still runnin' the bakery in Vilnius. See there wasn't enough dough in the bakery . . .' And he laughed merrily again.

Lewis wasn't sure how to play this. He wanted to set the record straight right away. Ross Boardman's last words still echoed in his head. He didn't want his book to be a *biography* of George Gibson. That wasn't the point . . . but he felt too tired, too jet lagged, too . . .

'Jerry . . . have I played you Jerry's stuff?' George Gibson set off on another track. 'Jerry's gonna be the new Andrew Lloyd Webber . . . this boy can write tunes . . . an' I gotta tell you . . . that's a dying art . . . Also I'm wrestling with this problem, see . . . how d'you measure out exactly equal portions of ice-cream? Any ideas?'

Confused, Lewis shook his head.

'I lose a fortune each week as the waiters put *too much* ice-cream with the apple pie. Too little's no good either. The customers complain. But you know those little scoops they use, they don't give *equal amounts* . . . ! That's my problem, see. I get my ice-cream from a little Italian guy in Queen's. Costa fortune. That's the price not the Italian's name . . . You like jokes?'

Gibson had a – was it a laughing or a coughing fit? Lewis was hard pressed to say.

'Okay. Here's a good one for you. This producer in Hollywood – one day his mother phones him at work . . . "Son, son", she says, "your cousin Mary . . . remember little Mary . . . well she ain't so little any more . . . an' she wants to see you" . . . "Oh no Ma'am" says this ganze film producer . . . "No, no Chaime, you gotta see her. She's 22" . . . So, anyway, finally the son agrees to see her – she phones an' makes an appointment to see him – 11.00 a.m. on the next day. Next day, dead on time the secretary says, "Your cousin Mary's here to see you." "Show her in," he says . . . an' . . . an' . . . in walks this beautiful girl – you know what I mean – model type – long blonde hair – and sits down . . . "Well," he says, the producer . . . "my, my you've grown up since I last saw you." "Let's get one thing straight," says cousin Mary right off. "I don't want to go into the movie business" . . . "Oh," says her cousin, a little suspiciously but she crosses her legs and says . . . "I don't want you to help me in any way . . . I just want to serve you . . . an' . . .",' Gibson begins to chuckle, ' " . . . an' I give great head"!' Gibson paused.

What's that mean? Am I supposed to laugh now! Lewis worriedly thought . . .

'. . . Then, then the producer looks at her for a moment an' says . . . "Okay, okay. But what's in it for *me*?" ' Gibson was wiping away the tears of mirth.

Lewis laughed politely but the joke had sailed right past him.

'Al Cohen told me that last night . . . Gaad he's a funny guy. You know him?'

Betty came in and said wretchedly, 'I can't find the tape, Mr Gibson. I think you took the last one with you to France.'

'Godamnit, you're right – I gave it to Doris. Never mind Lewis, go to the MCA recording studios at 7.00 p.m. – Jerry's playing Dee a demo of some new songs. Hot off the press. That'll start you off. Goodbye.'

And without further ceremony, George pushed Lewis out of the office and closed his door only to open it again immediately.

'BETTY! Give him some money. An' find him somewhere permanent to live, okay. Lewis, I'm gonna have to sit you down and give you the rest of my story for this book you're writing about me . . . Dinner tomorrow night! Be here at six.'

Jerry didn't just listen to his own music, he experienced it – bodily. His body, tuned like an instrument, moved as he listened and judged. He was highly motivated, self-critical – an utter perfectionist.

By the end of March he had completed 12 songs out of the expected 16. In the first days of April, with George's money, he had hired a studio at MCA, employed a dozen session musicians and laid down songs 10, 11 and 12. It had taken two all-night mixing sessions to please Jerry, and now, he was ready to let the people hear. Dee was special, so Dee was the first to experience it. He hadn't been too pleased to see Lewis bowl up, but Betty had rung saying George wanted it and Jerry was always prepared to go along with George.

Galileo was Jerry's first Broadway musical. He'd come a long way – and he was grateful. His mother, an illegal immigrant from Jamaica, had brought him to New York when he was two. She was penniless, he fatherless. She had found a job as child minder and general housekeeper to a young upwardly mobile couple with a child the same age as Jerry. In 1964, this young management consultant and his wife lived in a small apartment in Sutton Place. The couple were highly cultured and accomplished musicians – he played the piano and she the cello. Daily the young Jerry would accompany his mother to the apartment. He could climb on to the piano stool and bash away at the keyboard. The owners became increasingly successful and were invariably out or away on business. Thus Jerry's mother became an indispensable child minder. All the time Jerry's piano-playing improved – unnoticed by everyone except the little white boy who would sometimes stop playing with his toys and stare bright-eyed at the increasingly pleasing sounds Jerry would make. His playing was becoming structured. By the age of five he was composing – largely pastiches of stuff he'd hear on the kitchen radio that his mother never turned off.

In 1971 Sutton Place was sold and the family, now that a second child had been born, moved to a charming Brownstone on 53rd and First. Jerry and his mother moved into a room on the top floor. They were treated as members of the family. Jerry's brilliance as a musician was not lost on them – they recognised his enormous potential and were instrumental in finding (and subsequently paying for) proper tuition.

For his fifteenth birthday he was taken by his adopted family to see *A Chorus Line* and he was hooked. His destiny was mapped out. He wanted to do nothing else but write for Broadway.

In his early twenties, after majoring in music from Williams College, Jerry Trimlock wrote three songs that were recorded by Diana Ross, became million sellers and earned him a million dollars. Despite his success in rock and roll, he still yearned for Broadway and the American musical theatre. 'There's no-one writing musicals for today's kids,' he would say to anyone who would listen. 'Why should the Brits have it all their own way? You have to hand it to Lloyd Webber, he's captured the market; pop thro' semi-classical.' *Galileo* was his dream coming true.

Lewis yawned loudly.

'That boring?' Jerry asked testily.

'Oh sorry, no!' Lewis was mortified. 'No, I'm just exhausted from the flight.'

Dee was cooing. 'Oh Debbie, oh Jerry . . . that's just beautiful.'

The playing of the demo was over. Hearing the songs for the first time, Lewis thought they all sounded alike. One romantic ballad after the other.

As if to answer his thoughts, Jerry said: 'Yeah, but I still gotta tackle the political material that Michael and Ross keep comin' up with.'

'Can't you get Michael to come up with some lyric ideas?' Dee suggested.

'Yeah, I done that. I called him last night. He's full of good thoughts. He'll bring them from London at the weekend.'

'Do you and Michael Kershon get on well?' Lewis asked.

'Yeah. Why do you ask?' Jerry looked at him suspiciously. What was it about Lewis that Jerry didn't like? He didn't know himself. But if George wants this book . . . George always knew best . . .

Lewis plunged in. 'Well it's a difficult relationship between the composer and the book writer, isn't it? Especially when the composer's writing the lyrics as well. I've read a lot about it. There's been a number of such stormy relationships in the past . . . take Gilbert and Sullivan . . .'

Jerry interrupted him. 'Wanna eat?'

'Oh, that'd be great!' Lewis glanced at his watch. It was after ten and he hadn't eaten properly since that early breakfast.

But it soon became clear that the invitation didn't include him. Dee, who had been entrusted by George to look after Lewis, now politely got rid of him. En route home to the hotel he bought an over-stuffed roast beef sandwich from the Carnegie Deli and ate a few mouthfuls. Back in his room, fully dressed, he lay down on his bed and fell asleep at once, oblivious to the cockroaches on his bedside table feasting off the over-stuffed remains.

Jerry took Debbie and Dee to dinner at The Brasserie, where they drank three bottles of champagne and laughed a lot. Later, back at Jerry's apartment on 58th Street, the three of them, young, close friends, shared hits, drank Tequila, and Jerry, for old time's sake, made love to both girls on the thick pile carpet amongst the cushions. Debbie wasn't jealous as she watched Jerry and Dee. She loved Dee and Dee needed loving . . . Anyway Dee happy was Dee useful. She was Mrs Producer. Who knows what the future holds, Debbie was fond of saying.

After 3.00 a.m., Dee dressed and took a cab home to George and the cats, leaving Debbie curled up in Jerry's loving arms.

11

Suddenly good fortune seemed to smile on Lewis and things started to look up.

An early morning phone conversation with Betty in the office led to a meeting at 11.00 a.m. with the caretaker of a seedy block up on East 89th Street who let him in to view a curious one-room subterranean apartment. Despite high, dirty, barricaded windows, the spartan furnishings, the smears of grease and grime over the kitchen surfaces, and the general gloom barely relieved by the one source of illumination, an antique office desk light on a rickety table – despite all this, for Lewis it was love at first sight. And there were no roaches. This apartment *was* New York, New York.

By early afternoon he had left the Grand Lexington Palace and had taken up residence.

The apartment was owned by a would-be poet, a friend of a friend of Betty's, who had apparently removed himself to a cabin in Vermont to write amidst nature. Cleaning and tidying, Lewis discovered an abundance of evidence of frustrated literary endeavour. One particular cupboard in the kitchen (in which he expected to find cups and plates) contained neat piles of manuscript paper, each above a numbered label. Pinned to the inside of the cupboard door a yellowing list of contents. No. 15 caught Lewis's eye:

No.15. Strolling on the Knife Edge:
A cutting contemporary epic poem.

He picked up the three sheets above label No. 15. The top sheet bore the title, neatly typed, plus the author's name: Robert Berol. So this was Lewis's landlord.

Page 2 began:

Slicing langorously through the pulpy adipocere
Hermann perceived the corpse no longer matter,
Subject to natural forces,
Compliant to his surgeon's knife
But ethereal; non-temporal,
Elusive on Tom Tiddler's ground.

There followed several more similarly dense verses. The third page was blank but for the word 'and' in inverted commas.

Below the table in the bedsitting room Lewis made his most satisfactory discovery – a working electric typewriter. Certain a fellow writer would have no objections, he established it at the centre of the table and surrounded it with the tools of his trade exported from London: bottles of Tipp-Ex, boxes of Croxley paper, a Thesaurus and a Shorter Oxford English Dictionary. The machine now loaded with a pristine sheet sat waiting for action.

With the apartment as clean as it ever was to be, Lewis, with a cup of tea at hand, perched on the edge of a carefully cushioned seat, placed two hands on the table either side of the keyboard and prepared for work. He breathed heavily as if about to dive from the high board; picked his nose, bounced his legs, sighed loudly, and generally procrastinated. Then, suddenly, with an intense outburst of energy, he typed:

BROADWAY MAYBE

(provisional title)

An Artful Account of a Theatrical Journey

by John Lewis

April 1992.

Apt. 1D,
49 E. 89th Street,
NY, NY.

He had started and it felt good.

'Merv an' I call it the S.S.Q.,' Gibson was saying. 'An' let me tell you, young man, it not only applies to the delicatessen business – you can apply it to all walks of life – particularly the theatre. I'm telling this to Boardman all the time. Does he listen? What d'you think?'
Lewis had been studying the incomprehensible menu. Every-

thing had a grand title followed by an exhaustive description of the contents of the dish. By the time he had got to the end of the description his appetite had died. 'THE SHUBERT ALLEY SPECIAL SEA-FOOD salver. A schpritz of SEA-THIS and a schpritz of SEA-THAT, WOW! MAINE OYSTERS SEGGING INTO A CRAB MOUSSE CAKE IN A SAUCE OF DELI-SHOUS MUZZELS. MARKET FRESH ITEMS INCLUDING (GET THIS GUZZLERS!) SQUID, EELS, CLAMS, LOBSTER, SOFT-SHELL CRABS, BAKED TO PERFECTION ON OUR UNIQUE SALVERS. DISH INCLUDES HOUSE SALAD WITH *ANY* OR ALL OF OUR 75 DIFFERENT DRESSINGS.'

'Sorry,' Lewis looked at Gibson over the menu. 'What is SSQ? I didn't quite . . .'

Gibson was rolling carefully torn strips of paper napkin around the ends of several wooden toothpicks he had lined up next to his knife.

'I'm saying S.S.Q. – that's Speed, Size, Quality. In that order. Give 'em that to ten – and I'm talkin' ten outa ten – a triple–decker BLT or a musical comedy – it all oils the cabbage. Deliver it fast, make it big, cook it well. Whad'ya want? A Merv special?'

Lewis found 'THE MERV SPECIAL' under 'THE HOT-TO-TROT CHILLI'. He read: 'A DELICIOUS SPICY-PEPPER-SAUCE ATOP A CAJUN-BLACKENED MARKET-FRESH FLOUNDER ON A BED OF THE CRISPEST SEA-WEED MERV CAN FRY'.

'Who's Merv?' Lewis asked.

Gibson was cleaning his ears with his improvised swab. The waiter arrived and grunted something unintelligible. 'Merv's my partner in the food business. See this is our flagship – The DELI DELITE – but we got two others – two blocks both ways.'

Gibson turned his attention to the waiter. 'Two Merv specials, house dressing, okay I order for you? You like fish – you'll like this one.' The waiter nodded and moved on. Lewis felt no need to argue.

'You know how old I am?' Gibson asked.

'Sixty, sixty-five.' This was diplomacy: Lewis had done his research.

'Yeah – I look that, don't I? Well, I was born third year of the First World War – that makes me 75. An' I'm strong as a mule. Feel that muscle.'

He offered his bent arm and Lewis had no choice but to reach over and be impressed.

'Ski, play tennis at weekends – great game – keeps you fit. You play?'

'Actually I do, but I'm not very good.' Humble as ever.

'Pity. Otherwise I'd have given you a game.'

'I'm not that bad and I'd love to play you sometime.'

Gibson studied Lewis for a moment. 'What kinda woman you like?'

Was this a test question? 'How do you mean, Mr Gibson?' Lewis asked warily.

But Gibson wasn't interested in Lewis's tastes. 'See my ideal is a six foot blonde Scandinavian. Preferably deaf and dumb. I don't like women who talk much, an' they never listen anyway. A while back friend of mine calls me an' says he's found me my ideal woman. People are always trying to do me favours, you know Jaahn. He's found this incredible Scandinavian broad who's 6'2". And 100% deaf! So I arrange to meet her for dinner. She's perfection. At the end of the meal, I mouth, 'You wanna go to bed with me?' This girl reads lips perfectly. She smiles. Then writes me a little note, that I kept to this day. Says, *'Why not?'* Well, Jaahn, this girl has the strangest orgasm noise you ever heard! You written all that down?'

Lewis didn't know whether to be just shocked, or shocked and appalled. 'Er, not yet . . . no. I'll remember that one, Mr Gibson . . .'

The waiter brought them salad and water. Lewis checked his pencil. 'How would you define a producer?'

'He's the schmuck who raises the money, hires the director, buys the script, contracts the actors, pays for the set and loses his shirt when the director fucks up.'

'But who does okay if you get a hit?'

Gibson seemed to dismiss this notion. 'Sure, sure – but it needs one hit to pay for eight years of failures – and it's failures that are the norm. Only mebbe one in ten shows makes money. Did you know that? That's why it's getting harder and harder to raise money for shows. The more difficult it is to raise money the less shows are produced and the less producers we have – and so on. It's a descending spiral. Costs go up – ticket prices rise – less audiences.'

'Okay,' Lewis said, 'but let's start at the beginning . . .'

Gibson munched noisily and talked. He had a lot to say. 'Born 1915 Cleveland – get writing! Ohio born and bred. Great city in those days, can't take going back now. D'you know the Erie's so polluted a year or so back it caught fire. When I was a kid you could swim off the breakwater . . .'

Wait a minute, Mr Gibson. I thought you came over on an immigrant ship from Lithuania . . . Puzzled, Lewis chewed his salad.

'Rich city, back at the beginning of the century, rich in iron. We built more ships than any place else.'

This confusion needed clearing up fast. 'Er, sorry. I thought you said yesterday that you came over on a ship from Vilnius . . .'

It was Gibson's turn to look puzzled. 'Me? No y'got me mixed up with someone else . . . No – my father made nails. Big business: nails. You wouldn't think so – it made him a small fortune. My mother, God rest her soul, had loved the theatre. Did some amateur work – brought up me and my sisters.' His eyes filled with tears.

'Your mother was a big influence then?'

'She was . . .'

At that point the narrative was interrupted by the arrival at their table of Merv Baum – Gibson's partner. Merv was all stomach with no height to mitigate the grotesque proportions; just a small head perched on rolls of fat. Nevertheless Merv was usually smiling – not necessarily indicative of joy, more a function of the construction of his face. Lewis was struck by large warm twinkling eyes.

'Hiya boys,' Merv said, lifting a stubby hand in greeting. Huge patches of sweat spread across the front of his short-sleeved white shirt. He was picking the seeds off a sesame bagel.

'Hiya Merv. Merv, this is Jaahn Lewis from England. He's writing a book about me.'

'Yeah?' Merv grinned.

Lewis and Merv shook hands. *A book about the show not about him.* Sweat and bagel crumbs changed hands.

'So this book's fiction or whaat? My boys not looking after you? No drinks. Hey, what is this. What d'you want?'

'Gimme an orange juice,' Gibson said. 'Same for you?'

'Lovely,' said Lewis.

Merv bellowed out the order over the din of the restaurant.

'You wanna sit and listen while I tell him my life?'

'Na. I lived too much of it widja – I'll sit with ya later . . . Hiya boys . . .' And he drifted off to another table at which four Hassidic Jews were huddled, arguing, waving arms.

'Round about the time I was being born, my mother's childhood sweetheart, fellow name of Francis Drury, was raising money for various charities. He was a charitable man. My father didn't like him – see – guess it was . . . well, my father had this suspicion that my ma would have preferred to have married Francis – the goy . . . I mean he raised *millions* for the Church too . . . This stuff interest you?' He sipped the juice that had arrived. The waiter cleared the salads.

'You bet.' Lewis was obligingly enthralled.

'Beautiful girl, my ma. I'll show you some pictures. You can put them in your book. One of me in a kinda smock, lookin' very

67

serious, standing next to my mama. She's sittin' in an armchair smilin' an' holdin' cut flowers. I musta been seven or eight.'

He paused and his eyes were moist. 'I gotta tell you Jaahn. That's what we've lost in the theatre today. Goddamned plays about family life. Mother love. Know what I mean. Sentiment and compassion. I'm trying to get Kershon and Boardman to see that. Galileo was a family man, right! I mean that guy *loved* his mother. An' his sisters. Christ, he even loved their husbands. I mean that's a *great* guy – how many guys do you know who love their sisters' husbands, for Chrissake! That's why I wanna do a *musical* about Galileo! The guy was a hero. You agree with me, Jaahn?'

'I'm sorry, I'm getting a little confused here. You want to do a musical about Galileo because he loved his sisters' husbands?'

Gibson peered at Lewis as if he was a idiot. 'Sure. Politics, shmolitics. That's what they're giving me. People don't want politics, Jaahn. They're sick of politics. They get politics rammed down their throat day and night on TV. Now the viewing figures are dropping like shit. Berlin Wall falls, dictators get shot – no-one gives a fuck. Give 'em: "Momma Dies so Son can Live" and they switch on in the zillions. I know these things – I have a heart. Where was I?'

'Your mother and Francis Drury.'

'Oh yeah. My uncle Nathan, on my mother's side was a kinda bohemian. Black sheep of the family – as different from my father as you could imagine. My father's a hands-on industrialist – rolled up sleeves – he's out there next to the furnaces quality-controlling those nails himself. No supers for him. My uncle Nathan on the other hand, he's out on the lake in a row boat – dodging the lake traffic – painting Cleveland from the water. Uncle's got these fellow painters – making no dough you understand – these guys barely sold a single painting one month to the next . . . some painters huh? The guys want to start a theatre, these painters. It's not so surprising – I see surprise on your face, Jaahn . . . You like the flounder . . . one of our best-selling dishes . . . we get through 65 pounds of flounder every three days! Now that should surprise you. Hi Jackie.'

A short balding man stopped briefly at their table, exchanged a pleasantry and moved on to join the four, now laughing, Hassidim.

'That man's a great comedian, gonna give him his own show one day . . .' Gibson resumed his monologue. 'So these painters need money. My uncle Nathan asked my mother – who asks my father. He says he'll think about it. Anyway, she goes to her old flame, Francis Drury who takes the whole thing on board, lock stock and barrel. Charlie Brooks, Uncle Nathan's pal, becomes president of the theatre board and my father *likes* Charlie, likes him so much that he starts donating to the Playhouse funds . . . soon he's hooked too. Meetings are held at our house – our house becomes the fund's headquarters. So I grew up with the theatre. By the time I'm 12 the Playhouse is a two-theatre complex (they named the larger house after Francis – you should have seen my father's face at the naming ceremony – 1927 . . . I remember every second of that day. Boy, was I proud). Fred McConnell ran the place, he was always round with us – my ma, me hangin' in there – would go to meetings, arrange fund-raising galas – Fred became like a second father to me. If I have to name one person – only one – who made me what I am today . . . that was a great man . . . great theatre man . . . knew what made a play work . . .'

Lewis was having trouble with the fish. Blackening the fish, he decided, did little to improve the taste. Gamely he munched on.

'When I was 16 my father took me into the nail business, sure I was going to be a nailman. For ten years I worked my ass off. There ain't nothing I don't know about the iron business – but I gotta tell you I hated every goddamn second. Why didn't I get out? Mebbe I could have – but the pressure from my father was too strong – I was the only boy see – Rose and Lilian – my sisters – got out of the way as soon as they could . . . Then along came the war and, boy, was I glad – and saved. In '45 I came home wiser and clear about my future. It was bye-bye Cleveland, hello Broadway.'

'What happened to the nail business?' Lewis asked.

'Benevolent take-over in the late forties. My father retired in comfort and laid enough on me to finance my first coupla shows. You *need* dough behind you in this business, Jaahn, let me tell you. That's why I got all this.' He waved his arms possessively.

Lewis looked about: Deli Delite was airy, almost hospital clean. Tiled, gleaming floors – white tables, alcoves and benches. Opposite the door – the take-out counter, a noisy crowd, a cross-section of the theatre district, waiting for orders to be made up. Dancers, rehearsals over for the day, exchanged gossip leaning on sport sacs bulging with pumps, tights and magazines. Actors mingled with their audience. A whole life. For Lewis it was the life of the art.

'I'm the last of a breed, Jaahn; the last of the independent creative producers – something, I have to tell you, I'm proud of. I *get* in there, Jaahn, with my sleeves rolled up an' I *create* the show. When you see a billboard that says: 'A George Gibson Production', you know you're gonna get quality. But it's the riskiest business in the world. A show doesn't work and it closes in five days. Critic of the Times gets a bug, he hates a good show, it closes in five days. Six or seven million dollars down the tubes in five days. It's a mug's game. You have to be mishugah to do it. You think they teach you producing in college?'

Gibson leant forward, dipping his elbow into a pat of butter on his side plate. 'I'm gonna tell you something confidential. I've had eight years of semi-failure. One show after another. But, I'm telling you, *Galileo*'s going to change that. I've been working on this show for two years – and I got faith in this one.' He beat his chest. 'Unshakable faith.'

His eyes blazing with passion, he gazed deep into Lewis's and said: 'You like cheesecake? Whady'a want, blackcurrant or plain?'

The chauffeured Mercedes manoeuvred through the late evening traffic on Madison Avenue. George Gibson was in the back puffing angrily at his cigar, next to him Lewis, eyes streaming with tears from the acrid smoke, whilst the object of George's fury, Dee, sat in the front next to the driver, staring moodily ahead.

Dee had gone to a show, been picked up by the car and had collected the two men from the restaurant. Their conversation had continued into the car when Dee became involved. Attempting to be friendly to the foreigner, Dee had said: 'See that block over there – the tall one – that's called "The Actors' Hilton". Apartments are rented to actors and writers real cheap. I gotta good writer friend who lives there and . . .'

Before she could finish, George had interrupted. 'Why you always going on about that no-good cock-sucker claiming to be a writer?'

'He *is* good!' Over her shoulder to Lewis she had added: 'He thinks I'm havin' an affair with him, that's why he's always putting him down. Frank's had several plays produced in repertories in Illinois. He's real smart. One day he'll . . .'

'Okay, okay,' rejoined George. 'If he's so clever, how come he ain't rich?'

'Oh come on George . . . !' Dee argued fiercely back. 'Having no money doesn't make you less clever – or not a good writer . . .'

'Name me one good playwright who isn't rich. C'mon! You can't! But I'll name you a hundred who are.'

Dee had muttered something under her breath that Lewis hadn't caught. Both sunk into a furious silence.

The car turned left on to Madison and Lewis wanted to continue the interview. 'It must be great working with Ross Boardman again after twenty-five years. I'm a terrific fan of his, of course.'

George didn't answer immediately. After a moment, he leant forward and gruffly asked the driver to turn on the radio. The Bolshoi Ballet Orchestra was playing excerpts from *Les Sylphides*, and it was with this pastoral underscoring that Gibson said: 'You gotta genius there. Probably just about the ace of goddamn directors of musicals in this country. That's why I picked him. I only pick the best! You gotta be tough to direct a big new show. You gotta deal first with the script – I mean the writers – and not only clever ones living in the Hilton Schmilton!' George leant forward and shouted the last phrase at the top of his voice at Dee.

'Sure, sure George – I'm listening,' Dee sighed in the front.

'You gotta make that script hang together. Then you gotta have a helluva lot of visual imagination. Musical comedy, you gotta love jokes and gags. That's why I'm always jumpin' on those guys to get them to deliver more jokes! Boardman did that Shakespeare thing in Long Wharf. What was it called?'

Lewis looked blank.

'*Shoemaker's Holiday*,' said Dee.

'Yeah, that's what I said. Shakespeare, right? Great job,' George went on. 'Had it all. When that asshole gets it right he gets it right. I did a show coupla years back – oh Jesus what was it called – had that TV star in . . .'

'*Looking Sweet.*' Dee had curled up into the comfy leather.

'That was it . . . *Looking Sweet.*'

'Real flopperoo . . .' Dee added.

'Too much scenery, too many computers. They wired in computers to do everything – pull up the scenery, pull down the scenery – haul pallets in – haul 'em off. The only thing these computers couldn't do was rewrite the show. An' I told that guy who directed it – I forget his name – I told him way back at the beginning – keep it simple. It's a small show, don't try an' make a small show big. It won't work.'

'Why didn't he listen?' Lewis asked. He could see George grow tense.

'He was *second rate*. That's why.'

Dee turned round and answered for him. 'Gibs should have fired him. Nick Kodaly – that was the guy, the director.'

'Nick, yeah. Shoulda been a big hit. Too much scenery. See, if they won't listen – if they don't get it right – you have to fire them and get in people who are going to get it right. *Looking Sweet* could have been a great show . . . only show I never fired anybody – and my only big disaster.' George thought deeply about all this.

Lewis steered the conversation back to Boardman.

'I've only done two shows with Ross in the 35 years I've known him. I discovered him you know. He was putzing around Washington when I brought him to New York to do *Owen's Valley*. What a hit that was – a sensation at the time! You know, he's never done anything as good . . .'

'Have you, George . . .?' Dee was in a provocative mood stung by George's remarks earlier about Frank.

'Is that a question or are you trying to make me angry?'

'Sorry, sorry . . .' She held up her hands in mock surrender.

'After *Owen's Valley*, Ross was hot. Got asked to do a lotta shows. Some worked – he had a coupla hits, nothing as big as *Valley*. And it was a great time in the city. Big shows: *Pajama Game*, *Damn Yankees*. Then he drifted off to make movies . . . nothing great. He married, divorced – alimony, the usual. So in '64 I offered him *Love Boat*.

'I forgot *Love Boat* . . . ,' Dee said.

'You weren't born in '64, so you can keep your mouth shut . . .'

'It was a piece of shit . . .'

'SHUT UP, DEE!' George shouted.

'Shut up yourself!'

Lewis, caught between the sudden eruption, interceded. 'It wasn't a success, then . . .?'

'Bombed. Ran a month or so despite schlock reviews . . . cheap show – only a dozen in the cast – no chorus. I tried every which way to get publicity for that show, to sell it. I smelt we were in trouble before we opened. I said to the guys who ran my publicity: "Anything you have to do to sell this show you got my permission . . ." Nothing. An' I have to tell you, Jaahn, it was nobody's fault except mine. Ross did his best, Norman (you remember him – does my publicity) did his . . . but you can't make gold outa excrement. Funny thing about that show for Ross was that he became more serious, more mature. He's done some good work since. Lotta good plays – he's as hot again as he was – and he's a critics' favourite. Frank Rich loves this guy. I've hired Ross to do this piece because I think he can handle the romance *and* the politics. Make both work, make it entertaining . . .'

'Yeah,' said Dee grimly, 'I like to laugh.'

The Mercedes pulled up outside Lewis's 89th Street apartment. The evening was over.

12

The production conference had been called for 10.00 a.m. Coffee
and bagels were laid out at the centre of the table in the conference
room of George Gibson's office suite. In his eagerness, Lewis was
the first to arrive. He sat alone at the table and stared at the food.
If he'd known breakfast was going to be served here, he wouldn't
have wasted his money at the diner. But what the hell! Lewis was
now in love. In love with New York. And a man in love can afford
to throw away $3.75. He'd been here a week but it seemed a year.
The city gave him a buzz he had never before known. He felt alive
and exhilarated. The pace thrilled him. In London he woke at 8.30
rarely refreshed, here he needed no alarm, yet was fresh, ready for
anything at 7.00 a.m. He already had a favourite table at the mock
fifties diner at the end of his block. A New York Times propped
up against the paper napkin dispenser, a blueberry muffin half eaten
on his plate, his coffee cup continually refilled by the waiter: Lewis
breakfasted a most happy fella.

'Hi, Jaahn! How's the book goin'?' George strolled into the
conference room from his next door office and interrupted Lewis's
musings.

'Well, I haven't honestly got too far yet, Mr Gibson . . . I'm
hoping to get going with this conference . . .'

But George had already wandered off to talk to the Casting
Director, Cathy Newman, who had arrived with her assistant,
Miles Fox.

'Hi, John! I'm Fly Gold, Ross's assistant.' Fly, cheerful,
prematurely balding, was in his early forties. 'Ross has told me all
about you. Need anything, I'm your guy! And I mean *anything*,
okay?' He winked at Lewis, adding confidentially, 'Fr'instance,
there are a coupla dancers I know who'd give you an interesting
night . . . Or if your taste's the other way . . .'

He's pretty direct, Lewis thought. The last time he'd had an offer
like that was on a day trip to Tangier from Marbella. 'No thanks,'

Lewis said. 'But I'll let you know if I do.'

Lewis had exchanged a few words with Michael Kershon before the meeting started. They had met before – two years earlier. Lewis was writing a piece on First Night Disasters. Michael had just opened a play to crucifying reviews – and Lewis remembered being struck by a display of noble sang froid – a calm acceptance of the criticisms. Kershon had obviously been hurt by the personal malevolence of some of the reviews. Yet in the conversation, conducted on a beautiful hot day in his garden in Islington whilst a couple of naked children romped, ducking in and out of a sprinkler, he had been able to analyse in cool detail the deep flaws in his own text. Lewis found him honest, open, a playwright of great intelligence and pride.

Ross arrived, and with the assembly complete, began the meeting. 'Welcome to our first, full production conference. Enjoy; from now on it can only get worse!'

There was a smattering of laughter around the table. Lewis made notes. He found himself riveted by the designer Karl-Heinz. Buddha-like he sat, palms on the table, a slight smile played on a ghostly white face. His Vietcong Jungle cap appeared to hide a shaven skull.

'Most of you know each other, I think. But perhaps not everyone. On my right, my assistant and associate Fly Gold.' Lewis jotted down a description: *Fly's got a sort of pinched creased face that makes him look older than he is. I put him 35-ish but it's hard to be sure. Doodling on his schedule . . . seems to be a kind of fixer . . .*

'Tam Topp, our choreographer. This is Tam's first Broadway show – but I'm sure most of you know him from the excellent work he's done with the City Ballet.' Tam waved to the group and smoothed a neatly trimmed moustache with the thumb and index finger of his right hand. Lewis wrote: *Distinguishing features – what? Jet black hair worn long, swept into a pigtail fastened with a gold hair grip. Fastidious, precise. His script is festooned with yellow Post-it notes written in a tiny hand.*

'Gene Landau, General Manager, next to him Norman Naff, publicity . . .' Lewis noticed the edge in Ross's voice as he introduced Naff.

'Karl-Heinz Zeiss, our designer, and Chubby Moscovitz, his American assistant. Chubby will be your liaison on all design questions, including costumes. Karl-Heinz, I'm afraid, doesn't speak. He's a man of principle and has concluded that the world is far too noisy. Am I right, Karl-Heinz?'

The German designer nodded gravely.

'However, I urge you not to be put off by this. After all, this principled position is not far removed from vegetarianism. He understands English perfectly and he'll respond in aphorisms and drawings that you will doubtless find thought-provoking and amusing.'

Lewis wrote furiously. He was surprised and delighted by such eccentricity.

'The two Sams. Sam Lee, lights, sitting next to Sam Mole – sound. For those of you unlucky enough not to have made the acquaintance of these two gentlemen before – they're simply the best!' They returned Ross's smile. 'Our Stage Manager, the indomitable Charlie Brodsky. Casting, Cathy Newman . . .' Ross paused, and sipped some coffee.

Lewis fell in love and wrote: *She's mid-to-late thirties. Californian beach blonde grown older in an exquisite way. Married? Apparently, judging by the diamond rings.*

'Okay,' said Ross. 'Our writers, Michael Kershon, book; Jerry Trimlock, music stroke lyrics.'

There was spontaneous applause for the writers led by George Gibson. *That's nice of him,* Lewis wrote. *But they must be rich! Refer to last week's car journey with Dee and George.*

Jerry Trimlock and Michael Kershon made a very odd couple. Michael Kershon was tailored by Savile Row. He wore a dark blue suit with a red hanky 'V' peeking out of the breast pocket, a blue striped shirt and an MCC club tie. Jerry, in startling contrast, sat crosslegged, one basketball-Reebok-encased foot resting on a bare black thigh. He sported scissored-off jeans, exposing strong muscular legs. The front of his white tee-shirt read 'THE OPERA'S NOT OVER TILL THE FAT LADY SINGS'. (On the back, Lewis noticed, in full colour, a huge gaping mouth and tongue – at least Lewis thought it a mouth). Michael toyed with a silver Cross ballpoint, Jerry sucked chocolates.

Ross introduced Lewis. 'Treat him as one of the family – show him our pride in our work but let him see also the other side – our warts and blemishes.' Lewis thought this flowery but nice. George Gibson raised his eyes to heaven. Or was he just examining the cracks on the ceiling?

'One person missing. Stan Warburg – our Musical Director – supervising the National Company of *Happy Birthday, Mother*. He's in Chicago today.'

Introductions over, Ross asked George to speak.

'Doris says she's sorry she can't be here,' George began. 'We gotta great show here. I gotta tell you I've been working on this show for two years and I've put together the best team in the world. I'm proud that we've got you guys from Germany and

England over here working with us. Michael and Jerry, you're number one! By the time we get into rehearsal you'll have a great script for us.' He made that sound like a threat, Lewis thought. 'Norman's got plans for an eye-opener press campaign and we're gonna have a topline cast, right Cathy?' That sounded like a threat too. 'You promise me a smash and I'll make sure you're not short of anything. The game's too important. Right?' Everyone nodded. As if he wasn't happy with that, he said again: 'Right?'

This time they all agreed enthusiastically. 'Right, right, Mr Gibson!'

They got down to business. Gene Landau, the General Manager, began with the schedule: 'Rehearsals start last week October for seven weeks and we're into Washington for Christmas . . .'

Ross interrupted. 'Hey, wait up. I thought we had agreed eight weeks' rehearsal?'

Landau seemed at a loss. He looked to George who didn't react. 'Yeah, I know. George and I discussed this. George feels that eight's probably excessive for this show. The actors'll go stale with so much rehearsal.' He didn't sound convinced.

'No, that's unacceptable,' Ross countered strongly. 'We agreed eight weeks.'

'See, Ross, the extra week pushes up our costs by over $50,000 . . .'

'I need it,' Ross said quietly but firmly.

Stand off. Everyone looked at George who bounced his right leg nervously under the table. After a moment, he smiled. 'Sure, you can have it. I told you: the game's too important.'

'Okay, then,' Landau was adjusting his schedule, 'rehearsals commence third week in October . . .'

Lewis looked around the table. Nobody showed a reaction. He tried to make something out of the expression on Karl-Heinz's face but to no avail.

'We tech a week in Washington week one of December, open beginning of second week. I've given us a clear tech week – it's not long but it's all you got. Okay, Karl?'

Chubby said, 'Gene, it's Karl-*Heinz*, he doesn't like just being Karl.' The German scribbled on his pad. Chubby read out the message: 'The sands of time will cleanse the Elbe.'

'What's that mean?' Landau asked.

'All things will come to pass, I guess. We'll make the dates,' Chubby said. Karl-Heinz nodded slowly.

'We play six weeks at the Kennedy Center. This is a good date as I'm sure you all know. So end of fourth week in January we close DC. Tech here for one week, preview second week of

February – open March 3rd. Before all the other spring shows open.'

Ross said: 'Sounds good to me. Any questions? No? Then let's move on.'

'How is the casting coming on?' Michael Kershon asked. 'Any luck with Old Galileo?'

'Here's the scoop. Fact is we've been turned down by a number of stars,' Cathy Newman said, running her fingers through her hair. 'The general feeling now is we don't need a star. We're going to make our own. Right, Ross?'

Michael Kershon looked unhappy. 'Are you sure that's a good idea? Don't they like the book? Is that why they turned us down?'

Cathy shifted a little in her seat. George was about to speak but Cathy continued:

'It's not that they don't like the book . . . or the score. They're simply not available. Either they're carving successful movie careers, or tied into long TV runs. However, we've one or two tricks up our sleeve and I hope to have more news in a day or two.'

She looked nervously at George. He knew the truth. Several major stars had turned them down specifically *because* they didn't like the book. One or two didn't like the score but most had negative reactions to the story and dialogue. Cathy had shared this information only with the producer.

George leant forward and rapped the table forcefully. 'We gotta have a star! What d'you guys think about Pavarotti for Galileo? He's Italian and he sure sings okay.'

'I did check him, George,' Cathy said. 'He's not available till 2005. Anyway, I guess he'd have trouble with eight performances a week.'

Lewis caught Sam Lee winking at Fly. It made him wonder if Cathy was being serious.

'Yeah, okay. But that's the calibre of guy we need,' George continued. 'Somebody to sell the show on . . .We gotta be clear on this – I'm not gonna put 7.5 million bucks into this show without a major star. I'm with the English guy on this one!'

George had forgotten Michael Kershon's name.

'Hey, let's wait till 2006. Do two shows a week and get Pavarotti. I got some great music for him,' Jerry joked. The others laughed.

'Come on Jerry,' George said, 'it's a serious problem. We gotta solve this in the next week or two or I'll call a halt. We need a star.'

There was an awkward pause.

'How about Sir Harry Whitney?' Lewis said suddenly, surprising himself and the others. All eyes were on him. He felt impelled to continue. 'You know who I mean. He's a truly great old English actor and film star. I interviewed him once. Liked Toblerone, I remember. He was knighted in the 1989 New Years Honours, but unlike Olivier, Gielgud or Richardson the title never seemed right and it didn't stick. Harry he was and Harry he remained.'

'Great idea!' George responded enthusiastically, regarding Lewis in a new light.

Ross wasn't pleased. He neither liked Lewis's interfering nor the idea itself. He glowered at Lewis, eyes narrowed, cheeks puckered, sucking saliva. An icy stare.

'Can he sing?' Jerry wanted to know. 'I loved him in that CBS version of *The Return of the Scarlet Pimpernel II.*'

'I know him well,' Michael Kershon said. 'He played in *Flight of Fancy*, my last play for the RSC. I'm not sure he's right for *Galileo*. Ross?'

But Ross was occupied making a note on his pad.

'Yeah, but can he sing?' Jerry repeated.

Michael shrugged and they looked again at Lewis.

'Not a clue,' Lewis said, pleased as punch to be at the centre of such august attention. 'Couldn't you ask his agent?'

Ross tore off the sheet from his pad.

'He's difficult. Especially with directors . . .' Michael said.

'So I've heard,' Ross said, non-committally, passing the note down the table. 'And a celebrated bore.'

'For Chrissakes!' George shouted and ordered Cathy to check out if Sir Harry sang and whether he was available.

'If he is we'll audition him,' Ross said, regaining the authority which he felt he'd temporarily lost.

'Really?' Lewis said aghast. 'But he's famous!' Then the note appeared in front of him. He unfolded it and read: 'Never, *ever*, do that again. R.B.' He felt himself go crimson with embarrassment.

'Think Dee could play Marina?' George suddenly asked.

Dee, George's wife. Cathy glanced nervously at Ross. If he was shocked or surprised he didn't show it.

'There's maybe something for Dee in this, George,' Ross said. 'We should certainly consider her.'

'I'm not pushing,' George continued, 'but she's a damn fine actress.'

'Good singer too,' Jerry added. 'Dances from hell to breakfast. We gotta consider Debbie too.'

'Right!' George agreed. 'I played Doris the demo she made of "Play for Love". She went crazy for it . . .'

Debbie? Then Lewis remembered: *whopping tits,* Jerry's girl.

Ross pursed his lips – only Fly recognised the sign of tension.

78

'They're great girls and we won't ignore them . . .' He tried to turn his attention to Michael but George wasn't about to let go – just yet.

'You damned well won't ignore them an' you will consider them!' He shouted angrily. 'If I tell you to!'

Lewis was shocked but Ross was a picture of patience. 'Keep your hat on George. We're not the boys in your deli you kick around, okay? Treat us with respect.'

'Yeah. Okay,' George said sourly. 'Anyone want more bagels, lox . . . C'mon guys – it's on the house.' He looked around and smiled. After a moment, most ate. Happy to eat free.

Ross ignored the offer and turned to Michael. 'The two Galileos are our big problem. We have to cast the two parts together – we need a plausible pair – a Young Galileo who can realistically turn into Old Galileo.'

'Can't they be played by the same person?' Naff asked.

'You haven't read the script?' Ross asked grimly. Naff shook his head. 'They play scenes *together*.'

Michael Kershon explained: 'The last half of the second act is a resolution of dialectical opposite forces symbolised by the two Galileos. You see the synthesis asserts a primitive form of existentialism.'

Ross nodded. 'Early Sartre.'

'More or less,' Michael agreed.

Naff looked blankly at the director and writer. Lewis glanced around the table. George looked angry and tapped the table with his fingers. Gene Landau, the General Manager, nodded sagely but hadn't understood anything.

'Can you write exi-whatever music, Jerry?' George asked crossly.

'If I knew what the fuck it meant,' Jerry laughed.

'Get my point?' George looked at Ross.

'No, what point?'

'Who cares about all that! No-one. No-one gives a fuck. We gotta love story. All musicals are love stories. It's love turns the fuckin' world around. The rest is just crap. People come to musicals to hear the music an' cry a little. They want goddamn philosophy they go to college.'

'I don't want to get into this here, George,' Ross said quietly. 'This is a discussion for another time.'

'George,' Michael said, concerned to keep the peace. 'I don't want you to get the wrong end of the stick. Of course this is going to be entertainment first and foremost. We're just talking about an intellectual underpinning . . .'

'What . . .?!!' George seemed about to explode again.

Ross tried to come to Michael's rescue. 'Fact is, drama must be built around ideas as well as emotions, George. Style and form only evolve from content. The emotional impulse, like the conflict, must derive from a basic idea. Our basic idea here is: You have to see the world as it is not as you'd like it to be. Galileo's against a society that sees the world as it would *like* the world to be, not as it really is.'

The producer sighed deeply before muttering, 'This is shit . . .'

Ross finished making his point. 'No. It's a fun idea to work with. We mustn't be afraid of it! It's a vision of the piece – our vision, right?'

Michael nodded warily. Ross looked to Jerry. He smiled and shrugged. 'Hey, don't look at me. I don't understand that shit either. I just write the notes. I'm the music man. I write romantic songs best but I'm tackling the politics . . .'

'We'll keep it balanced, George,' Ross said. 'Don't worry.'

Don't worry? Lewis played with his pencil and considered this. The composer doesn't understand the book and wants to cast his girlfriend; the producer thinks it's pretentious and wants to cast his wife; the tensions between them all are manifold. *I'd say there was plenty to worry about.*

13

Alone in his apartment, Lewis, picking at a salad from the Korean self-service a block away, typed up and revised the notes he had made earlier in the day at the stormy production conference. A half-finished Coke sat by the typewriter.

He was writing:

. . . 'I'm left with the overwhelming sense that there are two widely divergent forces at work. Ross, on the one hand, wants to build a show with intellectual foundations. Gibson, on the other, appears simply to want a love story, full stop. Of course, it might be that these apparently opposite contradictory views could be combined. They might achieve an intellectual love story. Or it could be they've chosen a subject that simply won't work as a musical because it embodies too many contradictions . . .

Lewis looked up from the typewriter as he heard a key turning in the lock. Horror tales of muggings and knifings in the city flashed through his brain. BRIT SLIT IN BIZARRE MANHATTAN SLAYING . . . 89TH STREET DECAPITATION HORROR! . . . LEWIS FINALLY LOSES HIS HEAD . . .

'Hi, I'm Florence.' The grin said it all. She was freckly and friendly. 'Florence Hackstuber. Friend of Bob. Guy who owns this . . .' she looked around, ' . . . okay, this dump. Mind if I come in?' Without waiting for a reply she popped out into the hallway and immediately re-entered pulling a battered, bulging suitcase.

'Okay,' Lewis said a little late.

'You look kinda surprised to see me. Bob not call you?'

'No, sorry.' *Why am I apologising to her?*

She threw herself on to the sofa. 'Shit!' A Velcro strap had broken on her Reeboks as she pulled them off. 'Shit, shit! These shoes have seen me through dark days – now I'm gonna have to buy some new. Can you lend me 75 bucks? I'll pay you back when

I get a job.'

She kicked her once-white sneakers on to the floor and wiggled her toes. The legs above the naked feet (she was wearing no socks – which Lewis found slightly erotic) were tanned and shapely, encased in crudely cut-off jeans – cut-off high to the thigh. She was short, (Lewis reckoned about 5′3″), her brown curly hair fell thickly in all directions sometimes masking her freckled face.

'Well, I'd love to . . . only . . .'

'You as broke as me? Tough times, huh? You're British right?' Lewis nodded.

'Yeah! I'm good at accents. No, see, thing is I met Bobby in the Happy Veggy in Manchester . . .'

'Oh, you've been in England?' Lewis leant back in his chair – putting distance between himself and his work.

Florence laughed. 'No. Manchester, Vermont. I was travelling from Dorset, close to Mettowee Valley. I was staying with my friend who's gotta shack on Lake St Catherine. The snow's melted so skiing's finished. Hitching back to New York. Got any Seltzer? Travelling gives me wind.'

She wandered off to find the refrigerator.

'Why don't you buy Diet Coke?' she called back to him. 'Better for you. Mind if I help myself? You want another one?'

'Please . . .' Florence tossed him a can and threw herself back on to the sofa. She grimaced as she slugged her drink.

'You don't know Bob, do you? Well, I didn't either. I mean I thought my friends were nutty but Bob, wow! Man, soon as I'd paid for my salsa at the Happy Veggy, and I was looking around for somewhere to sit . . . I mean I was riveted by this guy. This guy sitting alone at a table. If I tell you he's been growing his hair for 27 years you can guess how long it is. He's been growing it since *before* Woodstock. Wow! I mean he's got this beard too. This guy is walking hair. Got these little eeny-teeny glasses, Lennon-like, but thick lenses, you know that act like magnifying glasses so his eyes are, I mean huge, pop-out. Like he's gotta thyroid problem. I say, 'Hey man, can I sit down?' He says nothing, just looks at me with those spooky eyes. I'm not comin' on or anything, just being loosey-goosey friendly.

'So I'm eating my salsa and casting looks. Finally I say: "Can I get you another Sprite?". He is so miserable his beard's practically curling up – if you see what I mean. "What's up, Doc?" I say, "you've got a mighty frown." An' then he tells me he's got this block. I say, "What like the drains in your cabin?" "No, no," he says, "writer's block." Seems like he's been fucked up for 'bout six years – left this city for the country to clear his skull. But his brain's still a no-go area for ideas.

'Then I see tears are coming. Double King-Vegi-Burger size tears rollin' down his cheeks gettin' lost in this grey tangled yukky matted hair. I swear to God it wouldn't surprise me termites were livin' there. "Hey man," I say, "maybe you oughta go back to the city." He says no 'cos it was worse there. Anyway, to cut a long story down to the pubic hair . . . Am I borin' you at all?'

Far from it, Lewis was hooked, fascinated. Every tiny movement of the thigh, the hand, the mouth was ecstasy.

'No, no! Please go on!'

'Okay, so I say, "Maybe you gotta have shock treatment of some kind, you know the way you sometimes can stop hiccups by scarin', that sorta thing." He didn't believe me but I know a thing or two – I been around. I'm an actress you know, well, kind of. So I seen it all. I seen how shock can alter a person's whole way of looking at things. I get this idea, see. It pops right into my head with no warning. You ever get those?'

'Ideas, you mean?'

'Yeah, right . . .'

'Sometimes – I hope.' Lewis looked at his notebook and neatly typed sheets.

'Well, I get this idea how I might unblock his mind jam. I say, "Finish your beer, man, an' come with me." We go out to the parkin' lot an' I ask him if he's got transport. He points to a Nissan.

'Next thing you know we're in the back of his Nissan pick-up parked in the woods by a fast-running stream. An' he's screwing the daylights outa me. I mean . . . what's your name, by the way?' Lewis gave his name. 'Oh okay, John, you gotta understand that this is not like me! I don't go with just *anyone*. Not like that. Not after ten minutes. Okay, not often. I like to work up to these things. But I gotta tell you this was just like *The Postman Always Rings Twice*. You see that movie? Wasn't Jack Nicholson great? I don't think Bob had had a bath for as long as he'd been growing his hair so if I say that man's Neanderthal you'll have a pretty cool idea of what my senses are going through. Of course, it's okay as I realise that I'm doing this for *art*. There is every chance that Bob will be unblocked by this experience and write *The Brothers Karamazov* or *Gone With the Wind* or some other high-art shit that'll win the Pulitzer – and it will all be thanks to me. Not that I'm not enjoying it. Yeah, well, it's true I didn't at first – in fact I gotta tell you I was repulsed – then as we get going it gets okay. Then it gets great. Suddenly he shouts in my ear, "Christ, it's been 32 years since I shot a load." That's it. I go over the edge – a double whammee – he does too – he comes maybe ten times, twenty times. Frankly I lost count. I mean I'm practically drowning.'

Florence stopped her monologue for a moment and thoughtfully sipped her Coke. Lewis had not moved a muscle for five minutes.

How long had she been here? Ten minutes, fifteen? She's telling me this story as if we've known each other all our lives.

'After it was all over, Bob certainly looked happier than when I was eating my salsa at the beanery. "It might work," he said. "What might?" I asked. "I feel . . . I feel different . . .," he said, " . . . about my art." "You mean you might feel unblocked now?" I guess I was excited and flattered. "Mebbe," he said, "I'll let you know. Where can I reach you?" I said: "I'm going back to New York to getta job but I got nowhere to stay." And so he says he's got this apartment that he's just rented out – but he's sure there'd be no problem me sharing . . . "Take my key," he says . . . and bingo here I am.'

And she smiled her freckled smile.

14

The four hundred and fifty guests, who had each paid $150 to eat the so-so sea-food linguini on the third floor banqueting room of Sardi's, laughed and applauded the after-dinner speech. The speaker was Conrad Livonia II, the President of the Claudette Millstein-Windsor Benefit. Claudette Millstein-Windsor was a lesser American poetess of the Massachusetts School. After her death in 1956, her poetry (mostly an evocation, in various forms, of the apple trees she observed from her window on the ridge above Sturbridge) became less and less remembered outside the coterie dedicated to ensuring her immortality; not as a writer but as a founder of a get-away-from-it-all country home for poets: a lodging where, as the board outside reads, 'Tranquillity allows the muse to guide the hand' of many a city-distracted artist. Much sought-after, the refuge turns many away (including on several occasions Lewis's own landlord, the unhappy Robert Berol). Once a year, the rich and worthy are invited by the committee to meet for dinner, honour the memory of Claudette, raise sufficient funds to maintain the house and the apple trees and to offer three-month bursaries to the lucky few.

Claudette's loving memory, however, was far from Ross's thoughts as he gazed beyond Conrad Livonia II through the window to lighted theatreland beyond. He had barely touched his food. Ellen, sitting next to him, had, over the last couple of months, become increasingly concerned about his lack of appetite and general demeanour. At first she ascribed it to tiredness and stress. The last show had been difficult and the subsequent journey to Europe so soon after the opening had been, in her opinion, folly. Since his return, however, she sensed a more general change in him. Always a somewhat remote man, he now frequently descended into periods of deep gloom. He had trouble sleeping yet was impossible to wake. 'It is as if he can't face the day,' Ellen confided to her friends . . . She watched him lost in his inner world and felt him a stranger, separated from her by . . . what? Another lover or just another show. As each show came and went, Ellen became accustomed to the idea that the show was Ross's mistress, at least for the rehearsal period. But this was different, more frightening. *Galileo* was only at the start of pre-production yet was already making demands on him like no previous show. She had tried to talk to him about it, persuade him to visit his doctor. He brushed her anxiety aside and refused another check-up.

Looking at him, his face barely illuminated by the restaurant's mood lighting, she was suddenly alarmed by the change. The face that Ellen loved had taken on a gaunt greyness. She at once experienced a fearful premonition of doom – she saw him dead, herself childless and alone.

Unaware of the profound passions stirring in Ellen, Ross was, in fact, still preoccupied by the production conference two days ago and the subsequent fall-out. One question went round and round his mind as if on a recorded loop: why had he again agreed to work for George Gibson after the nightmare of *Love Boat*? Twenty-five years ago the man was dangerously unpredictable; time had only made him worse. Had he really expected that it would be different?

Some were petty, these horrors thrown up during and after the production conference, easily disposed of. Others were mere hints at what was to come. Rational and methodical Ross was considering each in turn. The pressures to cast Dee and Debbie – he wanted neither. Both were good singer/dancers. Dee a strong dancer, Debbie a fine singer. Neither, he considered, were accomplished actresses – and this was the sine qua non. He was looking for strength in all three departments. And Ross, the puritan, also disapproved of casting husbands, wives and lovers – especially those of producers and writers. But this problem was containable. In the end he need cast neither. No, the real blow below the belt had come as the meeting broke up. George wanted to talk privately 'about the book'.

Ross was well aware the structure of the show was still a problem. They had been wrestling with it for over a year and it still wasn't right. The problem was quite apparent. Ross understood it well: writing by committee never worked – or rarely.

There were too many people pulling *Galileo* this way and that. It lacked a single inspired vision. George wanted spectacle and musical comedy – Michael's instincts were towards psychological exploration of the characters – Jerry was inclined to leave all that 'garbage' to Michael and concentrate on writing extractable rock 'n' roll that might get into the charts. Ross tried to steer a path to the magic land of the Unified Concept. Michael was always amenable to any suggestion – 'I'll try it,' he would say on the phone as he listened to Ross. Often he would fax back: 'Tried it – doesn't work.' Sometimes he telephoned back to discuss it further. Other times he would simply fax: 'Okay. Done.'

Galileo was Michael's first musical. An accomplished and successful playwright, he was a soloist – a virtuoso. Working closely with a composer was a new experience. He respected Jerry's work, even liked it. It's a mark of how good he is, Michael had once said to Ross, that our whole family likes his last album. From the kids to the adults. The basic idea had been Michael's. Michael and Ross were at the same small dinner party given by a mutual friend at the Caprice. Over coffee Ross was surprised to hear from Michael he had a desire to write a musical. 'A musical?' Ross had said amazed. 'Working on a musical is like swimming through shark-infested waters with a bleeding toe. You feeling suicidal?'

Michael had smiled and replied: 'The challenge is to make it work. I like musicals; I like the form, I like the joy they give. And what's more, I have an idea that's centred on the life of Galileo . . .'

Ross had been attracted by the idea immediately. He asked Michael to write a two-page treatment. Armed with this document Ross set about finding a producer. Cameron Mackintosh, David Merrick, Manny Azenberg turned them down. George Gibson was fourth on his list.

'There is no question,' Ross had said to Michael as he tried to convince himself it wasn't an insane idea involving George in this project. 'George Gibson is still in the top league players. He's a liar, a cheat, a two-faced-sonofabitch, in short, a producer. He's impossible, but he sells the show. He makes hits. And that's what Broadway's about.'

George Gibson had loved it. He immediately made a deal with Michael's London agent, hired Jerry and the show was on starter's marks. Five months later, Jerry and Michael produced a script and five songs on a cassette. George gave the tape and script to Doris – she read, listened and told George 'to include her in' with one reservation: the book needed fixing.

Everyone told George the book needed fixing. Dee told George, Lionel Cohn, an agent and George's closest friend, told George. Al, the barman at the Music Box Theater, who George swore 'always gets it right' told George. No-one had a bad word to say about the music. With accumulated opinions George was ready to pronounce. He summoned Michael to New York.

Over the year, Michael produced three drafts. Each an accurate reflection of the discussion that had preceded its writing. Despite

87

all the travail a final perfect structure had not emerged. It was passably good but not good enough.

Then, just after the end of the production conference, Ross, shadowed by Lewis, had been fixing schedules with Gene Landau, George's General Manager, when Betty approached.

'Can you pop into George's office for a moment?' Betty whispered into Ross's ear. She was gently tugging at the pocket of his trousers. Something she did often and it grated.

'About what?' Ross asked.

'I think,' she whispered, 'about the book.'

George closed the door behind Ross, shutting out Lewis. The two men were alone.

'I gotta hand it to you Ross, there's no-one handles a production conference better than you. You got that team lickin' outa your hand.'

He disappeared behind the desk rising a moment later with a cigar taken from the humidifier. He didn't offer one to Ross. 'Sit down. How d'ya think it went?'

He was all glitz and smiles.

'The conference?' Ross was short. 'We did what we had to do.' Something was up. He could feel it. George did not like one-to-one conversations with him. They made him feel uncomfortable. He didn't handle them well.

'That designer, the German, can't figure him out – what's his name . . . yeah . . . Karl. He don't say much. You sure he can deliver? You seen any drawings yet?'

Cat and mouse game. Did George not like Karl-Heinz? Certainly he didn't like non-US residents in the team. Too expensive – all those international Business Class flights and per diems. Did he want him out – or was this just an opening gambit? Ross sensed that he was embarking on a fight to hold on to his team.

'We're meeting this afternoon. He's excited about what he's done. I'm confident.'

'What's that crap about a vow of silence? I hired a meshugana? You wanna get rid of him? You just gotta say.'

'George,' Ross smiled patiently, 'Karl-Heinz is the best designer of his generation – either side of the Atlantic. He's a genius. Genius is allowed to be eccentric. Besides we all waste too much time talking. He can teach us a lesson.'

George understood. 'Well, thank God I've one genius on my team. You see the Rich review of *Red Poppy* in the Times?' He tapped the paper folded open at the theatre review section. 'That show'll fold Sunday. You catch it?' Ross shook his head. 'I did. Dee an' I went to the Gala. Piece of shit. No laughs, no jokes, just

88

all those kids bein' Chinese Red Guards. See, they took a good idea – American girl caught up in the Cultural Revolution – then threw it away. Red flags all over the stage – you know what I mean. Lotta chantin'. Where were the pretty songs? Who knows how to write a pretty song? Webber, he knows, but here? I gotta tell you. Jerry does. You like that song he wrote for Marina. Wassit called . . . "Play for Love"? It's a great song. Number one hit. You like that song Ross?'

'Sure.'

There was an uncomfortable moment of silence.

'Hey, it's good to talk to you Ross,' George said and, as if to prove his sincerity, relocated himself and perched on the front of the desk nearer the director. 'We go back, what, 35 years. Over half my life. You gave me my best and my worst show.' He jovially wagged his finger at Ross and smiled.

'And fuck you, George. We don't owe each other anything.'

'Don't get mad at me, Ross. I'm trying to be friends, okay? We gotta work together, we *gotta* be able to talk. Fact is we need each other. I need you, you need me.'

'No, George, that's bad dialogue. Clichés. You're employing me, George, because one: I brought you the project, and two: I'm the best you can get.'

'Okay, okay!' George retreated behind his desk and relit the cigar stub. 'What is this? You want me to clap you on the back? You need reassurance or something?'

Ross waited till the butt was lit. 'Let's just keep to a working relationship, George. I respect you; I understand you. I brought you this show because you're a showman. They don't make them like you any more. You and Merrick . . . What did you want to talk to me about? I got work to do. The boys are waiting for me out there.'

'What's eatin' you, Ross? I hold out my hand . . . Have I ever shown you anything but love . . .?'

'C'mon, George, I gotta go . . . ,' Ross got up and headed for the door.

'Ross,' said George, finally delivering the blow below the belt, 'I'm gonna fire Michael.'

Ellen leant over and whispered, 'Are you alright, darling?' Protectively she brushed some fluff from the collar of his DJ. Twenty-five years in New York City and she still sounded very English. Recently her accent had started to bother him.

Ross nodded.

'Then write the cheque.'

Ross surfaced. The third floor of Sardi's was silent except for the scratching of pens on cheque books – the annual ritual at the Millstein-Windsor Benefit.

'Pass the paper!' the chairman intoned. Another ritual. A blank sheet was passed around the table and the cheque writer wrote down the value of his contribution. No name, just a figure. Then each ten-person table totted up their total. The chairman called out the table number (1 to 45). A delegated spokesman rose and proclaimed the figure to much applause. Finally the chair announced that table 33 had won the coveted annual Millstein-Windsor Golden Orb for a donation totalling $6,275.

Table 9 cared little for all this. Their accumulated $460 was a fair reflection of their interest in the life and work of Claudette Millstein-Windsor. Ross and Ellen's guests were Michael Kershon and Karl-Heinz Zeiss. Ellen had wanted to meet Karl-Heinz (of whom she had heard a great deal) and renew her friendship with Michael (whom she had first met when she was still living in England). She had tempted them to the Benefit with a promise of good company and a small cabaret – Lena Horne *and* Michael Feinstein. Karl-Heinz had kept Ellen amused with caricatures of the other guests – Ross and Michael talked about the script unceasingly through dinner and were only reduced to a reluctant silence by the tedium of the speech.

'Ladies and gentlemen, the cabaret! The one-and-only, the incomparable, the GREAT . . . LENA HORNE!' Rapturous applause as Lena carefully picked her way on to the raised platform, acknowledged the hot welcome and launched into her set.

George had backed off quickly. Too quickly. Ross immediately suspected a ruse. He distrusted George to such an extent that he found conspiracies everywhere. Now he saw the ploy for what it was: a clumsy threat. Neither sensitive nor delicate, George, with all his customary vulgarity, was saying: get this script right. Or else. Or else what? Or rather whom? George knew as well as Ross that firing Michael would throw the whole show into disarray. How many good book writers were there in New York . . . or London? Ross had hardly needed to remind George of this – but he had, and forcibly.

'It's my view,' Ross had said, 'that the book scenes require substantial cutting. We do this and the story will emerge more clearly. It won't seem so heavy. Overwriting is a common fault when playwrights get to write musicals. I'm gonna lock up Jerry and Michael at Jerry's for the next four days and get Jerry to musicalise anything and everything he can, okay?'

'You think he can do it, Ross? I gotta tell you I don't agree with you there's no-one who can write good librettos. How about Conrad Rothstein? Guy who wrote that funny Off-Off-Broadway show. You like him? I gotta coupla more names up here.' He tapped his head but refused to divulge them. 'I don't see it just as a question of cutting. Sure anything can be helped by cutting, I know that. It's the humour of the piece. It's gotta be funny, Ross. It needs jokes! Michael good with jokes? I never heard him tell a good joke. He's a Jew with no jokes. You're a Jew, you know! Whoever heard of a Jew with no jokes. If he can't write 'em phone Lou Stern – he'll give you any number. Or Jackie Mason. Galileo didn't tell funny stories? Gimme a break.'

Ross liked and admired Lena Horne. He had worked with her on a picture ten years ago and Lena had since become a friend of both of them. Ellen and Lena made a point of having tea together in the St Regis once a month, drinking and laughing. Ross listened and relaxed – her songs and style, the equivalent of warm milk and a hot bath. His melancholy diffused as Lena sang and the events upon which he had been ruminating assumed different, less catastrophic proportions. We're mounting a musical for God's sake, he thought. It's hardly a life or death struggle. In the history of human achievement and endeavour, musicals don't figure much.

Besides which, in the end, his team had stayed intact.

He turned to look at Michael and Karl-Heinz. Both sat entranced; the German sketching, the playwright smiling happily, unaware that his future in his own project had been in the balance.

15

'You sure you're going to be all right on that sofa, Florence? I honestly don't mind if you want the bed.'

'No big deal, John. You sure you don't want some of this magic mushroom? It's good shit. No shag. Okay.'

'I'm fine thanks.'

'Okay. John?'

'Yes?'

'I gotta get a job.'

'Right.'

'An' I done some acting out west a while back . . . I was wondering if you'd like kinda mention my name to the casting guys for this show you're observing. Wouldy'a?'

'No problem, Florence, Cathy Newman's the Casting Director. Auditions are coming up next week. I'm sure they'll be delighted to see you . . . I'll mention it.'

'C'mon, Georgie, little Dee wanna cuddle with her big bear. You gonna spend all night sitting out there? Hello, George! You hear me? There's a hot bod waiting for you-oo in here! Hi, sweetheart. What's up? Surprise me.'

'I'm trying to work out how I'm gonna get rid of that English writer on *Galileo*. Coupla days ago I tried to make Boardman see why we gotta do it but he didn't bite . . .'

'You'll think of something Georgie – come to bed . . . forget work . . . little Deedee wants her big man . . . she'll make you forget the horrible world out there . . .'

'Jesus, Dee, gimme a break, will ya. This is important . . .'

'Christ, George, I'm important too you know . . . What's going on down here's important . . .'

'Sure, sure. If we don't get this friggin' script right . . . With this writer we got no show. I know it. An' I gotta trust my instincts . . . Whatever stunts Boardman pulls . . . Hey, c'mon that hurts . . .!'

'So Little Willy doesn't wanna come out an' play again . . . huh?'

'Remember Alberta Hunter, Ellen. Wonderful black singer. I think she was 82 when she made a comeback at The Cookery. The buzz of the crowd gave her the energy to keep going another seven years. I'm only 60, but the fizz has gone.'

'Mmm? Sorry, darling, what were you saying?'

'If you'd put your book down for a moment . . .'

'I wasn't reading, I was thinking about this evening . . . wasn't Lena wonderful! And I do so like Michael. I knew I would . . .'

'I keep replaying in my head the scene at the end of the film of *42nd Street*. Warner Baxter, the director is slumped on the fire escape stairs, smoking and coughing, all alone. Dying. He's given his last ounce of strength to get the understudy on to that stage, to give a great performance.'

'Would you like some of my tea, Ross? It's got honey in.'

'No.'

'You're obsessed with that image, you know. The tragic dying director. The hero. But you can't kid me. I know you love your work. The only similarity between you and Warner Baxter is that you too will go on till you drop.'

'All I'm trying to say is the joy has gone. I get no pleasure doing it any more.'

'Okay, then. I'll challenge you. Stop. You've done enough, sell the apartment and buy a little place in Florida. Write your memoirs and I'll give English pronunciation lessons and charge a fortune. You're smiling! See! I told you. I win.'

'I've four children, and three homes to support. I need one more hit, Ellen. If we turn *Galileo* into a *Phantom* or a *Les Mis* I can afford a graceful farewell to Broadway. We'll buy a boat and sail round the Antilles in ever decreasing circles . . .'

'Promise.'

'Maybe.'

'No. Promise.'

'Goodnight.'

'Turn your light off then.'

'Hey, Wise-Ass, mebbe if you hadn't opened your fat mouth.'

'Where d'ya throw that CD box, Debs?'

'I said talk to the Casting Director . . .'

'Jeez, the mess here . . .'

'Will you listen . . .'

'I'm listenin', but I'm also lookin' for that box! I don't like you messin' with my CD collection . . .'

'No way is *Ross* gonna buy me in the show, scumbag, if he thinks you're pushing.'

'I told you Debbie . . .'

'So Gibson's pushing Dee! He's the fuckin' producer and if he says Dee's gonna be in the show, Dee's gonna be in the show. If he says he wants George Bush in the fuckin' show, Ross'll put Bush in the show. He pays the piper, man. Gibson isn't gonna push Ross for me when he wants Dee in. We're too similar. I told you to talk to Cathy!'

'Now, I lost the shit . . .'

'So how're you gonna get out of it, Jerry? I wanna know. It's very important to me. I wanna get into this show. I don't want to be remembered for just singing the fuckin' demo, okay?'

Parker Meridien Hotel
119 West 56th Street, NY, NY

Late Sunday.

Darling H,

VIA FAX

I desperately miss you and the kids. Once the show gets into rehearsal we'll put the kids into school here. It won't do them any harm at their age. In fact they will probably find a New York school very stimulating. I know I would have at their age. I mentioned this possibility to George Gibson before the production conference on Friday. I must say he was charming about it. He even offered to help find a school that would be suitable.

Ross is working us hard. We have little time for relaxation. Tonight was an exception. Ross and Ellen invited 'the foreigners' (as we're called) to a bizarre fund-raising event. A pretty laughable affair apart from the cabaret. You would have loved it! Lena Horne (in all her glory) and Michael Feinstein. (He, incidentally, spotted Steve Sondheim in the audience and proceeded to play a medley of Steve's hits!)

Our day starts at midday. Jerry doesn't surface till 11.00.

Then it's just Jerry, me and the piano till about 3.00 p.m. (the local Chinese or Japanese send up delicious lunch). We effect Ross's notes from the day before. We're mainly cutting, cutting, cutting. Losing a lot of stuff that should go – but, I fear, also texture and meaning. I'm terrified that it's getting bland and (worse) anti-intellectual. Galileo, the fool. I'm exaggerating, of course, but, and I kid you not, George Gibson actually suggested (I think yesterday) that we give Galileo a joke or two. 'Let's make it a spaghetti musical,' I said – kidding. I'm afraid he took it seriously. I think he might have said 'Great idea!' But I don't object to more humour in this piece. It's just getting harder and harder to keep rewriting.

Jerry's very fast. If I (or Ross) suggest an idea for a theme or song – Jerry pauses a moment, listens (I assume to some muse singing in his head), his fingers lightly dance in the air (as if they already know what to play and can't wait to hit those keys) then he attacks the keyboard and out comes a delightful melody, or something appropriately dark.

Around 3.00 p.m. Ross arrives. He challenges us, line-by-line, lyric by lyric. I take notes. Sometimes he finds Jerry's lyrics jejeune or my scenes overwritten. He's forever saying 'can this be musicalised?' Reminds me of working on the film with Milos: 'Image, image, Michael, no words!' Remember? No-one likes words any more.

Next a novel! Or a biography.

Tired now. Bed calls. Night, night, my sweet. Love to the kids. I love you.

M

P.S. Would you look out that interview I did with John Lewis who writes for the Indie and fax it me. The little prick is here, would you believe, trying to write a book about the show. A stupid idea but George and Ross seem to support it. Anyway, I want to remind myself what it was he said about me so I can prove him wrong!!

M xxx

The first audition was scheduled to start at 10.30 a.m. and several members of the team met for breakfast half an hour earlier in the Green Room. This coffee shop is part of The Play Room, a converted fabric warehouse on Broadway in the Chelsea district. The building hums with activity. Not only do New York shows rehearse in it but also shows for out-of-town, across the country. Producers frequently hire one of its spaces for auditions. Its unprepossessing exterior hides a complex system of interlinked rehearsal rooms, music rooms, changing rooms, ranged over eight floors.

Sharing the table: Ross, Fly, John Lewis, Tam Topp, Molly Call (Tam's assistant), Cathy and her assistant, Miles. Each had a copy of the day's schedule that Cathy had prepared.

'What I've done', Cathy explained (between bites of toasted English muffin), 'is to put the final recalls, all our favourites, into the afternoon session and I've mixed in with them Dee and Debbie. You'll notice I've also slipped Sir Harold Whitney into the afternoon. He's in New York publicising some movie and so he's coming in. I don't know if he's going to sing . . . His agent said he had a cold or something . . .'

Ross sipped black coffee and asked if he had been sent a script.

Miles nodded. 'Sure – and a demo. We dropped it by his hotel yesterday.'

'Well,' Ross said. 'He can read today and the music department will have to meet up with him later.'

Lewis studied the audition list.

GALILEO AUDITIONS
THE PLAY ROOM – 890 BROADWAY

Note:

a.m.   Artists screened by Cathy and Miles *not* seen by
       Mr Boardman or Producers (Mr Warburg present for some)

ARTIST	CHARACTER
10.30 CINDY OXFORD	ANNA
10.45 JOYCE ALMEIDA	ANNA
11.00 JANE KENNETH	ANNA
11.15 PRICE GORDON	GUIDO
11.30 SOPHIE FORSYTH	MARINA
11.45 JAMES TRIPP	OLD GALILEO
12.00 QUENTIN KOLIOPOS	YOUNG GALILEO
12.15 ADELE LANTZ-COOPER	ANNA
12.30 LOIS CARPENTER	MARINA
12.45 TASHA PORTOVSKY	MARINA
LUNCH	
2.15 MICHAEL OLAF BRUN	YOUNG GALILEO
2.30 FRED BLENFORD	OLD GALILEO
2.50 DEE BRUNEL	MARINA
3.05 TARA MARTIN	MARINA
3.25 SAM BENN	YOUNG GALILEO
3.40 (SIR) HAROLD WHITNEY	OLD GALILEO
4.00 CARLY MALONE	MARINA
4.15 DEBBIE MAGUIRE	MARINA
4.30 ZIGISMUND BRONOWSKY	YOUNG GALILEO
4.50 LUCCA MAGGIORE	ANNA
5.05 ROMNEY JACOBS	OLD GALILEO
5.25 *ASSESSMENTS*	
5.30 *FINISH*	

Ross studied the list. 'It's going to be a long day.'

'True,' Cathy said. 'But I'd be very disappointed if we haven't decided on 60% of the principals by the end of the afternoon.'

'So long as we've cast the three leads, I'll be happy,' Ross said.

Cathy agreed. 'You think we'll be okay, Ross?'

'I've a hunch that we're gonna hire Tara Martin and Ziggy Bronowsky for the kids. The problem's still Old Galileo . . .'

Fly tapped John Lewis on the shoulder. 'Check out Miss 10.30 a.m.,' he whispered.

'Cindy Oxford, you mean?' Lewis was curious why they were whispering.

'You want her, I can get her for you.' He winked.

'If she's anything like Cathy, you're on,' Lewis whispered back. *Does he charge for this service?*

'That's your type, huh?' Fly appeared to take a mental note.

'Wait and see.'

'Let's go!' Cathy said. This was her big day and she was impatient to start. She picked up the check. 'Y'all owe me six bucks.'

Waiting at the check-out, Tam Topp asked Ross if Doris was coming to the auditions. Ross shrugged and said he thought she was in Paris.

'That's good,' Tam nodded happily.

'Not one of your favourites, right?' Ross grinned.

Doris had insisted on personally interviewing Tam when Ross proposed him for the job of choreographer. 'I *hate* dance,' she had told Tam. 'I don't know why Ross wants any in this show, for heaven's sake. A dancing Galileo, I ask you! Frankly, my dear, it embarrasses me. If I'm forced to go to the ballet I spend most of the evening reading the programme. I find the sight of men wearing tights repulsive. Those bulges are utterly distasteful. We call them "privates" with good reason!' She had regarded him with evident disdain. 'Well, if they want that prancing, I guess you'll do.'

Tam had not forgotten those words. As they headed for the elevator, Tam said, 'She gives me the creeps'.

As soon as the handler dragged the dog into the baggage area and it vomited blood at their feet – Doris, correctly, feared the worst. Roget, her beloved shih-tzu, was grievously ill. Up to this moment, she and Paul Etienne had had every intention of being at the auditions. The Concorde from Paris had been on time and her chauffeur was waiting outside to whisk them straight to 890 Broadway. But this incident happening at 9.00 a.m., in the Air France Terminal at JFK, apart from being an appalling shock, put paid to their schedule. Instantly flying into a rage, Doris demanded to see a supervisor, and blamed Air France for negligence. A veterinarian was called and Doris, physically supported by Paul Etienne, sat in a small uncomfortable waiting room, chewed on her nails and awaited his diagnosis.

Mercifully, this wait was short. The veterinarian soon came into the room and gravely informed Doris, Paul and the worried-looking Air France supervisor, that he suspected the worst. His preliminary diagnosis indicated stomach cancer at an advanced stage.

Doris put her hand to her mouth and turned a ghastly shade of pale. Paul and the relieved Air France supervisor helped her to a

VIP waiting room and plied her with cognac. When she had sufficiently recovered, she and Paul took the whimpering Roget out to the waiting chauffeur who drove them speedily back to her apartment in Manhattan.

'There, there, chérie,' Paul tried comforting her as they passed through Queens. 'We will call ze specialiste as soon as we get 'ome . . . maybe zis man is wrong.'

'It's the worst. I know it is. Look at the poor pathetic little thing!' And indeed Roget did look pathetic as she cradled him in her arms. 'Oh, Paul! How will I live if . . .? If he should . . .' Tears welled in her eyes.

'Excuse me, Miss Stein,' the chauffeur said politely after he had helped them into the lobby of their apartment block. 'Will you still be needing me to take you down to the auditions? I have that on my schedule.'

Doris looked askance. 'Oh, I forgot! Auditions!' She thought for a moment. 'Yes! I must go on . . . They need me there.'

'My brave, brave little sing.' Paul tenderly patted her hand.

'Yes. As soon as poor little Roget has been seen to we'll go . . .'

The ancient elevator that slowly took eight people up to the sixth floor was too small for the job. Lewis found himself pressed firmly face-to-face, body-to-body against Cathy for the duration of the voyage. It reminded him of rush hour in the tubes back home. *Must talk to her about getting Florence Hackstuber an audition.* But Cathy, smelling of lavender and things nice, was lost in thought, seeing nothing. Lewis, his face three inches from hers, gazed into her clear blue eyes. *God, she's stunning!* Suddenly, to his horror, Lewis found that the forced intimacy engendered by the crush, combining with the vibrations of the elevator, was producing an unwanted and embarrassing stiffness in his trousers. A hardness that very soon would become more than apparent to Cathy. *Oh Jesus!*

'Sixth floor!' The elevator man said loudly and impatiently into Lewis's ear.

Just in time, Lewis prised himself away from Cathy's body. As he did so, to his horror, he saw that he had been so absorbed he had failed to notice that everyone had already got out. Luckily Cathy seemed completely unaware of his presence, the trickle of sweat that ran down his forehead into his right eye making it smart, the erection that his notebook barely hid. She too had important things on her mind.

The room they were to use for the auditions was large. Mirrors covered the length of one wall. Sparsely furnished, it contained only a piano, a long table and a dozen chairs. Waiting for the group arriving from the Green Room were Charlie Brodsky, the Stage Manager; Michael Kershon; Jerry Trimlock and an accompanist. George Gibson stood apart from this group with a small, stubby man that Lewis didn't recognise – the Musical Director, Stan Warburg. Stan was the only person Lewis had yet to meet. Fly made the introductions. Lewis was immediately dazzled. Stan was short, plump and jolly but behind thick rimless glasses his grey-blue eyes gleamed; Stan had great éclat, and his splendour went before him. Every director on Broadway wanted him as MD – but few were chosen. Stan chose and whenever possible he chose Ross.

Charlie Brodsky called out from the door. 'People, it's 10.30! I got a line out here.'

'Okay, let's go!' Ross said firmly and sat down at the centre of the long table flanked by Stan Warburg and Michael Kershon. Next to Stan sat Jerry and George. Tam Topp was to Michael's left. Cathy and Miles pulled up seats behind Ross, Fly and Lewis sat on the periphery a little away from the main group.

'Cindy Oxford!' Charlie announced.

Cindy entered the room. Fly nudged Lewis and whispered. 'Wha'd'I tell you?'

Cindy was a tall, stunning, brunette with a ravishing figure. She wore a fish-net top that hung loose exposing the full glory of her naked breasts underneath.

'I see what you mean,' Lewis whispered breathlessly.

'Cindy, this is Ross Boardman,' Charlie said.

'Remember, if you wannit, you only have to ask . . .' Fly muttered to Lewis.

Cindy shook Ross's hand. 'What are you going to sing for us, Cindy,' Ross said with a welcoming smile.

' "Joanna" an' "I Got Rhythm." '

'Okay,' said Ross with a friendly smile. 'That sounds great.'

As Cindy took her music to the pianist, Cathy passed Ross her picture and résumé, which he studied carefully.

'I can get you pictures of this one *naked*,' Fly whispered.

'Oh, it's okay, thanks.' Lewis prayed he would shut up.

Cindy launched into her ballad, bravely thrusting out her breasts.

Everyone took notes. Lewis observed how the method of note taking reflected character. Ross wrote small, sparingly, discreetly. George scratched noisily: his writing large but tidy. As he wrote he sucked and blew through his teeth, his feelings on the surface, unhidden, obvious. Stan jotted down her vocal range and

100

whispered to Jerry. Michael just put a cross against Cindy's name.

'Well done! Thank you!' Ross said as the last chords of "I Got Rhythm" faded away. 'Will you read for us please?'

'I'd be delighted to!' Cindy said happily, convinced this was going well.

Lewis whispered to Fly: 'Does Ross like her? I didn't think she sang "Joanna" particularly well.'

'I doubt it,' Fly whispered back. 'But he's very courteous.'

Cindy read an extract from the script. Charlie, putting little expression into it, read with her. She read badly and Lewis felt sorry for her.

'Great tits but can't act, huh?' Fly said in the usual whisper. Lewis worried that Ross could hear these comments but his assistant continued regardless: 'You can fuck her if you want to. I can fix it . . .'

Cindy finished her reading and was politely dismissed by Ross. He scribbled more notes before calling for Joyce Almeida, the next appointment.

Despite Fly's constant muttering in his ear, Lewis enjoyed the early part of the morning – his first experience of Broadway auditions. The process, he discovered, was not as he expected – it was a quiet, orderly affair conducted by Ross in a manner far removed from the fiction of Broadway. Where was the darkened auditorium, the hassled director hunched up in the stalls shouting 'Next!'?

Sophie Forsyth was the fifth audition of the morning – a strong candidate for the female lead – Marina Gamba. Lewis remembered the script. Marina lives with and bears Young Galileo's children. Half of the plot of the musical centred around the romantic but stormy relationship between these two young people. Casting these two parts, Marina and Young Galileo, Ross had already declared his priority for the day.

Sophie Forsyth was to be put cruelly to the test. Having sung her ballad, she had just launched into the refrain of 'June is Bustin' Out All Over' from *Carousel*, when the door behind the long table burst open and, directly in Sophie's eyeline, Doris Stein marched in with Paul Etienne closely in tow. Oblivious to the sensitivities of the performer singing her heart out for a job she desperately wanted, Paul bustled round Doris helping her unload a capacious mink. Tam Topp caught Ross's eye.

Sophie gamely sang on watching events out of the corner of her eye . . .

'Buds're bustin' outa bushes
And the rompin' river pushes . . .'

Paul attempted to hang Doris's fur on a coat stand close by the table. The weight of the coat caused the stand to topple over and it crashed to the floor.

'Merde! Merde!' Paul said as everyone turned to look.

'Look what you've done!' Doris hissed at the Frenchman. 'The floor's filthy!'

Sighing loudly, she crossly threw herself into the empty chair at the end of the table next to George Gibson. Paul righted the stand and stood dutifully behind Doris, gazing blankly at Sophie.

'. . . Jest because the captains hanker
Fer a comfort they ken only get in port! . . .'

Doris sat pale, tight-lipped. Her hands restlessly fiddled with the lizard strap of a Hermes handbag. Sophie's confidence gradually ebbed away as she felt Doris's displeasure. She finished as strongly as she was able and Ross thanked her. As no apology was forthcoming from Doris or Paul, Ross said: 'You did great! I'm sorry for the interruption.'

'Thank you,' Sophie said, but tears were welling in her eyes.

Ross didn't notice. 'Would you like to read?'

Sophie found the tension too much to bear. She tried to say something but nothing came out and she fled the room. After a moment Cathy looked at Miles who slipped out of the room to give comfort.

'Stupid girl!' Doris said under her breath. 'Who's next? Who've you seen George?'

Cathy, eager to be effective, chipped in first. 'Hi, Doris. Good mornin' . . .'

'Hi, Cathy.'

'This morning's prelims. Any we like go into the afternoon. After lunch we see the real possibles.'

Cathy passed Doris the audition list. She scanned it rapidly. 'Is this it?' she said witheringly. 'This all we've got after four months' work?'

Cathy blushed. The team shifted uneasily in their seats. Charlie Brodsky put his head around the door and asked if they were ready for the next one.

'What's eatin' ya, Doris?' George asked. Charlie, sensing the atmosphere, waited at the door.

Cathy began to offer a careful assessment of the afternoon schedule. If she was hurt or angry she didn't show it. Lewis wondered why Ross remained silent. 'We have, Doris, three excellent choices for Old Galileo. Fred Blenford . . .'

Doris intervened. 'I have known Fred Blenford for years, Cathy. He couldn't sing in 1950 and he can't sing now.'

'If you'd allow her to finish, Doris,' Ross said sharply. 'I think you might . . .'

'And why, might I ask, have you put Romney Jacobs on the list?' She was not to be stopped. 'I thought I made it perfectly plain to you, young woman, that I will not have that man on my payroll.'

'What ya got against Romney, Doris?' George asked. 'He was great in *Looking Sweet*. He was the only guy in that show I never wanted to fire. Apart from Dee, that is.'

'You should have fired him, George. I *begged* you.' Doris looked at him. 'I'll never forgive him for what he did to me at the closing party.'

'Oh Christ, Doris', said George, 'the man was drunk, he didn't remember anything the next day.'

'Hey, guys,' Jerry asked. 'What happened? What's the story?'

'Sorry to hassle you, Ross, but I've got a line of people backing up out here,' Charlie said hanging on the door. He consulted his list. 'I've got Tripp, Koliopos, Lantz and Carpenter and some girl . . . Florence Hackstuber who's not on the list who wants to be seen.'

'Two minutes, Charlie . . .'

'Okay, it's your show . . .'

'So?' Jerry prompted. 'What's the big problem with Romney?'

George explained. 'He put the moves on Doris. It was the booze. Guy was outa his mind.'

'He musta been,' Tam Topp muttered to himself.

'What's that you said?' Doris had half heard.

'Nothing . . .' Tam replied with a disarming smile.

Doris looked suspiciously at him. Then, turning back to George, she said tartly: 'You know he practically raped me.'

'C'mon, Doris,' George said wearily. 'He jus' got y'against a pillar and breathed alcohol over you.'

'Don't you tell me what happened, George Gibson!' Doris shouted. 'I know what happened! I *felt* him! He should have been locked up. Putting his filthy hands everywhere on me. It was disgusting, nauseating . . .'

Paul Etienne nodded and sniffed.

Ross concluded the matter, 'That's irrelevant I'm afraid, Doris. We're going on. We've a lot to do. Charlie, Mr Tripp please.'

Doris sat smouldering. Paul stood behind her, his eyes twitching nervously. Her tension was palpable and, like a virus, was transmitted to everyone in the room. The atmosphere in the auditions had changed radically. Lewis felt sorry for the actors. As soon as they stepped into the room, ice hit them. Ross became impersonal, clipped and businesslike, George scowled and even Cathy who had been charming and considerate (understanding the tensions the actors and actresses feel at auditions), had sunk into a sullen silence. No smiles now from her. The actors were quickly dispatched. And then it was lunchtime.

As they dispersed, Charlie sought out Cathy who was standing talking to Ross. Lewis lurked nearby. 'There's a gate-crasher out there, Ross. Says she was told to come by our English friend here.' They looked at Lewis, He blushed. Charlie consulted his list: 'Name of . . . Florence Hackstuber.'

'We've got a full afternoon, Charlie. Tell her to leave her résumé,' Cathy said and moved off towards the door.

Lewis chased along after her. 'Er, thing is, Cathy . . . She's a friend of the man whose apartment I'm renting, you see.'

Charlie, at the door, cupped his hands and shouted to the group. 'Okay! Hey, everybody, can I have your attention a minute before y'all leave? Mr Gibson has invited us to join him for lunch downstairs in the Green Room. Big table's booked. Gimme some idea of numbers . . .'

They streamed out of the room and into the corridor leading to the elevator. No-one paid Florence any attention as she waited patiently, perched crosslegged on her chair, a fat paperback with a lurid cover on her lap. She looked up expectantly as they passed.

Lewis was still trying to explain the situation to Cathy when Florence suddenly jumped up in front of them. 'Ah,' said Lewis, slightly nonplussed. 'There you are.'

'Leave your résumé with the Stage Manager,' Cathy said abruptly. 'Sorry we can't fit you in but we have a full afternoon.' She walked on down the corridor toward the other members of the team waiting for the elevator.

Florence was persistent and followed along. 'Hey, Cathy, it's okay. It's cool. I'm no dragon lady. I understand the business, you know what I mean. I'm no Desperate Daisy who needs the ducats but I gotta tell you that you'll be flunking your responsibility if you don't put me in front of these guys . . .'

'No, sorry. It's absolutely impossible,' Cathy said firmly. The elevator arrived and they piled in.

As they rattled downwards Florence suddenly caught sight of Doris pressed against the opposite wall. 'Hey, Cathy, is that Doris Stein?' she whispered.

Cathy, who was becoming increasingly irritated, nodded.

'I was at school with her daughter,' Florence said excitedly. 'I must go say hey okay.'

And she did, pushing her way through the throng as the elevator stopped on the ground floor.

A few minutes later, through the plate glass window of the restaurant, Lewis watched in amazement, as Florence, talking animatedly, index-finger stabbing the air, disappeared into the back of Doris's limousine.

Dee arrived for her audition, dressed to kill, in a cream Ralph Lauren suit. Her hair, cascading in blonde curls about her shoulders, was fixed with a cream chiffon scarf roughly tied and flowing free – a gesture towards the Italian peasant look. Although she knew everyone she was far from relaxed. Ross chatted casually to her for a few minutes before asking her to sing.

They had never worked together but Ross had known Dee for the last ten years, first as Dee Brunel, an ambitious young singer/dancer, always in the front row at dance auditions, eye-catching and sexy, later as George's wife. Dee's professional career was not blessed with good fortune. She was too striking to be in the chorus, not good enough an actress to be cast in featured parts. She played a small part in the ill-fated *Looking Sweet* which was where she met George Gibson. She was 25, he 70. The girls in that show were known on Broadway as 'The Gold Diggers of 1987'. Dee bet the girl who shared her dressing room she'd get George. She played hard-to-fuck and George, frustrated beyond reason, swept her off to Tijuana and married her. As it happened, the other girl, not wanting to be left out, put out and got the composer (who left his wife and baby daughter). Subsequently George gave Dee the lead in a couple of touring shows. She gained valuable experience.

'George, I thought you were gonna . . .' Dee cocked her head towards the door.

George looked at the door, puzzled. 'What?'

'Leave . . .' She smiled at the others.

'I think she wants you out of here, George,' Doris said.

George eventually understood and left the room. Dee took her music to the pianist. After a brief consultation about tempo, she turned and announced she was going to sing one of Marina's songs from the show – the romantic ballad – 'All I Ever Gave'.

Outside in the corridor, George sat on a chair as far away as possible from the actors and actresses anxiously awaiting their turn. He briefly acknowledged Tara Martin, an actress he knew slightly, who was considered the hot tip for Marina. As Dee began to sing behind the closed doors the corridor quietened down to listen.

Deedee's got quite a voice, he proudly thought to himself. *Yup, she's quite something.*

'Excuse me, Mr Gibson. Can I have a word with you?'

George looked into a freckled face smiling down at him.

'Hi, I'm Florence Hackstuber, Mr Gibson, I jus' wanted to say that I think your wife sings like a bird.'

They both listened to the muffled voice for a moment.

'Thank you,' George said. 'She sure does.'

Florence pursed her lips and smiled sweetly. 'Please can I ask you a small favour, Mr Gibson.'

George eyed her suspiciously. He cursed himself for sitting amongst the artists but he had wanted to hear Deedee sing. Now he was trapped. *What's this girl want?*

'Can I take your hand a minute, Mr Gibson . . .'

'Excuse me?' Had he heard right? Was this a pick-up? He looked her over. He didn't like the bird's nest hair but otherwise . . .

'As well as bein' an accomplished actress I practise palmistry an' I heal. For example, see I just went back to Doris's apartment. Turns out we have a great deal in common, an' she has this real sick dog. I'm about to cure her little doggy of a horrible illness the nasty vet *says* is incurable. Well, I said phooee to that! I have healing hands, Mr Gibson. Look.'

She showed George hands that looked cute but were otherwise unexceptional. Then, lowering her voice and putting her head close to his, she said softly, 'I can read the future in *your* hands, Mr Gibson . . .'

Gently she reached for his right hand. He offered no resistance.

'The key to the future for all of us, George, is right here.' She looked deep into his eyes and gently caressed his hand. 'You are our life force. Feels good, me doing this right . . .?'

It did. Florence's hands were seductive instruments. Her left hand held his, her other travelled delicately over his skin creating erogenous zones wherever it went. Slowly she raised his hand towards her mouth, so close that he could feel her hot breath.

'This will bring you luck,' she whispered.

Palm reading forgotten, Florence lightly kissed his hand. Once, twice . . . Then some more. George felt her tongue, wet and warm, lick the insides of his hand. He closed his eyes for a moment, temporarily overcome.

Suddenly, eyes still closed, he realised it had gone quiet. Dee had stopped singing, no-one was talking or moving in the corridor. A sense of horror gripped him. Had he been taken for a fool! Was everyone looking at him? He'd be the talk of the town. Cautiously he opened one eye. To his relief, Charlie Brodsky was idly picking at his teeth with a toothpick, Tara Martin was studying the scene she was about to read for the team; others were reading magazines. No-one was looking at him.

Florence was smiling sweetly at him. 'Like it?' she said. 'Did I give you pleasure?'

George nodded.

'Then there's one little thing you can do for me . . .'

Jerry gave Dee an approving smile and for a moment or two after she had finished singing nobody said anything. Lewis judged it better than anything they had heard so far and, as it turned out, so did Ross. He smiled at her. 'Beautiful, Dee. I mean it.'

'Thank you,' she replied graciously.

'Sure was swell, Dee!' Stan said, twinkling with pleasure. 'You've never been in better voice.' This was praise indeed coming from Stan. 'I'm sorry George missed it.'

'It was better he did. I'm nervous enough. He's probably biting his nails outside.'

Ross said: 'Let's read the scene. Call Charlie to read with Dee, Miles.'

MARINA. And now there's Livia to support! Pass me that cloth. (YOUNG GALILEO *sighs, leaves his books and his lenses and collects a cloth from a basin.*) We can hardly make ends meet as it is! I need clean water.

YOUNG GALILEO (*returning to his work*). I have to work! The lenses won't grind themselves.

MARINA. There's a man in Pisa who will marry Livia. The dowry is 1800 ducats but there's got to be 800 in cash.

YOUNG GALILEO. Michelangelo will share the burden . . .

MARINA (*getting angry*). Your mother had a letter from him. Now he's saying he can't pay you back the money he owes you. That's the money that got him to Poland! Wake up, Galileo! (*She comes to him and sits.*) You live in

107

the clouds. Your head's buried in your work. You grind lenses and think you see everything, but you don't . . .

She tried too hard and it wasn't good. Ross worked her hard. He wanted her to do well. The team knew it.

'Do the last speech again. Take a beat after "Poland", so that you can play the moment before "wake up, Galileo". But don't let him see how emotional you're feeling! Use the power of silence. Talk *to* him, not *at* him. Hope he'll take you in his arms – he won't – he lives in his head not his heart – Marina of course is the opposite. Okay?'

Lewis found that hard to follow but Dee nodded and seemed to understand. She took the beats – tried her best. But it wasn't there. As she finished she winced with the pain of it . . . She knew it wasn't good and said so. She tried again. This time it was marginally better. She knew they were disappointed but no-one said anything.

'Tam,' Ross said. 'Your turn.'

'You look in great shape, Dee,' Tam Topp said.

'Yeah, thanks,' Dee said, relieved the hard part was over. 'I work out every day. You want me to do a few steps for you.' Dancing came naturally.

'No. I know your work,' Tam said and smiled.

After she left, Charlie asked if they were ready to continue. Ross nodded and wrote notes.

'Get George back in,' he ordered.

'She's a great kid,' said Doris.

Ross grunted and wrote next to Dee Brunel's name: 'Vocal: strong, attractive, B–. Plenty of unforced emotion. Charm, yes – but abrasive enough for M?? Reading: Okay – limited range. Slight lisp. Dancing A+.' He found Dee damned attractive but casting her for Marina was something he had no intention of doing. George's wife in the show was out of the question. However good she may be. Her loyalty would be split. It could only mean trouble.

Tara Martin strode confidently into the room as one of Broadway's leading musical performers had every right to do. A three-times Tony winner, she was the hot tip to land the role of Marina Gamba in *Galileo*. Everyone on Broadway was saying it and the more everyone said it the more likely it was to come true. Tara was and looked Italian. Her parents ran one of the most frequented coffee houses in the Village. Her voice was a rich extraordinary instrument with a range that stretched from a delicate sensuality to a big, brassy, ball-breaking Ethel Merman belt.

And Tara was a character, a Broadway legend as famous for her voice as the stories about her. During a coffee break, Fly told Lewis one. 'Backstage, during the intermission of a musical she was once appearing in, she was disturbed by some screaming in the corridor outside her dressing room. She looked out an' saw one of her co-stars standing there naked 'cept for a microphone battery pack strapped high to the inside of her thigh, near her bush,' Fly said. 'This woman was screaming at a couple of young kids from the chorus. A stagehand passed and Tara muttered to him: "I always knew that cunt could sing!" '

Lewis was mystified at the tale but Fly found it hilarious. 'You don't get it, huh? Never mind. Thing is Tara Martin's name in a show sells tickets. If George wants a star then he'll go for her. Tara's talent with a capital T. Talent walking on two great legs. An' if you want I can . . .' But Lewis had stopped him.

Ross and Cathy were pinning their hopes on Tara. And Tara did not disappoint them. She sang 'Can't Help Lovin' That Man' with rich feeling and read the scene with technique, passion, warmth and humanity.

Tam Topp whispered to Ross, 'Can I dance her a little?'

Ross nodded and Tam and his assistant spent five minutes putting Tara through her paces. Tam returned to his seat satisfied.

However, one person was unsure. Stan Warburg, the Musical Director, asked Tara to sing a couple of scales. 'Just to la, Tara.' After she was done, Stan thanked her and she left. Smiles all round except from Stan: 'She can't sing it, Ross. It's too high for her.'

'Well, lower it, for Chrissake!' George said sharply. 'If we like her enough, Jerry'll rewrite the goddamned songs for her.'

'I don't know, George. It's a big deal,' Jerry said. He wanted to make sure Debbie stayed in the running. *When she sings it'll blow their minds . . .*

Stan shrugged, not wanting to take sides.

'Save it for 5.30, gentlemen,' Cathy pleaded. 'We're running very late and I don't want to keep Sir Harold waiting.'

Charlie jokily doffed an imaginary cap. 'Beggin' your pardon, guv, but he's already been sitting out there for ten minutes and I've also got that girl Doris wants us to see. Who d'you want first?'

'What girl's this, Doris?' Ross asked, shuffling papers. The group looked at the lady General Partner.

'Florence er . . .' But she couldn't quite remember the name.

Lewis helped her out. 'Hackstuber.' He blushed and felt them glaring at him.

'Why're we seeing her, Doris?' Ross asked.

'Just a hunch. Humour me, Ross. Call it animal instinct – smell, you know.' Doris tortured her face into a smile.

'Doris, this is final recalls,' Cathy said. 'I've got Florence's résumé here.' She brandished a handwritten note scrawled on the back of an envelope. 'It says and I'm quoting: "Training: Californian Institute of Life (on the beach)!!! Ha, ha!!! Work Experience: healing hands; animal counsellor; couch potato." '

Jerry was the only one to find this funny. 'I was a beach bum once too,' he said.

'It doesn't hold out much promise, Doris.' Cathy could see the smile freezing into a steely glare.

'I sink you should see ziss girl, Cassy, if I was you.' Paul Etienne said gently and added, 'She was so good wizz Roget. Such sensitivity . . . such feeling.'

Then George Gibson, who had been sitting there quiet as a lamb, spoke up: 'Yeah, I'm with Doris on this one. We should give this girl a break . . .'

'You know her too, George?' Ross asked, surprised.

George seemed uncomfortable. 'Nope, but I got this instinct too . . .'

That was the clincher.

Tasha Portovsky, recalled from the morning, left just after 6.15 p.m. The auditions were over and everybody took five minutes' break to stretch their legs and sip the beverages supplied by Charlie Brodsky. Ross sifted through his notes and the résumés piled before him, gathering his thoughts. Tam Topp explored some dance steps with Molly in a far corner. George Gibson and Doris Stein, with Paul Etienne hovering quietly, compared notes. Fly stood with John Lewis at one of the large picture windows explaining something about the problems of lighting the top of the Empire State Building that could be seen over the roof-tops.

'Hey Ross, c'mon, let's get moving. I gotta dinner in half an hour!' George Gibson testily called down the table. Everyone reassembled and prepared to decide who to cast.

'Don't you think Florence Hackstuber could play Anna?' Doris said as casually as she was able. 'I thought she came over delightfully.'

Ross tapped his pencil on his pad. 'She was terrible, Doris. I doubt I have seen a worse audition.'

'Well, I'm sorry Ross, but I just have to disagree with you. You were put off by the fact she sang an atonal Indian love poem. I happen to think that mighty original.'

Triumphantly, Doris sat back feeling convinced her point was well made.

'Are you kidding us, Doris?' Ross enquired gently.

'I got three and three quarter million dollars riding on this show.' Her voice rose an octave and increased several decibels. 'So if you THINK I'M KIDDING, YOU'D JUST BETTER KNOW I'M NOT!'

George held up his arms. 'My God, what is this? It's half-past six, I gotta dinner in twenty-five minutes! I got a seven-and-a-half million dollar show an' we haven't gotta single fucking actor yet! For Chrissake!' He stared accusingly at Ross. 'Anyway, I liked that Florence whatever-her-name-is. Her audition stank but she'd be damned handy in the company.'

Doris beamed happily at George. Ross wondered if his two producers were losing their minds. 'This girl knows Doris's daughter,' Cathy whispered. Then Ross understood.

'Okay, George, wanna know my choices?' Jerry was addressing himself to the Producer.

'Sure, Jerry,' George said. He turned to Stan Warburg on his left and muttered, 'Jerry's a genius, Stan. Next Richard Rodgers.' Stan nodded distractedly.

'Debbie for the female lead . . .' Jerry said, parking the gum in a corner of his mouth. He waited for reaction, support. Jerry knew he was in for big trouble if he came home empty-handed. *You promised for fucksakes, she'll scream. I tried, Debbie, I tried.* 'What you think, Ross?'

'No deal, Jerry,' Ross said quietly. 'Sorry. Sure she's a wonderful voice but she can't act. It's that simple.'

'I agree,' Michael said, joining in the discussion for the first time. 'Neither Dee nor Debbie have sufficient acting ability to sustain a performance in the book scenes.'

No-one rescued Michael in the silence that followed his polite dismissal of the wife of the producer and the girlfriend of the composer.

Ross watched, listened but was detached. He was uncomfortably aware of a low-grade ache in his side. It had been there since early morning and had persisted.

'Let me tell you what I feel,' George said, leaning forward and glaring at Michael Kershon. 'I feel that I'm gonna hire Ziggy Bronowsky to play Young Galileo, Tara Martin to play Marina and Harry Whitney to play Old Galileo! I'm gonna get stars in this show!' He rapped the table with his fist.

Ross said, 'We've only read Harry Whitney, George. We can't book him till we know he can sing . . .'

111

'If he can't sing it, teach him!' George shouted. 'That's what I'm paying you for, for Chrissakes!'

'Ross?' Cathy looked at the director for confirmation. 'Are we set? Ross?'

Ross was caught up in a bizarre fantasy in which a rejected actor at the end of his audition suddenly pulls out an automatic weapon and sprays bullets over the production team.

'Ross, are you okay?' Cathy's voice broke through the daydream.

He smiled at her. 'Sure.' He glanced at his notes. They looked at him and waited. Even Doris. He was in no hurry. A little suspense did no harm. He wanted to get this right and be seen to get it right. It was important to retain authority. To yield at this or any stage meant future decisions would be made by George Gibson, with Doris wielding a meat cleaver at his side.

'Ziggy's swell. I can't think of anyone better. So offer him Young Galileo, please Cathy.' Ross extracted spectacles from a leather pouch. Wearing them gave him somewhat of a donnish look. 'For Anna I agree with Stan about Lucca – she's on the button. Great company member. Solid, solid performer . . .'

Lewis again referred to his notes. *Which one was Lucca?*

'. . . She has wit and grace. But she's also got an edginess that'll give Anna an interesting complexity. Okay, George?'

But Doris got in first. 'What about Dee, George? She's got the best voice . . .'

'Hey wait a minute!' Jerry interrupted. 'If we're talking voices here, Debbie's got the *best* voice . . .!'

'I vote for Dee . . .' Doris said.

'Debbie! Debbie!' Jerry shouted, drowning out the Lady Producer.

'For Chrissakes!' George shouted and banged the table.

'Doris,' Ross said quietly. 'We want you to spend your money wisely. We're destined for Broadway not oblivion.'

Then George, to everyone's surprise, terminated the discussion by acceding to Ross and confirmed Lucca as Anna. Cathy made a note.

'Why has George given in?' Lewis whispered to Fly. He was thoroughly confused. He had expected auditions to be carried out in an orderly fashion and rational decisions made. This seemed a madhouse.

'Who says he's given in,' Fly whispered back as the conversation carried on around them. 'George makes the contracts. Tomorrow he says to Ross, Lucca's too expensive so I booked Dee . . . She was our second choice, right?'

'God knows,' Lewis sighed. 'I'm totally lost. Surely George

wouldn't do a thing like that . . .!'

Fly gazed at him with pity.

Ross continued, 'I too would like to see Marina played by Tara Martin . . .'

'So you're expectin' me to change the whole fuckin' score to get it into Tara's range,' Jerry said excitedly.

'Think about it, Jerry,' was all Ross said.

'What about Old Galileo, Ross,' Cathy asked. 'You didn't like Whitney did you?'

'I'm not crazy for that English mannered acting except in English plays,' Ross said.

'I gotta dinner date! We've got our principals except for Old Galileo,' George said getting up and gathering his notes. 'You're the big director, but don't tell me that Englishman Whitney can't act this part, okay? C'mon walk me to the elevator. Bye guys and thank you.'

The rest of the team muttered polite goodnights. George propelled Ross firmly through the door. He marched him down the long corridor away from the niceties of civilised behaviour. Out of earshot, George went on the attack. 'Listen Ross, we gotta get a few things straight! Predicated by the fact that this is gonna be my last show I'm damned if I'm gonna let you fuck it up! I bin in this business a damn long time.'

'Longevity,' Ross said, 'doesn't guarantee good judgement.'

'Don't get smart-assed, Ross. One: I'm gonna hire Whitney and you're gonna make him act it right. You see him do that fox play at the Lincoln Center?'

'*Volpone*? Sure Harry Whitney's a star, and swell in the right parts. I've seen him play Lear at Stratford . . . But we don't know he can even sing . . .'

'Excuse me, George,' Doris joined them in the corridor. Paul Etienne held her coat and stood a respectful pace behind her. 'But do you think I could have a word with Ross alone?'

'Yeah, okay,' George said suspiciously. 'I gotta coupla things to say to Cathy . . .'

Ross popped a piece of dental gum into his mouth and chewed carefully. Then he noticed that Doris was crying.

'You're a great director, Ross,' she began, as soon as George left. 'We've known each other for years, haven't we, and I know we haven't always got on. Maybe you don't respect me.' Before he could reply, she added, 'But I haven't had an easy life, Ross . . .'

'Sure,' Ross said. 'Money isn't everything and too much money is a terrible burden, right?'

Missing the irony, she agreed and gently laid a well-manicured

113

hand on his arm. 'My little Roget is dying, Ross.'

Ross was puzzled but sympathetic. 'I'm sorry, Doris. Who is Roget?'

'Why my little dog!' she exclaimed, surprised the dog's plight was not more widely known. 'When someone close to you is passing away you can see clearly how finite life is.' The tears welled again. 'I want you to do me a favour . . .'

'Well?' he asked coldly. He had guessed how her speech would end.

'Please find a part for Florence in our production. She means so much to me and I know how much she can contribute to the show. She's a very special person, Ross.'

He thought for a moment. 'She was at school with your daughter? I never knew you had a daughter, Doris.'

Doris managed to laugh through the tears. 'Why, heavens, no! I've no daughter. I just met Florence today. She's very special, Ross. She can save Roget. She has magic powers and healing hands.'

'How do these things equate, Doris? A part in our show and healing hands? You've lost me.'

At that point George accompanied by Cathy emerged from the room.

'I'm sorry, Ross,' Cathy said. 'We've all got things to go to. We need to finish off.'

'Sure,' Ross said. 'Excuse me . . .'

Doris held him back a moment longer. 'I'm desperate, Ross! I'm a co-general partner and nothing can be done without my say-so. Tell him George!' She paused and looked at him. She wanted an answer. She meant business.

'I hear what you're saying Doris,' Ross said. 'But I don't like threats.'

'Whassis about?' George asked, looking from one to the other.

'It's nothing, George,' Doris said, putting a Kleenex back in her bag. 'Ross and I have . . . an understanding let's call it, don't we? Just so long as you promise to think about it. Promise?'

'I think you should go now, Doris,' Ross said.

'You wanna tell me what that was about?' George asked as soon as the elevator doors had closed on Paul and a smouldering Doris.

'Keep her away from us, George,' Ross said. 'She's a very dangerous woman.'

George, happy for once that someone else was the butt of Ross's displeasure smiled. 'You betcha! I'm the one calling the shots, okay! You got problems you tell me. You too Cathy . . .'

'Sure,' Cathy said. 'I'll tell the guys you'll be a coupla minutes,

114

Ross.' And she disappeared back into the room.

Ross and George were alone again.

'Fact is, Ross, we need each other,' George said. 'And we're good together. Sure we're different – you had plenty as a kid, I had zilch – but we both did okay, yeah? We came through because we're fighters! Hey, I'm remembering that scrap outside the theatre before the opening night of *Love Boat*. You remember?' He laughed and playfully punched Ross on the shoulder.

Ross stood rooted to the spot feeling unable to handle the encounter or to escape from it. Some members of the team passed them offering goodnights.

George became confidential and pally. 'I got great instinct Ross. I can *smell* the good things: lockshen soup, chopped liver, hit shows. *Galileo* smells $600,000 a week. Things have changed since we did *Owen's Valley*, Ross. We got two years outa that show on Broadway an' thought we did great. It was great for the fifties. We used to take 80 g's at the box office a week! Remember! We danced in the streets! We gotta tour outa that show went round the country for a year. We cleaned up. But it's changed, Ross, last coupla years. You been out of it but you read those grosses in Variety. Shows like *Phantom*, they're still playing in the city grossing more than $600,000 a week. There's four companies out on the road each grossing the same amount again. That's three million bucks a week! Way over 150 million bucks a year! And these shows have been running five years, Ross! That's as much or more than those nebbische blockbuster producers from Hollywood dream of making!'

As his lecture continued, George's face pressed close to Ross, reddened, his eyes darted hither and thither never settling, never making contact with Ross.

'And it's all ours, Ross. We don't have to share it with majors and distribution companies so you never see a dime. You're in for 2%. If the show's another *Phantom*, you'll make over a million bucks a year. That's a beach house on the Keys and a pension for you and Ellen.'

At that moment Florence emerged from the elevator next to the two men.

'You seen John Lewis, George?' she said gaily.

'Er . . . No. Yes! He's in there.' George said pointing towards the room. He was alarmed by her familiarity. *Had Ross noticed?*

'Yah, ta! Night, George, night Mr Boardman!' As she squeezed past she innocently touched George's hand. 'You sleep well now!'

Ross stared after her. 'Something odd about that girl,' he said.

'Never mind her. I was saying *Galileo* could be an asset that will

115

see you an' me out, Ross!'' George continued, his energy somewhat dissipated though by the encounter with Florence. 'It'll put your kids through school . . .'

'My kids have long left school, George.'

'You know what I'm saying, for Chrissake. You gotta problem with one of 'em, right? That Chloe. Still on drugs is she? But we get Harry Whitney and we gotta hit! It's as simple as that! Trust me. Then we gotta goddamned goldmine!'

17

It wasn't the Julie he remembered. That Julie was the girl with the laughing face joking over a ploughman's lunch in the pub next to the offices of the Independent. The sort of girl Lewis wanted to introduce to Dad as his wife-to-be. Kind and gentle – 'his' girl. This Julie, superficially identical, was wild and wanton and – *naked*. Where am I? What am I doing here? Why am I subjecting myself to this appalling sight? But Lewis was riveted. He wanted to look away, to block his ears, hold his nose. No deal. The sight, sounds and the smell of Julie making love to Clive North were awesome. The worst aspect of the spectacle was that Clive North was not even undressed. In fact he was immaculately attired in formal evening wear. Nonchalantly sitting on a chair, one elbow casually resting on a dining-room table, Clive was smiling at Lewis as Julie bounced up and down on his lap, her eyes closed, moaning loudly, lewdly, happily. Steadily her lust for the Senior Guardian Arts Correspondent drove her into ever more frenzied writhings. Suddenly Lewis realised where they were, the three of them – at his table, in *his* sitting room, in Willesden! Why? How? Oh God, he cried, distressed beyond words, aroused beyond endurance, fit to burst.

It wasn't the first key turning in the lock that woke him – but the second, the heavy one – the one that best secured him from the skulking horrors of the city. The room was hot and humid. Lewis, prising open his eyes, saw that no light lit the chink of sky that was observable over the broken shutters – New York was still enclosed in night.

Lewis just managed to cover his embarrassment. In the brief interval between Florence extracting the key from the lock, picking up her bag and cautiously opening the apartment door, Lewis found the sheet that had been kicked to the floor. Florence crept in and did her best to close the door quietly.

Their routine had become well established over the past two

weeks. Lewis spent most evenings alone at a movie or occasionally in the theatre – usually off–Broadway, where the prices were affordable and the shows were better. Amongst his new acquaintances, only Fly offered him any hospitality, but the invitation was to a club where, Lewis gathered, bizarre sexual acts took place. Often between the clients, Fly had said. Lewis didn't feel quite up to that kind of experiment . . . yet. He was not lonely; he was too wrapped up in his work. Just happy to be fulfilling his dream; observer, eavesdropper, biographer – a latter-day Pepys. It was no misery to walk back alone to the apartment at 11.00 p.m. through the balmy streets, stopping at the deli round the corner, picking up a couple of peaches and a carton of milk. Then between 11.00 p.m. and two in the morning, came the happiest hours of the day, transcribing the day's notes into a first-draft narrative.

Lewis had seen little of Florence since the day of the audition. A creature of habit, he would leave the apartment at 9.00 a.m. for his breakfast. Florence in tee-shirt and panties, curled up on the sofa, barely covered by a twisted sheet, never woke before 11.00. She spent most of her days nursing Roget in Doris's penthouse apartment on Fifth Avenue. A bedroom had been converted into a highly automated canine care centre and Florence was in charge. The ailing animal lacked for nothing and did seem calmed by Florence's healing hands. As Roget's life ebbed away, the relationship between Florence and Doris grew. Grief bound them together and they were rarely apart. In the evenings the two women, with a hapless Paul Etienne in tow, dined at 21 or the Pierre, before hurrying home to continue their sad vigil. Doris had tried without success to persuade Florence to move into the apartment. For reasons beyond Doris's understanding, Florence wanted to retain a modicum of independence.

And in Robert Berol's one-roomed apartment, when she finally arrived home, John Lewis was usually asleep.

Lewis's erection and Julie's image faded as he lay there listening to Florence preparing herself for sleep.

She sensed his wakefulness. 'Hi,' she whispered.

'Hi,' he whispered back as if there were six other people asleep in the room.

'You okay?'

'I'm fine, thank you. How's the dog?'

'Fading.'

'Oh, sorry.'

'How goes the preparation for my show?' she gaily shouted from the bathroom as she brushed her teeth.

'We've got chorus and dance auditions tomorrow,' Lewis

replied, sitting up, trying to beat some life into dead pillows.

'What about the rest of the cast? Mind if I switch the light on?'

As Florence switched on and looked toward the bed, the sudden illumination from the bathroom caught Lewis, bare-bottomed for a moment, hastily turning back and covering his nakedness.

'There were terrific rows. They went on for days after those auditions. I don't know how Ross copes with the conflicting pressures. In the end he sort of compromised – well I think he compromised – but you can never tell with him. Everything is bottled up. Gibson is the opposite. He wears his opinions like clothes, a different set every day, and everything is emotion.'

Florence sat on the edge of the bed manipulating dental floss around her teeth. 'So who're the chosen few, apart from me, I mean?'

'Old Galileo's under offer to Sir Harold Whitney.'

'That was your idea, right?'

'At the production conference, yes. He sort of passed the singing audition yesterday. He complained of a sore throat. Young Galileo's going to be Ziggy Bronowsky.'

Florence examined the floss. 'Oh yeah, I liked him. Hot bod. I ran my eye over him before his audition.'

'Tara Martin's been offered Marina but she's up for a movie. No-one knows if she's going to accept. They finally offered Anna to Dee.'

'Gibson's wife? Hey, let's play Happy Families, right.' She was rolling the floss into a ball.

'Dee's a great singer and everyone says her acting's improved no end. It was going to be Lucca Maggiore, that's who Ross and Michael wanted, then suddenly it had changed. It got very confusing. I think Ross must have given in. There was a lot of pressurising and bargaining going on. And you got Giulietta, right? I haven't seen you for a while . . .'

'Yup!' Florence beamed at him. 'I got one line! I guess I owe you one, Jaahn.'

'I think it's Doris more than me,' John said modestly.

'Yeah, probably. George Gibson too, y'know.' She flicked the ball of floss across the room aiming for an overflowing bin next to the table.

'I didn't know he'd helped,' Lewis said, with a twinge of jealousy.

'Oh, he was jus' *handy-dandy*,' Florence said and laughed at a private joke.

The conversation died and they found themselves gazing at each other the way two people do who find themselves largely naked on a bed at 2.30 in the morning.

'You horny?' Florence asked.

'Sorry?' Lewis feigned incomprehension even as his pulse quickened.

Florence giggled. 'Is that for me?' She looked at the growing mound below the sheet. Gently she reached out.

'Oooh, it feels big and strong and ready for some action.'

Bells rang in Lewis's head. And it was only after Florence released her grip, he realised the phone was ringing.

'God, it's 2.30!' Lewis exclaimed, feebly. 'Who on earth could that be?'

Florence answered and Lewis covered himself as though the caller could see his shrinking nakedness.

'Hello,' Florence said evenly. 'Oh hi! Aaa-ha. Yeah. About to, yeah . . .' She leered at Lewis then winked. 'Why, you wanna join us? Aaah, aaha . . . yeah . . . when . . . ?'

She looked around the room. 'Sure, right . . . Yeah, if you want some fanny humping. Oh, hey, you get a haircut?'

She slammed down the phone and threw herself on to Lewis's bed, laughing wildly.

'My landlord?' Lewis asked.

'Sure is . . .'

'Why are you laughing . . .?'

'He's unblocked, round the corner and comin' on over!'

Bob Berol, sitting on the sofa next to Florence, closely resembled the picture Lewis had painted in his mind. Little of his face showed. His dense, frizzy hair grew from every available inch of his head and cascaded in waves across and down his back to his waist. His moustache, unaccountably, was less busy but grew long over his lips, hiding his mouth. Likewise his eyebrows lolled full and complacently over his kindly, grey-blue eyes. No question, this was a gentle soul, Lewis thought. His tee-shirt, covering a growing belly, carried the message: 'Life Stinks, So Hold Your Nose' in gothic print. Lewis, noting this, mentally added it to his growing list of tee-shirt quotes he hoped to use in an article for the Independent. He had it mentally entitled in his mind as 'Aphoristic Fashion: the New Maxim Gun'.

Florence was smiling happily at her man, savouring every word of his travel monologue.

'The pick-up lay abandoned outside the shack – its big end snapped an' there was nothing else to be done except hitch.' He noisily scratched his scalp. 'Reminded me how I used to do that

120

back in the sixties. Hitched 'cross to Berkeley in '68 to see what was doin' . . .'

Bob gave a minute-by-minute account of his hitch from Vermont to New York featuring the driver of every car who had picked him up. Lewis, sitting in his bed, feeling like a hospital patient with visitors, became completely engrossed in one particular incident described by Bob in graphic detail. It was an account of an apparent Damascene Conversion on the road to Mystic.

Bob had accepted a lift 'in a tuna wagon' from a 57-year-old widow, a *grandmother* (Bob had said with relish) and her *older* sister. Not dogs, he said, no, these were two hot little ladies. 'Damn attractive!' They were on their way home. Their way was his way, and it didn't take him long to accept their offer of coffee and apple flapjacks in their pretty little house on the outskirts of Mystic, near the waterfront. Once there, it transpired that the ladies wanted to offer Bob more than apple flapjacks. Much more . . .

Then 'it' happened, Bob said, during a two-hour bout of rolling around on their wooden floor. 'To be precise, between orgasms two and three and I mean theirs, not mine,' he said proudly, adding, 'Because I have total control. I gotta quit working on the Great American Epic Poem and change direction.'

Florence's novel unblocking procedure had succeeded. Berol called it ' . . . shifting frequencies'. He described to his two rapt listeners how, in a post-coital glow ('having performed magnificently'), cradling the two old ladies in his arms as they fed him perfect applejacks with whipped cream, he suddenly understood that Florence had been right. 'Yeah, Flo. Remember the letter you wrote me last week . . . One about the synergy of poetry and music could be the missing link in my creative development. You said opera's dead, man, like the novel. How there was only one true blending of all the arts: poetry, drama, dialogue, music, design, an' performance. One truly popular. An' you wrote, Bobby, you gotta get into this shit, remember?'

'The musical?' Lewis asked, ahead of the game.

'Yup, the musical!' Florence said beaming at the two men with pride and joy.

'When the revelation that you were right exploded in my brain with all the force of the Hiroshima bomb,' he said, 'I let out a whoop that scared the old ladies shitless. I kissed 'em an' thanked 'em an' said they would never understand the precious gift they had bestowed upon me. "You mean the applejacks?" they said. No, I explained patiently, the gift of understanding. The pot of gold at the end of the rainbow, the land of Oz. "Oh," they said, understanding nothing.'

121

Bob could see only one problem ahead in his life's work – he knew nothing about music or the theatre. 'But I guess that won't be an insurmountable problem,' he declared confidently.

'We could introduce him to Jerry!' Florence said excitedly. 'Maybe they could work together on their next project.'

Lewis was sceptical. He just yawned and glanced at the travel clock next to the bed. Christ! 4.30 a.m. He immediately felt completely exhausted and craved sleep. But how and where? His absurd English politeness made him offer to give up his bed to the two of them.

He fully expected them to refuse. But they accepted and soon Lewis found himself on the sofa curled up under the sheet whilst Florence and Bob crawled into his bed.

Lewis was suddenly angry. *I'm bloody paying rent! I'd every right to sleep in that bed! I hardly know these people!*

But sleep temporarily overcame these irate reflections. After what seemed to Lewis moments, but in fact was over half-an-hour, he was awake again. Woken by a crescendo of grunts and moans from the bed, only feet away.

And so a miserable Lewis, feigning sleep, was witness to Bob's immense reserves as he athletically satisfied his third lady of the day.

18

The same night the '4A's' New York fund-raising committee met in an upstairs book-lined room at the Players Club. The Club is housed in a large brownstone on Gramercy Park and resembles at least in feel its English counterpart, the Garrick. It's respectable and old-fashioned and counts amongst its members the cream of the New York theatrical establishment. It is also where the American Artists Against AIDS holds its monthly committee meeting. Serving on the committee were Ross Boardman and Dee Gibson.

Ross, a member of many committees, gave as much time as he could. He cared for his profession and felt it important to work for its welfare. Dee Gibson felt the same way and, working infrequently, had the time and energy to be an active participant. The NY 4A's were planning a major musical fund-raising event to be held at Lincoln Center in the late autumn.

Ross had forgotten Dee might be there. He spotted her soon after she had arrived. She looked great. Every inch the producer's wife, dressed expensively but soberly in a beige business suit. He avoided coming into contact with her during the first part of the evening. He was still enraged at the way she had been cast. Not that any of it was Dee's doing – or at least not overtly. The pressure to cast her had come from many quarters – Jerry, Stan and finally Michael, orchestrated, he guessed, by George. And he had caved in. He was, therefore, mostly enraged with himself. That decision, taken with his climbdown over Sir Harry Whitney (who had, it's true, more-or-less, received Stan's approval: 'With work I can get him to sing it . . .'), were signs, he thought, of great weakness. Diminished authority. *A clear loss of will. What's happening to me?*

However, in the coffee break, Ross found himself next to Dee.

'It's just fine,' Dee said, helping herself to a cup. 'A little work now, then we can sit back in October an' enjoy the show. Always provided, Ross, you don't call me for evening rehearsals!'

There was a certain sensual ambiguity in the signals Dee sent out

. . . a sauciness . . . that was sometimes intended and sometimes not. She could turn it on when it suited her. It suited her now.

'We'll use what time we have. It's going to be a difficult show.' Ross looked round hoping to be rescued. On the one hand he was attracted to her (as most men were), on the other she was an actress in his company and George Gibson's wife. She was in the enemy camp.

'Aren't they all?' Dee agreed amiably. 'Maybe this one's more difficult than most, huh?'

There was to be no escape. She steered him towards a book-lined wall away from the other members of the committee.

'By-the-by, I'm glad I've got you to myself a moment, Ross. I want to say thank you. I know it's been a tough decision. But I'm not about to let you down. I'll work till my bones crack, okay? I've got a great acting coach and I'm doing vocal training through the summer, I'll be in shape.'

Ross nodded. 'Good. I'm sure you'll be okay.'

Her eyes flashed with anger. 'I want to be better than okay!' She gazed into her cup thoughtfully for a moment. 'You don't think much of me, do you?'

Ross didn't want to get into this. 'Sure I do. I thought your reading was terrific.'

Dee laughed. 'You don't sound very convincing. Anyway I'm not sure I meant that.'

Ross glanced at her properly for the first time. 'Then what did you mean?'

'I meant me as me. I caught you looking at me earlier in the evening just after I got here. It was as if you hated me.'

It was Ross's turn to laugh. 'You'd be surprised how many people say that to me. It's something about the way my face is set.'

'Maybe you should have plastic surgery. Anyway . . . that's a relief. Because, you see, I find *you* a very sexy man.'

The conversation had taken an unexpectedly dangerous turn and Ross didn't like it. Red stop signals flashed in his brain. But before he could reply, the chairperson recalled them to the table and the final part of the session. As they resumed their place she said to him. 'George is in Washington for two days. Take me to dinner after the meeting.'

They ate Brandelli of Pasta with a morel sauce and drank two bottles of Barolo '84 in a trattoria in Chelsea. Three-quarters of the way through the second bottle, Ross relaxed and began to enjoy listening to Dee dish.

'. . . Sometimes, y'know, I think the only reason George married me was to get me into bed. I gotta tell you I was *very* hard to get!' She giggled into her wine glass. 'I found old guys kinda creepy, right? Always wanting to touch an' *feel*. Yuk! George wasn't like that. Wasn't typical, more old-fashioned. He wooed me you know, in the way younger guys don't know how. Caviare, red roses, champagne. An' the more I said I wouldn't go to bed with him the more he wanted me an' the more stuff he'd send round to my apartment or dressing room. Finally, I guess, because the show was closing an' he *still* hadn't scored, he said he was in love an' how about marriage . . .'

Ross finished the bottle and ordered another. He was nicely mellow. 'You didn't love him . . .?'

Ross found it hard to picture anyone *loving* George.

'Sure I loved him! You think I'd have married him if I didn't love him? Did you notice if they got Tiramisu on the menu?'

Ross shook his head and smiled.

'It's the greatest dessert. You like it?'

'I never eat desserts.' He asked her to continue the story.

'I was 25, from Arkansas, doing my first show on Broadway, an' this *legend* asks me to marry him! Of course I fell in love with him, with the whole idea. We went to Tijuana an' got married. An' five years later I'm still Mrs Gibson and George an' I are getting older.'

She didn't look happy until the waiter told her they had Tiramisu. Ross ordered a double Espresso and an Armagnac.

'George has been seeing Leman again. Did you know?'

'No, I didn't. Why?'

'Because I made him.' She laughed and swayed in her seat. The wine had made her quite tipsy. 'Ironic, I guess. I'm the one who used to be screwed up now he's the one seeing the shrink.'

Ross was interested. 'You want to tell me why?'

'Yeah. But not here. Take me home.'

The wine made him happy and he raised no objections. He paid the check and they found a cab.

In the cab she said. 'He can be manic, Ross. Violent, abrupt changes of mood, you know. An' he doesn't sleep. I wake up an' it's maybe three in the morning an' the bathroom light's on. He's cleaning his teeth. Washing his hands. Inspecting his skin.'

'That's unusual?'

'Sure. You do that? See he does it five, six times during the night. In the morning I say, "George, why do you do *that*?" An' I swear to God, Ross, he remembers nothing.'

'That's sleepwalking – not serious.'

'I did psychology at college an' I know the symptoms of obsessional behaviour. Like he's obsessed by you, for instance . . .'

Ross was staring out of the window. The route took them through the Park. Close to midnight and tourists were taking buggy rides in the warm night air.

'He talks about you a lot . . .'

'Yeah?' Ross was being non-committal.

'He envies you I think. Envies your *power*.' She studied his reaction. 'You see, he wants to do it *all*. Everything. He can't bear to share it. An' as his power wanes . . .'

Ross interrupted. 'This is nonsense, Dee. He is not waning . . . and this talk of power . . . We're creating plays. That's what we're doing. We're not running armies, fighting battles.'

'That's not how he sees it, Ross,' Dee said vehemently. 'Believe me. He *does* see it as a battle. He sees life like that. Who wins? It better be me! That's how he thinks. He talks about *control*. That what's important to him. That's what he wants over me, over you, over everything. An', as I said, as his powers wane . . .' She leant heavily against Ross as the cab rounded the corner too fast and came to a stop. They had arrived.

Dee insisted on paying.

She held his hand and walked unsteadily across the pavement towards the lobby.

Ross thought, what am I doing here?

The Gibson apartment that Ross and Dee walked into was on the 6th floor of the Dakota. The rooms were spacious, tastefully furnished and well lit. On the walls of the main reception room were several fine examples of 19th-century American art and Ross was immediately drawn to a magnificent Maine landscape by David Johnson and several pictures by Edwin Lord Weeks that were astonishingly exotic.

'You've been here before?' Dee said, kicking off her shoes and tossing her purse on to a sofa.

'Never. I recognise the style of the settings, however,' he said glancing about. 'Early eighties Robin Wagner.'

Dee laughed. 'On the button. When George had Robin design some show back then he'd just bought this place. He commissioned Robin to fix it up. Great job, huh? Wanta drink?'

She passed him an iced bottle of California champagne taken from a small refrigerator built into the drinks' cabinet.

Ross began to open it. 'George only collects 19th-century?'

'Ross, George just writes the cheque. All this was chosen by Aimi Schumacher at Sotheby's. It's just something to hang up –

fill wall space. Aimi sends over a Polaroid and says it's a good deal. Cheap. George gives the photo a glance an' if he likes it okay and the price is right, he gets Betty in the office to give Aimi the go-ahead. Simple, huh?'

She paused to sip the champagne.

Ross sat on the sofa and said: 'Everything is simple when you've money.'

'You survive okay. You never stop. Keep talking. I'm gonna change. If you see my kitty, pour it some milk from the refrigerator, will you?'

She trotted into the bedroom taking her glass with her.

'You know how many shows I prepare never get on, how many filmscripts I read, never made. Sure I'm always busy – but real hits are few and far between. The royalties dry up. I gotta lot of wives to feed, kids to support.'

'Don't worry, kitty's in here. On my bed. How's Ellen?' Dee called from the bedroom.

'Away in LA.'

'That's nice . . .'

'Vocal coaching at the Pasadena Playhouse.'

'While the cat's away the mice can play . . .'

'Coincidentally it's a revival of an early Michael Kershon comedy – *Inns and Outs*. She's trying to get them to speak proper English . . . She says she's partially succeeded.'

Dee laughed. 'Maybe she can coach me on one or two things about you, huh?'

Ross liked women, he relished their company and he enjoyed variety. So why resist? Because Dee was in *Galileo*? He had rules he tried to keep and one was: *Don't mess with the cast*. This was modified on occasion to: don't mess with the cast till *after* the rehearsals are over. (Out-of-town, on tour, was the time for trouble.) But Dee was something else: irresistible. Plus she was George's wife. To the sexual expectation was added the sublime piquancy of danger.

And triumph.

She came back into the room unsteadily, holding a Siamese. She'd changed out of her suit into jeans and a plain white tee-shirt. Ross had expected her in a robe, naked underneath. *I watch too many movies*, he thought.

'Say hello to Ross, Chai-Chi . . .' And she disappeared this time to the kitchen to fix the cat some milk.

'How long have you an' Ellen been together?' she called out.

'Fifteen years . . .' He didn't want to talk about this. A refrigerator door closed in the kitchen.

'An' you never married, right?'

In Ross's experience, women in these situations rarely wanted to talk to men about their other women.

'No.'

'An' you two are happy together, are ya?'

'Sure.' Loyalty overcame truth. Ross was, in fact, bored with Ellen's English steadfastness, her evenness. There were few surprises, little *drama*.

'Well that's *great!*' Dee, having satisfied the cat, came back into the room, poured herself a refill and lay down sprawled on the carpet fixing cushions for comfort. She seemed to lose interest in Ellen. 'You know I was telling you about George an' his waning powers an' things . . .'

Ross nodded and topped up his glass.

'Well he's become impotent.' Dee waited for a reaction but got nothing. 'Over the last coupla months.'

The liquor was making it tough for Ross to think clearly, to understand motivations. 'Why are you telling me this?'

Dee leant forward swaying slightly and rested her elbows on Ross's knees. 'Because I think he's going crazy.'

Her eyelids drooped. He didn't take her seriously. 'Dee, I've known George over 35 years – he's always been crazy. You married an old man. Old men get problems.'

He smiled at her.

'Well, it's not fair,' she said petulantly. 'What am I gonna do? I even phoned Leman and asked him if it was a permanent condition.'

'What did he say?'

'Maybe yes, maybe no. But probably yes. Be understanding an' imaginative, he said. Well, I've tried Ross. I've been understanding *an'* imaginative.'

She stared into his eyes before twisting away and then leaning back, sitting between his open legs, poured herself another glass from the bottle on the floor.

'Oops.' She'd tipped the bottle over, putting it down. The frothy liquid gushed over the carpet. 'S'alright, girl'll clean it up tomorrow.' Turning again, rubbing her body between Ross's thighs as she did so, she gazed up at him.

'You wanna make love to me, Ross?'

Gently he touched her face and she smiled at him, Then she drew him down towards her and kissed his closed eyes.

On the carpet now, next to the spreading stain of the spilt champagne, Ross made love to Dee carefully and considerately. He was slow and inventive, Dee was responsive. He felt vibrant, powerful, *triumphant*. Yes, he thought, this *is* a form of triumph. Possessing George's beautiful wife! It qualified as a morsel of sweet revenge for those humiliations inflicted through the years.

Into his ear she said something about this is why she likes older guys. 'You calling me an older guy?' he managed to say. She laughed.

19

The buzzer woke Ross the next morning at 8.15 a.m. – an hour before his alarm and four hours before his body wanted. He struggled towards consciousness and realised that he felt acutely nauseous. Tying Ellen's bathrobe about him, he headed unsteadily towards the apartment door. En route, he decided that the malaise was probably due to booze and lack of sleep: it was only four hours since he had prised himself away from Dee and ridden home in a cab.

A Federal Express package propped against the door fell in as he opened it. In the kitchen he laid the pack on the breakfast bar and poured himself an orange juice. He sat and stared at the glass thinking about Dee, his emotional frailty, his immaturity. *Sixty and still a child!* He knew that sleeping with Dee was madness, an appalling mistake. *A one-night stand, okay, but should it turn out to be more . . .* He took a sip from the glass. The orange juice did immediate damage. The acid burned into his stomach lining making him retch. Instead he settled for sipping some chilled water.

The Federal Express package was from Michael in London and contained draft number 4 of *Galileo*. Michael had pinned a letter to the front page.

Dear Ross,

Well, here it is! I finished it late last night as I told you I would. I'm nothing if not punctual! I hope you'll be pleased with it – I am. It's much funnier (George'll be happy, I think) yet it hasn't lost what *you* like – it's still historically accurate and (I hope) intellectually honest.

Enjoy! Phone me when you're done. (The director's temporarily kicked me out of rehearsals so I'm working from home.) Heather sends love,

– Your friend, Michael

Ross, sitting for 60 minutes at the kitchen table was totally immersed in Renaissance Italy. He read the fourth draft as if it were the first, attempting to put himself into the shoes of a first-time audience. He succeeded to the extent that he forgot his stomach ache.

It was not, however, with increasing pleasure that he read, but with steadily mounting gloom.

Something had gone radically wrong. Ross finished the last page and sat back. The charm had gone – and the wit. George had asked for more jokes and Michael had tried to fulfil the request – there were some poor, crude jokes scattered through the draft, largely unfunny, giving the whole less wit not more. In the process, Galileo who had had strength, charm and intelligence was portrayed in this draft as a buffoon. It reminded Ross of Peter Shaffer's treatment of Mozart in *Amadeus*. This was far from the original intention. Their Galileo was to be tough, witty, idiosyncratic – of the people. The first drafts had portrayed him as a great lover and sensualist – a man of vision wrestling with a society trapped in concepts fashioned centuries before – concepts palpably and demonstrably false. Some of that was still there, but hidden in false theatrical glitter. The heart of the piece seemed reduced to dross. What had begun as a poetic vision had become prosaic or, Ross feared, just plain awful.

How had this happened? Michael was one of Britain's best playwrights, winner of five Olivier awards for Best Play, twice nominated for a Tony. An intellectual like Ross. Michael must surely have sensed something was awry? Five days ago Ross had called Michael to see how the new draft was faring and Michael was joyful. He had reported himself delighted, yes, that was the word that stuck in Ross's mind, *delighted*. George's instincts had been right. Adding crudeness to Galileo completed his character. It will give Jerry another angle and colour for the music, he had said. The warning signs in this transatlantic conversation were all there.

The worst of it was that Michael, whom Ross loved and respected, was *delighted* with what he had done. *Delighted*. *Delighted*.

The word went round and round.

Ross sipped more water. The nausea had gone but had been replaced by that worrying ache. He rubbed his tummy and promised himself he would call Dr Lipschitz.

What was to be done? Michael had to come to New York and

they would work through it again. This time he would insist Michael rewrite it here, not just take notes and return to London. Ross had tried to persuade Michael to fax the scenes page-by-page but to no avail. *Better to see it revised and complete,* Michael had said – *changes I make at the end of the script could necessitate further changes in earlier scenes etc.* This was writer's nerves – Ross recognised the signs. The truth, however, had to be faced. Michael had written so many drafts, he had lost touch. He was writing to order, not from instinct. Determined to oblige producer, co-general partner, director, composer, he had ended up ruining the script.

Ross decided it was crucial no-one else read this draft. If George got his hands on it, Ross worried, there was a probability he would *like* this crude showbiz version of the story, and it would become the rehearsal draft. The prospect of six weeks' rehearsals followed by six weeks of previews with a script he now hated and couldn't support was intolerable. There was still time for major alterations. It was only early August – nine weeks to go before rehearsals started – plenty of time for another draft.

Ross put the glass in the dishwasher and went into the bedroom to shave and dress. At eleven he was due at the Gershwin Theater for the principal dance and chorus auditions.

The nausea had passed, the pain gone. Once again he put off calling Lipschitz.

They had begun lining up at 10.00 a.m. By 10.45 a.m. when Lewis turned the corner on to 51st from Broadway, 150 singers and dancers were sitting on the pavements, standing in groups, leaning on walls, sunbathing or dishing, enjoying an unusually cool, clear August morning in New York City.

Lewis found his way to the stage door of the Gershwin Theater. With some difficulty he persuaded the stage doorkeeper that he wasn't a dancer or singer trying to get in early but a bona fide member of the production team. The unshaven hulk, sucking a stogie, sitting on a broken chair, seemed unconvinced by the reporter's notebook Lewis waved in his face. Passing Cerberus, Lewis found his way to the stage where Tam Topp, the choreographer and Molly Call, his assistant, were working out a short dance routine to teach the auditionees. Lewis recognised the accompanist from the previous auditions. As Tam and Molly put their dance together, the pianist improvised on a theme from one of Jerry's numbers. Clustered in the stalls were some of the production team: Stan Warburg; Fly Gold; Charlie Brodsky, the

Stage Manager; Gene Landau, the General Manager, and Cathy Newman. Lewis made his way down the rickety steps from the stage to the stalls, and was welcomed by the group. Almost immediately they were joined by Ross and, hard on his heels, Jerry Trimlock clutching a Hershey Bar.

'Jerry's in a good mood. Ross seems gaunt and pale,' Lewis wrote in his notebook.

'We got a coupla hundred kids out there, Ross, Stan. We gonna type first, sing, then dance 'em?' Charlie shouted from the stage.

'Yeah – usual Charlie.'

Ross called Tam and Molly into the stalls. Tam was out of shape and sweating. Molly cool and serious. Ross addressed them. 'Just to remind you, we want dancers who can sing and singers who can dance. I want faces, characters. I want to make Renaissance paintings out of these people so don't offer me fruit. Group of boys, Charlie, group of girls. Mix 'em up . . . Ten at a time. Remind them we're typing.'

Charlie disappeared towards the stage door to organise.

Lewis asked Fly what typing was.

'You'll see,' Fly said.

Charlie led ten young men on to the stage where they stood in line facing out towards the auditorium. From each he collected a card which contained a name, Equity number, skills and a three-line résumé. He said, 'Sorry guys. We're typing. You know the score. If we call your name, please wait over there. You'll be singing, then dancing. If we don't call your name, thanks for coming. Okay?' Charlie headed into the stalls and gave the stack of cards to Ross.

Stan whispered to Ross: 'Third guy on left's a great bass. Good type for you?'

'Yeah, okay.' Ross found his card. 'Anyone else? I like the look of the end guy on the right. Anyone know him?' No-one did. Ross extracted his card and gave the two cards to Charlie who called out the two names. 'Everyone else – thank you.'

Lewis was shocked. 'Is this typical?' he whispered to Fly who was standing next to him.

'Typing? Sure. Everyone's used to it.'

Well, they might be, but Lewis clearly saw the disappointment on the faces of the other eight.

'There's no other way to do it,' Fly explained. 'We can tell immediately if the guys are okay lookswise and we know the best singers. Otherwise, we waste time. There's too many out there. Also, remember Stan and Tam already have six or seven people earmarked for the show. This is to fill out the gaps.'

133

'Tough business,' Lewis noted, watching the next ten wheeled in.

It was during the gap between one group and another that Jerry leaned into Ross and asked him what he thought of Michael's new draft.

'You get a copy?' Ross asked.

'Fed Ex yesterday. What d'ya think?'

'Michael's lightened it too much,' Ross said cautiously. 'I don't think he's done Galileo's character any great favours. Plus the change puts the text at odds with the music in places.'

Jerry looked surprised. 'I don't agree at all. Michael's done everythin' you asked him to do. And more!' Jerry grinned. 'Hey, didn't you like those jokes? Wow! Made me finally wanna write some musical comedy.'

He offered Ross a square of chocolate. Ross declined.

'Next group for you, guys!' Charlie shouted, and ten girls were standing on stage.

Fly appeared next to Lewis. 'Check out that one, fourth from left,' he whispered. 'You ever seen gazoomas like those?' Lewis had to admit he hadn't.

'I don't know her but if you want I can look thro' the cards . . .'

'I can find my own girls, Fly,' Lewis whispered. 'But thanks anyway for asking.'

'So what you wanna do, Ross?' Jerry asked in the next gap. 'Get Michael back and clean it up again? When are you gonna be satisfied with it, for Chrissake?'

'When it's right!' Ross said loud and sharply, causing heads to turn. *This boy has never written a Broadway show,* Ross thought. *Nothing's right till it's fixed and when it's fixed, don't mess with it.*

'Okay. But how d'you know when it's right, man?' Jerry didn't want to give up. Ross may be older but it was time for his generation to roll over. 'I say it's right, you say it isn't.' He shrugged. 'Who says who's right?'

Now everyone was listening. There were ten more girls lined up on stage. Charlie, seeing the discussion in the stalls, chatted amiably to a couple he knew. Lewis made notes.

'Ross has to take an overall view,' Stan said. 'If he thinks it's not gonna work, you better believe it . . .'

'You think Michael an' me are *stupid!*' Jerry said passionately. 'We can't tell if a thing's a crock of shit?'

'Slow down, Jerry!' Ross said, not liking the way this was developing. He knew Jerry felt a junior partner in the team. 'All I said was it's not right *yet.* It's the book. The music's just fine.'

'Christ, Ross, don't patronise me!' Jerry shouted. 'If the book's shit, it's all shit. Everything's interconnected!'

The team looked away, embarrassed. On stage, Charlie and the girls had stopped chatting. They watched, fascinated.

'What's this about, Jerry?' Ross asked quietly. 'Not about the script, is it?'

Ross turned away from Jerry. 'Hi girls. Sorry to have kept you waiting.'

As Charlie began to marshal them into a neat line, the stage doorkeeper lumbered gracelessly on to the stage.

'Hey, Boss, phone call, stage door,' Charlie shouted from the stage. 'Washington. You can take it in the wings. Godzilla'll put you through. Sorry, Tiger, just a joke . . . Relax *again* girls!'

Jerry, who was still smouldering, caught up with Ross in the aisle. 'You got to let me call some of the shots, Ross, okay? Not many. Just some.'

'This is about Debbie. Am I right?'

Without waiting for a reply, Ross walked up the steps on to the stage and disappeared into the wings. Shocked, Jerry stared after him.

Ross instantly knew who it was. The choking cough was the giveaway.

'Ross? George. You busy?'

'Auditions here, George. We're working for you . . .'

'Okay, okay. You heard anything about that musical just opened in London?'

'No.' Ross, looking from the wings saw the girls sitting on the floor chatting and laughing.

'Friend of mine produced it in London, *Dance Steps.* Wondered what you'd heard.'

'George – nice of you to call – I gotta get back . . .'

'Yeah. Okay. Justa minute . . .'

In Washington, at the other end of the line, George was coughing and spitting. Ross waited. 'What's on your mind, George. I've got 100 kids to see . . .'

'I gotta give up these cigars. I'm smuggling Havanas and they're costing me half the budget . . .'

'George . . .'

George came suddenly to the point. 'You read Michael's draft?'

So Michael had mailed three – to Jerry, George and himself. *Jesus!* Ross muttered an affirmative.

'It's crap, right?' George said. 'I mean it's not just bad, it's a complete stink bomb. Guy can't write a book, Ross. I gave him every chance. He's blown it. He's out. Okay?'

Ross thought quickly. Fire the writer at this stage and you're in

135

deep trouble. Who can come in at short notice and re-write someone else's script? Ross had been through this only once before with disastrous results. In the end rehearsals had been postponed and the show, when it finally opened, had a different director as well – Ross had resigned.

'George, you're full of surprises. When I read that script this morning, I said to myself – "George is going to love this . . ." '

'Yeah – why?'

'I thought you'd like the jokes.'

'What jokes? I didn't see no jokes . . .'

'It's fixable . . .' Ross said.

George interrupted him. 'You've been trying to fix this for a year, Ross. You can't work miracles. I hired Michael to write the book – he can't do it. I'll get someone who can!'

'Not at this stage, George. If you fire Michael, we're through. The whole project will collapse. Remember *Lucky Lucille*. Writer got fired from that and the show never made it.'

'Writers are two a dime out there. There's a whole block of 'em on 41st and 7th . . .'

George, I screwed Dee last night and it was great. Whilst you were futzing around Washington, your wife and I . . .

Charlie was suddenly next to Ross. 'Do you want me to stand these girls down, Boss?'

'Look, George. Don't do anything till you get back to the city. Then we talk. Okay? I gotta go . . .'

'It's too late, Ross. I already done it. Betty faxed his agent in London one hour ago. Michael's out . . .'

The team worked until they had reduced the dancers and chorus to a manageable short list of 35.

Ross had returned from his phone call stiff with rage. He didn't volunteer any information and no-one asked. The team had to be told but he needed time to think. At 1.00 p.m. Charlie had taken lunch orders and Ross had requested the team eat together as there were matters to discuss. At 1.30 p.m. Charlie called an hour's lunch break. Ross broke the news.

'Hey!' Charlie said. 'I've won the sweepstake! I drew Michael to be fired first. Wha'd'I win?'

'$55,' Fly said, checking his notebook.

As Ross expected, Jerry took it badly. He and Michael had established a close personal relationship over the 18 months they had worked together. Not natural collaborators, nevertheless the bond they formed was strong, maintained by mutual respect for each other's skills.

Lewis was taking copious notes. This was good stuff. 'Back in London,' he wrote, 'must interview Michael K.'

Stan spoke for them all. 'George has made a tough decision, Ross. I can't say I think it's right. He's living in the past. We should have gotten beyond the days of doing business like this . . .'

'Sure should have!' Cathy added.

'Does George have someone in mind?' Stan asked.

Ross shrugged. 'I doubt it. George acts on impulse. He's back in the city this evening – I'm seeing him first thing tomorrow . . .'

Lunch arrived and Charlie sorted out the sandwiches. The food lifted their spirits. They were still a team. A team of freelancers – at the top of their profession. And they were the survivors. Lose one overboard – the showboat sails on.

They knew it must be soon for his breathing had become fitful and rasping. The veterinarian had called at around 8.00 a.m., injected a powerful painkiller and offered sincere condolences. There was nothing else he could do. Doris, with Paul lightly holding her hand, sat staring at the dying dog. The maid, offering breakfast, was turned away.

Florence arrived at 9.30 a.m., after receiving a call from Paul. She had brought Bob Berol to add moral support. Doris sat immobile and white-faced, unable to even lift her eyes as Florence introduced him. The only movement she made was to take a Kleenex from the box immediately on her right and dab at her nose. Roget whimpered feebly. Bob sat down quietly in a corner, folding his burly arms, watching the deathbed scene. *Alas, poor Roget,* he thought.

Florence moved straight to the crib and stroked the dog's head. Immediately his breathing eased and the fearful whimpering stopped. He even appeared to sigh with a rare pleasure. One eye opened briefly and glistened wetly at Florence. Then he slept, breathing gently.

They all relaxed.

Doris looked at Florence in wonder. She saw before her not Florence Hackstuber, born in Queens 24 years ago, but Florence Nightingale, saviour of souls, blessed with healing hands. Doris's heart melted, tears flowed, not with thoughts of imminent death but with gratitude and a deep love for the freckle-faced healer.

The phone rang. Someone, somewhere in the large apartment

answered. Almost immediately the extension rang in the sick room. Paul answered it. 'Doris, chérie, c'est George à l'appareil. 'E is in Washington. It's urgent 'e must speek wiz you.'

Reluctantly Doris took the call, and with little preamble, George asked if she'd read the new draft Betty had sent over.

'Christ, George. I'm in no fit state to read anything.' Her voice was thick with emotion. 'This is a house in deep distress.'

'Listen, Doris, I'm in deep distress too. It's a piece of shit, Michael's work, I gotta tell you. The damn thing's gotten worse – not better. That guy couldn't write a joke if it was written on a label tied to his dick! An' Ross keeps trying to defend him! I want your agreement to fire him *an'* Ross. I wanna hire another writer to work the book scenes an' we'll hire a younger director who's got some fire in his nuts. Marty Rice. You know him? What d'you say?'

'I'd say you're going a bit fast for me, George. Hold on . . .'

She covered the mouthpiece and asked Paul to get her a small brandy. 'Let me get it straight. This draft's shit. Okay, doesn't surprise me. You should have dumped Michael months ago. You've got too soft, George.' The colour was coming back to Doris's cheeks.

Florence stroked the dog's face apparently oblivious to the phone conversation. Bob watched Doris.

'If we dump Michael,' Doris asked, 'you got someone else in mind?'

'No. D'you think Jerry could do it? Guy's a genius you know, Doris. You heard the new stuff he's done? I'll have Betty send you a tape . . .'

Doris thought for a moment and sipped the brandy Paul had given her. 'No, George, not Jerry. No experience. You gotta get a Doc in: Neil Simon or Peter Stone. Someone good at fixing books.'

Florence pricked up her ears and looked thoughtful.

'Betty's already faxed Michael's agent,' George was saying. 'What about Ross?'

Doris didn't want to disturb Roget so she moved to the phone in her bedroom. Moving gave her a chance to think. She felt no compunction in removing Michael Kershon. She'd never liked him or his work and she knew the feeling was mutual. The writer had pointedly ignored her or simply brutally dismissed her ideas out-of-hand. Good riddance.

Ross was a different matter. Firing Ross would be folly. Not that she felt any warmth or sympathy for him either. But Ross had built the team. Chop off the head and the body might die. Doris sat on her bed and picked up the extension. Down the line in Washington she could hear George clearing his throat, hawking, snorting, mucous everywhere.

'No, George. Jerry needs Ross. We gotta big show. We need experience at the top.'

'Doris, I think I made a mistake from square one hiring Ross. I shoulda looked for young and hot.'

'George,' Doris said. 'It's too late. If you want to put the show on ice for a year to 18 months okay. Fire 'em all, we start again.'

'I been thinking about that too, Doris. We could cut out now . . . Delay till next season . . .'

Doris kicked off her shoes and lay on the bed. 'Then count me out, George. I'm in for this season and this season only. Look, you gotta find an American writer to replace Kershon, George. Transatlantic writing partnerships are too expensive. I was looking at the statements before I left France – we've already spent over $60,000 in airfares and subsistence – and we're still four months away from rehearsals. We got to sell a lot of tickets to recoup that! George? You there . . ?'

'Okay. We don't fire Ross,' George said grimly. 'I'm gonna look for someone to fix the book an' we go this season.'

Doris went back to Roget's room. The scene was apparently unchanged. Bob sat motionless in the corner. Florence, lost in thought, an idea crystallising in her mind, was mechanically stroking the supine animal. Paul Etienne had dozed off.

But Doris knew immediately. She let out a small involuntary shriek and pointed into the crib. There, on the satin cover of the tiny pillow with the embroidered heart, was a trickle of blood oozing from the dog's silent fixed mouth.

20

Ross and George met the next morning to discuss writers but got nowhere. Ross was unco-operative and negative. The last 24 hours had not reduced the rage and frustration Ross felt about Michael's firing. A late-night phone call to Michael in London had only added fuel to the fire. Heather, Michael's wife, said Michael was out. Ross knew she was lying. He told her to tell him how sorry he was. She thanked him and hung up. He decided to write a letter but fatigue overcame him.

For a week George chased several well-known writers. They all turned him down. Fixing someone else's work is not such a desirable occupation.

Meanwhile, Ross concentrated on design. Karl-Heinz flew in for four days with a to-scale card model of the set and a suitcase full of costumes sketches. This part of the process still excited Ross when so much else fatigued him. Consequently, the champagne was chilling in an ice bucket when the German, with Chubby Moscowitz in tow, presented himself at Ross's apartment in the afternoon.

The model was unwrapped and prepared for viewing whilst Ross took a phone call in the kitchen. Dee, with a new intimacy, wanted to talk.

'Honey, I'd sort of hoped you'd call me you know. Okay, we were both smashed but the *intensity* wasn't something *I* could forget. Is Ellen still away?'

She knew perfectly well Ellen was in LA for another four days till her show opened. Ross tried to detach himself from this conversation, hoping that a businesslike approach might bring this affair to a speedy conclusion.

But was this what he really wanted? Was Dee a casual affair? A one-night craziness?

He tried to put her off but his body told him something else. The sound of her voice was a sufficient reminder of champagne-perfumed pleasures to make him want a repeat performance. Her lovemaking had been intoxicating, exotic and relaxed, guiltless and liberated. Afterwards there had been no remorse – only tenderness and sleep. This was a narcotic and, in the final analysis, Ross wanted more.

'Okay,' he said to her. 'My place tonight? TV supper and the Movie of the Week?'

'It's a deal,' she said. 'Oh and by the way, Ross . . .'

'Yeah . . .' he said.

'You wanna know something. George wanted to fire you but Doris talked him out of it. I just thought you might need that information . . . like for ammunition. See you in three hours . . .' And she was gone.

Five minutes later, Ross returned to the sitting room where the designers were silently sipping champagne in front of the carefully arranged model. Tiny model chairs and tables were laid out on ground plans ready to be slipped into the set as they went through the show scene by scene.

Karl-Heinz held his hand up for silence. He nodded to Chubby who switched on Ross's CD player – Fauré's Requiem at 55 watts. Karl-Heinz thought this appropriate accompaniment to the set. It didn't occur to any of them to play the tape of Jerry's score. The lights were turned off, the blinds drawn. His mind preoccupied with Dee's imminent arrival, Ross watched and listened in a state of erotic expectancy – his senses were alive, vibrant and excited.

It was Chubby who reverently described the set. Karl-Heinz had designed three concentric hemispheres that could revolve and move to make extraordinary images: a giant globe – the earth – lit, using the Planetarium projection principle, slowly turned around. Suddenly, it was transformed into the solar system with shooting stars. Using an ingenious (Ross was assured, foolproof) system of multi-tracking and gearing, the hemispheres could be separated, set spinning, moving across the floor to establish chapels, small rooms, an exquisite ballroom – or the Doge's bedroom. Triumphantly it solved the trial scene – the three half-globes placed across the stage and lit with brilliant projections of stained glass windows. The two designers put on a show, using torches and mini-spots to give a sense of how it would look under lighting.

When it was over, Ross sat back, thrilled. This, he knew, would take Broadway by storm – and bring design forward to the mid-nineties. Karl-Heinz had the qualities of Boris Aronson at the peak of his powers.

'It's so *sexy*, Karl,' Ross said. 'It's erotic and wonderful. You've given me more than a set. It's a work of art – a moving sculpture.

I can see the show and know it will work. This is poetry and it's what theatre should be.'

Karl-Heinz took off his sunglasses and wiped away the tears that were streaming down his face. Tears of joy at Ross's words. Pleasing the director was the imperative – as long as Ross was happy, everyone else could go hang. On a scrap of paper he wrote: 'THE MOVING BOSOM OF WOMAN IS, FOR MAN, THE LAMB OF GOD.'

Ross looked puzzled for a moment.

'The set has a certain convexness,' Chubby elaborated, 'a *breast-like* quality that Karl-Heinz sees as fundamental to the design of *Galileo*.'

This was fine by Ross. He was accustomed to this way of thinking. The designer of Dekker's *Shoemaker's Holiday* had begun his conception with an erect phallus centre stage and developed his design from there. By the end of the process this erection had become a turret on a street house with smoke drifting from a chimney.

'Karl-Heinz would like to show you his costume drawings,' Chubby announced reverently.

The costume drawings were ravishing. The period was perfectly captured with meticulous attention to detail – from wigs to shoes. If the costume-makers reproduce these accurately, Ross thought to himself, the actors will appear to have stepped out of an early 17th-century painting. He was very happy. Chubby and Karl-Heinz finished their presentation and sat back to bask in Ross's effusive praise. The choir sang 'In Paradisum Deducant Angeli', and Ross, in perfect bliss, knew why he loved theatre, this project, and despite all the shit, one way or another, he was going to make *Galileo* into one of the great 20th-century musicals.

21

Doris ensured that Roget was interred with as much pomp as her father. The service, conducted by Rabbi Goldmark of the 75th Street Reform Synagogue, was on a hot summer's afternoon in the Where Our Friends Repose private Pet Cemetery in Queens. In attendance, with a mourning Doris and Paul, were Florence, Bob and Lewis, and to Lewis's surprise – George Gibson.

'You wanna have dinner with us, George?' Doris asked in the limo afterwards. Paul, Doris, Florence and Bob sat squashed together at the back. Lewis and George faced them on the jump seats.

George looked at his watch. 'It's 5.00 p.m., Doris, an' I've gotta meeting with a writer in my office at 5.30. It's important – an' I'd like you to come to it. I didn't wanna worry you with this prior to the internment.'

So that was why George was there, thought Lewis.

Florence and Lewis pricked up their ears. Everyone connected with *Galileo* was eagerly awaiting news on Michael Kershon's replacement.

'Okay,' Doris said. 'Tell the driver, George.' George gave the directions. 'After dinner? You wanna ask Dee to join us?'

'Yeah – okay. Pass the phone.'

Bob obliged.

As he dialled, Florence could contain her inquisitiveness no longer. 'Who're you seeing, Mr Gibson, which writer?'

George chose not to hear. This matter wasn't for public discussion until settled. 'Dee, it's me. If you get this message in time – you wanna join Doris an' me for dinner at the . . .'

He put his hand over the mouthpiece and looked at Doris.

'Le Giraffe d'Or,' Doris said.

'. . . Le Giraffe d'Or at 6.45.' He passed the phone back to Bob. 'I doubt she'll come. She does committee work in the evening. They're producing an AIDS Benefit in October.'

'Which writer did you say we're meeting?' Doris asked.

'I didn't,' George said, looking out of the window.

Doris persisted. 'You can talk in front of my friends, George. I love these people. They're my family.'

'Mais oui . . .,' said Paul, nodding.

Florence beamed at Doris. Lewis looked surprised and Bob sat expressionless.

George pulled out a cigar from a leather traveller and thoughtfully sucked its end. 'You're gonna find out soon enough, Doris.' And he refused to be drawn further.

Bob, Florence and Lewis sat outside George's office flicking through magazines whilst Doris and George were interviewing the writer. Betty sat behind her desk filing. Filing her nails.

'Who's he got in there, Betty?' Lewis asked.

Betty looked up from her nails. She felt friendly to this group; delighted finally to meet Bob and proud of having helped Lewis get accommodated. Only Florence she had not taken to. *Something about the girl's eyes,* she told herself.

'Conrad Rothstein,' she whispered confidentially.

'Never heard of him,' Florence whispered.

'Me neither,' Lewis whispered back. 'What's he written?'

'Not very much,' said Betty. 'He wrote a kinda revue a season ago that George liked. Off-off-Broadway.'

'What kinda revue?' Florence asked.

'Well, I didn't see it,' said Betty. 'But it was called *Torah! Torah!* Some kinda Jewish thing . . . You'll have to ask George . . .'

At that moment, grim-faced, George, Doris and Conrad emerged from the inner office. Lewis stared at Conrad fascinated. He was an exotic specimen. An Orthodox Jew from head-to-toe, he appeared to have stepped straight out of the Warsaw ghetto.

'Hi, guys!' he said waving cheerfully to Bob, Lewis and Florence who gazed back at him somewhat surprised at the ordinariness of his accent and manner. Doris and George accompanied him to the door where he took his leave. 'So – er – so, sorry I've wasted your time, guys . . . Right?' And, with a brief wave, he was gone through the door.

George and Doris were depressed. 'Didn't work out with him, huh?' Florence said sympathetically.

'Nope,' Doris said. 'He's got a development deal with Paramount to write a comedy feature.'

'Guy's a genius,' George said. 'New hot-shot comedy writer.

S'pity . . .' He shrugged disconsolately. 'I don't know where to turn. I'm blocked.'

This was the first time Lewis had seen George so down. *Got to remember this moment.*

'Can I have a word with you, Mr Gibson?' Florence said, 'in private . . . in your office. Why don't the rest of you guys go wait in the limo with Paul . . . We'll only be five minutes . . . Or so.'

She gave them a warm smile. Lewis wondered what she was up to. He noticed George seemed unsure whether to follow Florence who had already disappeared into the office. Doris led the others into the lobby towards the elevator.

'Close the door, Mr Gibson, will ya?' Florence said when they were alone. 'You wanna sit on that sofa . . .?'

Not used to being managed in his own office, George neverthe-less followed her instructions. Florence sat down next to him.

'I jus' thought you looked real depressed out there, Mr Gibson . . . what with the funeral . . . an' then this *disappoint-ment* . . .'

'Yeah,' George agreed. 'That Conrad's perfect for this show. I just don't know why I hadn't thought of him earlier . . . now he's not available . . .'

'There must be other guys,' Florence said thoughtfully, reaching for George's hand. 'D'y' think if you could *relax* a bit you might come up with some alternatives?'

George shook his head. 'It's a tough one. Sure writers are a dime a dozen out there – but I gotta hire someone who fits – who can deliver . . .'

Florence squeezed his hand tightly. He looked at her intently.

'You know what, George,' Florence said brightly. 'If you're *blocked*, you said you were *blocked*, right? I gotta great way to help . . .'

'They're taking a helluva long time,' Doris said. The engine of the limo was turning over and she was hungry. 'What could they be doing?'

Lewis shrugged. Florence worked in mysterious ways.

'Pass me the phone, Paul.'

Doris dialled George's private line.

'Yeah, Florence? That you?'

'Hi, Doris,' Florence said.

'How long are you guys going to be? We're hungry.'

'We're almost coming, Doris . . .'

145

Florence put down the phone and looked at George, sitting motionless on the sofa, his underpants and trousers still at his ankles.

'They're gettin' impatient, George . . . You want me to try some more – or you had enough?'

George came out of his trance and looked down at his spindly white legs and his limpness. Florence had worked her fingers to the bone but with limited success. For a brief moment she had felt a little stiffening. George had groaned and tried hard – but he was too tense.

'I guess we better go . . . Or . . .,' George paused.

Florence smiled. 'You would like one last little try, huh?' She moved to the sofa and looked down at him. 'I got one last trick to play, okay?'

George looked up at her towering above him. 'One last trick? What's that gonna be?'

'You'll see,' she said putting a finger on his nose. 'You jus' relax George, an' let me do the work. Close your eyes now . . . C'mon George, do as I say . . .' She knelt on the floor in front of him and squeezed open his legs. 'C'mon now, baby . . . relax. If my fingers doin' the walkin' didn't help, maybe my mouth doin' the talkin' jus' might . . .'

Moments later she was able to say with satisfaction: 'Now we're gettin' somewhere . . . aren't we?'

The limo pulled up outside Le Giraffe d'Or on 3rd Avenue and 65th Street. This was Doris's favourite Manhattan restaurant – cool and chic – all white and gleaming chrome. It was already busy and Doris demanded a table in a quiet corner away from the door and the kitchens.

The six sat quietly studying the menu. Doris was still pondering their predicament. Damn it, she thought (she didn't read the menu she always ordered the same dish: 'Lotte à Moutarde Ancienne'), if I can't come up with the perfect writer for this show, no-one can. But her mind was a blank. The Maitre D' arrived to take their orders.

Lewis had gone native. The menu no longer held terrors – he knew what he liked and what he wanted. Patiently he listened to the specials of the day, then chose the broiled lobster decorated with soft-shelled crabs in a champagne sauce. This seemed the lightest item on the menu. He watched the others choose. Doris ordered her usual; George, Lewis noted, was in high spirits and ordered a New York steak with salad; Florence, breast of duck with French fries; Bob Berol, pork in a wine sauce; Paul a truffle omelette. Bob's choice was particularly noteworthy – one of Bob's many transformations in the last week was the renunciation of vegetarianism. As if to make up for missed carnivorous years, he feasted now on meat three times a day. The result of this carnivoraciousness was a new rosiness in his cheeks.

Lewis smiled at the world. He was enjoying life amongst the millionaire class. Hanging around with Florence and Doris meant they all got to travel first-class and eat like kings. If this was Broadway, Lewis could take it.

Doris had ordered cocktails. Fortified by her Kir Royale, she returned to the other subject that had been preoccupying her: how quickly she could find a replacement shih-tzu. 'Maybe it seems a little undignified to talk about finding a home for another little creature when pauvre Roget's still warm in the ground but we're going back to France next week and there's little time. Besides I'm sure it's what he would want.' She smiled wanly and Florence sympathetically patted her hand. 'You don't think I'm hard-hearted do you?'

Florence energetically shook her head. 'Doris, you gotta keep jumpin' to the beat. Granma Hackstuber used to say "the sweetest flowers grow on old bones".' Florence thought for a moment. 'Sounds better with a German accent!'

Lewis was interested in George's demeanour. He was serene, like a calm sea. 'What happened in the office?' Lewis whispered to Florence whilst Doris talked at George.

'Wouldn't you like to know!' teased Florence. 'I gave George a hard time . . .' And she laughed gaily.

'I wrote a poem 'bout death once,' Bob suddenly said to the table. He'd spoken little all day and they were surprised to hear from him. 'Wanna hear it? It's called "Death Snow". It went something like this:

> Luis up on 120th pock-marked;
> Night masking the whiteness of his lips
> Gives with green gripe-wracked eyes
> To the desperate honkies on the sidewalk.
> 'Buy my stuff' the look says
> Offering a twisted paper roll
> Not worth a rat's ass –
> The Death Snow sold by Luis.

Bob looked round for approval.

147

Florence offered plenty. 'Jesus, Bob!' she glowed. 'That's sensational. I mean REALLY.'

'Yes, well done!' said Lewis, who hadn't understood a word.

'Zis death snow is slippery ice?' Paul asked.

'No man,' said Bob. 'Fucked Coke'.

But Paul was none the wiser.

'What did you think, George?' Florence asked.

'Yeah, it's pretty good,' George agreed. 'I like the bit about green-gripped eyes.' He turned to Bob. 'You ever get that published?'

'Sure. Magazine called "Continuing Street Poetry Volume Twelve, issue 4".'

'You mean the whole magazine was called that?' Lewis asked.

'Yeah. Neat. Every month it came out, each one called volume twelve. Had eighteen issues before it crashed. Got known in the end as just Volume Twelve.'

'I got an idea,' said Florence quietly. 'You open to this, George?' She put an elbow on the table and supported her chin on her hand. 'Bob's a great writer. Why not give him a shot at rewriting *Galileo*.'

The audacity of this suggestion silenced the table. Lewis caught Florence and Bob exchange a quick look. *Had they pre-planned this?*

'You ever written a musical before?' George asked as the caviare Doris had ordered for hors d'oeuvre was set before him.

'Everything Bob's done has been developing towards this moment, George,' Florence said.

'Why can't he answer for himself?' George spread a few eggs on to thin toast.

'Sure he can. He's just modest, George. Go on Bobby . . .'

'I could have a damn good crack at it, sir.' Bob stroked his grey beard. This was considerably less alarming than heretofore: Florence had insisted on trimming his hair and beard after she'd bathed and shampooed away deep filth. 'Fact is, as Flo here has said, I've been writing poetry pretty damned successfully for the past 25 years. Recently I've completed three novels which are gonna be published soon – I'd let you see these but the proofs are in my house in Vermont – an' I'm crazy about music. It all fits, right! I was looking at myself the other day – you know analysing the state of my art. You know what I saw there, sir? Why, all the components of a Broadway musical – America's greatest contribution to dramatic writing an' art. I had it all. Words, poetry, music and imagination. The last attribute, I'm pleased to say, I have been plentifully endowed with.'

George stared blankly at Bob, unable fully to comprehend what he was saying.

'What d'you think, Doris?' Florence said, her healing hands gently caressing the older woman's.

Doris looked into Florence's caring eyes and a picture of Florence bending over Roget's crib, stroking his lovely furry face, rose before her. How could she refuse? Florence had magic on her side.

'I think it's worth a shot, George,' Doris said. 'Anything's better than what we've got right now. Put Bob together with Ross and Jerry and see what happens.'

Ten eyes watched every nervous twitch and tic in George's face as he struggled to come to a decision.

'I dunno,' he said. 'I'm gonna have to think about it . . .'

'Oh George . . .,' Florence said smoothly. 'I'm sure you don't have any doubts about Bob's *ability* do you? I've read his material. It's fabulous.'

Lewis watched goggle-eyed as Florence whispered something into George's ears. Did he see her hand lightly brush George's thigh?

George visibly weakened. 'You got some work I could look at, Bob?'

Bob picked at an irritating blackhead under his beard and looked thoughtful.

'What about the poems in our kitchen cupboard in the apartment?' Lewis suggested helpfully.

'Might be something there, sure,' Bob said doubtfully. 'I'm gonna look for you, George, an' bring 'em over to your office, okay?'

'Yeah, okay,' George said warily.

Doris beamed happily. 'Great! Then let's celebrate.'

22

The designers had been gone an hour. Ross was sitting in his comfortable chair, script open but unread, TV on, sound to mute, waiting for the buzzer, doing nothing. *What is keeping her?* She said she'd arrive by 9.00 p.m. It was ten past. Punctuality's the sine qua non in the theatre. *If she were as hot as me she'd be here . . .*

He picked up some new lyrics Jerry had faxed but he read the same line over and over – nothing penetrated. His mind was overwhelmed with Dee. Then he realised the telephone was ringing. It was Jerry.

'Hi, Ross! Can we talk! I hope this isn't inconvenient?'

When you're waiting for your lover . . . anything is inconvenient.

'What's on your mind, Jerry? I haven't had a chance to look at the new lyrics . . .'

Down the line came a torrent of words. 'This writing shit, man. George's got us in a helluva mess. I'm completely fucked up . . . I can't sleep . . . I got Debbie buggin' me about castin' . . . everything's cascadin' down . . . a fuckin' waterfall of shit. I done my work . . . an' it's great, right? The fuckin' songs are hits. Christ, Ross, I got Warner Records beggin' me to give them the rights to the album – it's all sewn up . . . but we haven't gotta fuckin' show to go with it . . . you got any ideas?'

Ross was calm. 'We're okay, Jerry. We've got a script. We've got a show . . .'

'Yeah, but you say it's totally fucked . . .'

'If you'll let me finish . . . we've got a script that's 60% okay. If George had let us continue work on it we might have got much closer . . .'

'This is a complete fuckin' farce, Ross . . .'

'Jerry, we could go into rehearsal with what we've got. I've gone into rehearsal with far less than this and had hits.'

'So who's going to fix this . . .?'

Ross glanced towards his apartment door. The buzzer had gone.

She was there.

'George is working on it, Jerry. I've got to go . . .'

'DON'T FUCK WITH ME, ROSS!' Jerry was suddenly shouting. 'He's out of fuckin' ideas. I told him this morning that I done 90% of my work – I've written the music and the lyrics . . . I worked closest with Michael. I think *I* should fix it – rewrite the book . . . integrate the fuckin' book with my work. I don't want some shit-ass comin' in and start tellin' me I gotta change this an' that. If Michael's gone – it's my show now. Will ya support me, Ross?'

The buzzer went again. Ross had instructed the doorman to show his visitor right up. He put Jerry on hold. His heart thumped with excitement as he went to the door. And there she was. Beautiful, proud and real.

'Hi!' she said and kissed him.

'I've got Jerry on hold. Make yourself at home . . . Get a drink.'

He went back to the phone but watched Dee's every move.

'Yeah, Jerry . . .,' he said.

She stands for a moment. Looks round . . . absorbing his place . . . looking for signs of Ellen.

'Are you goin' to support me, Ross?'

'Doing what?' He can't think straight.

She flicks him a glance and her face dissolves into a smile. He responds and relaxes. His eyes indicate the drinks. Before Dee, there was nothing.

'Takin' over the book, for Chrissakes, Ross.'

'I can't, Jerry . . . support you.'

At the other end of the line Jerry audibly exhaled. 'Why the fuck not? You don't think I can do it?'

She's taking a whisky and Coke . . . wandering towards the CD player . . . Ross and Ellen's CD collection . . . browsing . . .

'Maybe yes, maybe no, Jerry.' Ross said. 'Michael is highly sophisticated and very British. To fix this script's . . .'

'Bridge Over Troubled Waters' . . . third track . . . 'Cecilia' . . . Volume's down low . . .

'. . . going to require an equal measure of witty inspiration . . .'

'An' you think I can't give that! What are you sayin', man? The lyrics stink?'

'No, I'm not saying that . . .' Ross became irritated at the way this conversation turned. He'd always had good relations with Jerry. This wasn't the time for the remainder of the team to start losing their cool . . .

Dee's sensing it. She comes over to him and places her ice-cold glass on his forehead . . . teasing . . .

151

'MY LYRICS ARE FUCKIN' WITTY! OKAY!' Jerry yelled down the phone.

'I'm going to go now, Jerry. We'll talk when you're calmer . . .'

Jerry suddenly was. 'Okay, hey, sorry man . . . I told ya . . . I'm all fucked up . . . Lack of sleep . . .'

. . . Kissing the back of his neck . . . running her hands through his shirt . . . gently caressing his chest and lower . . .

'It's just I care, man, you know . . . This show means everythin' to me, Ross. I've worked my butt off draftin' and redraftin' these songs . . . an' I know they're good.' Jerry paused for assurance. Got none. 'Hey, you there, Ross?'

With Dee's hands roaming, he was miles out in space . . .

'Jerry, I've got to go . . .,' he said. 'Why don't we meet tomorrow . . . say 2.30 p.m.'

Reluctantly, Jerry agreed and the conversation ended.

'Missed me . . .?' Dee said, releasing him, moving to the sofa, lying down.

'Uh, huh.' He already missed those roving hands.

She stretched out – a cat wanting to play. 'Uh, huh? Only that much? What's for supper?'

'You like sushi?'

'Great,' she said.

He watched her slowly take off her earrings, her watch and place them carefully on the coffee table. She looked at him, her eyes narrowing.

'Want me as an appetiser?'

'My mouth's watering . . .,' Ross said.

'C'mon. Go for it then,' Dee said. 'I know what you like . . .'

Hungry after making love, they ordered up a banquet from the Japanese restaurant on the next block and tried to watch *Chinatown*, the Movie of the Week, but the phone kept ringing: Ellen from LA to see if he was okay; Stan to discuss the writer vacuum; some friends from out-of-town . . .

Finally, Ross took the phone off the hook.

'Seems to me, George,' Bob was saying, his double decaffeinated Espresso suspended in mid-air, 'it's lacking in just about everything anybody could want. See, I don't know what *they* were getting at. I mean that stuff about seeing the world as it is, not as you'd like it to be. Kinda hit that idea over an' over again – an' that's not a poetic thing, George. It's gotta have more poetry see. Then the poetry . . . they're Italians yet they read like they're Brits. It's so fucking *laid* back. I wanna charge it up – put in some hot pepper – Italian hot, you know, George – heat it up – cut the science shit – the materialism.'

Bob leant back in his chair and thoughtfully sipped his coffee.

'Yeah! Right on Bobby! You tell 'em!' Florence said, encouragingly.

George looked impressed, Lewis thought. Was Bob expressing much of what the producer himself felt? Could this ex-hippie fix the material . . . with Ross's guidance?

The meal at the Giraffe d'Or finished in relatively high spirits. Only George kept himself to himself, refraining from too much conversation. Before leaving, George and Lewis found themselves together in the toilet. Lewis, standing at the urinal, watched George extract a miniature dental kit from his pocket, assemble a toothbrush, apply toothpaste and methodically clean his teeth.

'How do you really feel about Bob maybe rewriting the show, Mr Gibson?'

George was now washing his face with a small sponge he had extracted from the dental kit. 'Doris is my partner. We're in this fifty-fifty. If she wants to give it a try . . .' He shrugged and packed away his implements.

'How d'you think Ross will feel?' Lewis asked, drying his hands.

At the door of the bathroom, George said: 'He supports new playwrights. This guy Bob's not young but he's new . . . an' we need to encourage new talent. He might look on it favourably.'

They wove their way back through the tables.

'When are you going to speak to Ross? Is there any chance of letting me come to that meeting, Mr Gibson? It would give me real insight, I'm certain.'

'His phone's permanently busy,' George said. 'I've already tried to talk to him. I pass his building on the way home. I might call up from the lobby or leave a message . . .'

They left the restaurant together. On the sidewalk, George and Doris's limousines waited nose-to-tail.

'Goodnight, George,' Florence said, kissing the producer on the lips. 'An' thank you.'

George blanched, coughed and snorted.

'I'm not gonna let you down, sir,' Bob said as he pumped his hand. 'You better believe it.'

'Yeah, well I gotta discuss it with the director . . . He gotta agree . . .' George was keeping his options open.

'If anyone can persuade him, you can, can't you George?' Florence said encouragingly.

'Sure, he will, Florence,' Doris said.

153

'Mais oui!' Paul agreed.

'Mr Gibson said he might call round this evening,' Lewis said.

'Did you?' Florence said. 'That's great! Let's all go!'

'No, let's not all go!' George said sharply. 'I'm only gonna call from the lobby. It's too late to go up. I'll take Lewis – you all go home. We'll talk tomorrow.'

'Chicken à la King three Mondays running!' Dee was naked, curled up in Ross's arms, laughing. 'Three benefits, three Chicken à la Kings!'

'Caterer's revenge,' Ross said, still intoxicated by her nearness and smell. 'They hate us and consider boredom appropriate punishment.'

She laughed and twisted out of his arms, giving herself space. For a moment she lay with her back towards him before turning on her side and half sitting up – her elbow on the pillow, her hand holding her head. Hair cascading.

She studied his face.

'I like you,' she said. 'You're funny.'

Lewis looked at his watch as he and George Gibson entered the lobby of Ross's apartment. It was 10.25 p.m. A solitary doorman dozing on a chair woke, startled, as George jabbed him with his fingers.

'We wanna talk to Mr Boardman. His phone's permanently busy. You gotta house phone?'

The doorman, struggling to wake, looked confused and frightened. 'No understand . . .,' he said in a thick continental accent.

'Mr Boardman!' George shouted. 'I gotta call him! Or leave a message!'

Pointing to himself, the doorman tried to explain: 'Albanian . . . Yugoslavie . . . famiglia kaput . . .' By way of clarification, he drew his finger across his throat.

George looked blankly at him before turning to Lewis. 'What's he saying?'

'I think he's saying he's Albanian . . .'

'What's that? I thought those were guys with blond hair, white all over . . .'

'No. That's albinos . . . This chap's a Balkan . . .'

'Whatever he is – ask him to phone up.'

Patiently, Lewis tried to explain in pidgin English using big gestures. 'We-want-your-phone-to-use-please.'

'Ah, ja!' said the doorman with a winning smile then shook his head.

'What mean you?' Lewis said loudly.

'Phone kaput.' And once again he drew his finger across his throat.

George was getting impatient. 'This is hopeless. We'll leave him a message an' I'll talk to him tomorrow . . .' George turned to the hapless doorman. 'Gimme a piece of paper! I wanna write the party a message.'

The doorman's eyes brightened. He had understood something. 'Party! I know party! Dance ja?'

'I think he's got the wrong end of the stick, Mr Gibson,' Lewis said, then tried himself. 'Mr Boardman's the party . . .'

Suddenly everything was clear to the doorman, his eyes brightened. 'Okay! Okay!' he shouted at them happily. 'Come! Come! Mr Boardman's party. Dancy, ya!'

And without further ado, he pulled them into the elevator talking ebulliently in Albanian. They were too confused to protest. The Albanian deposited them on the sixth floor. 'Gut party! Gut party!'

There were three doors leading off a small lobby each with a brass tag above the bell push – 6A, 6B, 6C. No names. Nothing could be heard from behind any of the doors. The only sound was the dull whine of the elevator descending to the ground.

George hesitated. 'Which is it?' he asked Lewis. 'A, B or C?'

'D'you think this is a good idea, Mr Gibson?' Lewis asked, anxiously looking round at the three doors. 'I mean supposing he's having an early night . . . or entertaining . . .'

'Well, we're here now,' George said. 'Press the bell. That one.'

His finger pointed to apartment C. Lewis had little choice and quickly pressed the button. From the far recesses of the apartment a small bell could be heard. No-one answered. He pressed again and they both waited. No-one appeared.

'Try B,' George said impatiently. Reluctantly, Lewis did as he was told.

After a few seconds they heard rattling chains and sliding bolts. The door opened a few inches and an old gentleman in a paisley dressing gown peered out.

'Yeah?' he whispered, eyeing them suspiciously through thick glasses.

'I'm sorry to bother you,' Lewis said full of English politeness. 'Do you happen to know where Ross Boardman lives. We've tried apartment C . . .'

A hostile look stole over the old man's features. 'Check wid de doorman,' he said and slammed the door shut.

Lewis turned to George. 'Don't you think we should call it a night, Mr Gibson?'

But George had already pressed the bell on apartment A.

Dee was lying on the quilt smoking. Lazily she turned on her side and called into the bathroom: 'You want me to get that?'

Her lover emerged drying his hands. He hadn't heard the bell.

She said again: 'You want me to get the door, Sweetie? Pass me a wrap, will you?'

'Maybe we're on the wrong floor, Mr Gibson,' Lewis said – 'I'm not sure he . . .'

But Lewis was interrupted by the Albanian doorman reappearing in his elevator.

'Party! Party!' he shouted at them gaily depositing Karl-Heinz in the little lobby.

The designer was dressed in a Bavarian winter hunting outfit: knee-high leather boots with brown corduroy trousers tucked in at the top, a leather coat lined and trimmed with fur and a dark green deer-stalker pulled low over his eyes. Behind the black shades, his gaze was, as always, impenetrable. His wintry aspect was in marked contrast to George and Lewis who were dressed for hot summer in the city. Lewis, having finally discarded his Marks and Spencer checked shirt, was wearing a tee-shirt which read FISTING CAN BE FUN. Luckily, as Lewis had no idea what this meant, the slogan was partially obscured by his denim jacket.

Karl-Heinz nodded curtly, but politely, in their direction then fished around in his khaki ex-East German army shoulder bag until he discovered a packet of gum.

'Are you here to see Ross?' Lewis asked pleasantly, needing something to say.

The German stared at him as if he was an idiot then nodded, wearily closed his eyes and leant against the wall to wait.

At least now they knew they were at the right door . . .

'No,' Ross said as he passed through the bedroom towards the front room and the door to the apartment. 'Better I go.'

'You expecting someone?' Dee called out. 'Another girl to make a triptych. I kinda like those. Or maybe it's Ellen home early . . .? Ask her to join in! I'm broad-minded . . .'

Ross laughed, confident Ellen was safely in LA. 'It'll be the Super . . .'

Then the phone rang. It took Ross by surprise. He'd forgotten he'd put the receiver back. It was his lawyer and friend, Joe Nunzio.

'Maybe he hasn't heard us,' George said crossly.

'I think I heard the phone ring,' Lewis said.

George angrily pressed the bell three times and from inside they heard Ross shout, 'Hold on, for Chrissakes!'

'Yup,' George said. 'He's there.'

Then, incredibly, as if they were all in a Marx Brothers movie, the elevator doors opened again and into the confines of this small space on the sixth floor, the Albanian released Doris, Paul Etienne, Bob Berol and Florence.

'Party! Party!' said the Albanian again, waving to Lewis as if he was an old friend.

'Hi, guys,' Doris said.

'I've just gotten through the draft of your contract with Gibson, Ross. I got to tell you it stinks.'

Joe Nunzio is the best, but the most expensive, showbusiness lawyer in town. He's 45 but looks and sounds ten years younger. A compulsive workaholic, none of his clients is surprised to receive calls any time from 6.00 a.m. to 1.00 a.m. He operates on a person-to-person basis only: his client list is top-drawer and he makes each feel special. Joe has been Ross's lawyer for 20 years and doesn't bullshit. It took him 50 seconds to put Ross in the picture.

'The nitty gritty is that the money's okay, we agreed that months ago. It's top of the range as you know . . . but the billing is totally unacceptable. Okay so he's going to give you 75% of title size on the publicity, the poster . . . no-one has bigger than you . . . even the stars . . . What's unacceptable is *Gibson's billing*. He wants and I quote: "George Gibson's *Galileo*".'

Ross said grimly: 'I don't approve of anyone having that kind of

157

billing. This is team work. I never accepted billing like that for my movies . . . even when the studio offered it.'

'Sure,' Joe agreed. 'I'm gonna tell George this is a deal breaker, okay?'

Dee wandered about the room wearing Ellen's robe loosely tied, partially exposing her body. Ross, watching her, suddenly conscious of the eccentricity of the situation. *This is George's wife, for Chrissake.* Joe was waiting for a reply.

'Okay, Joe. Sure.' Ross was in a hurry to terminate this. 'And while you're talking to him ask him where the first payment is? Tell him no pay no play. Look I'm kinda tied up right now. If you want to talk more about this, call me in the morning.'

Dee was at the door. 'Sounds like there's more than the Super out there, baby,' she whispered. 'Listen.'

Outside, the atmosphere in the lobby was, true to the Albanian's predictions, becoming quite party-like. Everyone chatted noisily. Florence explained to Lewis how she had persuaded Doris to turn the car round and head back to Ross's apartment. 'I didn't trust Georgy-Porgy to get the story straight, you know,' she whispered. 'I mean to really *sell* Bob. If Ross meets him personally, like face-to-face, he couldn't turn him down. I mean could he? Jus' look at him.' She smiled lovingly at the poet. However, a strange vacant look had come into Bobby's eyes. Lewis wondered if he'd overdosed on protein in the restaurant.

Next to him, Doris was engaging George in a heated discussion. Over Florence's shoulder, Lewis could see Paul enigmatically eyeing Karl-Heinz. Lewis was slowly coming to the conclusion that there was something quite equivocal about the Frenchman. AC/DC? He couldn't be sure.

'WHAT THE FUCK'S GOIN' ON!'

Jerry, looking flushed and excited, had suddenly emerged from the elevator and unexpectedly encountered his colleagues gathered en masse. Nobody had noticed him arrive.

Florence reacted first. 'Hi, Jerry . . !'

'Doorman says there's some kinda party . . .'

'Ah,' Lewis said. 'No. He's sort of missed the point . . .'

'What are you doin' here, Jerry?' Florence asked. Lewis noted that the smile had disappeared from her face. Did the arrival of the composer upset her plans, he wondered? Presumably, Jerry had no inkling of Florence's attempt to team him up with Bob. Maybe, Lewis thought, maybe he might get a bit upset when he finds out.

158

'What the fuck are you all doin' here? Are you havin' a meetin' with Ross and not tellin' me, for fuck's sake! C'mon George! I KNOW I'M ONLY THE FUCKING COMPOSER!!'

'JERRY!' George shouted back. 'Getta fucking control of yourself!'

'Don't open the door!' Dee shouted as quietly as she could.

Ross, absent-mindedly, still absorbed in the implications of Joe's call, had his hand on the door handle.

'That sounds like Jerry an' George!' Dee whispered and she peered through the spy-hole.

'Jesus Christ,' she said pulling away from the door. 'Take a look at that!'

Ross squinted through the little fish-eye lens and saw most of his production team in the hall. Centred in the perfectly framed but grossly distorted picture, was Dee's husband, being harangued by Jerry.

'What can they all want?' she whispered and backed away from the door. Then she collapsed into uncontrollable giggles. 'Have you ever, I mean *ever*, seen such a sight in your life? What the hell are we going to do?' More giggles. 'We're trapped! Shall I hide in the closet?'

'If you keep quiet maybe they'll go away,' Ross said hopefully.

'Didn't you shout "hold on" a minute ago?'

'Oh, yeah,' Ross said.

23

They didn't go away. They were too busy.

When Ross finally opened the door, it caught them by surprise. They froze into a melodramatic tableau. Ross smiled at the picture.

'Isn't this a little unusual, George?' Ross commented wryly. 'To convene a production conference at this hour without warning me first . . . I'm busy. Goodnight.' He started to close the door.

'Yeah, I'm sorry, Ross,' George appeared contrite, but held the door open. 'This wasn't planned. We've all kinda met here by chance . . .'

'Zis is absolument correct, Ross!' Paul Etienne said with a glance towards Karl-Heinz.

'You're the centre of our universe, Mr Boardman,' Florence said sweetly, attempting a joke and touching his arm. 'We're humble planets circling a sun.' She spotted the disdainful expression on Ross's face and got to the point. 'George wants to introduce Bob Berol here to you, Mr Boardman. Bob is a . . .'

She got no further. George, with Jerry breathing heavily behind him, had suddenly realised the potentially explosive nature of this situation. 'Ross, I gotta apologise to you!' he blurted out. 'We're gonna talk about this tomorrow. You're coming into the office after lunch, right? Goodnight . . .'

He released the door and turned to go, hoping to lead the group towards the elevator.

But Jerry was not going to be put off so easily. 'MEETIN' TOMORROW? WHAT FUCKIN' MEETIN' TOMORROW! I don't know about that! We gotta talk about this now . . . !'

And he pushed past Doris and an alarmed Florence. Ross, guarding the door, was no impediment to his forceful progress as he marched determinedly into the apartment and threw himself down on the sofa. Florence and George hurried in behind, anxious to keep the peace. The others followed. Paul Etienne, Doris, and Lewis hovered nervously at the door. Karl-Heinz strolled calmly in, slipped Ross a note, and installed himself comfortably in a leather armchair.

'C'mon Jerry,' pleaded George, 'Let's go. We don't wanna intrude on Ross's privates, okay? Guy's entitled to be private when he wants. We'll talk tomorrow . . . c'mon.'

Jerry, far from removing himself, curled up into a ball, burst into tears, and howled wildly. This unexpected behaviour was received in embarrassed silence. Florence seized the moment and flew to his aid. With unerring instinct she cradled him in her arms.

'Who is this guy and *what* is he on?' Bob Berol whispered to Lewis. 'Crack, Coke? Does he deal?'

'He's the composer and your putative partner. I think he's a bit overwrought,' Lewis whispered back. 'Florence, do you think we should call Debbie to take him home?'

At that moment Florence saw them sparkling prettily next to the telephone. She wouldn't have given them a second glance, those earrings and that jewel-encrusted watch, had not the latter been upside down so that the tiny inscription on the back caught her eye:

TO
DEEDEE
FROM HER GEORGIE, 1985

Her mind raced. Deedee's watch and earrings on Ross's table? She could imagine few circumstances that could lead a girl to leave her watch and earrings on some guy's table around midnight. Only one delicious conclusion presented itself to her and it took great effort on her part not to smile with the piquancy of it. She glanced at George then at the others. Nobody else had spotted them although the strange guy with the pipe seemed to be watching her closely. The little devils, she thought with a thrill. That's why it took Ross so long to answer the door! Maybe, just maybe, Dee was still here. Where? The bedroom?

'Yeah,' she said. 'It's a good idea. Poor Jerry. Shall I call from the *bedroom*, Mr Boardman?'

Florence looked directly at Ross hoping to catch a guilty look. At the same time, with a sleight of hand, she managed to sweep the three articles into her lap and out of public view. I'm doing them a favour, she told herself.

'No need,' Ross said smoothly and looked towards the bedroom. Florence's heart missed a beat. *She's in there!* 'I think he's perfectly able to get home on his own. Now, c'mon Jerry! Let's go!'

Ross attempted to get a grip on Jerry's arm but Jerry angrily shrugged him off.

'George!' Doris suddenly said.

161

'Yeah?' George replied.

'Tell Ross why we're here.'

'Look Doris,' George said. 'We gotta go . . .'

'For Chrissake I'll do it! Ross, I'd like to introduce you to Bobby Berol.' She had kept quiet for three minutes and this had required an enormous effort. 'We want to hire Bob to re-write the book and we want you to agree. He's a writer, a poet and a very, very, good friend of mine.'

Good, Lewis thought. No beating about the bush! Straight to the point and to hell with the consequences! But Ross was not listening. He was attempting to decipher the enigmatic note Karl-Heinz had passed to him a few minutes ago:

THE FOOL'S CAP RESTS AT THE EPICENTRE OF THE THIRD GLOBAL. REVOLVE IT AND YOU SEE IT REVEALED FOR WHAT IT IS!

K-H.

'Hi, guys!' Bob cheerfully raised his hand in greeting. 'Glad to be aboard.'

Jerry's hysteria had abated enough for him to absorb this information. He sat up wild-eyed to look at Bob. 'Whaat?!'

'I'm sorry,' Ross said. 'What was it you were saying, Doris?' Ross had decoded the designer's message and folded it away. (He kept Karl-Heinz's messages in a scrapbook.)

'I need a Hershey bar,' Jerry said weakly.

'I need the bathroom,' George announced. 'Ross! Your bathroom's through the bedroom, right?'

But Ross wasn't listening to George. So George set off towards the bedroom door. Florence observed this with alarm. 'Wait!' she shouted to George. If anybody should be going into the bedroom it should be her. *This needs discretion* . . . She had no wish to throw open the bedroom door and say 'Voilà! Caught in flagrante!' as she exposed Dee curled up naked on the bed (for this is how she imagined the scene on the other side of the door). No. She just had the feeling that the information might come in useful. Particularly useful if Ross didn't respond to the suggestion that Bobby rewrite the book.

'Are you sure you want George to go to the *bathroom*, Ross?' Florence said loudly.

However, Doris was keen to press her advantage and so Florence's question remained unnoticed and unanswered. George paused at the bedroom door to listen to Doris.

'To be frank,' Doris said, 'we have approached a number of

experienced writers and got nowhere. Ross, our position is that the time has come to approach this problem in a different way. A well-known producer once said to me about some show we were doing together, "Doris, we don't need experience, we need O and E." "What's that," I asked. He replied, "Originality and Enthusiasm". Bob Berol has both.'

'Hold on, Doris, for Chrissake!' George said re-entering the discussion. He had stood at the door fuming at Doris's attempt at manipulation.

'I gotta tell you, Ross,' George continued, nervously picking at the wrapping of an Havana he had found in his breast pocket, 'we're not committing ourselves here. Doris got this idea, okay. That's all.' His bladder began to feel uncomfortably full.

'But Mr Gibson . . .George,' Florence said. 'Why, I thought you had agreed. You heard Bob's poem and you were impressed, right? Bob, let Ross and Jerry hear something. It's only fair that you audition for them.'

Ross got the smell of a conspiracy and he didn't like it. 'I think,' he said tensely, 'that you should all go and we'll discuss this tomorrow.'

'Is your bathroom through here, Ross?'

'Wait a minute, George!' Florence ordered in a tone of voice that cut through everything. Turning her attention to Ross she said, 'Please, Mr Boardman, just listen to one of Bob's poems. It won't take a moment. Then we'll leave you. Promise! But if you don't hear anything, how will you be able to judge? An' I heard you support new playwrights . . . C'mon Bob! How about the one where the two guys are rimming?'

'It's kinda rude for this company, Flee,' Bob said. 'I'll sing "Jag House Rag" instead. It's in the same vein.'

He perched on the edge of the heavy coffee table and cleared his throat. Florence sat at Bob's feet and watched Ross's reactions. Doris moved to the sofa and summoned Paul to her side. Lewis craned forward to see that Karl-Heinz had, interestingly, started a pencil portrait of Florence. George discarded the wrapping and lit his cigar.

Bob began to sing. His delivery was slow; his voice high pitched and nasal as if he was suffering from a badly blocked nose. The tune was indecipherable. Ross, despite his annoyance, found himself riveted by the weird spectacle.

'Scratchy bebop blasts from the record machine
Unintelligible to Billy as he hugs the man;
Dancin' in a feeble attempt to lose the pain.
No, the hurt is psycho-meta-physical!
Mind tortured with horror at the realisation:
Yes! The phantasm he perceived,
Ghostly in the slime-smeared mirror,
Was him. Him! Him! Him!'

Bob paused after intoning the last three 'hims', overcome with the emotion associated with the imagery. Florence thought that Ross didn't look as impressed as she thought he should.

'Okay, I get it,' Ross said. 'But writing the book for a musical is something quite different. It's difficult and requires skill. That's why so few are any good at it. The book writer needs to have a sense of the whole structure; he's constructing an edifice, brick-by-brick. He has to write short scenes that nimbly make plot points, get out of a song and lead effortlessly into the next. A musical is like an Impressionist painting. Study it close up and it's a collection of songs and scenes; stand back and it's a work of art. An artist only masters his craft after years of trial and error. It's arrogant to assume that anybody can do it because they can string a few words together.'

'Now that's not fair to call us arrogant, Mr Boardman!' Florence cried passionately. 'We're only trying to do the best for the show. Okay Bob maybe doesn't have any experience working on one of your famous musicals . . . but then again maybe, just maybe he can do better than that preppy Englishman you had working on it before! How long did he have . . . one year . . . two . . . and what did he come up with?' She squeezed the earrings and the watch tightly in her hand.

'Yeah, you're right,' George growled, entering the argument. What was it about Ross that so irritated him . . . made him want to say the opposite? 'For a year and a half he wrote crap and wouldn't listen when I told him. What did I tell him? I told him it was crap! Where's the jokes? I asked him. It's got no wit, your book, I said to him. I thought we was gonna have a musical comedy! How can you have a musical comedy with no jokes? You want the audience to come out depressed, I asked him! Okay so the guy can write plays . . . I even liked one of them . . . What was its name? . . . Ach, I can't remember . . .'

The situation was ludicrous. It was hard to believe these people could be serious. But he knew they were. He'd been in the business long enough. Even so, Ross had had enough. There was little point in further discussion. The reason for this appalling girl's passionate defence of the would-be writer was obvious, the liaison transparent. But who was he to judge with the smell of Dee still about him. *Christ could George smell it!*

'Tomorrow we'll . . .,' he began but the phone rang. 'Excuse me,' Ross said, taking the call.

'I'm gonna take a leak then we're going!' And, before Florence could say a word, George opened the bedroom door and slipped inside. Florence, with a gasp of horror, leapt up.

'You okay?' Doris asked worriedly. 'What's up?'

Without replying and, to everyone's amazement, she dashed into the bedroom and slammed the door behind her.

'Hi,' Dee said quietly. 'Is everyone still there?'

'Oh, yeah.'

'Then I guess we gotta little problem.'

'Oh?'

'I've left my watch and my earrings on the table by your telephone.'

Ross, who had been watching the exodus into his bedroom, looked down and could see nothing. He caught no-one's eye but could feel them watching him. He hated this farce. 'I think you're mistaken,' he said.

Dee understood. 'Then where the devil have they got to? I know they were there, Ross . . .'

'Oh . . .'

'Shit! Shit! Shit! As soon as I got down to the bottom of the fire stairs I realised I didn't have them. I couldn't very well come back up, could I? You'd better keep a look-out, the watch is inscribed . . . What's George doing? Don't answer that! I'll try to call you later.'

He hung up as George and Florence came out of the bedroom together.

'Thank you for coming,' Ross said politely. 'Karl-Heinz, you might like to stay and we can pursue your idea about putting the Papal Court set into the third revolving hemisphere. Yeah, I deciphered the note quite quickly!'

The designer looked up from his almost complete drawing of Florence and smiled. Lewis saw that he had chosen to represent the girl as a mermaid with a cascade of golden curls tumbling over a nude upper torso, her lower half complete with fishtail and oversize genitalia.

'I gotta poem about the Vatican . . .,' Bob said helpfully.

'Better leave it, Bob,' Florence said. 'I don't think Mr Boardman's too receptive tonight.'

'Yeah, we gonna talk about this tomorrow,' said George, re-lighting his cigar and sending clouds of acrid smoke into the room. 'Nice place you got here Ross. C'mon Jerry, let's get you home to bed. We're meeting at 2.30 in my office. Bob, we're gonna talk about you then, so if you've got anything else for us to look at you better get it round to my office in the morning.'

They filed out into the lobby and awaited the arrival of the elevator.

Florence was the last of the group to leave. Judging the others out of earshot, and choosing to ignore the presence of Karl-Heinz, Florence said goodnight to Ross and at the same time passed Dee's jewelry into his hands, carefully interposing her body between him and the open door to the lobby. 'I palmed those to avoid any embarrassment,' she whispered hoarsely. 'Gibsy would have been, I guess, pretty pissed. Dee'll no doubt want them back but I thought you'd like to do that rather than him or me.' She stood on tip-toe to give the director a goodnight kiss. 'Mmmm, you smell sexy,' she said with a mischievous grin. 'Same perfume in the bedroom. Lucky Gibsy' jus' smells smoke. You will give Bobby *special* consideration, won't you. 'Night!'

And with a friendly wink, she joined the others noisily getting into the elevator.

'Party over? Party over?' the Albanian shouted at them. 'Jus' like Communist Party!! Ho-ho-ho!'

Ross stared after them through the open door.

166

24

The next morning Ross made several futile attempts to interest other writers, some of whom were close personal friends, but he found they had little desire to fix *Galileo*. Everyone he contacted was happily working on an original idea of his own.

Everyone, that is, except Bob Berol.

Florence and a reluctant Lewis spent the morning with Bob planning the campaign. Florence told him that convincing Ross was the key. He'd be tough, she said, but if he wasn't persuaded she would have to try other means.

'Like what?' Lewis asked.

But Florence wouldn't be drawn.

'You must go to the meeting with a detailed new scenario,' Florence said. 'We gotta lay out a storyline that'll knock 'em off their feet. Give 'em tone and substance, baby. You heard George say he wanted jokes. Well you're gonna give him his jollies. Before you woke kiddo, I strolled along to Doubledays and picked up these joke books. Hey I've even done some of your work for you . . . I've marked the Italian jokes with Post-its.'

Lewis read out one of the jokes Florence had marked: 'An Italian papa brought his baby to be baptised in Pennsylvania. 'Now,' he said, 'you see you baptise him okay. Last time I tell you I wanna my boy called Tom you call him Thomas. Thees time I wann him called Jack. I no want you call him Jackass . . .,' Lewis paused. 'Is that funny?'

Bob shrugged and said: 'It sounds pretty funny to me.'

'It didn't make you laugh,' Lewis said.

'Not all good jokes make you laugh,' Florence declared protectively.

But in the end it was Lewis's ideas for a radical change in the plot-line that formed the basis of Bob's presentation to Jerry, George and Ross later in the day. Bob delivered his prepared speech in George's office clearly and energetically, injecting passion where

Florence had decreed. He seemed confident and convincing. George even laughed at a couple of the jokes they had found in the books.

'Whad'ya think, Ross?' George asked.

But Ross sat there mute, refusing to be drawn. He was overwhelmed with a profound sense of doom. He felt lost, bereft of ideas, impotent, comatose. *What's wrong with me? I gotta pull myself together.* Events would have to take their course, for the moment, without him.

Jerry, chatting merrily away, said the alterations to the storyline might work. He was greatly relieved he wouldn't now be responsible for the book. 'Guys, this is a mega-weight off my mind. I guess that's why I was so, y'know, fraught yesterday.'

'So that's it, is it?' Bob said as he left the meeting, surprised and delighted at how easy it had been. Luckily Ross had said practically nothing. He occasionally muttered 'Gotcha' and left it at that.

George Gibson patted Bob on the back. 'That was a swell presentation . . . Could almost have been rehearsed. What you gotta do now is lock yourself away an' write, write, write!'

'Yeah,' Bob said. 'Er, do I get to meet with Jerry?'

'You bet,' Jerry said. 'Soon as you have something we'll talk. When you done a draft I'll know what I gotta do . . . Most important you bang it out fast as possible . . . right Ross?'

Ross grunted and Bob took his leave.

'By the way, guys, Florence sent her love,' Bob said, looking at Ross and George. ''Specially to you two . . .'

The next day they sealed the arrangement. George contracted Bob Berol through Doris's lawyer whom she had instructed to act impartially on Bob's behalf. Not surprisingly Bob came cheap: minimum royalties, minimum fee.

Four days after the late-night gathering at Ross's apartment, Variety carried the following item:

George Gibson, doyen of Broadway producers, announced yesterday a change in the line-up of creative personnel he's put together for his eagerly anticipated new musical *Galileo*. Out goes Brit author Michael Kershon (Tony nominee two seasons ago for his hit comedy *Comic Persuasions*) and in comes Robert Berol, an unknown and unpublished poet, as book writer. Veteran director and helmsman, Ross Boardman, capo of the project, said Berol turned up at his apartment one night and read him some poems that betrayed a hitherto hidden talent. 'We read Bob's poetry,' Boardman explained. 'And composer Jerry Trimlock responded very positively to the material.'

That was enough for Gibson who said he was delighted to be able to encourage bright new talent to the Broadway of the nineties. Gibson would neither confirm nor deny that *Volpone* star Sir Harold Whitney and Tara Martin have been offered lead roles. Gibson said, despite roster changes production's still slated to go in fall with Broadway opening scheduled spring of next year.

'You're outa your fuckin' mind!' Debbie screamed at Jerry. 'Outa your fuckin' mind! You let them all walk over you . . . You gotta stand up for yourself! Is this true! You were "responsive to the material". Are you crazy?' She hurled the paper at him.

'There was no fuckin' choice, man!' Jerry screamed back and walked into the tiny kitchen of their apartment. Anything to get away. 'It was stitched up . . .'

'Stitched up? By whom?' Debbie followed and stood squarely in the doorway watching him noisily forage through the deep freeze hunting chocolate bars. 'Ross? He stitch it up?'

'I dunno, Debb. Everyone got in the act.'

'George, Doris . . .?'

'Will you leave me alone, for Chrissakes! What is this, the fuckin' Inquisition? I told you, Florence, Lewis everyone . . . Yeah an' Doris . . .'

'Who the fuck's Florence . . .?'

'She's some girl that's attached herself to Doris . . . I don't know, Debbie.'

'You like this Florence?'

Jerry looked at her and read jealousy. 'Cut it out, will ya! She's nothing to do with me! She hangs out with Doris. She's a bright kid an' I think this was her idea . . .'

'Oh yeah . . .? You wanna fuck her?'

'Gimme a break. George picked it up an' ran with it. It doesn't seem a bad idea an' it's sure taken a weight off my mind.' He gave her a conciliatory smile. 'This guy Bob's pretty weird but he talks sense . . . shares an apartment with Florence . . .'

'Oh, yeah,' Debbie said sensing the conspiracy she'd been expecting. 'So this was her idea 'cos she's screwing Bob an' she gets Doris to support her, right? I see it all. Jesus, you're a sucker . . .'

'He's a poet. Some of his stuff's okay.'

'An' why is this the first I get to hear about all this?'

'We got *any* candy bars?'

'When did this happen?'

'When did what happen?'

'These decisions 'bout who was writin' the book . . .'

"Bout four days past . . . Soon as it was settled George put out a release.

'Surprise, surprise,' Debbie said.

'Are we outa candy? I'll have to go to the store . . .' Jerry moved out of the kitchen past Debbie, back into the sitting room, searching for his jacket. 'Anyways why you so mad?'

''Cos I'm lookin' after your interests, asshole. We're supposed to be a team, right? That was the deal as I remember it. You write, I perform. One for all, all for one. Only it hasn't worked out like that. Now you write an' I sit it out. You broke the bargain, shithead. All I got is what you got an' I wanna hold on to that!'

'It wasn't my fault they didn't cast you, okay! I been beggin' you to go to those fuckin' actin' classes . . . You went . . . what was it . . . twice!'

'It was shit . . .'

'You say . . .'

'Yeah, I say . . . I was fuckin' there . . .!'

'Yeah well, that's why you didn't get the fuckin' job because you didn't fuckin' deserve it 'cos your actin' stinks!'

Debbie burst into tears, the frustration overwhelming.

'Asshole! Asshole!' she cried, picking up Jerry's rhyming dictionary and throwing it at him as powerfully as she could.

Ross had woken at 5.00 a.m. feeling unwell. Alone in his bed he was, at first, aware only of the nausea. Soon, however, in addition, he began to experience a dull ache in his abdomen and he was bathed in a cold, clammy sweat. Deciding to get some Evian from the refrigerator, he swung his legs out of the bed but experienced an immediate dizziness and the room swam before him. He lay back, closed his eyes, his heart pounding. The transition from nausea to vomiting was sudden. It allowed Ross only enough time to lean away from the bed. When it was over he knew that he could postpone no longer fixing an appointment with Lipschitz.

'How long have you been experiencing this discomfort?' Ninety minutes later, having completed his examination, Dr Lipschitz sat back in his chair and put his hands behind his head.

'Since early this morning.'

'Otherwise you've been in good health?'

Ross thought for a moment. He had to face the truth. He hadn't been feeling good for several months. Not since before *Shoemaker's Holiday* at Long Wharf. Suddenly the prospect loomed of hospitalisation, tests and the implication for the *Galileo* schedule.

'I been kinda tired and tetchy for a couple of months.'

'Loss of appetite?'

'Yup. A bit. I've been working hard. Travelling. Preparing a musical. It's heavy on stress.'

'Yeah, I heard,' said the doctor. '*Galileo*, right? Sounds a great idea for a musical. I saw that Brecht play a few years back. My wife and I see all the musicals in the city . . . Last one we saw was *Miss Saigon*. I loved it but Sylvie didn't. Couldn't remember any of the tunes, she said. Must be tune deaf!' He laughed at his own joke, scratched at his arm and looked wistfully at Ross. 'It's an expensive racket you're in! I guess the evening, with parking, cost close on 400 bucks . . . I gotta treat a lot of patients to cover that kind of money . . . Talking of which . . . Oh yeah . . . you've been shaky for a month or two . . .?'

An injection of Prochlorperazine dealt with the nausea and, just as Ross had feared, Lipschitz ordered him to New York University Medical Center for immediate tests.

'Is it bad?' Ross asked.

'You want the truth?'

'Yeah,' Ross said. 'I've directed a lot of melodrama. I know the score.'

'Well it could be. You'll have to wait and see. That'll be $250, please,' Lipschitz said, scrawling something on his pad. 'You wanna pay me a cheque now or I mail you an invoice . . .?'

Ross thought a moment then said: 'You know how many theatre tickets we have to sell to cover that kind of money . . .'

Ellen arrived home from Los Angeles in the evening to find Ross lying on his bed pain free but fatigued. She was alarmed by the change in his appearance during her two-week absence. He had clearly lost weight and there was something odd and disturbing in the greyness of his demeanour. It didn't take her long to discover the truth then dismiss it.

'It's probably an ulcer. Or just stress. I've been telling you to slow down. Catch! – I bought it at the airport.'

She threw him a small package.

'What is it?' Ross asked, gloomily.

'Open it and you'll find out.' Whilst he did, she unpacked and chatted. 'You haven't asked me but yes the show went well. They spoke beautiful Queen's English. Thanks to my brilliant coaching, I got rid of the odd twang in the American actors but the LA papers accused the only genuine English girl in the piece of having a lousy accent. Sometimes I think I should just give up . . . And no, since you didn't ask, Michael didn't show up for the opening. They said he might. Probably had it with America after the way you all have treated him. By the way I saw the piece in Variety . . .'

The wrapping removed, Ross turned the gadget over in his hands casually inspecting it.

'You like it?' Ellen asked.

'A Wizard, huh.'

'Haven't you always wanted one? Now you can throw away your diary and address book. You can store a thousand names and numbers. You can plan your schedule till the year 2093 . . .'

Ross smiled. 'Appropriate present under the circumstances.'

'Well I thought it was,' Ellen said testily. 'If you don't like it I'll use it . . .'

'Sure,' said Ross. 'Take . . .'

She snatched it from him and stalked out of the room.

25

Each working day, Bob, at home in the little apartment on 89th Street, worked with the up-and-coming writing team of Lewis and Hackstuber. The driving force as always was Florence. Sadly Bob, they found, was largely incapable of original thought and hamstrung by his lack of knowledge of musical theatre structure. So Lewis took over the typewriter and, together with Florence, planned and wrote scene by scene. Lewis derived enormous pleasure from the creative writing he now found himself doing. His journalist's prose, a short and pithy style, flavoured with appropriate jokes culled from the books Florence had assembled, peppered with aphorisms (from *The American Collection of Famous Aphorisms*, Volumes 1–3) was, he hoped, ideally suited to writing dialogue and constructing tight scenes. As far as he knew, no-one guessed, not even Jerry, that the words and song suggestions tabled at their occasional meetings, were mostly his, Americanised by Florence with Bob adding the odd poetic flourish. Once or twice George rang the apartment on the pretext of enquiring how Bob was progressing but really wanting to talk to Florence. Lewis took the calls and Florence was always 'out'. They never heard from Ross.

Ross largely disappeared from view during the ten days it took for Bob and his partners to complete a first draft of their new version of the script but he was constantly on the phone, determined to carry on as if nothing had changed. He spoke to Tam, Cathy, Stan and Fly, continuing the detailed planning. Every morning he called Chubby, who was presently with Karl-Heinz in Germany, to check that work on the model and technical drawings was moving speedily ahead. Michael's third draft script was still the only script they referred to.

The day after Ellen returned from LA, Ross met Dee briefly for a drink at the Players, a locale where such a meeting would not be misinterpreted. The nausea was under control and apart from a low-grade ache in his stomach, Ross didn't feel bad. He returned the jewelry. They both found it difficult to talk.

Finally Dee said, 'I'll leave him. If you want me to.'

That wasn't what he wanted to hear. 'We have to cool it for a while. At least for the moment . . . My life's complicated enough.' Now that Ellen had returned, he was afflicted by virtue.

'I'll wait . . .'

He looked at her through his glass and knew she meant it.

One day later the results of the lab tests came through. He had, without realising it, been mentally preparing himself for the worst and when the worst came he faced it with a fortitude that was completely in character. Ellen had no such reserves of strength nor did she see the need to hold back the enormous despair she felt. Ross was everything; life without him could only be bleak and forbidding. They walked down First Avenue away from NYU Medical Center unable to talk. A helicopter roared away from the 34th Street Heliport but Ellen found herself only dimly aware of her surroundings. She looked at Ross marching grimly beside her, pale and withdrawn; his state of mind mirrored in the tautness of his features and the stiffness of his walk. They walked along 38th Street and turned right into Third Avenue, full of bustle and shops. She reached out and took Ross's hand. The gesture brought Ross back to her and he smiled.

'Let's have a coffee', he said leading her into a coffee shop on the corner of 39th Street.

'Cancer of the liver, huh. What did Rudnitsky say? Genetically imprinted. A time-bomb indestructable, ticking remorselessly away. An Act of God!' Ross laughed and sipped his coffee but Ellen watched his hand shake.

'What are you going to do?' she asked quietly.

'I'm going to run down Broadway.'

'What on earth do you mean?'

Ross smiled at her. 'It's just a dream I once had as a kid. I must have seen a late-night movie or something. I was running down Broadway, in this dream, late for an opening night. I could see the theatre in the distance, the crowds were outside, there was noise and light and limousines . . . but no matter how hard I ran the theatre never got any closer. Freudian as hell, right?'

'If you say so. How old were you?'

'God knows. Maybe eight or nine.'

'Already dreaming of being the great director?'

'I suppose so. I watched too many movies and I was ambitious.' Ross smiled again. 'I'm not going to have the operation, Ellen. Or the chemotherapy.'

'But that's insane!' Ellen said, alarmed. 'Why ever not?'

'Because I'd have to abandon the show. Don't look at me like that. I'm not crazy. You heard what he said. Operating would only postpone the end. There's no cure.' He reached across the table and took her hand. Not given to tactility the gesture made him uncomfortable. 'We're not going to tell anyone. Not my ex-wives, my children, not our friends, no-one connected with *Galileo*.' He looked out of the window on to the street where life went on. 'I'm going on with the show . . .'

'You're serious, aren't you?' Ellen said. 'You don't see that as melodramatic crap?'

Ross looked at her for a moment, unsure whether to commit to words what was in his mind. 'I can't bear the thought of doing nothing, waiting to die. You know that old expression: Doctor Theatre. Working is the best cure. Well maybe cure is the wrong expression in my case. But it will prevent morbidity if I totally absorb myself in the show. You heard Rudnitsky . . . he said keep your mind occupied . . . fulfil some goal . . . Bringing *Galileo* successfully to Broadway will keep me going. I'll keep running, even if that theatre keeps getting further away . . .'

'Remember that image in *42nd Street,* the film I mean,' Ellen said stirring her cappuccino. 'The last shot, Warner Baxter, sitting on the fire escape, knowing it's his last show . . . the shot you once said you kept replaying in your head . . . ?'

'Sure . . .' he said.

'Well, I always think that shot describes the difficulty of separating life and art,' Ellen said. 'Your life is, has been, your art. I mean that in the sense of practising your skill, by the way. I don't classify what you do as high art. You've sacrificed more than one family to it, let's face it. That said, what would be the point of giving up now?'

Ross looked at her. 'You're a smart woman, Ellen. I always knew that.' He ordered more coffee and while they waited they sat in silence staring out of the window on to Third Avenue. Ellen knew arguing was useless. Ross lived his own life, she hers. It wasn't only his illness that had separated them. The waiter returned.

'There's another reason too,' Ross said, not drinking the coffee, just playing with the sugar sachet. 'You think I could quit and let George, that asshole, wring his hands with joy. After what we've been through. I didn't tell you but at the same time he fired Michael, which I might add he did without consulting me, at the same time he wanted to fire me . . .'

'How do you know that?'

The directness of Ellen's question momentarily startled him. It crossed his mind to tell her about Dee. He found himself wanting to share with Ellen the joy that Dee gave him.

'I can't remember, Gene Landau, I guess, told me . . . Doris talked him out of it. But the point is,' Ross said hurrying on, 'I can't let George have the satisfaction of capitalising on my resignation due to ill health. I can just see it . . .,' Ross said bitterly. 'All over the Witchel column. Besides I can't afford it. Whilst you were away I had a letter from Mary-Anne; Chloe's disappeared somewhere in Europe. That kid's been nothing but trouble. God knows where she is or what she's up to . . . and Chrissy wants to go to ballet school . . .'

'I get the point . . .,' Ellen said. 'You've got to do what you've got to do, Ross. I could offer you the next six months in Florida sipping orange juice but . . .,' she shrugged knowing it was hopeless. 'You might just as well go down captain of your ship . . .'

26

Dee hadn't meant to spend $18,500 in one hour in Bergdorf Goodman but there was a sale and that somehow seemed to justify it. Made it sane. She bought with a reckless abandon, hurrying from one boutique in the store to the next, as if the cops were on her heels. She charged to George's account: $11,600 for a Patek Philippe watch with a gold bracelet, $2660 for a Nicole Farhi combination, $550 for a Montana leather jacket, $340 for Ferragamo shoes, $150 worth of Clarins Skin Care plus other smaller items. She bought as if she sensed this might be the end.

Out on Fifth Avenue, clutching a bag stuffed with smaller goodies – perfumes, Belgian chocolates, two tins of Beluga that she had bought earlier – she suddenly felt cheap.

'Hiya! Deedee! You sleepwalking or what?'

It took Dee a moment to realise that Debbie Maguire was standing in front of her, smiling.

'Christ, Debbie, you gave me a turn,' Dee said putting her hand to her chest. 'I was miles away . . .'

'You looked it. That what spending George's dollars does for you? Can I peek? Knick-knacks, huh. You wanna buy me lunch, looks like you can afford it. I haven't seen you in ages . . .'

'One last scene to write then . . . ,' Lewis's tummy rumbled loudly and he wondered if his Sony dictaphone had picked it up. Bob and Florence were out buying rations, leaving him precious minutes alone to talk fast into his new acquisition.

'I didn't think we'd do it, but we have . . . We've just discussed the one scene left to tackle tomorrow, and it's a crucial one. Galileo, on his deathbed, with his younger self watching, horrified. Bobby suggested writing Galileo's death in the form of a hallucinatory acid trip. It would have turned out little better than Michael Kershon's version: a kind of post-Freudian metapsychical exploration of the interface between life and death. Jerry hadn't grasped the intellectual daring of Michael's idea hence no song existed for the scene.

'I suggested we start with a bright white light to symbolise death. Parenthesis: I'm sure I've seen that used before: close brackets. They love it. I suggested Old Galileo says something simple and memorable like . . . "It's a far far better thing I do . . ." Or "Bugger Bognor . . ." Something like that. They got the idea and Bobby came up with Old Galileo saying: "Hey, the end's cool, y'know." Oh Christ. I offered Milton's:

And for the Heaven's wide circuit, let it speak
The Maker's high magnificence, who built
So spacious, and his line stretched out so far,
That Man may know he dwells not in his own –
An edifice too large for him to fill,
Lodged in a small partition, and the rest
Ordained for uses to his Lord best known.

'We could get Jerry to adapt it as a song, I suggested. I think Bobby looked depressed. Poetry was his domain. End.'

Lewis snapped off the machine and wondered about lunch.

'You're kidding me!' Debbie said. 'You and Ross Boardman!'

'For heaven's sake, I don't want the whole restaurant to hear . . .' Suddenly Dee wasn't sure confiding her secret to Debbie was such a good idea. Debbie seemed changed, colder, more distant. But, Dee thought, at least I've told someone.

'When did you two get it together . . .?'

'Coupla weeks ago . . .'

'State of grace, right? Judging from your expression,' Debbie said.

'Uh, huh.'

'What d'you see in these old guys, Deedee? I'm interested not in a negative way . . . just might be something *I* should be thinking about.'

Dee laughed. 'They make me happy . . . Young guys just aren't fulfilling I guess.'

'I know what you mean,' Debbie said, toying with her untouched Caesar Salad, thinking about Jerry.

'When George an' I were in France in spring, we were driven by this cute chauffeur to Doris's place in the hills,' Dee said lowering her voice. 'An' when I say "cute" I mean like *real* sexy cute. George and Doris were talking business so I went exploring the garden an' I knew this guy was there somewhere in the dark, waiting for me. Thinking about this now, I can't believe I did what I did . . . but I stripped . . . everything, right . . . an' went skinny dipping in Doris's pool . . . knowing that this guy's watching . . .' Dee paused, remembering.

Debbie's face was expressionless as she listened intently. 'Yeah. What happened?'

'Nothing. We got interrupted. But nothing would have happened anyway. I was interested but not that interested,' Dee said thoughtfully. 'In the end I prefer guys with *power*.'

'Well you certainly can pick 'em, Deedee. George, now Ross. George presumably knows nothing about you an' Ross . . .?'

'You're the only one who knows, Deb, and I'm relying on you not to tell *anybody*, okay? Not even Jerry. *Please!* George'll kill me! You're my best friend and I trust you, okay. For old times' sake.'

Debbie smiled and patted Dee's hand. 'If you can't trust your friends, Deedee, who can you trust . . .'

Bob, Florence and Lewis silently munched jumbo sandwiches at the kitchen table, each absorbed in his own thoughts.

'What if they don't like it?' Bob broke the silence. 'I mean if they *really* don't like it . . .'

'Nah,' Florence said. 'We done good work. They're gonna love it.'

Lewis admired Florence's confidence. 'It's only Ross I'm concerned about pleasing,' Lewis said.

'Yeah,' said Bob searching for a cigarette stub lost in the hair behind his ear. 'Jerry keeps saying George is gonna love it. Ross is the key guy, right, Flo?'

Florence beamed merrily at them. *Ah ha,* Lewis thought. *She knows something and she's not telling us.*

'Do you wanna know a secret, guys?' Florence asked, rolling her tongue around the inside of her mouth, clearing crumbs.

She knows something and she's about to tell us.

'Guess who's having an affair with who.'

Bob and Lewis stared at her. Bob found the stub and shrugged. Lewis said, 'I'll play. Er. Cathy and Miles?'

'Who? Nah! Try again . . .'

'Members of the production team, right?' Lewis said, putting his elbows on the table, crinkling up his face as he concentrated.

179

'Gettin' warm . . .' Florence said.

'George and you!' Lewis said putting two and two together.

'You gotta diseased brain, y'know that John,' she said, disgusted. 'No, c'mon guess again!'

'Okay,' Lewis said. 'Ross and somebody . . .'

'Now you're gettin' real hot . . . C'mon Bob. Join in!'

'I can't think of anyone, Florence . . .' He was concentrating hard on drawing smoke from the dog-end.

'I give up too,' Lewis said.

'Well you got close . . . Ross and Dee! Mrs Gibson! What d'you think about that, huh? Pretty hot stuff. So I was thinkin' if Mr Boardman doesn't like our work . . . well . . . we could spread some nasty rumours.'

What! Was this true? It sounded preposterous. If it was, Lewis thought, blackmail? 'Are you sure?' he said, appalled.

'I cannot divulge my source,' Florence said proudly. 'You're gonna have to trust me on this one. Lunch is over, guys, let's get back to work.'

27

Ross, pen in hand, stared out of the window. In the distance an illuminated sign displayed the current temperature, 91° and the forecast: *Sunny, Warmer.* The apartment was cool, the air-conditioning maintained a comfortable 70°. His mind had drifted back to a holiday he and Mary-Anne had taken with the twins, Chloe and Chrissy, then five years old, on Amelia Island, off the Florida coast. It was there he had taught the twins to swim. Looking back, it was the exultant expression on Chloe's face as she successfully swum her first width that he now so vividly remembered. *Was this the best time?*

He glanced back at the half-finished letter addressed to his second wife. '. . . if Chrissy wants to go to ballet school and you think she'll stick it this time, send her and bill me. I'm anxious you call me as soon as you hear of Chloe's whereabouts in Asia . . .'

The phone rang.

'Ross, it's Betty.' Ross could hear the rasping sound of Betty filing her nails into the mouthpiece as she talked. 'George wants to know if you've read the new script from Berol.'

Bobby Berol's typescript lay close by, read and digested.

'Tell him, yeah.'

'Then he says can you come to a meeting 2.00 p.m. in the office. Jerry'll join at 2.30.'

'You inviting Berol to this?' Ross asked.

'No,' Betty said.

'I'll be there,' Ross said.

Ross told the cab to drop him at 49th Street. He wanted to walk the remaining five blocks down Broadway. The air was stifling but it didn't bother him. As he strolled, the past strolled with him. Every street, every corner, had a memory attached. Ross was given to looking back, now, under sentence of death, he could indulge his predilection to the full . . .

He stopped on the corner of 45th Street. Crowds were pouring into the theatres. He'd forgotten it was Wednesday, matinée day. *Will* Galileo *make it here? Will I? Six months to go.*

In the elevator going up to George Gibson's office a young director he knew from somewhere spoke to him. 'Hi, Ross! How're ya doing? What you up to?'

The cheerfulness grated. *Was I once like this?* 'Working on a musical,' Ross said, 'how about you?'

The elevator stopped at George's floor. 'Oh, not a lot,' said the young man, 'I'm hoping, y'know. Just hoping this or that turns out . . .' The elevator swept him away.

Ross pushed the buzzer and the door to the office suite opened. Betty sitting at her desk looked worried and unwelcoming. 'You'll have to wait. He's out to lunch.'

'Isn't he always,' Ross said.

Betty was puzzled. 'How d'you mean?'

Ross said: 'It doesn't matter,' and settled down to browse through the weekly Broadway grosses in Variety. He read:

Miss Saigon	$771,233
Cats	$453,419
Phantom of The Opera	$620,000

He couldn't resist a small calculation. *Assuming each director receives 2% . . .*

George was 15 minutes late. He swept into the office shouting instructions. 'BETTY! Call Jerry an' cancel his appointment!'

'He'll already be on his way . . .'

'BETTY! When he gets here say I'll call him later! Ross come with me! We're going on a journey.'

'You going to tell me where?' Ross said as they travelled back down the elevator.

'You know a writer, Nathan Rothstein?'

'*Conrad* Rothstein, yes,' Ross said. 'I suggested him to you as book writer, remember?'

Clearly George didn't. 'Yeah, well I talked to him five or six weeks ago about coming in on the book. He couldn't 'cos he'd signed some development deal with Paramount, right. Yesterday his agent calls me up. His deal with Paramount's fallen through, for why? I didn't ask . . . Guy's available.'

Inside George's limousine, they glided through the dense after-lunch traffic, heading downtown to the Lower East Side.

'I get it,' Ross said. 'You read Berol's book, right?'

'I think this guy's the answer to our prayers. It's still August,' he said. 'Nathan says . . .'

'It's *Conrad*, George . . .'

'Okay, this Conrad says he writes best fast, under pressure. He can deliver in under three weeks. That'll be a week or so before your design production conference out in Westport. Still a month before rehearsals start. It'll be the third writer but what the heck, it's only money, right?'

George laughed and heartily dug Ross in the ribs.

What's he after? The bonhomie didn't ring true.

'You mind me telling you something, yeah well I will anyway . . . you gotta eat more. You're getting too thin. You, me, Ellen an' Dee oughta go to one of my eating places one night. Y'know make a night of it! Whad'ya say? I don't want you fading away on me thru' this show!' Again he poked Ross in the ribs and it hurt. 'You an' Ellen having problems? Y'know, couple problems.'

'Let's keep this strictly business, George,' Ross said, beginning to feel trapped. The limo had come to a stop, hemmed in on all sides in a mid-town street.

'Sure, okay, but we oughta be friends. Think about that dinner. I got something else I wanna talk to you about . . .'

Christ! What am I doing trapped in here?

'. . . That lawyer of yours, Joe Nunzio, he's driving me nuts with unreasonable demands, Ross. You sure he's straight? Y'know, not *Mafia* connected . . . He's Italian, right?'

I'm dealing with the enemy, Ross reminded himself. *Dealing with the enemy . . .*

'I leave business decisions to my representatives, George,' Ross said. 'That's what I pay them for. Where are we going?'

George didn't want to let go. 'We got an agreement but he's kvetching about the billing. Billing schmilling, what does the billing matter? Who gives a shit about the goddamned billing . . . !'

Ross reminded himself of the problem. 'He wants to call the show *George Gibson's Galileo*.' That's what Joe had told him on the phone several weeks ago. He hadn't heard from Joe since. Clearly the problem hadn't gone away. 'I don't want to get into that, George,' Ross said. 'Where are we going?'

Again George wasn't to be diverted and Ross caught himself staring at Gibson's bulbous nose, the duct for those snorts and sniffs. 'You gotta look to the future, Ross. That's what's important. That's why I want Lewis writing his book about me. So there's a record. Future generations are gonna be able to look back an' say, yeah, Gibson and *Galileo,* so that's how he did it! An' that's why the billing's important . . .'

'You just said . . . ,' Ross attempted to point out the contradiction but the streamroller couldn't be stopped.

'This is gonna be my last big show, Ross, an' I want it *memorable*. Then I'm gonna retire to San Diego with Dee, to the house I'm building on the beach. It's a dream this place, only damn thing I ever wanted! But you, you're gonna walk Broadway for ten more years! This sure ain't gonna be *your* last . . .'

Yeah, I get the message . . . Ross looked at George oozing vulnerability, pleading pity. 'How long have you been building?' Ross asked trying to be as pleasant as possible. *Dee, beach houses. A future.* Since discovering the cancer, Ross sensed time in a new way. The future didn't exist. Only the present and the past.

'Four years. Dee fell in love with the place. She's a sea person, y'know. But I guess you don't know her too well, huh? She's a great gal, Ross. You're gonna love having her.'

This is the enemy. This is the enemy.

'She's taking acting lessons, day'n night! She's not gonna let us down . . .' George looked at Ross, coughed and snorted mucous. 'Oh yeah, you said where we going? Nathan, no *Conrad* right, Conrad's Jewish bookstore down on the lower East Side. He'n Myra are expecting us . . . How about we re-title the show *Stars in His Eyes?* Friend of mine who works in the Imperial thought of that. Pretty catchy title huh?'

184

28

On the Thursday after Labor Day, that is at the beginning of September, one month before rehearsals began, Ross had scheduled a two-day production conference in the meeting room of a quiet hotel in a leafy suburb of Westport, Connecticut. The day before Jerry said wouldn't it be a good idea if someone told Bobby Berol that he was no longer the writer of *Galileo,* now officially re-titled: *Stars in His Eyes.*

Only Conrad, Jerry and Ross had worked through the latter part of August. Their deadline for completing the new version of the show: the production conference. With the casting and design in place, George and Dee had disappeared to California until Labor Day. Betty told everyone she couldn't reach them. Everyone but Florence, Bob and Lewis knew this to be a lie.

Four days after they submitted their script, Betty told Bob over the phone that George loved it, had a few 'problems' but had taken it away to read again on the plane to San Diego. 'He'll be in touch soon,' she'd said. Jerry had called immediately he'd read it. 'Hi, Bobby!' he had shouted ecstatically down the phone. 'Love it! Great! Well done! We'll meet soon!' Only Ross's attitude remained a mystery. On Florence's urging, Bob left several messages on his machine. Finally, several days later, when they were out, Ross left an enigmatic reply: 'Sorry not to have got back to you sooner. We're all thinking.'

Lewis thought this didn't sound good. He said nothing lest Florence take up her threat to broadcast the news of Ross and Dee's affair. Florence had Bob leave another message on Ross's machine: 'Ross, hi! Shouldn't we meet to discuss music changes as soon as possible? The big production conference in Westport's scheduled in two days. Gonna soon be too late . . .'

But it was Jerry who replied, leaving a message on their machine at lunchtime the next day: 'Great to hear from you, Bob! Great! By the way, I'm no longer at my previous number. Debbie an' me aren't speaking anymore so I'm kinda upset. Here's my temporary number.'

Bob called that number and heard a recorded voice say: '. . . and please leave messages for Con, Myra or Jerry after the bleep . . .'

'Who the fuck are Con and Myra?' Florence whispered as Bob held his hand over the mouthpiece. 'Tell him he must phone us back about a meeting . . .'

The next day Jerry phoned and they were in.

'We gotta meet to talk music, sort out changes,' Bob said with unswerving machismo carefully bolstered by Florence. 'We . . . I mean, I'm real worried about time slipping away.'

'I'm kinda busy right now,' Jerry said. He sounded anxious. 'Debbie and I have busted up . . . an' I've been kinda shocked y'know by the whole thing . . . I can't get anything together at the moment, man. Should be okay in a few days . . . *after* the conference tomorrow . . . No . . . No I haven't seen Ross . . .'

As soon as Jerry hung up the phone in Myra's kitchen, he went into the sitting room to report this conversation. Conrad and Ross were poring over the new text.

That night Ross arranged to see Bobby Berol.

Lewis, clutching his copy of the Berol version of *Galileo,* arrived at Grand Central Station at 8.05 a.m., precisely the time stated on his schedule, and found himself the first there. The train was not due to leave from Westport until 8.43 but Charlie said he didn't want people late. Lewis looked anxiously around the busy station. He re-checked the schedule, yes, he was in the right place at the right time on the right day.

Spotting Fly trotting towards him was reassuring.

'Hi, Jaahn!' Fly said cheerfully. 'Had a nice summer? Where'd you go? Meet any nice chicks?'

'No,' Lewis said. 'And we stayed in the city. You?'

'Minneapolis . . . saw my folks . . . annual pilgrimage . . . but I spent more time downtown in the clubs . . . Jesus, John, the clubs in that city these days, I gotta tell you, they're something else . . . One night in The Parisienne . . . there was me an' three women an' one other guy . . . you wouldn't believe the combinations . . . the *gymnastics* . . . Oh boy! . . . Sometimes, I wonder why I left . . . You first here, huh?' He looked around. 'Okay, betcha Charlie's next. You're looking worried, what's up?'

'Bob Berol didn't come home last night after meeting Ross.' Florence and Lewis had stayed up till 3.00 a.m. talking, reading, waiting. At 7.30 a.m., when Lewis crept out of the apartment, Florence slept alone. No sign of Bob.

'So? He's a big boy right,' Fly said, distracted by two passing girls in tight, short skirts.

'No, it's not that. I'm just keen to know how Ross liked our . . . Bob's script.'

Fly's smile disappeared, and Lewis noted his expressive face registering what . . . ? Concern?

'You don't know, huh?'

'Know what?' Lewis asked, suddenly feeling the ground shifting underneath, the old Lewis returning; uncertainty, doom and dread. Fly crouched down and began to rummage in his suitcase. Then Charlie arrived full of hustle and bustle.

'You guys first here? It's 8.15 an' I told everyone they gotta be here by now . . . I'm gonna go buy a Times, watch out for the others . . . Hiya Ross, you wanna paper?'

Ross arrived at the same moment that Fly produced a script out of his case. 'Morning Ross!' Fly said.

'No, I got one,' Ross said to Charlie before acknowledging Fly and Lewis.

Fly passed Lewis a blue-covered script, boldly emblazoned with *Galileo's* new title *Stars in His Eyes*.

'What's this?' Lewis asked, catatonic. He turned to the title page:

STARS IN HIS EYES
A Musical Comedy
Music and Lyrics by Jerry Trimlock
Book by Conrad Rothstein

Book by Conrad . . .! How is this possible? Lewis's mind went into overdrive. It was a deception and the scale of the deception was astounding. 'Where's Bob?' he rudely asked Ross. 'Does he know about this?' He waved the Conrad script in the air.

'Good morning, John,' Ross said politely, if a little weakly. 'Yes, I explained the situation to Mr Berol last night.'

'And . . .? How did he take it?'

'Bob? He took it fine. Why?'

'He didn't come home last night and I wondered . . .'

'He said little then left my apartment after fifteen minutes . . . I've no idea where he went after that . . .'

Others started to gather and Ross turned away. Lewis, left to nurse his wounds on the periphery of the cheerful group, decided Florence had to be told. He called her from a nearby phone. As he had expected, she was mad as hell, swearing biblical vengeance.

Eventually, his nerves jangled from the torrent of expletives, he extricated himself from the conversation and hurried to join the others lining up at the platform entrance.

They started the conference after lunch.

At one end of a long table Chubby Moscowitz sat by a model of the set with the first scene in place: three silver convex spheres filling the little model. Next to him Karl-Heinz, dressed in a brightly coloured caftan with a Cincinnati Reds Baseball cap askew on his bald head, puffed nervously on a cheroot. The whole team was present. Stan Warburg, the Musical Director, was next to Ross and on his left, Fly. Sam Lee and Sam Mole, the Lighting Director and Sound Designer, sat with ground plans and rig designs on hand for reference. Conrad Rothstein, less orthodox today, dressed in a black suit and yamulka, sat with Jerry and looked nervous. Charlie Brodsky, on Conrad's left, sat with Tam Topp.

Ross tapped the table with his pencil. 'For those of you who haven't worked with me before, I guess a little explanation is in order. We've gathered for a concentrated two-day work-through away from big city distractions; the telephone, families, girl-friends . . .' Ross looked at Jerry and smiled. '. . . Even producers.' There was laughter. Ross grinned again and sipped some water. His lips were parched, his left eye was inflamed, bloodshot and irritating. Sunken cheeks exaggerated the jaw and an emaciated neck cruelly exposed his Adam's apple. There could be no mistaking the change in him.

As the grin faded he said: 'We're going to go through the show line by line, lyric by lyric, and we're going to talk about the set movement, and I mean by that the general staging and the choreography. We'll discuss how we move from scene to scene, the underscoring, and the overall style.

'Let me begin with the last, the style. We're starting with the premise that the production is free-flowing or continuous. We're not stopping for scene changes, or setting stuff behind drops. We have a brilliantly conceived multi-dimensional set, thanks to the genius of Karl-Heinz, and we're going to use it every way we can. One of the purposes of today's exercise is to discover, together, just how far we can push this set. You got to fire off ideas, however goofy you might think them. Fear not that you will be laughed at . . . out of the craziest notions can come best moments.'

Stan played the songs on an upright in a corner of the nondescript conference room with Jerry turning the pages and singing the lyrics. Jerry wore a lurid tee-shirt depicting in comic book style a B52 dropping a payload of bombs on to a theatre. A caption underneath read WE BOMBED IN IRAQ. As a singer he was no big deal, frequently out of tune. Fly read Conrad's short, sketch-like scenes in a flat voice. The team made notes, asked questions, offered up suggestions. The work was painstaking but the hours passed quickly.

It took Lewis several hours to come to terms with rejection. But now, part of the meeting, involved despite himself, he was impressed at the sheer scale of the changes that had been made. The new title said it all. The show was now vaudeville, revue, Las Vegas.

They stopped at 6.00 p.m. to shower and change for a 7.15 dinner. Lewis phoned Florence from his room. She sounded depressed and different.

'Yeah, he's back – he's asleep.'

'Bob? Where was he?'

'He got back this afternoon. Walked the city for 18 hours. Didn't sleep, didn't eat.'

'Pretty pissed off, is he?'

'Yeah, real pissed off . . . ,' Florence was silent. This wasn't a Florence Lewis recognised.

Lewis tried cheering her up. 'Meeting's going well, though, you'll be pleased to hear. This new version's very different though rather good, I think . . .'

That was too much for Florence who exploded with pent-up anger. 'Don' you take their fuckin' side! Those assholes! Cock-suckin'! SCUMBAGS! After everything I've done for them!'

'No, really, Flo,' Lewis said reasonably. 'I do think this is better than ours. It's wilder, more anarchic.'

'Traitor!' Florence hissed down the phone and hung up.

The conversation upset Lewis greatly. His heart was still thumping as he made his way to the bar to join in a pre-dinner drink. The bar of the Westporter Inn was dark, moody, wall-to-wall velvet. Surveying the room from the door Lewis saw only Fly, Charlie and Sam Mole nursing drinks.

'No-one else down yet?' he said jauntily from the door. He set out to join them, blissfully unaware of the velvet pouf, lurking innocently but invisibly on the velvet carpet.

'You okay, Jaahn?' Fly asked anxiously, bending over the groaning Englishman sprawled on the floor, his face buried in the velvet pile.

Lewis mentally checked over his parts. Apart from the crack the left side of his face had received from the corner of a solid wood table as he went down, no other damage seemed evident. He picked himself up.

'No – I'm okay – thanks,' he said, gingerly touching his face, feeling a bump growing.

'I'll get you an ice-compress from the bar,' Fly said solicitously. 'It'll reduce the swelling. Sit!'

Lewis's face, like his pride, hurt like hell. Through the pain he heard the barman say to Fly: 'Happens twice a night. Who gives a shit . . .'

The ice-pack and the brandy Fly supplied helped Lewis's spirits recover. 'Old dancer's trick,' Fly explained. 'But you're gonna have a black eye tomorrow.' Charlie, who had enjoyed the episode hugely, suggested they bet on who would tumble next but no-one took him up. The conversation turned to the events of the day.

Sam Mole said: 'New script works swell. I read that last version. Personally, I thought that total shit. You too?'

'Oh yeah,' Charlie said. 'Robert Berol. God knows where George dug him up. You meet him, John?'

Lewis felt himself blushing. Trying to talk he could only stammer: 'Er . . . yes . . . he's a pop-poet. Nice chap.'

Fly lowered his voice: 'Conrad Rothstein has been working with Jerry for the past couple of weeks and they've become real buddies.'

'That's nice,' Lewis said with as much false enthusiasm as he could muster. He sipped his brandy.

'Sure is,' Fly said. 'First time in this whole game I got real confidence that we're getting somewhere.'

'I'm afraid I'd never heard of him,' Lewis said.

'Really?' Jerry said surprised, unwrapping gum. Lewis hadn't noticed him arrive. 'Con had a coupla big off-Broadway hits coupla years ago. First play he wrote was *Gumbo Riley*, a re-working of a Grimm's fairy tale set in a graveyard in Louisiana, second was a small-scale musical revue that Ross saw, called . . .'

'*Torah! Torah*', Charlie said. 'Yeah, I caught that. Funniest show I ever saw.'

Jerry grinned. 'Yeah, it was. He's a smart guy. It was his idea to use that Commedia dell'Arte shit in *Galileo*.'

'Right! Makes it live.' Sam agreed. 'Last draft gimme the flop sweats.'

'Flop sweats?' Lewis asked.

They laughed at his ignorance. Fly explained: 'It's a cold, clammy sweat that crawls over your body as it dawns you gotta flop. Friends ask if you're okay. You say "It's just those old flop sweats breakin' out, man" . . .'

They laughed comfortably together.

'I done shows where I got the sweats about now,' Sam said to Lewis. 'I sit in meetings like this knowing I gotta keep working on the garbage for seven more months.'

'Well, why do it?' Lewis asked naively.

They looked at him as if he was insane.

' 'Cos you could be wrong . . .,' Sam said, losing interest.

'An' then it's farewell megabucks,' Fly said, adding jauntily, after examining his eye. 'Pip of a shiner y'got there, Jaahn, ole fruit . . .!'

It was half way through the following morning session that the door to the conference room opened and George Gibson unexpectedly walked in. Jerry and Stan were in the middle of a ballad, 'Long Forgotten Moments', and nobody paid much attention. Except Lewis.

George, tight-lipped, sat in an empty seat next to Sam Mole and glowered in Ross's direction. When 'Long Forgotten Moments' ended, one or two people said 'hi', but George pointedly ignored them.

Something's up! George looks . . . peculiar.

Ross continued work, pointing out a set movement and lighting change. After a few minutes sitting stony-faced, apparently listening, George abruptly drew a white envelope from his pocket and skimmed it across the table. The envelope nudged Ross's legal pad, face down, challengingly delivered. Ross appeared not to notice, he remained hunched over his script, listening to lighting Sam discuss the positioning of some lamps with Chubby. Ross let time pass. It wasn't until Stan and Jerry had launched into the next song that he finally opened the envelope. It contained a single sheet of paper.

Lewis surreptitiously leant back in his chair and thus was able to read the message formed with letters cut out of newspapers:

HEY CREEP PRODUCER . . . WHY DO YOU ALLOW YOUR WIFE TO BE MULTIFUCKED BY THE GREAT DIRECTOR, HUH?

Lewis was shocked. No signature. *Who could it be from?* Christ! *Florence?* It was a strong possibility. His sore left eye, which had blackened further overnight, throbbed alarmingly. Lewis felt implicated, guilty and sick.

Ross betrayed no emotion. Without looking up, he carefully folded the paper, put it back in its envelope, and deliberately replaced it face down on the table.

The song was finished and everyone looked at the director. George stared at him. Analysing his passivity, Lewis reckoned. The room had been reduced to silence as the tension between the two men became apparent. Finally, Ross wearily lifted his head. 'Guys, take a ten-minute break will ya while I have a word with George.' Without a glance in George's direction, he pushed back his chair and headed for the door. George followed him out of the room.

Inside, nobody moved, nobody spoke; gloom descended. Soon they began to hear snippets of the conversation outside the door and they listened in embarrassed silence.

'Y'gonna tell me this isn't true? YOU'RE NOT STICKIN' YOUR PUTZ WHERE IT'S GOT NO DAMN BUSINESS BEING?' They heard George shout. 'Why would ya do this to me, Ross? What have I done to you? I give ya the best work in town. How many musicals get done on Broadway anymore? Y'can count them on one hand . . . an' I give ya one of them. Y'THINK IT'S GODDAMN EASY TO RAISE MONEY FOR SHOWS! Well, I'll tell ya the heartaches that this gives . . . the tsuris.' There was a silence. 'Why ya not saying nothing, ya stinker? Y'gonna neither confirm nor deny nothing?'

'You better speak to your wife, George,' Ross said.

'No! I wanna hear it from you. Or is your silence indicating this shit is accurate?'

'You believe what you want to believe, George. Now I've got . . .'

'I WANNA KNOW AN' I DON'T WANNA KNOW. CAN Y'UNDERSTAND THAT!' George shouted.

'Jesus Christ, George, keep your volume down . . . you want all the guys in there to hear!' Ross took a breath, containing his anger. 'You think I need this? Well you've got another think coming. I've had it with the lies, the inanities. I'm resigning. I'm out!'

The door half opened and the team glimpsed Ross about to enter before suddenly disappearing, pulled back out by George. The spring hinges gently closed the door.

'Ross screwing Dee . . .?' an amazed Tam Topp muttered to no-one in particular.

'Somebody's gotta do something about this,' Jerry said anxiously.

'What's going on?' Stan asked from the piano. 'Does anyone know?'

'It's a domestic,' Fly said. 'Better not to know.'

Lewis knew but wasn't about to tell. His thoughts had once again turned to the authorship of the blackmail note. Florence's name played in his head on a closed loop. 'Isn't it *fun!*' she had said. Lewis had asked her how she had found out. 'That's telling,' she had said, 'keep it to yourself.'

And he had.

Having heard Ross threaten to resign, apprehensive conversations were taking place around the room. The fate of the show appeared to hang in the balance. Lewis got up and moved near to the door, hoping to hear more clearly. He did.

'I GOTTA CONTRACT WITH YOU, ROSS!' George was saying. 'Y'just betta remember that y'can't walk out on me. All I'm trying to say to ya, is "keep your fuckin' pants buttoned".' He paused. 'You think I'm being unreasonable?'

'You're wrong, George,' Ross said calmly. 'We haven't got a deal. We're in dispute over the billing. I can walk any time I like and you can't stop me.'

George laughed. *Like a hyena,* Lewis thought.

'No, you got it wrong, Ross! All wrong as usual. WE GOTTA CONTRACT! A watertight contract. I agreed it all with Nunzio *this morning.* I gave you everything you asked for . . . including billing. Y'get better billing than me, Ross! I agreed to take my name off the top an' that yours goes in a box. I even sent round to Joe the first instalment of your fee and gotta *written* acknowledgement!' he shouted. Lewis imagined him waving a paper like Chamberlain. 'You're all mine, Ross. You pull out an' I'll sue you through every court. Pull out an' I'll make sure as hell Ellen and the city know why. You pull out, I'll ruin you!'

'You're such an asshole,' Ross said evenly.

It went quiet outside. Lewis moved closer to the door, straining to hear. Behind him, Ross's team muttered unhappily.

'Who sent you this, George? Do you know?' Ross said.

'Some nudnik. A well-wisher.'

'Have you shown this piece of shit to Dee?'

'No. And I don't intend to.'

'Don't.'

Boardman thrust open the door to the room and Lewis, still lurking behind the door, received a nasty crack on his forehead close to his right eye. Oblivious, Ross returned to the table. Lewis, however, clutching his head in agony, staggered out of the room into the corridor where he collided with a shell-shocked George Gibson.

'Oh sorry,' Lewis spluttered. 'Need bathroom . . . sorry.' And he rushed off down the thickly carpeted corridor and disappeared.

The collision brought George to his senses. Turning on his heels, he strode purposefully down the corridor away from the conference room. A few minutes later, he was being driven back to New York.

'We don't always see eye-to-eye,' Ross declared to the team. 'You all know he and I have a history of going 15 rounds. Then we wrestle in mud.'

He looked at them and smiled wanly. They laughed uncomfortably with him.

'We throw shit but the show goes on,' Ross said. 'Now where were we . . .?'

29

The team travelled back together to New York on Amtrak that evening. Everyone was relaxed, the crisis apparently passed. Jerry and Stan drank beer and played backgammon; Others read; Karl-Heinz drew pictures of the landscape. As the train rumbled towards Manhattan, Lewis, now sporting two black eyes and feeling he'd been in a war, cornered Fly in the Club Car eager to hear his reactions to the morning's events. Fly was untroubled and philosophical.

'You gotta understand,' he said. 'It's a question of *power*. Why d'you think George turned up today?'

'Because he found out about Ross and Dee . . .'

'That was the excuse. He couldn't sit in New York knowing Ross was leading a production conference in Westport . . .'

Lewis looked amazed. 'I can't believe that. Anybody who finds out his wife's cheating on him would be bound to do something . . .'

'Think about it a moment,' Fly said. 'George bursts into the meeting raging an' he makes damn sure everyone knows why.'

'You mean he wanted us to hear?' Lewis said, touching his tender right eye, unable to grasp the subtleties of George's behaviour.

'Oh sure,' Fly said as if it was so obvious only an idiot could fail to follow. 'See if you look at everything from the point of view of a power struggle between Ross and George then everything becomes clear, okay?'

Fly started to count out points on his fingers. 'One: Ross calls this Westport meeting and specifically excludes the producer, knowing it's going to get George mad. Which it does. One round to Ross. Two: George finds out Ross is having an affair with his wife. He's found a perfect excuse to come to Westport to assert that he's the number-one guy and nobody better forget it. It's a double whammee because he figures that we'll feel sorry for him and think Ross an asshole for fuckin' his wife. Two rounds for

George. Looked at this way, George wins two to one *and* Ross comes out severely weakened.'

Lewis's brain worked overtime trying to come to terms with this kind of alien behaviour. 'You actually mean,' Lewis said slowly, lowering his voice though no other team members were around, 'that George has no qualms about publicising his wife's affair so long as it helps him assert dominance over Ross?'

'Sure,' said Fly brightly. 'George must see this as a heaven-sent opportunity. The very guy with whom he's fighting for power is dumb enough to weaken his position by futzing around with his wife. You gotta understand, John, that George would sacrifice anything or anyone for control over the show. Anyone.'

'Does Ross understand this?' Lewis asked.

'You thinking of telling him?'

'No, of course not!' Lewis replied. 'I just wondered how conscious Ross is of these games.'

'He's conscious,' Fly said and smiled into his plastic cup.

Ten minutes later, as the train passed through the ruins of the Bronx, Ross came into the Club Car with Jerry.

'Those are two nasty bumps,' Ross said, sipping a diet calorie juice. 'You should get that looked at.'

Lewis felt his face. Looking up he could quite easily make out the lumps. One on either side. *Like horns, my God!* They felt tender and peculiar. 'They're okay. First, a table in the bar, then a door. I haven't had much luck . . .'

'How's the book coming on?' Ross asked pleasantly. 'You finding this process interesting?'

Interesting? Are you kidding!

'Absolutely,' Lewis gushed, eager to please. 'Everything's still a bit disorganised . . . I haven't had much time to get any order in it. I think my problem is that I feel so close to you and it, I might lack objectivity.'

'You must have formed some impressions?' Ross leant against the window and the Bronx, a panorama of wanton destruction and urban decay, unrolled behind him.

'Oh sure!' But Lewis's brain, trapped by the question, went blank. The old panic returned. *Brain damage!* Concussion caused by confrontation with door and table. Then, an answer popped into his head: 'It's much more combative than I had expected.'

'In what way?'

That was a tough one to answer without getting personal. 'Er, well, you know, you and George don't always see eye-to-eye, as you yourself said back in Westport . . . this morning.'

'Ah! Producer-director relationship, you mean. Well this isn't conventional, you know, this set-up. You'd better not think this typical. Usually it's fairly harmonious. There are always disagreements, but not usually like this. Fact is the chemistry's wrong. Always has been . . .' The train stopped in the middle of the wasteland. Ross turned and gazed out of the window. It was night but nearby, illuminated by the street light, a fast game of basketball was being played by black kids in a parking lot.

'Then why do you two continue to work together?'

Ross laughed and Lewis noticed that the tension seemed to drain from his features. 'Seems pretty dumb, huh? But I'm a hired man, John. I sell my services to a producer. You know I even sell him the copyright to my work. I don't even get to keep that. And whatever my personal problems with George, I respect him professionally. He's been one of Broadway's most successful producers.'

'I understand that,' Lewis said. 'But presumably you and Michael could have had the pick of the producers for this project. Wouldn't anyone have wanted to come in?'

'No. They wouldn't touch it. Thought it too risky. It wasn't musical comedy, kinda more like an Italian *Les Miserables*. They couldn't categorise it and therefore wouldn't touch it. George welcomed us with open arms. At the beginning we said we'd put the past behind us, agreed to look to the future. Our prior disagreements, we said, wouldn't interfere with what we both thought to be a potential hit. This time we said we'd make the partnership work.'

'So what went wrong?'

'I went wrong. I forgot George sells pastrami on rye.'

Lewis looked puzzled.

'He gets confused between his two businesses, John. He thinks the theatre's a deli and the deli's theatre. He treats his waiters like actors (and most are). Us he treats like waiters. He orders and expects us to serve up anything he wants. Well I'm too old to do that, John. I guess he's too old to change and that's the problem.'

'Maybe his attitude is traceable back somehow to his upbringing in Cleveland.'

Ross looked puzzled. 'Cleveland? George was born and brought up on the East Side. Here in New York.'

'Oh,' Lewis said. 'That's funny. He told me his mother started a theatre in Cleveland. It was wonderfully romantic. Chaps on boats painting the city from the lake. That sort of thing.

Ross smiled knowingly. 'Garbage, I'm afraid. He musta got that tale out of someone else's biography.'

'He didn't arrive on a boat from Lithuania either?'

197

'Nah,' Ross said. 'That sounds more like Sam Goldwyn.'

Confused and dispirited, Lewis fell silent and stared out of the window. Nothing seemed to be turning out right. The train restarted with a lurch and the two men paused and watched as the window filled with the city's lights, shifting and fluctuating, a mesmeric kaleidoscope. They were nearly home.

'Did you enjoy working on the book?' Ross suddenly asked.

The question caught Lewis by surprise. Assuming Ross was still asking about his journalistic efforts, Lewis replied: 'Absolutely, yes! It's as if this is what I've always wanted to do.'

'I see,' Ross said. 'Well, maybe you'll have better luck next time.'

What on earth can he mean? Lewis thought. Then it dawned on him. *Christ! He means the book for the show.* It had never occurred to him that Ross knew everything. He had assumed that Ross, like the others, had been successfully fooled into thinking it was a solo work of Bob's.

'What . . .?' was all he managed to utter.

'Don't take it personally, John. You tried your best.' Ross smiled at the hapless Lewis. 'Writing books for musicals is tough. Maybe there's a slim chance complete amateurs could crack it first time around – but I doubt it.'

'What makes you think . . .?' Lewis felt his face go hot and red. Sweat trickled down his back.

'It wasn't difficult. I suspected it from the start. Here we go again, I thought, a certain English feel to the dialogue. The Milton quote was the giveaway. Wrong dramatically, wrong coming from Berol. Thing is I recognised the quote right away then it didn't take me long to figure out the team.' Ross sniffed, blew his nose. 'Maybe you've gotta future in writing musicals, John, but this one wasn't it.'

30

'Sure he's depressed! I'm fuckin' depressed! What d' you think?' Florence was still mad as hell and Lewis didn't find it a pretty sight.

The apartment was a mess. The writing process had generated much paper waste, not manuscript but takeaway food wrappers and cardboard drink containers. This detritus was scattered everywhere. Neither Bobby, Florence or Lewis had taken the time (or had the inclination) to clean or tidy because the writing had gone on round the clock.

Lewis sat on the edge of the unmade bed and looked morosely at Florence. Even the tantalising glimpses he had of her breasts and thighs as she stormed furiously about the apartment failed to lift his spirits. Bob was out buying bagels and pickles for dinner; a spartan diet but money was scarce. They had hoped to persuade George Gibson to give Bob an advance for the book but Doris's lawyer said George's lawyer was not returning calls on that one. Now they knew why.

Mysteriously, a week ago Betty had stopped paying Lewis's per diems. When he'd asked for the reason she'd shrugged. 'Ask him yourself,' she'd said. But Lewis hadn't. His reserves were not dangerously low. Seeking independence and drawing heavily on his list of the slogans on Jerry's tee-shirts, he had at last rattled off a 2000-word article to the Independent now entitled: 'SHIRT SPIEL: A WORKING CATALOGUE OF APHORISTIC VESTS' with an accompanying letter to the Arts Editor offering to provide a weekly article on Manhattan subculture. If his editor bought the proposal he reckoned he might get paid enough to get free from George.

'An' another thing!' Florence said from the kitchen as she crashed shut the door of the refrigerator. 'I didn't send any fucking note to George. I wished I'd thought of it – but I didn't. You wanna soda?'

Lewis looked at his watch. 8.35 p.m. He was hungry, having not eaten since lunch in Westport. 'Okay. Bob's taking his time. I

199

thought you said he was only going round the corner. If you didn't send that note, who did?'

Florence shrugged as she came back into the room. 'Could be any one of a zillion people. Those guys got plenty of enemies . . .'

'Have you talked to Doris?' Lewis asked, opening his can. He had to mop himself down as the fizzy liquid fountained over his trousers.

She shook her head. 'Since Roget's funeral the fight's gone out of her. Anyways she's in France . . . I could get the number . . . but what's the use . . . We lost.'

It looked to Lewis as if some of the fight had gone out of Florence also. His stomach, craving food, rumbled angrily. But it was another hour and a half before Bob returned. He entered the apartment grimly clutching the brown paper bag containing their meagre supper.

'Hi Bob!' Lewis said cheerfully. Bob didn't reply.

'What's up, man?' Florence asked as Bob tossed the bag into the kitchen, then threw himself on to the sofa. Lewis and Florence watched from the bed. Bob covered his face with his hands and lay back.

'You okay?' Florence asked again. Lewis hauled himself off the bed and headed for the kitchen and food. Returning a couple of minutes later with tomato and cream-cheese imprisoned in a poppy bagel, he found Florence sitting next to Bob on the sofa.

'He's still upset about the script, I guess,' Lewis said to Florence with a mouth full of bagel. 'The conference went well, Bob. I got back 'bout three hours ago.'

Suddenly Bob dropped his hands and stared wild-eyed at Lewis. His face, Lewis saw, was drained of colour. The whites of his eyes were bloodshot. He seemed in shock.

'He wasn't as bad as this when he left here,' Florence said to Lewis. 'Something occur at the deli, Bobby?'

Then Bob spoke, hesitantly at first. 'I thought it might do me some good, y'know, clear it outa my system, to go to the Metropolitan Grand . . .'

Lewis looked at Florence, puzzled.

'You mean the hotel where the theatre is?' Florence asked Bob.

Bob nodded. 'Yeah, right. Times Square.' The theatre where *Stars in His Eyes* was scheduled to open in February was built on the third floor inside a new 54-storey hotel. Lewis had attended a show there but had been more impressed with the vastness of the theatre lobby rising up 37 floors. Four elevators encased in glass rushed up through the theatre lobby, racing up to the 40th and disappearing upwards again into the 41st floor. Floors 3–40 were ranged around the lobby each with their own balcony. Lewis had found it breathtaking and awesome and couldn't resist taking an elevator to see the view from the revolving bar on the 54th.

'I guess I thought seeing the theatre might kinda make the pain go away,' Bob said. 'Anyway, I go up to the glass doors that separate the theatre from the lobby an' this guy in a suit stops me. I say "Hey, man, I thought no shows are playing here," an' he says it's a trade show for the launch of a new car or something. I say can't I just put my head round the door, please, 'cos it's for psycho-medicinal purposes. He says "no" an' pushes me away from the doors like I'm a kinda leper or something. "Is there an intermission?" I say to the guy, not wanting to give up. "Yeah," he says, "in ten minutes" an' he adds he don't want his clients seeing my face in the lobby when they're taking of refreshments so I gotta get out.'

'Well, you gotta picture this scene, okay. There's me an' this guy standing in the middle of this deserted lobby, exchanging opinions. Suddenly it's like we're in the middle of a gothic horror fantasy, okay, because something catches my eye, falling thirty feet away, across the other side of the lobby. It's falling almost in slow motion, turning over as it falls, an' lands maybe 30 feet away with a dull thud. I realise what's fallen's a *body*! Then maybe a second or two later, right in front of us – and I mean not 2 feet away – lands this severed arm.'

Bob paused for breath, his eyes straining in their sockets. Neither Lewis nor Florence moved. An unchewed morsel of bagel grew soggy in Lewis's mouth.

'Guy jumped musta been 35 floors,' Bob said, resuming his narrative, 'I swear to God, that as me an' the guy stared in horror at this arm, the fingers twitched once, an' blood oozed from the other end on to the grey carpet. Then I saw the fingers had released a black Berol pencil, you know the kind . . . I buy 'em. Same name as me. My dad used to say we're a branch of the same family. Anyway, I think of this pencil as the *writer's* friend, okay, 'cos it's got this firm eraser on the end.

'I'm rooted to the spot an' I hear myself say: "We gotta call the cops, man . . ." I look at the guy in the suit. He looks like he's gonna throw up. He says to me: "No, wait." He grabs *my* arm. "I got five hundred salesmen coming out for champagne in five minutes – we gotta call the cops *after* the intermission." I say: "Hey, wait a minute, man, you can't do this . . ." He says: "I'm gonna pay you 100 dollars to get that Chinese screen from over there and put it around this arm. I'm gonna get the other one an' put it around the body. Then when my delegates come out in four

201

minutes they're gonna be untroubled and happy. Okay? We been planning this show," he says, "for nine months an' no fucking jumper's gonna screw it up." '

Bob stopped again, emotion welling up in him. Florence gently prompted him. 'So? What? You got a screen . . .?'

'Yeah,' Bob said. 'I gotta screen for the arm. As I passed the body, I saw it was a guy I knew a bit, he was a writer, a gay poet lived up near Zabar's . . .'

Bob wiped away a tear.

'So I got the screen an' I put it round the arm hiding it from view. An' I stayed inside the screen with the arm as the break arrived an' these car salesmen with their wives poured out of the theatre into the lobby for their refreshments. I stood there guarding the arm for twenty minutes as conversation an' laughter swirled round me. When it was all quiet again, the guy in the suit comes back and lets me out. "That went okay," he said to me, clearly relieved. Guy was amost *smiling*. "No-one knew anything," he said "Now we can call the cops . . ." '

'Did you take the $100?' Lewis asked.

Bob shook his head. 'I needed air, man. I needed to breathe. I knew every detail of that guy's arm an' hand by the time the break was over.'

Florence stretched her legs. 'How'd the arm get severed, Bob? You thought about that at all?'

Bob thought about it then. 'Body musta hit something on the way down . . . So much for being a writer, huh? An' I never did get to see the theatre.'

'Don't take it personal. Lotta guys with AIDS are jumping in that lobby, Bob,' Florence said. 'I read it in the Times.'

'Nah,' Bob said morosely. 'Guy was a writer. That's why he jumped.'

31

The next evening, Conrad and Myra Rothstein gave a small cocktail party in their apartment. They lived on the 16th floor of a building west of Lincoln Center on 66th Street. The apartment had one bedroom, a kitchen, a bathroom, and a sitting room cum study. Books were everywhere: two deep on shelves, in dusty piles in corners, open and abandoned on book-supported rickety tables. The piano, at which Jerry and Conrad had worked, was laden and overwhelmed with manuscript paper and yellowing sheet music from the twenties and thirties. In the bathroom, heaps of old Times' colour supplements made a journey to the toilet a hazardous obstacle race.

'Rare editions I keep here, the store carries books for the trade. We get a few passers-by, not many, plus I inherited a lot of books from my great uncle.' Conrad, airily waving an almost empty glass of California sparkling white, was explaining the super-abundance of books to Lewis: 'He was a Talmudic scholar who, one day in the late thirties, took it into his head to travel to Montana and introduce the cowboys to the Torah, or the other way round . . .'

'That sounds interesting,' Lewis said politely, perusing a dusty volume of Hebrew philosophy.

'I based the main character in my revue, *Torah! Torah!* on him.'

'Oh, really,' Lewis said finding it hard to be civil to his host. 'What was the revue about?'

'Kinda Tale of Two Cultures. It's set in 1910. Rabbi Goldberg of Brooklyn treks to the North-West to introduce the cowboys to the mysteries of the cabbala. He's following in the oral tradition handed down from Moses to the Rabbis of the Mishnah and the Talmud.'

Lewis looked blankly at him. 'Does he succeed?' he asked. *This is the guy who they thought could do a better job than us!*

'See his problem is that he is dressed inappropriately for the terrain. Goldberg makes no concessions! The cowboys think he's a nut; they don't take his learned opinions seriously but they don't mistreat him. The show isn't about anti-semitism . . . far from it . . . fact is they've never heard of a Jew, let alone met one.'

'So what happens?'

'What d'you mean what happens?' An edge crept into Conrad's voice.

'What's the story?' Lewis said testily.

Conrad was equally testy: 'I just told you the story. East meets West. That's it. It's a revue. It's told through songs and vaudeville-like sequences.'

'Oh, I see,' Lewis said, relieved that Conrad's wife had joined them.

'I do hope George and Ross are going to come. I did so want to meet them,' she said.

Myra Rothstein was plain, petite and plump. At the moment, her already nervous disposition was aggravated both by the presence and the non-arrival of her husband's high-powered colleagues. For all was not well. Conrad had invited George, his wife and some of the production team to the soirée with their companions. It was 6.30 p.m. and neither George nor Ross had turned up. The invitations had clearly stated *Please arrive at 6.00 p.m. prompt*. Myra hadn't wanted that phrase included on the invitations but Conrad had insisted. 'Otherwise,' he had said, 'people might just turn up when they please. We must be precise.' Myra admired his fastidiousness. That punctilious attention to detail was why he was already a success. What had Frank Rich said: 'Rothstein's attention to the intricacies of Talmudic scholarship is a wonder to behold . . .'

'Help yourself to more appetisers, Mr Lewis,' Myra said.

'I talked to Ross this afternoon,' Conrad said. 'He said "See you at 6." I said "Be sure not to be late" . . .'

Myra checked her watch. 'Well, both of them are . . . Oh dear. And Woolly's getting hungry.'

'Have you put the canapés in the oven?' Her husband asked.

'An hour ago . . . I'd better check. Can you smell burning . . . ? Oh, dear!' She hurried to the kitchen.

Lewis wandered over towards Jerry who was sitting cross-legged on a cushion talking to Fly. Jerry seemed relaxed and at home here having moved in with the Rothsteins following the deterioration of his relationship with Debbie. This didn't please Myra but Con was happy and business is business . . . Fly, cradling his wine glass and nibbling pretzels, was perched on a chair, smiling benignly.

'Hi!' Lewis said to them. 'Had a good day? I was zonked after those two days in Westport.'

'Yeah,' Fly said. 'Tam's been in the studio working on routines with Molly and Stan. I been in the office preparing scripts to send out.'

'Right. Only three weeks to go before rehearsals. Excited? I am.'

'I'm an ole pro. Take more than that to get me excited. Now two naked women on a rug by a log fire an' we could be talking.'

Lewis laughed. 'Yeah, I could do with a bit of that myself.'

'Me too . . .' Jerry said.

'Oh yeah? New York making you horny?' Fly asked Lewis. 'Not getting enough company. I keep telling you I got friends I could interest you in . . .'

'We talkin' orgies here . . .?' Jerry got up and wandered off to refill his glass without waiting for an answer.

Lewis changed the subject: 'You hear anything more about that scene in Westport, Fly. You know . . . Ross and George?'

'No,' Fly replied abruptly, unwilling to be drawn. They munched pretzels and ran out of conversation.

'Say hello to Woolly,' Myra had joined them. She was clutching a small stuffed, cuddly, pink pig.

'Sorry?' Lewis blinked.

'This is Woolly and he's been getting restless in the bedroom since the movie finished. He loves 42nd Street, in the new colourised version. Black and white he hates but I don't know why. Go on say hi!'

'Hi,' said Fly.

'Hello,' Lewis, deeply embarrassed, said to the pig. He caught Jerry's eye across the room and smiled wanly.

Jerry ambled back: 'Hi Woolly! Fly, you know when Ross or George's gonna to get here?' He helped himself to a biscuit smothered in chopped liver. 'Coupla things I wanna discuss with them . . . rehearsal pianists, that kinda thing.'

'Maybe I should phone them,' Myra said. 'After all, if they're not coming, I could serve up. George's home number's on the contact sheet. George'n Dee might still be there . . .'

'I wouldn't do that,' Fly said.

'Oh?' Myra said.

Fly looked uncomfortable. 'Give 'em time an' they'll show.'

'Okay,' said Myra and wandered off with Woolly and a tray of canapés to Stan, Conrad and Gene Landau.

Jerry looked suspiciously at Fly. 'You hidin' somethin'?'

Fly wouldn't be drawn. Jerry tried again. The more Fly wouldn't be drawn, the more persistent Jerry became. Finally Fly gave in.

'Dee and Gibs have split,' he said.

'Jesus!' Jerry exclaimed.

'Wow!' Lewis added. 'When did this happen?'

'After lunch. I was in the office getting ready to mail scripts and call sheets for the first day of rehearsal when I hear terrible screaming coming from some woman in Gibs's office. I look at Betty who's on the other side of the office. She kinda shrugs and mouths *Dee* at me. I mouth what's going' on? to her. 'Better not to ask,' she says out loud. Then I hear Dee screaming, 'Don't you ever call me that word again you asshole! I'm 28 an' I need a little love an' affection. Is that too much to ask!' Then she must have dropped her voice because it went quiet an' we couldn't hear a thing. A few minutes later the door of the office crashes open an' Dee comes flying out in floods of tears. She stops by me an' says I gotta come right in to witness the lies that are being spoken about her. Well, of course, I wanna stay out of this. I'm standing there wishing I'm someplace else, when George comes out. He's yelling that they're not finished yet. She says sure we're finished, finished for ever, finished years ago. That kinda thing. Then in front of Betty, who's pretending not to listen, messing with a filing cabinet, Dee says to me, 'You know Ross better'n anyone.' I say sure I do. I'm proud of it. I bin his Assistant twenty-four years. 'THEN,' she shouts, 'YOU TELL THIS ASSHOLE THAT ROSS AN' ME GOT NOTHING GOING ON!' Well see, we know that's a barefaced lie . . .'

'Yeah,' Lewis said sadly.

'Mmmm,' Jerry muttered. 'Dee told Debbie. What happened then?'

'I said I dunno anything about anyone's personal life. I mean it was a fuck of a position to put me in, right? Then George says to me she's a whore and at that point Dee socks him in the jaw. She's a tough lady, right, an' he's an old man. He totters back an' somehow saves himself from tumbling on to the furniture but knocks over my pile of scripts ready for mailing. Betty rushes over to him and fusses awhile. Dee's shocked at what she's done but she's still mad as hell, naturally. She picks up her Bergdorf Goodman bag, she been doing shopping before she stopped by the office, an' she storms out. "Mebbe she's broken my jaw," George says to Betty, who examines it like she's some kinda nurse or doctor which I have to tell you she isn't. "Na," she says, "it's just bruised." I gotta tell you I'm shaking an' I'm thinking about the show . . .'

'There's a good Stage Manager for you,' Jerry said to Lewis. 'Always gets his priorities right.'

'I'm thinking we're going to have to recast Dee . . . An' with Ross ill . . .'

'Is Ross ill?' Jerry stopped eating. He was half way through a cold potato latke.

'I thought so,' Lewis said. 'What's the matter with him? He's changed incredibly.'

Fly wished he'd kept his mouth shut. Ross had sworn him to secrecy. If the illness became acute during rehearsal, he had said, he wanted Fly, working with Tam, to see the show through to the New York opening.

'Jesus . . .,' Jerry said under his breath. 'It's not . . .?'

'What? Not AIDS?' Lewis looked in horror at Ross's assistant.

'No, no, for Chrissakes!' Fly said angrily. 'If I tell you, you gotta promise to keep it quiet, okay?'

'Sure,' Lewis and Jerry said simultaneously.

'It's the big C.' It was a relief to share the burden of the news. Fly had kept his word until now and told no-one.

'Curable?' Lewis asked.

Fly shook his head. 'At least I don't think so . . . he's not having any treatment.'

'An' how's this gonna affect *us*! Christ!' Jerry said, the magnitude of the problem dawning.

'How's what going to affect us?' Conrad said, arriving with Tam Topp.

'Oh, my God, oh my God . . .' Jerry said under his breath.

Fly cast looks at Jerry and Lewis, silently pleading with them to keep their mouths shut.

'You had a good day, Tam?' Fly said cheerfully, trying to change the subject.

'We've been working on the Act Two "March of the Archbishops and Princes",' Tam said joining them on the floor. 'It's terrific. Con, you'll love it. It's gonna start with Harry Whitney, Old Galileo, on his deathbed exchanging jokes with Ziggy, y'know Young Galileo, about his election to the Academia. Then, as Ziggy sings "Long, Long Ago", Jerry, we go into the dream dance sequence as Old Galileo remembers his success amongst Rome's intelligentsia, okay. This afternoon with Molly, I put together this incredible stylised triumphal entry into Rome. Blow your mind! Galileo's gonna remember it like the Triumphal March from Verdi's *Aida* . . . You okay Jerry?'

Jerry was lying back on his cushion glassy-eyed, staring into space, oblivious.

'He's just a bit upset,' Lewis said hurriedly, eager to make a point. He turned to Tam Topp who was still flushed with the excitement of his afternoon's work. 'I don't understand. Verdi's 19th century. How can Galileo who died in 1642 possibly remember something in the style of a composer who lived two hundred and fifty years later? It doesn't make any sense.'

Tam looked at Lewis as if he was a creature from another planet. 'It's musical *comedy*! You wanna explain, Con?'

'Anachronism lives, okay!' Conrad said, fire in his eyes. 'Old Galileo's on his deathbed looking back at the mosaic of his life. He sees it like an impression . . . an impression of an existence . . . I mean that's exactly what happens with people dying, right?'

'Yeah, poor Ross . . .,' Jerry muttered, surfacing to catch the end of Conrad's speech.

'Poor Ross?' Tam was confused.

Myra bustled over, clutching Woolly and looking at her watch. 'Woolly's ever so worried! D'you think that Ross is going to make it . . .?'

'Who knows, Woolly,' Jerry said numbly. 'Who knows . . .'

32

'. . . an' to change the subject away from Dee for the moment, I'm party to a little information about Ross you might find interesting,' Gino Bernstein said, stretching out on his office lounger.

'Yeah,' said George, full of curiosity. He was deep in discussion with his confidant, friend and lawyer, in Gino's well-appointed second floor office. Gino was a Senior Partner in Bernstein, Kraus and Dubitsky on 57th Street, almost next door to the Russian Tea Room.

'Did you happen to know that Ross is a very sick man, George?'

'Sick? How d'you mean sick?'

'Like very, very sick.'

'Like dying sick?'

'So I'm told.'

George leant back in his chair. 'When d'you hear this?'

'Today. Lunchtime. I was gonna call you.'

'Who told you this?'

'Can't tell you George. You know that.' People trusted Gino, shared secrets with him. Unburdening oneself to Gino made you somehow feel better . . . cleansed. It was like receiving absolution.

'You sure . . .?'

'C'mon, George. Trust me.'

George, showing no emotion, digested the information. There was a lot to consider. 'How long's he got?'

'Long enough they say to do your show.'

'What's that mean? We open on Broadway in four months. What happens if it gets delayed . . .? You saying he might die on me?'

Gino shrugged. 'What can I tell you? As your lawyer and your friend, I'd suggest you start looking fast for another director.'

'You think it could be quicker than four months?'

'For Chrissakes, George, I'm not God!'

George fell silent, thinking deeply.

209

Gino watched him for a moment. 'Didn't you have an appointment, George? It's 7 o'clock . . .'

'Jus' drinks at Conrad's . . .' George said. 'I gotta tell you the truth about something, Gino. I don't know why I kept it from you all these years . . .'

Gino sat up a little and looked interested. George, he saw, was choosing his words carefully.

'You remember Dee an' I went to Tijuana to get married those years ago . . .'

'Yeah, sure . . .'

'Yeah well I never told you what happened did I?'

'No, George, I don't believe you did . . . ,' Gino said, wondering what was coming.

'We never got *married* . . . '

Gino sat up in his chair in amazement. 'What! You mean you and Dee aren't married . . . ? Jesus Christ, George!'

'Yeah, you got it. See no-one knew, Gino. I didn't tell you or anyone – not even *Dee* . . .'

'I'm sorry, George. You're gonna have to repeat this. I'm not grasping what you're saying . . . Dee doesn't know you an' she are divorced?'

George smiled wryly. 'Not exactly *divorced*, more like it never happened. See the day after we got married I paid a little money to the guy who'd married us . . . y'know the score . . . he jus' pretended it never happened . . . erased the record . . . took back the papers . . . there were no problems . . . I couldn't tell Dee. Would that have been *nice*?'

'You can do *that* in Mexico? I had no idea . . .'

'With enough dough you can do *anything* in Mexico, Gino.'

'Well you sure do continue to surprise me, George. It may be kinda stupid to ask but . . . why would you do something like that?'

'You're a smart man, Gino. Why d'you think? What were we discussing jus' five minutes ago . . .? You asked me if I wanted to divorce Dee an' I said no. I don't *need* to divorce her as we're not married. Christ, Gino, you think I was born yesterday. I *covered* my ass, my position . . . That bitch isn't gonna get a dime outa me . . . she can go screw herself.'

'What you gonna do about Ross, George?'

'I'll figure something out. Something good.'

Dee had crashed blindly out through the glass doors into Times

Square crowded with mid-afternoon strollers. Clutching her shopping bag firmly to her, she had run across the road and started up Broadway without any sense of what to do. When the heat and breathlessness finally reduced her to a walk, her brain started to function again. *I hit him! Jesus, I hit him.* She knew it was the end, there could be no going back. The bridges had been burned.

She stopped at the 53rd Street intersection and waited to cross the road. *Must call Ross.* All the phone booths next to her were occupied. *Yeah, but what would I say to him? Guy's about to start a show, all he needs is me right now.* The lights changed and she walked on with the crowd. Someone jostled her, a cab forced its way amongst them, horns blared, pneumatic drills hammered the ground. *Hiya Ross! I've split from George, yeah we bust up an' I socked him on the jaw. Can I move in with you? How's Ellen, Ellen, Ellen, Ellen . . .?* Ellen's name reverberated away like a sound effect. The conversation didn't go well in her head. *Okay, I gotta get a lawyer to handle the divorce, no good asking Gino, he's George's, maybe Ross has someone. Hiya Ross! George an' me are gonna getta divorce, could you suggest someone to represent me on this one?* More horns angrily drumming in a crazy rhythm. A roller skater's lying on his side in the gutter on 57th, motionless, surrounded by a growing crowd. Someone's holding his head . . . the traffic's backed up, a cop car and an ambulance are fighting to get through. Dee skirts the incident avoiding looking at the injured man. Her mind is on a call to Debbie. *Some scuzzbag sent George a note about me an' Ross, Debs. Can I stay with you till I get somewhere? I'm already packed . . .* Dee realised with a shock that she had prepared herself for this. She had been on a three-week shopping spree and had unpacked nothing. *D'you think I should pull out of the show, Deb? Or say, hell no! I won my part fairly and squarely. I wanna do the show, Deb. I love that part. An' I'm sorry you an' Jerry have split . . . you're still my best friend . . .*

The security guard outside the Dakota gave her a friendly wave as she passed through the courtyard towards the lobby. 'Afternoon, Mrs Gibson,' the doormen shouted cheerfully as if nothing wrong existed in the world. As the elevator ascended towards her floor, Dee, reviewing her 28 years, perceived her life structured in cycles. Childhood, puberty, college, marriage to George. Now the cycles were changing again. Life with George had been full of excitement, an adventure. She regretted nothing, except, maybe that it had to end this way. The elevator sped upwards. *I don't need much. The settlement should be fair – I'll insist on that. This split is my fault.* She laughed out loud. *Poor George! The look on his face after I belted him!* The elevator stopped. Dee walked along the shadowy corridor towards her door, fishing for the key in her purse.

211

She tripped over a shoe box first. Then she saw the pile of half-opened suitcases. Dresses, shirts, underwear, trousers spilt out on to the floor. The contents of drawers had been unceremoniously tipped out, her most personal belongings including letters from her father, her grandmother's jewelry, medicines, memorabilia from her childhood lay scattered outside the door to her apartment. At first she thought there must be some mistake – someone had broken in and ransacked the place.

She tried her key in the lock, it wouldn't fit. *Is this the right apartment?* Then she noticed that the old, yellowing familiar lock had been replaced by one that was new and gleaming.

Utterly humiliated, Dee sat down on the floor opposite her belongings. *Whore!* he had called her. *Tramp!* Now she was glad she'd socked him, only regretting she couldn't hit harder. *I hope I broke your jaw, fuckhead! Okay, George. I get it. But I'm gonna squeeze you for every nickel an' dime!*

33

'Excuse me butting in Sir Harry but we're almost all here, Ross.'
Fly had appeared at the production table clutching a contact sheet
with names ticked off. The production table was set up in front of
50 chairs that Fly and his team had gathered for the cast, general
managers, producers, casting directors, and press agents. 'Wanna
start? Only Dee's missing. She is coming right?'

'Sure she is.'

'Just that George's gettin' nervous.'

Ross said 'I'll start when I'm ready. Give her a coupla more
minutes.'

Lewis, standing behind Ross, notebook in hand, was trying to
suppress the surge of adrenalin that was making his heart pound.
All the work, all the effort and finally they had made it to the first
rehearsal! Although the call was for 10.00 a.m., by 9.45 a.m. the
large room on the 4th floor at 890 Broadway was already filling
up. No-one wanted to be late for the first day of rehearsals. The
actors, mingling with the production team enjoyed the plentiful
supplies of bagels, lox, cream-cheese and coffee supplied by
Gibson's Deli Delite at cost price.

Sir Harold Whitney had made a loud and grand entrance 10
minutes earlier. Dressed to resemble an English squire, complete
with bow tie, checked shirt and Aquascutum jacket, he had trapped
Ross and Tam at the production table and was recounting a tale.
Lewis watching the room fill up, half listened: '. . . My heart was
thumping: everything seemed on the move; the TV, the lamps
even *me* on my bed! I grabbed my watch which was rolling around
the bedside table. 4.10 a.m. Of course, old son, it was an LA
quake. I had experienced one before. Suddenly it stopped. Dead
quiet! I thought I'd wander up to the roof to get some air and have
a gander at any damage to the city. Well, my dear fellow, I don't
know if you're familiar with the roof of the Hotel Le Ciel on La
Cienega, but it's got a sports complex on it. You know, pool,

jacuzzi, tennis court . . . that kind of thing. I opened the door from the stairwell and was presented with a bacchanalian *vision*. For there was Phillipe Rolande, you know, the very fastidious French actor also in *Sidewinder 2,* the movie I was making, in the steaming jacuzzi, drunk as a lord, two bottles of champagne on the side, naked as nature intended, frolicking with an equally naked voluptuous make-up girl called Monica something. They were too busy to notice me so I cautiously retreated and took the elevator to the ground floor where I passed three security guys watching TV. "Any news," I asked, "about the quake?" "No," they replied, "we're watching something much bouncier." I looked and saw that they were tuned in to the security camera focused on the rooftop jacuzzi. Phillipe and Monica, now out of the pool, in blissful ignorance of the security camera, were humping away in full close-up! Then one of the security guys, his eyes riveted to the spectacle, said: "Sure looks like the earth's moving for someone." ' Harold Whitney's huge laugh filled the room. 'Next day on the set, I told Phillipe *and* the crew. Told them I hadn't seen any *faces!* But he knew I knew alright! Ho ho, ho ho . . .'

Charlie Brodsky came and took Tam away.

'I doubt you'll have such opportunities for voyeurism on this show, Harold,' Ross said having hardly listened to a word. His mind was preoccupied with the reading: how the show would sound, whether it would hang together . . . Dee's lovemaking.

'Can't pretend I'm not nervous, Ross.' Harold, suddenly serious, paused, lowered his voice and added confidentially, 'and the fact is . . . I've been wanting to tell you . . . couldn't really tell Stan or Jerry . . . I'm having some trouble with my voice. Saw my doctor in London a fortnight ago. He said I might be getting nodes. Nothing serious, and they should probably clear up soonish . . . So I'm not going to give it my all today. Ça va? Ah, there's Tara . . . Tara darling . . .'

He disappeared into the throng leaving, Lewis thought, a worried looking Ross.

'. . . An', Mr Gibson, ticket sales in Washington are going okay?' On the other side of the room, George Gibson and Doris Stein were surrounded by some members of the chorus, eager to be friendly.

'Yeah. Doris and I are real pleased. The National doesn't have a subscription like the Kennedy Center . . .'

'Weren't we at one time going to play the Center, Mr Gibson?' a singer asked.

'One time . . .,' George said distractedly, watching Ross across the room now talking to Ziggy Bronowsky and Norman Naff.

Where's Dee and why wasn't that asshole getting started? Then he noticed Dee slide unobtrusively into the room. Ross noticed her too. Her eyes sought him out. He smiled. She winked. George watched.

Florence, already seated next to Lewis in the back row, also witnessed that moment. Despite the fact she had just one line and was to be a part of only three chorus numbers, Florence was as thrilled as anyone to be under starter's orders. Fully reconciled to the status quo, she had decided to join in and enjoy.

Lewis, absorbed in jotting down his impressions of the gathering, was in fine fettle. The mail, that morning, had brought a letter from the Independent in London warmly accepting his tee-shirt article and requesting more. *Lewis wins Pulitzer!* His imagination had gone into overdrive as he read it again and again. Working now on his next award-winning piece, he had written the title: 'First Steps'. Then underneath: 'There's a palpable sense of excitement and comradeship. At the piano. Jerry and Stan are discreetly preparing the score, going over points, quietly playing difficult passages. Tam and Molly lean against the piano, chatting to three singers. Anthony Bauer, the orchestrator, only half listening, is gazing at a lissome dancer exercising at the bar, watching herself in the mirror . . .' God, she *is* sexy, Lewis thought, sucking his pencil.

Florence interrupted the thought. 'It's getting better an' better. See how George is watching *them*. That look in his eyes! Oh boy, the *hate!*'

'Take your seats, ladies and gentlemen, please,' Fly and Charlie Brodsky shouted together.

'Hiya Doris!' Florence shouted as the lady producer hunted for a seat. 'You gonna join us on the back row?'

'Isn't this exciting,' Doris said as she sat next to them.

'Where's Paul?' Lewis asked politely.

'France. I've just flown in for two days. Since Roget went I . . . I . . .' Doris sniffed a little. 'I've told George that he can't count on me being round much . . .'

Florence was alarmed. 'But you're our protector, Doris . . .'

Ross began the rehearsal. 'Hi everybody!'

'Hi!' a number of eager chorus members shouted back spontaneously. General laughter relieved tension.

'Let's start. We're going to introduce ourselves. I'm Ross Boardman, Director. Fly . . .'

Fifty-four people nervously introduced themselves before Ross set the agenda: 'In a moment you're going to hear the whole show. Read your scenes, sing along with Stan and Jerry if you can. After lunch I'll make some comments about style and rehearsal techniques. Chubby will give us a conducted tour through Karl-Heinz's magical sets and we'll look at some costume drawings. Before you leave for the day, wardrobe has asked you check they have your measurements. Gene Landau wants to say a few words.'

Landau stood up and took off his rimless glasses. 'Welcome to the show. I'm going to distribute lists of Washington addresses so you can be thinking about where you wanna stay. Heeere's George!'

'Doris Stein and I are mighty proud of this show,' George began. 'Jerry's a genius and Conrad ain't bad neither. Believe me these guys are the dream ticket and you're gonna be hearing a lot more from these two in the future. We're glad to have Franz-Joseph from Germany designing and who could be in better hands than having Stan as MD. You all gotta work hard and we'll go gangbusters in Washington then knock 'em dead here in New York.'

'He didn't mention Ross,' Florence whispered to Lewis as George sat down. 'Wow!'

The read-through started well, Lewis thought. Conrad charmingly laughed at his own jokes and rubbed his hands with glee at unexpected treasures. Each of Jerry's songs were received with whoops and cheers. But the undisputed star of the morning was Ziggy Bronowsky. Not only a formidable singer, he brought to Young Galileo zest and wit, mining every laugh. Ross was clearly delighted because Ziggy had, along with a classic handsomeness, a strong chin, twinkling blue eyes, a fresh complexion – Star Quality. He was irresistible.

Florence fancies Ziggy! Three-quarters of the way through the first act Lewis became aware that Florence, who had given her one line forty-five minutes ago, was gazing rapturously at Ziggy. At first he thought nothing of it. But then, as minutes ticked by, songs came and went, jokes enjoyed then forgotten, and Florence was still locked on to Ziggy, he became increasingly disturbed. Lewis had last seen that particular look in her eyes the night that Bob Berol, back from Vermont, first turned up at the apartment. She was, he decided, on heat.

Sir Harry, too, watched jealously as Ziggy came to dominate the proceedings. Not to be outdone, from the start of the second act, he decided to try his luck with a song or two. The result was an embarrassment. His pitch and intonation were bad and the vocal quality unpleasant. There were some worried shufflings amongst the cast. Harry was important to them. No good Harry; no good show. Bleak prospects.

Ross, listening to Harry's attempt at song, realised they could soon be on the hunt for a new lead. He sighed and looked at his watch on the table. 12.45 p.m. *Christ!* They had started reading the second act at 11.45 a.m. and one hour later they were only a little over half way through. The second act was, and felt, long. Drastic cutting was needed. Ross looked at Dee seated among her fellow actors, thoughtfully sucking a finger, her face buried in the script. His mind wandered away from the room, the reading, the singing, away to the events of yesterday, Sunday, trauma. *After rehearsal I'm going to have to tell Dee . . .*

The company went wild for Tara's ballad, 'Play for Love'. Harry and Ziggy picked up their cue and embarked on the next scene. Tara glanced at Ross for approval but Ross was whispering to Tam.

'It's not going to work.'

'What isn't?' Tam whispered back.

' "Play for Love" . . . Despite the company's reaction, it's extraneous. It holds up the second act and doesn't advance the plot. It's going to have to go. We'll talk about it later.'

Tam nodded, not surprised.

'What's that you're saying?' Conrad, on the other side of Ross, had been trying to hear the conversation.

'Nothing,' Ross said. 'Music problem . . .'

'Okay,' Conrad said, relieved.

Thirty-five minutes later they finished. The company applauded vigorously, but knew there were problems. 'Obviously we've gotta do some cutting in the second act,' Ross announced. 'That read at almost one hour 45 minutes. It's 30 minutes too long. Something's gotta go. Have lunch.'

'Back in an hour please, ladies and gentlemen,' Charlie shouted. With the tension released everyone was talking at once.

'Wha'd'you think, George?' Jerry had immediately found the producer. At the same moment Doris, Florence and Lewis arrived.

'Great! Great! Great!' George said, beaming.

Doris lowered her voice. 'What about Harry's voice?' she asked Jerry. 'Don't you think it's a bit . . . rough?'

'Nah,' George answered for him. 'First day nerves, that's all. He sang just fine round the piano few weeks ago. Harry's a *genius!* You ever see that wolf play he did . . . How many nominations he get for that? Three, four? The boys wouldn't have hired him if they'd been worried.'

'Wasn't Ziggy wonderful!' Florence raptured.

'And Tara.' Lewis's adrenalin level was still high. 'Didn't you think that "Play for Love" was superb!'

George looked at the composer with tears welling. 'I gotta tell you Jerry, that *song!* I consider that *our* song, right? It's the most beautiful song you ever wrote . . . I ever heard . . .'

They all nodded enthusiastically.

Ross had closed his eyes, his energy vanished. There were too many problems to solve. *Just a five-minute sleep, and I'll be okay.*

'What d'you think, Ross? I mean apart from cuts in Act Two.'

Ross opened his eyes. Jerry had arrived wanting more praise.

Before he could reply, Stan, who had returned to the desk with his score, said: 'I think we gotta talk fast, Ross.'

'About what?' Jerry was immediately worried.

'You want me, Stan?' Conrad asked.

'Yeah. We can talk in the production office.'

Charlie was checking through his props list at the desk in the small office adjoining the main rehearsal room. 'Gimme a couple of minutes would you, Charlie,' Ross said.

'Can we get you guys some lunch?' Charlie asked. The boys ordered sandwiches and coffee. 'Don't forget we gotta do a schedule for the day after tomorrow, Ross.' Charlie said as he left.

Ross knew what was on Stan's mind. 'Harry, right?'

'Right.'

Jerry concurred. 'Sure's hell gone downhill since we first saw him. Last week when Stan and I worked with him he was real edgy and nervous, y'know. Said he had a cold comin' on.'

'Yeah. I put it down to nerves. And maybe that's what it is,' Stan said. 'But I gotta tell you, Ross, he's a big risk.'

'He told me earlier that it could be nodes.'

'Christ, Ross,' Stan exclaimed. 'Get him checked out immediately.'

'Will somebody please tell me why you ever cast this guy,' Conrad asked. 'I didn't like his reading either.'

Ross sighed. *Dee sleeping, Dee laughing, Dee holding him in her arms, Dee . . .*

'Because when we auditioned him,' Stan said, 'this was a different show. We had another writer . . .'

'I like the way he *reads* . . .,' Ross said, defending his choice.

'Yeah,' Jerry said. 'I remember you saying after his audition it was remarkable how someone with no brains could persuade you that he was an intellectual . . .'

'Who we talking about here?' Norman Naff asked from the door. 'Glad I caught you fellas. Just wanted to make sure you're leaving space in the schedule for press interviews . . .'

'We haven't fixed the schedule yet,' Ross said.

'See, I'm getting a lot of interest in Ziggy and Tara. Got a fashion thing going with the Sunday Magazine Section on both of them.

I'm going to need a few hours on that, Ross. I mean you're going to have to let them off rehearsals. But I gotta tell you I'm getting *most* feedback on Harry. The press are going crazy! They love him. I already got the Times, Mel's going to do an in-depth feature. Sixty Minutes may do an item and . . .,' he lowered his voice, 'confidentially, I got great hopes that we gotta chance with both Carson *and* Letterman. Wouldn't that be something!'

Stan was puzzled. 'Me, I don't see it. What do they like?'

'He's a swell raconteur, Stan,' Naff said and scratched at a blackhead on his balding pate. 'You not heard his stories. He's a wild guy.'

'Well you could have fooled me,' Stan said.

'Me too,' Jerry had been rummaging through the box of sandwiches Charlie had delivered trying to find his order. 'Shit! No pickles and the beef ain't rare enough.'

'Have mine,' Stan said.

'Enjoy your lunch!' Norman was ready to go. 'By the way, guys, well done. George said he loved the reading. Especially Harry and Zig! We're gonna have a hiiit!' And he was gone.

'Wild,' Jerry said, biting into Stan's pickle.

34

'Phone call for you, Ross,' Charlie whispered in his ear. 'And don't forget we have to do that schedule.'

It was mid-afternoon and everyone was growing sleepy. Karl-Heinz's set, described in hushed tones by Chubby, had impressed everyone and the designers with Ross were now going through the costume drawings with each member of the cast. Sir Harry was shown sketches for his three costumes first and found fault everywhere. They were too dark, too light, too heavy, too smart, too old, too this and too that. Karl-Heinz regarded him with distaste, leaving Chubby and Ross to show extreme patience, offering compromise where they could, insisting when necessary.

Thus Ross was not unhappy to be summoned to the phone. Not unhappy until he found out who was on the line. Then he was very unhappy indeed.

'Mr Boardman?'

'Yeah.'

'Tony Knight, on the Post newsdesk, Mr Boardman. I wanna ask you a few questions to confirm a story we're gonna run tomorrow . . .'

Ross knew all about Tony Knight.

'Interviews have to be arranged through Norman Naff's office, Mr Knight.'

'Gee, I'm sorry but I got so little time. Thing is, Mr Boardman, we're running a story says you're having an affair with Producer George Gibson's wife, who's also acting in your show. I'd like to know whether you're going to confirm or deny the story.'

Jesus! How'd they get on to this?

'You there, Mr Boardman?'

Ross was there. His mind raced through options but anything he said, he knew, would be misinterpreted.

'Aw, come on Ross. Get off your high horse. Keeping shtum isn't going to do you any good.'

Fuck you.

'Have you left Ellen Frazier, the woman you live with? Are you and Mrs Gibson going to shack up together?'

Piece of shit.

'How's all this affected your relationship with Gibson . . . If you don't mind me saying so, you seem to make a habit of this kinda thing . . .'

'Go fuck yourself,' Ross said quietly and hung up. Immediately he dialled Naff's number.

A secretary answered who didn't know who he was. Then she said Naff was out. 'Maybe Mr Gibson's office knows. Gee I'm sorry.' Ross didn't believe a word.

Jerry breezily entered the production office and found Ross sitting at the desk lost in thought, doodling on a pad. 'Hey, Big Guy, what's up?' he said.

Ross needed to talk to someone and why not to Jerry. If the press knew, Jerry knew. Nevertheless it came as a shock that Jerry had clearly known for some time.

'Sure, I know about you an' Dee,' he said. 'See that's why Debbie an' me split, okay?'

Ross looked puzzled.

'Debbie told me she sent that anonymous letter to George. She was wild, Ross. Crazy. I never saw her like that before. She hated me, you, Dee, George, everyone connected with this show thing. All because Dee got the part an' she didn't. I couldn't take the hassle any more an' left.'

He paused to check out the reaction. 'Sounds like a storyboard for a soap, right, but it's got out of hand. We've been working on this for nearly two years Ross, we can't fuck up now. Dee's problem with George is their affair, right? But I'm asking you, for all our sakes, Ross, do stop going with Dee. Christ, Ross, why're you shitting on your own doorstep? I mean that's why George is mad as hell. An' I can't say I blame him . . .'

Jerry left a moment for Ross to say something, anything. But he didn't. He sat at the desk fiddling with his pencil, not looking at Jerry. Jerry had no choice but to go on.

'An' . . . An' one more thing, man, I gotta tell you a few of us know about your illness an' . . . an' we're . . . I'm really sorry. If there's anything any of us can do, you know . . .'

They know everything!

'Stay out of it, Jerry!' Ross finally said sharply, slamming the pencil on to the desk. He had listened with growing rage as it became clear his private life was the talk of Broadway. 'How I manage my affairs is my business, you understand. You just concentrate on the show.' He kicked back the chair and stood up to leave. 'We've got our time cut out to make this show work because the show's flawed, Jerry. The reading exposed the problems with the second act. To cure second act problems you have to go back to the first act. That adds up to a lot of work. Save your energy for that!'

'Okay an' the same to you.' Jerry didn't like being treated as a kid. 'Save your energies for the show. I know Dee an' she'll kill you.'

'Yup,' said Ross, a shadow of a smile appearing on his face. 'It's going to be a beautiful way to go.'

As soon as he re-entered the rehearsal room he was accosted by John Lewis. 'Dee's looking for you, Ross. Have you seen Charlie? I want to ask him about accommodation in Washington. You okay? You're looking a bit pale.'

'I'm fine.' A conversation with the Englishman was not what he needed. He made a move to pass on.

'Oh, Ross,' Lewis said, putting out his hand to stop him. 'I just wanted to say how terribly sorry I was to hear about your . . . your . . . er . . . you know.'

'My what?' Ross said sharply.

'You know . . . your . . . well . . . illness. If there's anything I can . . .'

'I'll let you know,' Ross interrupted sharply.

'About that schedule, Ross . . .?' Charlie again.

'For Chrissake!' Ross shouted. 'Will you all leave me alone!'

Most of the actors had left for the day, the production team had gone about their business elsewhere and there were only a few chorus members left viewing costume designs. His outburst was not witnessed by many. Charlie looked at Lewis and raised his eyes to heaven. 'Strain,' Charlie whispered. 'Wanna have a bet who else cracks?'

'No, thank you,' Lewis replied politely.

Dee was reviewing a song with Stan at the piano in the far corner of the room. Her singing had drowned Ross's cry. Ross waited for a suitable moment to interrupt.

35

They shared a bottle of Sancerre at a round table in a quiet bar round the corner on 20th Street next to a Korean grocers.

'I haven't spoken to you for five days, Ross. I've missed you.' She reached for him and he took her hand. 'A lot's happened.'

'You're not kidding,' Ross said and allowed himself to smile.

'To you too?'

He nodded.

'You start . . .'

'No you.'

'Okay,' she said brightly. 'Well guess what I heard today from Joe Nunzio . . .?'

'George's going to give you the house in California and half of everything . . .'

Dee laughed. 'Got it in one . . . Actually no. He's not going to give me a cent. I don't know why I'm laughing.'

'And Joe thought that fair?'

'Yup. See it turns out that . . . My God you gotta hand it to him . . . We were never married. Or rather we were . . . then we weren't.'

Ross found the Tijuana story barely credible. 'You sure about that Dee? It's not just another of George's slick moves?'

Dee shrugged and refilled her glass. 'Who knows? Could be the whole wedding was a sham in the first place. I told you, didn't I, it was the only way George could get me in the sack. Then I kinda stuck, he couldn't get rid of me. Plain fact is, Joe says I'm not married. How'd you like that! God, those wasted years.'

'That's an extraordinary story, Deedee . . .'

'Deedee. That's what he called me. I'd rather you didn't.'

'Okay. You're taking it well . . .'

'Yeah I am, aren't I?' Dee laughed again. 'Tell you the truth, I'm relieved it's over. I need never have anything more to do with him. I guess that's why I can laugh. I'm free an' I feel young again.'

She pressed her wine glass to her forehead. The coolness was soothing. 'How 'bout you? What's the scoop? Notice we haven't talked about the show . . .'

'I've left Ellen,' Ross said simply.

'My God! Did she find out about us?'

'I told her. I'm amazed she didn't know. Everyone else does.'

Dee laughed. 'Are you surprised? Of course they do. This is Broadway.'

'I guess I forgot.'

'Poor Ellen. I feel sorry for her.' But she didn't look sorry. 'When did it happen?'

'Yesterday. Sunday. On the ferry back from Fire Island. We'd been staying with friends . . .'

Ross and Ellen sat on the crowded 6.10 p.m. boat from Ocean Beach to Bayshore waiting for its departure. Even on the upper deck the air was hot and humid, unusual for late September. Ellen read her way through the Sunday Times. Ross stared at the last remaining passengers scurrying along the quayside, heading for the boat.

They were returning to Manhattan after spending the weekend at the beachside house of their close friends, Elaine and Joe Blech. Ellen had thought Fire Island the perfect antidote to the anxiety that immediately preceded the start of rehearsals. The Blechs were management consultants and the absence of showbusiness gossip was refreshing. It was, said Ellen, the real world.

But Ross seemed unable to relax. On Sunday, waking at 7.00 a.m., she found that he was already up and gone. Opening the curtains, through the early morning mist, she saw him sitting on a sand dune, wrapped in a blanket staring at the sea. In the kitchen thirty minutes later, drinking tea alone with Elaine, she shared her worries. 'The pills keep the pain away. Two days ago he forgot to take them. He was very sick in the evening . . .' Ellen had confided in their friends and sworn them to secrecy.

'You can't help but see it,' Elaine said. 'I don't just mean physically. He seems so remote.'

'D'you find that?' Ellen lightly touched her friend's arm. 'Sometimes I think it's me. Something I've done. We have arguments over nothing.'

'It's just coming to terms. An attempt to find a strategy for dying.'

'It's a lonely business.'

224

'For both of you.'

Ross hadn't seen the man at first, certainly hadn't seen him fall, but he knew he was dead. Close to the ferry, on a nearby jetty, the man was stretched out on the weathered planking, illuminated almost theatrically by an intense white light from the setting sun. He wore a light cream suit, Armani, Ross guessed, under which was a silk shirt, open at the neck. His longish, greying hair was swept back and a neat moustache gave the impression of a broker or banker, certainly a man of substance. Ross guessed his age at between 35 and 40.

A woman breaking into a run heading towards the prostrate man caught Ross's eye. As she came closer Ross saw that her mouth was wide open. In terror? The ferry was ready to depart and the woman's screams were drowned by the roar of the engines. The boat moved away and Ross was left with an image, a tableau: the victim, the woman cradling the man's head in her arms, two others on their knees offering help, and several onlookers.

'Did you see that?' Ross turned to Ellen.

'No, what?' She was absorbed in a long article about the Art Market.

'Someone just died on the quayside.'

'Mmm, probably, darling,' Ellen muttered, struggling with the newspaper in the wind.

The boat sped towards the mainland. Ross closed his eyes and felt the warm wind caress his face. The randomness of the death on the quayside had shocked him. At least his own end, although close at hand, was a finite time away. He wasn't there yet, lying on that quayside, observed by 300 people on a boat. No, he had six months, maybe more. *Time, time, time.* And not to be wasted. Nothing must be put off, nothing must be left undone. There must be no regrets.

'I have to talk to you, Ellen. Please put your paper down.'

'I've nearly finished this . . .'

But he sharply cut her off. 'Please! We have to talk. This isn't easy . . .'

Ross knew he would never forget the look on Ellen's face. After he finished telling her it was over she said nothing. She didn't cry. She just looked enormously . . . *disappointed.*

They travelled back from Bayshore to Manhattan in a crowded taxibus. Neither of them spoke during the two-hour journey. But walking back along 73rd Street, Ellen said: 'You keep the apartment . . . well it's yours anyway, isn't it? I'll pack some things right away . . . stay with Nancy. I'll have the rest picked up as soon as possible.'

'You don't have to do it tonight for God's sake . . .' Back in city reality, Ross felt dreadful. Her coldness distressed him. *What did I expect! She'd thank me?*

'It'll be better this way,' she said.

Ross, sitting like a granite statue, immobile on the sofa in their main room, watched as she packed. He felt no pity now, no remorse, not even sadness for Ellen. On the ferry he had wiped away the last 15 years and was ready to move on to the final phase of his life. The past, unchained, was floating away behind.

'However, what is more disturbing is that the Post has got the story,' Ross was saying. 'I've just had a call from that asshole Tony Knight . . .'

'Shit!' Dee said. 'Well that's got to have come from Norman an' Norman would never do that without George okay-ing it.'

'That's incredible. Surely even George wouldn't want this in the press . . .'

'Don't you believe it. He would shit on his own mother to sell a show *an'* get even with you at the same time.'

'Even with me?'

'This is the real war, Ross. Up to now it's been just skirmishes. It'll be a war of attrition fought cunningly so you'll never be sure the battle is on. But it is. He hates the power you have, Ross. He wants it all for himself.'

'Okay,' Ross smiled. 'I'll take him on at his own game. He wants a fight I'll give him a fight. Trade punch for punch. He won't have it all his own way.'

'But you got me now, Ross. We can fight together.' She squeezed his hand. 'I love you.'

'I love you too,' he said meaning it.

'We're going to treasure every minute . . .'

'I'm going to be a great burden . . .'

A man at the bar glanced their way. Dee smiled at him. Then, transferring her hand to under the table, she said: 'I can put up with you if you can put up with me.'

As she gently stroked the inside of his thigh, her hand moving higher and higher, Ross finally understood that Dee supplied what he craved – the life force. It made facing death almost bearable.

36

Doris took Florence and Lewis for an early supper at 'Mr Lee's'. Florence was full of Ziggy. 'I mean he's not just Mr Hunk he's gotta voice to die for. And it was all so effortless, so unphony. I mean I closed my eyes and he kinda wafted over me, like . . . like a silken feeling.'

'Frankly, I don't think he's as good as you're making out. I thought he lacked a lot of passion . . .' For the past two hours Florence had talked of nothing but Ziggy, and Lewis was heartily sick of it.

'You've gotta be joking!' Florence gasped. 'No passion! Why that's what he had in zillions. When he and Tara played that love scene I was practically orgasmic . . .'

'Talking of passion,' Lewis turned his attention to Doris who was toying with a dish of crispy beef with scallions, 'what do you think about this business between Ross and Dee?'

'I try not to think about it at all,' Doris said. 'It's too upsetting. Poor George.'

'Well I'm glad it's out in the open,' Florence said. 'I guess I was one of the first to know about it and, confidentially, I don't think Bobby would have gotten to write what he did but for the fact that I knew.'

Doris seemed surprised. 'You knew? How'd you know, Florence.'

'That night we were all in Ross's apartment. I found Dee's earrings and her watch,' she said proudly.

'You didn't have to be Sherlock Holmes to work that out.' Lewis found himself unable to be civil to Florence at the moment. Everything she did irritated him.

'You knew and you didn't tell me,' Doris said, quite distressed. *Good*, Lewis thought, *Doris is upset with her too.*

'It's Doris Stein, isn't it?' A familiar, cultured English voice declared from behind Lewis's chair. *Oh my God!* Lewis didn't need to turn around to recognise the supercilious tones of Clive North.

Doris became European. 'Why, Clive chéri! How delightful to see you. Let me introduce John Lewis, a fellow countryman of yours . . .'

Clive beamed. 'Well, hi, old fruit! We meet again.'

'How delightful!' Doris repeated. 'You know each other.'

'We're in the same business, that's all,' Lewis replied ungraciously averting his eyes.

Doris chose to ignore that. 'And Florence Hackstuber. A dear friend . . . most of the time. At least when she's honest with me.'

Florence looked peeved.

'Having a good time, Lewis? I read your little piece today on the plane. Passably good.'

Lewis brightened up appreciably. 'I didn't know it was today. Glad you like it.'

'It seemed over-edited. Did the sub cut a lot?'

'I don't know . . . I – I haven't seen . . .' Lewis couldn't control his stutter.

'What are you doing here, Clive?' Doris asked.

'A couple of articles on the present Broadway season.'

What! Christ and shit! Lewis was ready to kill.

'Did you like my pieces on Impressionist Modern Art in Japan?'

I wouldn't read them if you paid me.

'They were reprinted in the New York Times. Rumour's about that they want to give me a Pulitzer.'

Over my dead body. Or yours . . . anyway, I thought you had to be American to win the Pulitzer?

'How's the show going, Doris? I heard some funny stories as soon as I touched down.'

'Like what?' asked Doris.

'Oh, you know, usual malicious stuff. Gibson separated from his wife who's run off with the director. Even heard that Boardman's suffering from a terminal cancer. Must say I had to laugh. It all sounded too ludicrous, too ridiculous. Kind of story I give bad reviews to back home. Ah, here's my date. Hello darling . . .mmmm.' A miniskirted backside was thrust into Lewis's face as its owner gave Clive North a wet kiss hello. 'Julia Roberts, Doris Stein. Doris Stein, Julia Roberts. Doris is producing *Galileo* with Harry Whitney on Broadway . . . I'm doing a piece on him next week. Wonderful actor.'

What! Norman promised me exclusivity. What's going on?

'Come darling, our table is over there I think . . . Ah Mr Lee . . .!' And, with a flourish, Clive North and his date swept round a decorated column and disappeared.

'Wow,' Florence said. 'He's carrying energy. And isn't she beautiful . . .'

'He's not one of my favourite people,' Lewis said bitterly.

'Oh I don't think he means any harm,' Doris said.

'You're joking!' Lewis exclaimed unable to let that pass. 'He's one of the most dangerous people in my business. The stuff about us will be in his column before you can say boo to a goose or Jack Robinson or whatever the damn expression is. Oh God!' Lewis sank into a sullen despair as he saw his exclusive series of articles from Broadway had suddenly become less and less exclusive.

The gloom was not confined solely to Lewis. Doris was still smarting at the news of Florence's traitorous misbehaviour. It niggled. 'What hurts, Florence, is that you didn't care enough to share the news with me; to understand that the news would be important to me. I have three and three quarters of a million dollars invested with George.'

'Doris, I didn't want to hurt either you *or* George. I was trying to protect you both! I was so shocked, all I could think to do was to keep it to myself an' hope the thing would blow away.'

'Well it hasn't, has it. And now who can tell what'll happen.'

'There must be something we could do . . .' The sparkle was returning. 'If we three put our minds together I bet we could come up with some plan that would . . .'

'You and your plans, Florence . . .,' Lewis interrupted rudely.

'I'm not kidding. Doris is naturally worried about the show. It's a major investment, right, Doris? If we can untangle the triangle maybe everyone will go back to concentrating on the show. An', wow! I just thought how to do it!'

Lewis eyed her with great suspicion. The last plan she devised had given him two weeks of secret toil for nothing. But Doris was more interested.

'It's a piece of cake,' Florence said. 'I'm gonna arrange it so Dee falls in love with Ziggy and Ziggy with Dee. That way Ross is out an' George isn't mad at him no more.'

She looked at them with satisfaction.

'Are you serious, Florence?' Doris said.

'And how, may I ask, are you going to do that?' Lewis asked sourly.

'Simple. See I'm gonna let Ziggy think *I'm* in love with him. I'm gonna date him, etcetera, etcetera. Then when we got it together I'm gonna fix it for Dee.'

'How?' Lewis asked bluntly.

But Florence would give nothing more away.

In the limo, with their mood improved, Florence and Doris sang songs from the show. Lewis felt sufficiently relaxed to contribute an occasional smile. Doris dropped her passengers on the corner of 89th and Third. She was catching the Concorde to Paris the next morning and had no plans to return to the US until the dress rehearsals, some six weeks away.

'Take care, you two. Good luck with the rehearsals, Florence. Learn your line now . . .!' Doris laughed loudly as the limo drove off into the late night traffic. Florence and Lewis lamely waved goodbye.

'Can I borrow your Walkman tomorrow, John?' Florence asked as they climbed the stairs towards the apartment. 'It's one that records too, right?'

'Yup,' Lewis said, carrying the provisions they had just bought at the deli. He was trying to remain huffy.

'I can? Great! Stan's asked us to record tomorrow's rehearsal. Help us learn the parts. There's a lotta harmony stuff.'

They were at the door of their apartment. Lewis pushed the bell as Florence fished around in her purse for her key.

'Isn't Bobby in?' Lewis asked.

She found the key. 'Probably crashed out,' Florence whispered as she opened the door. 'Don't turn on the lights. No point in waking him.'

They went into the dark apartment. Florence headed for the bathroom, Lewis made for the sofa and his corner of the room.

En route he crashed into something soft and unexpected. There should have been a clear path between the door and the sofa. He knew the layout of this place intimately. But now there was an obstruction, an object that swung back and forward after the collision like a punchbag. Lewis grasped it to him. A click and light from the bathroom illuminated Lewis, clutching the burly body of Bobby Berol. Bobby was hanging by his neck, suspended with an electrical flex from the water-pipe than ran along the ceiling.

It turned out that Bobby had died at around 7.00 p.m., more or less at the same time that Doris, Florence and Lewis had sat down to dinner at 'Mr Lee's'. Before the police arrived, Florence discovered a note typed on the back of a brown envelope and propped against the kettle:

It was better bearded, blocked, amongst the grasses,
Than bare-faced, lonely in the caverns of glass and concrete.
To Florence, whose cunt lips eased my day
I leave this tawdry place and make my literary
executor,
To Lewis I bequeath Florence.
Hang in there, Guys (Oops, sorry)
Sorry to leave you this mess.

.... Bobby

Neither Florence nor Lewis got much sleep that night. By the time the police had finished their examinations, taken statements and carried Bobby away it was past 2.00 a.m. They were deeply shocked. Florence convinced herself, in her hysteria, that it was the writing of the musical that had been the cause of Bobby's death. He had failed at that as he had failed at so much else.

'He died for nothing', she wailed at 3.30 a.m. Lewis, still haunted by the ghastly embrace with the corpse, tried to calm her down but she remained inconsolable. She spent the rest of the night on the bed drifting in and out of hysteria whilst he lay on his sofa, dozing fitfully.

37

Dee had dreaded going into work. She had left Ross's apartment at 9.00 wearing dark glasses and a headscarf to avoid being recognised. At the corner news stand she bought a copy of the Post. She hunted through to find the story: a column inch lost in a series of gossip bites about celebrities. Princess Caroline of Monaco's picture stole the attention, followed by a headline which read: **'Brit Royal Paternity Suit Riddle'**. At the bottom of the page under the by-line: **'Who's Got Stars in his Eyes!'**, Dee read:

> As rehearsals for new mega-Broadway musical *Stars in His Eyes* began Monday, the cast assembling at 890 Broadway were surprised to learn that featured player Dee Gibson has walked out on her marriage to George Gibson, Producer of the show, and into the arms of her Director, Ross Boardman. One member of the cast said last night they were shocked at the turn of events but that the show goes on. Should make for interesting rehearsals!

It could have been worse, Dee thought as she hailed a cab. In the rehearsal room she found Lewis and Florence the centre of everyone's attention aghast at the story of Bobby Berol's suicide. She was left alone. Her romance old news.

Ross stayed in bed after Dee had left. The music department had called the full company and he wasn't needed. A two-hour lovemaking session during the night left him drained, fatigued and slightly sore. Despite lying in a bed that remained suffused with the essence of Dee, the eroticism of the night before seemed pointless and banal. He tried to sleep but no sleep came. Instead his leaden eyes stubbornly remained open and he became fixated with the geometry of tiny cracks in the ceiling. Random thoughts and images flashed through his mind as if generated by an electrical storm. *Ellen dropping a six-pack of Perrier in Safeways; Mary-Anne caught in flagrante with her Mexican screenwriter; his father, naked on his deathbed, being turned over by nuns; his mother walking hand in hand with his baby sister along a desert road; Michael Kershon's wife leaning over her husband's desk as he worked at his IBM. Dee's face from below as his tongue brought her to climax.* He woke, but then doubted he'd slept. The images were neither from a dream nor real. He tried to summon up an image of his children whom, he realised with shock, he had neither seen nor spoken to for several months. *What kind of man am I?* He turned over on to his face and buried his head in his pillow. 'You're a mean selfish little guy who thinks of no-one but himself,' his father had said to Ross, aged 9, an only child. 'You'd better get your ideas in order or you'll be a man no-one will love.'

Ross pulled the telephone on to the bed and dialled Mary-Anne's number. The cleaner answered the phone. No, she was at work. *Kids should know that their dad was dying for Chrissakes! Will they care? The girls will. Chloe, Chrissy, Betsy. The girls loved me . . . the girls always loved me . . . In the end that's what's left . . . love. Dee loves . . . Dee loves me . . .*

The telephone woke him from a dreamful sleep. He felt dreadful. His stomach contracted in painful spasms and he was aware of a new ache in the lower reaches of his back. He had missed taking his pills at 9.00 a.m. and the pain was catching up . . . How long could he go on like this? Was it feasible to work under such conditions? *Give up. Go away; die under a stone. Phone Ellen. You're right. I was wrong. Come home. Take care of me. Don't leave me, Ellen . . !*

'Ross?' Ellen's voice on the phone. 'Ross? Are you there?'

'Yeah . . .,' he replied, finally convinced that this was real. His voice was rasping, his throat dry.

'How are you feeling?' she asked, betraying a genuine anxiety.

'Much better.' He didn't want to talk to her.

'Are you asleep? You sound dreamy.'

'Kinda dozing.'

'What about rehearsals?'

'They're learning the music.'

'Right.' Pause. 'Don't you normally go to the music rehearsals?'

'Ellen, did you want something?' He didn't mean to be cruel but it happened. He knew she'd be hurt. She was.

'I've got someone to help me collect the rest of my things,' she replied coldly. 'This evening. About 8-ish. It would be better if no-one's there.'

She hung up without waiting for a reply, unable to bear any more. Ross heaved himself out of bed and went to find his

233

medicines. Some time later, as the pains decreased, and he could begin to think of other things, he shuffled into the room that served as an office, rummaged in his desk for a red pencil, and reached for his rehearsal script.

38

The following morning, Ross arrived at 9.15 a.m. He'd called Fly, Jerry, Conrad, Stan and Tam to a meeting before rehearsal.

'Go okay yesterday, Stan?' Ross asked, as Charlie distributed coffees.

Stan said, 'Yeah, but then we didn't have Harry. Did he go to the hospital?'

Fly answered. 'He was supposed to. I left messages at his hotel but he never called back.'

'He's called for rehearsal this morning. He'll be here in 45 minutes.'

'Okay,' Ross said, reaching for his notes and script. 'Somebody better warn Cathy we might have to recast . . .'

'Let's wait an' see, Ross,' Stan said cautiously.

'Sure. Now, here's my suggestions for cuts and changes based on Monday's reading.' The team reached for their note-pads. 'We gotta lotta work to do, boys . . .'

He left what he correctly surmised to be the most contentious issue till last. "Play for Love" must go.'

'What!' Jerry could hardly believe his ears. Had Ross gone mad! *Everyone loved that song.*

'I'm sorry, Jerry. I know how much this song means to you but it stops Act Two dead.'

Jerry was stunned. 'You're crazy! One; that's gonna be the hit song of the show. Two; Tara will walk: it's her big ballad . . .'

'She has a ballad in Act One, then there's the duet, the . . .'

'You can't kill that song, Ross. It's the heart of my score!'

' "Play for Love" is like the Gershwins' "The Man I Love", perhaps their most beautiful song,' Ross patiently explained. 'They tried to interpolate that into three shows and each time *they* cut it. They were smart enough to know it wouldn't work. But it did have an afterlife – it didn't need a show to have immortality.'

But Jerry was prepared for a struggle. 'I tell you who won't let

235

it get cut, an' that's George. He loves this song. He feels it's his. You know how much he's worked with me on it.'

Ross knew indeed. The opportunity to enrage George was irresistible.

'Means nothing to me. It's either right or it's wrong. This is wrong.'

Jerry appealed to the others. 'Con! Help me! You said this was *your* favourite. Stan?'

Conrad shifted uneasily. 'We could always cut it later.'

Ross was having none of this. 'Cut it later and watch how mad Tara will get. Cut it now and sure she'll be mad, but she'll get over it.'

'Stan?' Jerry tried again. Stan had influence over Ross. Respect.

Stan shrugged and merely said, 'It's Ross's call.' He understood other forces were at play here.

'You have no opinion?' Jerry shouted at him.

'Yeah,' Stan replied. 'My opinion is that it's Ross's decision.'

'Jerry,' Tam said. 'We spoke about this song many months ago. Remember? It's a *great* song. I mean it. But it doesn't *move* and it doesn't advance the plot.'

One or two of the actors had begun to arrive for the morning rehearsal. The meeting was adjourned with Jerry still smouldering. He phoned George from the production office.

'He's done what?' George yelled down the phone. 'He can't cut anything without my permission! An' I don't give my permission! You tell him that from me!'

'I tried tellin' him that, George. There's other changes too . . .'

Jerry could hear George breathing heavily at the other end of the line.

'Get me Fly!' George commanded.

Jerry found Fly sitting with Ross. They were listening to the chorus rehearsing.

'Fly, George wants a word with you.' Jerry said, avoiding looking at Ross.

'Yeah?' Fly said.

Ross smiled.

'BETTY!'

In the outer office, Betty stopped typing.

'BETTY! Get Gino on two, and put one on hold!'

She thought for a moment then popped her head round George's door. 'D'you want Gino on one and the caller on one put to two

236

on hold after?'

'WHAT?' he yelled crossly.

Betty became flustered. 'Do you want one on two after I get Gino on two an' put *him* on one?'

'What the hell are you talkin' about, Betty? For Chrissakes just get me Gino and hold Fly.'

George sat back and swivelled his chair towards the window with its view of the waterfront, and thought deeply. In the outer office Betty was loudly telling Fly George would be with him shortly.

A few moments later, George was talking to his lawyer. 'Gino, I gotta problem with Ross. He wants to cut a song an' I don't. What's my contractual position?'

'What does Jerry want, George?'

'He sure as hell doesn't want it cut!'

'Then don't cut it.'

'Ross is insisting, Gino. It's an issue.'

'Let me ask you, George, is this anything to do with this game you're playing with him?'

'How d'you mean? What game?' George shouted. 'I don't play games!'

'Okay, George. You can, according to the contract, countermand his cut. If he decided to fight he could seek arbitration through the SSDC, the directors' union. It would be messy, expose you both to public scrutiny, and could end up with you losing and being undermined. You wanna get into all that? I'd advise you to reach a compromise.'

'I can bluff. I play a lotta poker, Gino.'

And he hung up.

'FLY THERE, BETTY?'

Betty entered the office looking worried. 'I put him on hold. Would you like me to transfer him to two?'

'No, you leave him where he is.' George pressed a button on the phone. 'Fly?'

'How're you doin', Mr Gibson?'

'Rehearsals going okay?'

'Yeah, just fine.'

'Good to hear. How's Ziggy and Tara?'

'Swell. Sound great.'

'Any problems I should know about?'

'No, everything's just fine, Mr Gibson.'

'Heard you had a meeting to re-arrange and cut some stuff this morning.'

'Yeah. Went well,' Fly said.

237

'Hear the director wants to cut "Play for Love"?'

'That's right, Mr Gibson. Would you like to talk to him about it?'

'You think it should go, Fly?'

Fly paused a beat. 'It's your show, Mr Gibson.' They didn't pay him enough to take sides.

'What the hell does that mean?'

'You an' Ross know what you're doing. It's your show'.

Suddenly George was shouting down the phone. 'Well, you tell that asshole I'm countermanding his decision! Does he think he's God? Got some divine right to see more than any of us? If he's got any arguments he'd damn well better look at his contract! That's a great song! Jerry's a genius! And that Gavin . . . Connell . . . whatever the guy's name is . . .'

'Conrad, Mr Gibson,' Fly said patiently.

'Yeah. Right. He's a genius too. I like what they write! Sonofabitch . . .'

And his voice trailed away to a rasping breathiness.

'Yes, sorry I'm late, Ross,' Sir Harry was saying cheerfully as Fly rejoined. Ross was drinking coffee out of a cardboard cup. Through the open door they could hear the chorus hard at work. 'Long chat to the agent in London. Couldn't get the old girl off the phone. Rabbits on and on. Ghastly line. Ended up having to say "over" when we'd finished our bit. Just like the old days of wireless telegraphy. Made a film about Marconi once, had to learn Morse code and . . .'

Ross could bear this no longer. 'Harry, what did they say at the hospital yesterday?'

'Hospital? What hospital?'

Fly looked puzzled. 'Didn't you go see Dr Kransky? I set it up for you. Remember?'

Harry's eyes widened as he remembered. 'Kransky! Of course! I cancelled. Couldn't face it. Feeling much better anyway. Nerves, you know. Hits people in different ways. D'you know I haven't *actually* sung on stage for years . . .'

'Harry, we'll monitor it,' Ross said.

Fly looked at his watch. Harry noticed and said: 'Ninety minutes late, I know. Where am I then? Here . . .?'

He wandered off into the wrong room.

Ross sighed and turned his attention to Fly. 'What'd George say? Was he angry?'

'Yeah. He was shouting down the phone. Called you unpleasant names, that kinda thing. Why you smiling?'

'Ring of confidence. I reckon I've got one crack at this show. If we're not right by Washington, we're dead in more ways than one.'

'That the only reason?'

'No,' Ross said. 'Because it made George mad as hell.'

39

The morning Bobby Berol was cremated, Lewis received a letter from Julie Page. Writing from London she was proposing a visit to New York. Could she stay?

> 'I'll be no trouble, but hotels are so expensive and I bet you've got a charming little place in the Village, with a fire escape and all that Neil Simon type stuff happening. I'm very happy on the sofa!! Don't bother to reply, as I'm on the move till I leave. I'll just turn up on your doorstep about 7.30 p.m. on Thursday, 7th. If it's a problem I'll toddle off. Lots of love, Julie. PS. I loved your piece about the tee-shirts. You sound as if you're having a fab time. PPS. Enclosing Clive North's *brilliant* Guardian article about current state of Broadway just in case you haven't seen it. Caused quite a stir here!!!'

There were three people at the simple ceremony: Florence, Lewis and Bobby Berol's 84-year-old mother who had flown in from Atlanta. Florence, having recovered much of her old form, took great delight in shepherding the old, distraught lady from La Guardia to Our Lady's Orchard of Eternal Rest across the river in New Jersey near a parking lot and a high-rise.

Lewis looked in vain for the orchard, but found only two trees, one stunted, the other suffering from blight. Surprisingly, he found himself in tears as Bobby's coffin disappeared behind the curtains. Thinking about it, he couldn't remember the last time he had cried. Watching the pain on the face of Bobby's mother made him feel guilty about his own father. He'd written twice but had received no reply. Aunt Mary, in a PS at the end of a postcard Lewis had received three weeks ago, had written 'your father's okay, but misses you'. Poor, lonely old man, Lewis thought as the electronic organ played a hymn. *How can I be a better son?*

Florence, with her arm around the weeping old lady, caught

Lewis's eye and winked.

They deposited Mrs Berol for her flight home at the United check-in at La Guardia. Florence, who had begun to treat the old lady like her mother-in-law, promised to write.

'What we gonna do with the rest of the day, John?' Florence said cheerfully as they sat on a mostly empty subway train heading back into the city.

'I should get back to rehearsals.'

'When are you gonna let me read some of your stuff?'

'Well, it's still notes, really. When I've got it into some kind of shape.' Lewis watched a black family noisily get into the carriage. 'You're going to miss him, aren't you? We haven't really talked about him since that night.'

Florence thought for a moment. 'I got this theory about death, y'know. Like before we're born we got nothing . . . I mean we remember nothing. All that history happened and we know nothing about it. I mean why aren't we in heaven *before* we're born? What's so special about *afterlife*? Why's there no *beforelife*? So I figure that if there's no before there's no after. We gotta make heaven here on earth.' She demonstrated with her hands. 'So we got *before* then *life* then *after*. It's the rule of three, right? Birth marks the transition between *before* and *life*. Death marks the transition between *life* and *after*. So birth and death are like a kinda conduit from one state to another. One's not more important than the other. Follow?'

'Make hay while the sun shines,' Lewis said, with little joy.

Florence looked at him with pity. 'Your problem, John, is that you never see things *positively*. You gotta walk along the street with your head up. Not down, like you're researching dog doo. That's the difference between us.' She paused for a moment and studied her nails. 'I think, when he was working on the show, y'know, for a while, Bobby had a positive attitude. He kinda had: Vermont, then life, then death. Rule of three. When we made love, he lived. He really lived. I read somewhere that the pure act, I mean the really like mega-orgasmic fuck, is like death . . . like being dead for a moment. Well I don't agree with that. I think it's like being more alive than you've ever been. I think that Bobby experienced that, y'know, John.'

'You're telling me? I was two feet away.'

'So the guy lived a little before he died.'

Lewis looked at her and an image of Julie in the Angel in City Road popped into his head. Suddenly he thought of London: his home, the pubs, the games of tennis, his father . . . Julie.

'I've never told you about what happened to me before I came

241

here, have I?' he said to Florence.

It took the rest of the journey into the city to recount in detail his immediate past; his near suicide; the vomiting in the Savoy; his subsequent revelation on the carpet. 'You see how much I owe George and, I suppose, in a funny way, Ross. Without them, I might have been, well, like poor old Bobby, incinerated in Our Lady's Orchard.'

'Wow!' Florence gasped. 'You an' Bobby are more alike than I dreamt. Both of you into killing yourselves. That's *weird!*'

Lewis was silent for a moment. 'It's pretty frightening really. I hadn't seen the similarities. My contemplating doing it and Bobby actually . . .'

He couldn't finish the sentence. Enough was said.

That night, for the first time, Florence and Lewis made love. The trauma of the funeral gave Florence a voracious sexual appetite that Lewis found hard to satisfy but nevertheless made the occasion memorable.

40

There had been no resolution of the problem of 'Play for Love'. It was a standoff. Ross had no contact with the writers who had closeted themselves in Conrad's apartment to work on the changes. George had not been seen or heard from since the Tuesday phone conversation with Fly. Tam Topp had started to choreograph the big numbers, Ross had begun character work and book scenes with the principals, and the music department continued to teach songs.

Early on Monday morning, Ross received a message asking him to phone Conrad and Jerry when he had a moment. It wasn't until mid-morning that he had a break.

Conrad spoke to Ross first. 'We're ready to show you what we've done. How are you fixed to meet up?'

'This afternoon. Around 2.30,' Ross said, looking at his schedule.

'There's a couple of things,' Conrad said. 'We've not cut "Play for Love". Jerry feels passionate about this, and he's supported by George. When we played the new and cut stuff for George last night . . .'

'I'm sorry,' Ross interrupted. 'When you did what?'

Conrad was expecting Ross to be outraged. That's why Jerry had said, 'You speak first . . .'

'Now don't get mad, Ross. We had no option. We took him through it last night. He had quite a bit to say and, I gotta tell you, it wasn't all garbage. He's gotta pretty sharp mind when it comes to seeing the problems. Or at least knowing there's a problem there. He might not know the solution but he can . . .'

'Let me get this straight, Con. You took George through my changes *before* you took me through them?'

'We didn't have an option, Ross.' Conrad sounded wretched. 'Here, talk to Jerry. He'll explain.'

Jerry came on the line trying to sound cheerful . . . 'Hi Ross! How're you doin'?'

'What's been going on?' Ross asked grimly.

'Oh come on, Ross. No point being mad at us. You know George has a perfect right to hear what we're doing. He hates being left out in the dark. I don't blame him, it's his show too. He had no idea what you were askin' us to do, man. An' he's right about "Play for Love", Ross. About not cutting it! He was right about a coupla other things that we should talk about when we meet this afternoon.'

'Like what?'

'He's given us a list of changes, bits here and there . . .'

But Ross had already hung up. *How dare they do this! Why have they done this behind my back!*

Harry Whitney, at a loose end, wandered into the office, sipping from an Evian bottle. Only after Ross had been forced to listen to another interminable story and his rage had subsided, had he perceived he'd lost his temper with the wrong people. This wasn't the writers' fault, he realised. This was a skirmish in the war. George was using the writers to get at *him*, and he cursed himself for not anticipating it. The writers were in the middle, caught in the powerplay, and he was acting *petty*.

During the afternoon meeting with them, Ross gave in. He accepted defeat to win them back. The price: 'Play for Love'. It stayed in. At least for the moment. Conrad and Jerry were so pleased they quickly agreed to dismiss George's other suggestions.

That was a small victory.

George Gibson hadn't realised how much he had needed Dee until he had lost her. When he was finally able to admit to this, it made him enormously angry. This anger first materialised as he entered 1515 Broadway. It grew as he crossed the lobby, increased markedly as the elevator ascended, and became unbearable as he sat at his desk staring at the photograph of Dee he'd left standing in its silver frame next to the fading sepia picture of his mother.

'BETTY!' he yelled.

With some trepidation, she popped her head around the door. He had hurtled past her a few minutes ago with such speed, had slammed the door to his office with such force, that there could be no mistaking his mood.

'Gotta rehearsal schedule out there?'

'Yes, Mr Gibson.'

'Check and see if Dee's rehearsing.'

She did and a moment later popped back. 'Yes. She was in at

10.00 for a dance call.'

'Have her call me.'

'When?'

'NOW!'

Betty beat a hasty retreat and left a message with Charlie in the rehearsal rom.

Ten minutes later Dee called. Betty liked Mrs Gibson.

'George wants a word.' Betty had been saying that to Dee for years but somehow, today, it didn't sound the same.

'What about, Betty!'

'I dunno, dear. You'd better ask him . . .' She put her through.

'Hi, George,' Dee said as pleasantly as she could after his gruff greeting.

He didn't beat about the bush. 'You wanna come home?'

'Home? Are you kidding me? You cheating asshole! You got some nerve! No, George, I'll never get over how you wasted my life. It's over.'

'You stayin' with Ross?'

'What's it to you? I love him.'

'What d'you expect me to say to that?'

'Nothing. You asked.'

Dee listened to him noisily clear his throat. Familiar sounds.

'An' how is the great man?' he finally said.

'You mean his health? He's sick but he's hangin' in there. He'll see the show through.'

'Is he having treatment or what?'

'He's refused the operation an' treatment. He says he wants to do the show then pass away peacefully.'

'HE WOULD SAY SHIT LIKE THAT, THE SHMUCK! THE ASSHOLE!'

'George! Stop it! You wanna have a conversation with me or you wanna shout at me?'

'Okay, okay. But you can tell him from me, that I'm not gonna open this show then have him die a martyr.'

'Oh? You surprise me, George. I thought you'd love that.'

George didn't understand. 'Whad'ya mean?'

'Just that I wouldn't have put it past you to try and sell a few extra tickets on the back of Ross's misfortune.'

An idea popped into George's head.

'You think I'm that callous!' He shouted angrily into the phone. 'That's all the respect you give me!'

'George we had a lousy life together an' now it's . . .'

Dee had planted a seed. As she talked the seed grew and grew in George's mind. Soon it had developed into a plan. A plan so

245

audacious even George wasn't sure he had the guts to carry it through.

'. . . How long you say he's got?' he interrupted, having no idea what she was saying.

Dee sighed at the other end of the line. 'You haven't been listening to a word I've been saying . . .'

'For Chrissakes, Dee! I gotta know this for the show. How long's he got? What are the doctors giving him?'

No harm in telling. He had a right to know. 'Five, maybe six months. They can't say for sure. It could go quicker, it could . . .'

On his fingers, George counted out the months . . . October to November, to December, January, February . . . March. Five months. *Maybe he'll live to April!* He had planned to open the show late February, early March. Dee says that's comfortably within Ross's lifespan. Could he dare postpone till *April*. A helluva risk. But maybe worth it. Worth it if the plan's to succeed . . .

Betty knocked at the door and put her head into the office. 'Advertising people outside waiting, George,' she whispered.

He put his hand over the mouthpiece. 'Call Gino and ask him to meet me for lunch at the Russian Tea Room. An' book a table.'

George got rid of Dee as quickly as he could. A series of meetings: with the agency designing the poster, with Norman Naff on marketing strategy, with Eugene Landau on the budget (a regular start-of-the week review), occupied the rest of his morning.

When lunchtime came around, he was impatient to get to the Russian Tea Room and start asking questions, planning the coup de grâce.

41

Lewis's relationship with Florence had subtly changed since they first made love the night of Bob's cremation. '. . . To Lewis I bequeath Florence.' Lewis had taken Bobby Berol's suicide note very seriously. From his sofa, he had witnessed every trick and knew how Bobby had excelled in that department. Lewis had a lot to live up to and he tried his damnedest. Unfortunately the harder he tried the worse he became.

'It doesn't matter, Jaahn,' she'd say as he came too quickly. 'Next time it'll be better.' Sometimes it was, sometimes it wasn't. But life had become serious and they no longer enjoyed the free and easy camaraderie of before.

Julie's arrival in New York, however, was to change everything. Lewis was, at the same time, nervous and excited about seeing her. Some of this he transmitted to Florence who became, uncharacteristically, jealous. He tried to explain the superficiality of his relationship with Julie.

'We worked in the same office. We went out once . . . for a drink. That's all.'

'Yeah?' Florence had said, unconvinced. 'You don't talk like that's all there was.'

'I've hardly *ever* talked about her,' Lewis said.

'Oh yes you have,' Florence said. 'More'n you think. I don't care anyway. I'm gettin' it together with Zig. He's asked me out on a date.'

'Oh, really,' Lewis said glumly.

He had booked Julie into a cheap hotel on Lexington. It was the best he could find, for the price. The room was on the 26th floor. He apologised for its squalor but she found it charming. 'It's just *so* exciting and magical,' she commented as she surveyed the city through the hole she'd wiped in the grime on the window. 'I'm ready for anything this city has to offer!' A remark Lewis pondered on for some time.

Julie was a breath of fresh air. She was on holiday; happy and relaxed. And Lewis relaxed with her. He decided to take time off from rehearsals to show Julie his New York.

Rehearsals, Lewis found, were no longer as interesting as they had been. By the end of the third week little new creative work was being done except by Tam Topp. There was constant activity but little new to interest Lewis. Julie was much more stimulating.

He didn't mind missing a few days for another reason. As the days had flowed into weeks, the workload had eaten further into Ross's fading strength. His decline greatly depressed Lewis. Despite the ups and downs in their relationship, Lewis's admiration for Ross was undiminished. He had been a rock, but the rock was crumbling. It pained him to bear witness. Ross, now, confined himself to making artistic decisions. Seated, rarely moving, he quietly issued directions to the actors. Constantly sipping water and forcing himself to drink thick broth for lunch, he husbanded his depleting resources. Fly assumed more and more responsibilities: scheduling, handling production conferences, liaising with the sound and lighting departments.

There was more.

Ross's behaviour and deteriorating health had begun to affect morale. The company knew Dee had moved into Ross's apartment, into the bed he had shared with Ellen. Was this sapping his strength? Unable to infuse his rehearsal with much energy, the actors became petulant and bored. The only excitement was to be found in Tam Topp's rehearsal room. Fly spoke to Ross and, finally, with Ross's encouragement, Tam began to stage more and more of the book scenes. Ross watched, suggested and made notes. Morale, then, began to improve.

'I find New York ever so *sexy*,' Julie said, holding on to Lewis's arm, as she surveyed 8th Avenue at its seamiest. They were standing outside a cinema advertising a movie *Hot Nurses Lick Dick*.

'Fancy lunch in Chinatown?' Lewis asked.

For three days they had had fun behaving like tourists; taking the boat round the island, glorying in the view from the Empire State, savouring the Museum of Modern Art, mooching through the Village, queueing for movies and off-Broadway shows, eating pasta late at night on the pavement in SoHo. As they wandered through the city, Julie gossiped about London, about the paper. He, in turn, had entertained her with stories and anecdotes, recounting in detail what had happened since he'd been in the city.

'You sure you're not making this up?' she asked sceptically picking at the Dim Sum.

'No, I'm not, honestly.' Lewis realised it sounded incredible.

'There's been more drama off-stage than there is on.'

He watched her choose another dish from a trolley wheeled by.

'D'you think that the West End is like this?' she asked before taking a bite.

'I've no idea,' Lewis said truthfully. 'I doubt it somehow. This is all very un-English.'

'Mmm, delicious,' she said, licking sauce off her lips. 'What are we going to do next? I want to have some serious fun.'

What on earth did she mean? he wondered. He had been under the assumption they'd been having lots of fun.

'Let's, tonight, get blind drunk and see what this city's got to offer, okay?'

By late afternoon they were back at the apartment on 89th Street. Florence was out and Lewis didn't expect to see her till late that night. She had a late rehearsal followed by her first dinner with Ziggy. 'I'm dating him for the good of the show, Jaahn,' she had said in the morning, as she rushed out the door, late as usual.

'You want to take a shower while I make some tea?' Lewis said. The weather was unusually hot and humid for late November and, after a day roaming the city, they were bathed in sweat. 'You'll find a clean towel in the cupboard. Help yourself.'

Julie nosed around amongst Florence's belongings. 'You haven't told me a lot about the girl you live with.'

'Haven't I?' Lewis said emerging from the kitchen drying a cup. 'There's not a lot to tell actually. Would you prefer tea or something cold?'

'Something cold. Have you a Diet Sprite? It's much better for you.'

Why did that ring a bell? 'It's what my room-mate drinks.' He chose his words carefully. Room-mate sounded unequivocally asexual. He disappeared into the kitchen.

'Do you sleep together, you and Florence?' Julie called out. She sat on the bed.

'I'm sorry?' Lewis said, coming back out with her soda.

'Are you and Florence an item?'

Lewis felt himself blushing. He wanted to lie. *Why?* The image of Julie in his dream bobbing up and down on Clive North's lap popped into his head. Yes he fancied *her*, but what did she think of *him*. Julie had treated him like a good mate, nothing more. He realised with a shock that he knew very little about her. If he closed his eyes he would be unable to describe her in any detail. So he studied her now. Light-brown hair already bleached by the summer sun; twinkling, smiley, blue-green eyes; a small birth-mark, unobtrusive, in fact cute, on the left-side of a delicate chin;

impudent breasts lurking beneath a damp, clinging white tee-shirt; roughly cut-off jeans exposing plenty of leg. Maybe, a little too much weight on the rear but . . .

'Are you going to give me that Sprite, or am I going to have to come and get it?' she asked.

'Oh, gosh, sorry!' Once she had dropped a hint about some 'bloke' she had been seeing in London, but hadn't gone into details, and anyway he hadn't really wanted to know.

And just then, as he was passing her the can, before he was forced into replying, Florence turned up.

'Hi!' Florence said cheerfully. 'Am I interrupting something?'

'No!' Lewis was more forceful than he meant to be.

'Hello,' Julie said, giving her a friendly smile.

After making introductions, Lewis said, 'I thought you weren't coming back this evening.'

'My rehearsal got cancelled and so did my date. I'm free as a bird tra-la.'

'That's wonderful!' Julie said delightedly. 'Why don't you spend the evening with us. We're going to a movie then we're going to get incredibly drunk! Aren't we, Johnny?'

'Yes.' Lewis was unsure if he could manage both girls. *And who was going to pay!?*

They took it in turn to shower. Lewis went first. He dressed and undressed behind the locked door of the bathroom. After, he watched goggle-eyed, assuming complete indifference and pretending to read the Times, as Florence and Julie, who had instantly taken to each other, undressed in front of him and wandered in and out of the bathroom stark naked.

They queued for the new Kevin Costner/Julia Roberts movie, enjoyed it, then went to a noisy bar on Second Avenue, where they started to drink California white. The girls talked unceasingly, leaving Lewis mostly the listener, the observer. On this occasion he enjoyed it, he was thrilled to be with two such lively, attractive girls. Julie became increasingly tactile the more she drank, he noted. Her hands became a permanent fixture on Florence's bare arm. As they shared secrets, giggled or rocked with laughter, Lewis saw their legs touch, casually at first but then, as the third bottle was consumed, shamelessly.

Are they lesbians? he wondered blearily, as the cheap wine went to his head. *Am I going to get a look in? Or is it back to the sofa?*

'What's the matter, Johnny?' Julie suddenly asked. 'Why are you so quiet?'

'Am I?' Lewis said. 'I don't mean to be. I'm enjoying watching you both and the wine's making me fuzzy.'

'Yeah,' Florence agreed, gulping down another glass. 'S'good. An' I like your friend, Jaahn.'

Julie patted Florence's arm. 'Aren't we having the best time. I'm hungry. Let's eat! Dinner's on me!'

They ate at the Trattoria Toscana, and, after several more bottles, Lewis reckoned the girls had little left to discover about each other. Two drunk businessmen from Nebraska, at the next table, invited them to a club but, after leading them on, the girls gave them short shrift.

'Didn't fancy them at *all*,' Julie said as they headed for home. They marched up the road three abreast, Julie in the middle, her arms linked through theirs. 'Only man we fancy tonight is you, Johnny. Right, Flo?'

Florence howled with laughter.

Was that a joke? Past caring, Lewis clutched Julie's arm tighter and joined in the merriment.

They staggered back into the apartment, laughing and singing, high as kites; Florence holding a bottle of peach brandy they bought at the liquor store round the corner; the girls so chummy they might have been friends for years. This is the way to be, Lewis thought: *embracing everything.*

The two girls sat giggling on the bed whilst Lewis fetched three glasses from the kitchen. By the time he re-entered the living room he wasn't entirely surprised to see Florence and Julie, locked in each others' arms. He sat on his sofa and watched. It was good spectator sport. For a while the girls kissed, oblivious to his presence. Then Julie, opening an eye, saw him watching. She pulled away from Florence and smiled tipsily. 'Don't just sit there! Come and join us.'

'It's party time!' said Florence with an attempt at an Albanian accent.

'Oh, I don't know, really . . .' His courage was at bay.

Florence glanced at him then whispered something to Julie that Lewis couldn't hear.

Julie giggled then sang, 'Florence wants you. She wants you to make love to her. Come on, I'll help.'

Gingerly Lewis made his way over to the bed. *Who does what and to whom?* He tried desperately to remember something he had read that might give a clue. But Julie expertly took charge of the arrangements, helping them undress, aesthetically deciding positions, proffering advice and aiding in extensive foreplay. This managerial side to Julie's character came as a surprise to Lewis.

Bringing Florence to a climax proceeded carefully and slowly. Lewis and Julie's mouths explored every inch of Florence's body. *This is a bloody funny thing to be doing,* he thought. The slow pace of the proceedings gave Lewis time to think. Head-to-head with Julie, licking away in the hot damp darkness between Florence's legs, Florence moaning way above them, Lewis found himself thinking about his life. Stopping to rest, he laid his head on Florence's thigh . . .

Then suddenly, in the musky darkness, just as he was contemplating joining in again, he had another revelation. A revelation as dramatic as the one those months ago on Ross's carpet in the Savoy. He was homesick. *Homesick?* He couldn't believe it. A mist had lifted and he felt able to see things clearly. Or at least differently. London no longer seemed a place to escape *from* but somewhere to want to go *to*. The past seemed fictional, to belong to another John Lewis. This John Lewis could see a future. In London. And somewhere in that future he could see a place for Julie.

He sneaked a look up at Florence. Judging from the increasing groans and sighs, she was on the verge of orgasm. This therefore didn't seem the appropriate moment to discuss revelations with anybody.

'Put it in her now!' Julie whispered urgently to him. 'Quick! Hurry or you'll miss it!'

'Oh, right,' Lewis whispered back and obliged.

Despite (or maybe because of) his intoxication, Lewis found all this exciting beyond his wildest dreams. He and Florence performed magnificently. Bobby Berol, he knew, would have been proud.

Now it was Julie's turn. After the first climax of the evening had been achieved, Florence, stripping Julie of her tee-shirt and knickers, began to return the favours. Lewis, propped up on a pillow, taking a well-earned rest, watched Florence work Julie into a frenzy. Looks like she's done this before, he thought. The sight was wildly erotic. Lewis, surprised and pleased at finding himself ready to go again, found he had an irresistible impulse to possess and satisfy Julie. Whilst Florence took Julie's breast in her mouth, Lewis, groaning with pleasure, did his duty.

For the first time in his life, Lewis felt grown-up.

42

Ross woke with a pounding headache. Norman Naff had woken him at midnight with a piffling question about scheduling an interview for Harry. This call at an unsocial hour wasn't an isolated event. Most mornings, around 7.00 a.m., Gene Landau called wanting to discuss something or another. It had only occurred to Ross over the last couple of days this might be part of an organised campaign to prevent him from sleeping. *Christ, is this real? Or has paranoia taken hold?*

On this, the morning of the first run-through of *Stars*, Ross, at last, received news from his eldest daughter, Chloe. She had, she wrote, been travelling in the Far East and was now in Europe. Chloe was headstrong and rebellious. Despite being a difficult kid, she was Ross's favourite, probably because she was most like him. In her letter she asked for money: $12,000. 'I'm totally desperate, Pop, or I wouldn't write. I can't explain why I need the money or why it's so much but if you love me you must try to help me. Please, please, don't contact Mom. I need this in cash, so if you can help, please send me American Express travellers' cheques to . . .' And she named a Post Office box at an all-night Post Office in London's West End.

The same mail brought a letter from Ross's Investment Broker warning him that recent withdrawals had resulted in his capital assets falling below $50,000, a sum below which they would be unable to continue to handle his affairs. 'We would be grateful if you could transfer into your account at least $15,000 to enable us to maintain our services.' His guaranteed fee of $40,000 for *Stars in His Eyes* would be now fully committed. The show needed to start earning money fast. The letter continued, 'Further, it has been brought to our attention that there may be new circumstances with regard to your health. If this is correct can you furnish us with details that may affect your insurances . . .'

'Brought to our attention'? *What the hell does that mean?* Who brought it to their attention?

The first run-through took place half way through the fifth week of rehearsals and was a mess. Ross insisted that no-one apart from the immediate members of the production team be allowed to attend. George was infuriated. He knew, however, that there was to be a second run-through the following day, which Doris, who was flying back to the city that evening, would also attend.

The show had been rehearsed in bits and pieces. When it came to be put together for the first time, few of the actors could remember the order. The result was that scenes fell apart, songs were forgotten and performances disappeared, sacrificed in the attempt to keep going. The chaos was a shock and depressing. The question asked afterwards was: Can we learn anything useful from this?

Ross felt enough objectivity to be able to ask Jerry and Conrad for yet more changes to the script.

'Christ, Ross!' Jerry exclaimed. 'Are we never gonna give this a rest?'

'Remember what George Kaufman said, "A musical isn't written, it's rewritten." '

'You've said that before,' Jerry retorted. 'Anyway, who can tell anything from that mess?! If there's a problem it's in the production, the performances. Not in the writing.'

Stan defended the production. 'We've got another run tomorrow. That's going to tell us a lot more.'

'Yeah,' said Jerry, 'an' George, Doris and the others will be watching. They'll tell us the truth.'

'Or possibly not,' Ross said quietly.

The second run did go better. The actors, learning from the previous experience, had gone home, studied their scripts and had come back with a feel for the continuity of the piece. Performances began to re-emerge. Ziggy, whose efforts the previous day had been lacklustre, began once again to show his mettle. Harry Whitney's voice no longer embarrassed. Tara had arrived for the run-through dressed in an approximation of 16th-century Italy from clothes she'd improvised from the back of her wardrobe. Her hair had been tied back in a *paysanne* look. She delivered 'Play for Love' magnificently; her voice, imbued with passion and commitment, soared and flew.

Dee, however, was unnerved by the presence of George. He wrote notes continuously with a gold Cross pencil on a legal pad. She missed several high notes, nervously glancing around to see what impression she was making. The more notes George made, the more tense became her performance.

254

Doris sat with a tanned Paul Etienne. Myra Rothstein, sitting with her husband, irritated everyone by timing each scene with a stop-watch. Perched next to her on a seat of his own was the omnipresent pig, Woolly. Myra was now a familiar figure having, for the past five days, taken to arriving each lunchtime with a hot kosher meal in a thermos for Conrad. Seated next to Woolly, Lewis made the occasional note but kept thinking about his sexual adventures. Embarrassingly, therefore, he spent the run-through in a state of uncomfortable priapism.

'Thank you everyone!' Fly called out on Ross's behalf, as the pianist played the final chords at the end of Act Two. The run over, George immediately summoned Conrad and Jerry into a corner leaving Ross with the rest of the team.

'What d'you wanna do with the company?' Fly whispered to Ross.

'Give me a minute with Stan and Tam. Then call the company together for notes. Let 'em know.'

Fly made the announcement and departed to type a schedule. The actors milled around, chatting, drinking sodas, waiting for the director.

Florence was talking to Ziggy and Dee.

'Thing is, if I *knew* what to play in the first act I could play it,' Ziggy was saying. 'But I don't know what my *attitude* is.'

Florence said it didn't show but Lewis, who had just joined them, disagreed. 'I thought you did look uncomfortable. There's such a mixture of styles that it's nearly incomprehensible.' The new text still rankled slightly.

'You think so?' Ziggy asked interestedly. 'I guess that's what I'm feeling. How about you, Dee? . . .' And they wandered off.

'You gotta funny look in your eyes, sweetie,' Florence said, after they'd gone.

'Truth is,' Lewis said confidentially, 'I can't stop thinking about, well, the three of us. You know, you, me and Julie.'

Florence laughed delightedly. 'Fun, huh. You wanna find somewhere quiet . . . there's an empty office down the corridor. We can lock it from the inside . . . You can think of Julie . . .'

And they slipped out of the room.

'You're right about "Play for Love", Ross,' Stan was saying to Ross. 'Tara sings it just great but it retards the second act.'

'Yeah,' Tam agreed. 'It takes ten minutes for the show to pick up.'

The Musical Director and the Choreographer watched Ross agonise.

'Okay let's cut it.' Ross declared. 'Stan, ask Fly to call the company together.'

Stan looked worried. 'You'd better tell Jerry first, Ross. Once we tell the company it's cut, it's cut. We've been through this before.'

They looked over to the other side of the room where the Producer was still huddled with the two writers. 'We're getting split, Ross,' Stan said. 'Split into two groups. It's not good.'

'George always works like that,' Ross said, watching Jerry and Conrad nod in agreement with some point George was making. 'Divide and rule. That way he retains as much control as possible. You know how he operates. They're caught in the middle.'

'Is George talking to you, Ross?' Tam asked.

'No,' Ross said simply. 'But we communicate by ESP. I always know what he's thinking. He has no secrets from me.'

'So what's he thinking now, Ross?'

'He's thinking about empirical relativity . . . and bagels.'

Tam laughed.

'Stan, see if you can prise the writers away from him?'

Jerry refused point blank to cut the song. He had been buoyed by George, who continued to love all the music. 'He's written you and Tam this note,' Jerry said, giving Ross a folded sheet of legal paper.

Fly arrived back and said the company were getting restless. Would Ross rather give his notes tomorrow? Across the room, George watched impassively, waiting. Ross read the note before replying:

Some of the first act's okay but the second act stinks. The choreography is klutzy and looks like sub Tommy Tune. The actors don't look like they know what they're doing. I want amateurs I go to Peoria social club. There's no problem with the writing. I like all the songs. The problem's yours and you know it. *There's no passion, no moments.* I thought we were doing musical comedy but you don't make me laugh. I've given detailed notes to the boys.

Signed. G. Gibson.

Satisfied, George beckoned to Doris and together with Paul Etienne, they slipped out of the room.

Ross sighed and passed the note to Tam. This continual harassment was hard to bear with low resistance. He felt George was destroying him bit by bit. What had Dee called it . . . a war of attrition? Suddenly he glimpsed what George was after. Not just humiliation, no, George was out to kill. Hence those phone calls late and early.

'Fly, assemble the company please,' Ross ordered weakly.

'So what you gonna do, Ross?' Jerry asked fiercely.

'I'm going to give my notes, Jerry. Tam's going to give his and you and Stan are going to give yours.'

'What about George's?' Jerry pushed his pad at Ross.

'I'm not interested in anything that man has to say, Jerry,' he said quietly, refusing to look at it. 'I'm going to give my notes and they're going to include cutting "Play for Love". I know what's best for this show and we're going to do it my way.'

The company had drawn up chairs in a semi-circle around the production team and listened.

'That's fuckin' unbelievable, man!' Jerry shouted. 'You know better than anyone . . . do you! WELL, YOU'RE AN ARROGANT ASSHOLE! THIS IS MY FUCKIN' SHOW TOO . . . !'

Ross laid his arm on Jerry and said softly, 'I think we should discuss this after, Jerry.'

'Yeah,' Fly said joining in. 'We got the company here, Jerry. Let's just get on with the notes.'

The company of actors stared blankly, uncomprehendingly at the discord. Fly knew that their impassivity was a front. For some this open conflict was deeply disquieting and gave rise to fearful foreboding; to others it was grand stuff to spread around Broadway at dinner time. *Jerry and Ross have fallen out. 'Stars' in deep shit.* But Jerry wasn't to be put off. If Ross announced to the company he was cutting 'Play for Love' it became a fait accompli and Jerry knew it.

'If you cut this number right now, Ross,' he whispered, tensely, 'I'm gonna walk.'

The room was silent. Everyone listened. It was a nightmare scenario.

Ross didn't reply. He turned to the company and winced in pain, the persistent ache in his side becoming, suddenly, a stabbing pain aggravated by, he guessed, the tension. In a small voice he addressed them.

'Company, that was a good run. Thank you. We learnt a lot from yesterday. Your performances are returning as your confidence builds. Fly's going to give you individual notes but before he does, I want to say a few words about the shape of the whole show. The road to perfection is strewn with obstacles. Finding your way is difficult, painful. Act Two is full of obstacles and we haven't yet found a way to clear them . . .'

'Can I interrupt a moment, Ross.'

'Sure, Ziggy. Go ahead.'

'Speaking for a few of us, we feel we got problems with the first

257

too. Once we're in the vaudeville style, we kinda feel comfortable, the problem is before that. It's kinda serious, then seems to change abruptly. Then it even goes back again. It's hard to get your toe in the right door, if you follow me. I gotta tell you I have a real block about this.'

Florence, who had just snuck back in with Lewis and was sitting directly behind Ziggy, pricked up her ears.

'Help me, Tara,' he added.

'Yeah, I kinda know what Ziggy means, Ross. We have to play two styles in Act One: vaudeville and real. It's been left vague as to when we do which. So we don't know what to play when. I don't think that helps Act Two either because we haven't gotta firm enough base from the top. Sorry, Ross.'

Florence leant forward and whispered into Ziggy's ear: 'I might be able to help you with that block, Ziggy.'

Sir Harry had stood up to make a speech. 'You boys can see it better than us, but watching the other bits played out, Ross, I found it a trifle confusing. I mean the two styles. When I first read the script, in the old version, it was conventional, right. I mean, scenes followed by songs. We're now playing mostly revue *with* remains of the old version. Frankly I thought the old version better.' He sat down abruptly.

Ross was thoughtful. 'I hear what you're saying. As a matter of fact, I don't agree. The very thing you're criticising, namely its inconsistency, gives it uniqueness. But Ziggy's instincts are good. If you've problems in the second act, look to the first. It's a point well taken and we'll look at it. Fly, Stan and Tam'll give you notes.'

Ziggy's interjection had been timely. Ross had said nothing about cuts. Once again 'Play for Love' remained in.

'I missed the first part of the note session,' Lewis whispered to Charlie who sat near him marking his script. 'Did I miss much?'

Charlie shrugged. 'Nah. Just civil war.'

'Oh, right,' Lewis said smilingly, enjoying what he took to be a joke.

258

43

The company moved to Washington early in the first week of December to prepare for the technical and dress rehearsals. There was an almost party-like atmosphere on the Metroliner as it sped from Penn Station through Philadelphia to Washington. Rehearsals were over, the die was cast. Ahead lay the stage of the National Theater, technical rehearsals on the set, with the crew, the sound and the lighting. Hard, tiring, exciting work.

Ross stayed behind.

Dr Rudnitsky, who pleased Ross with his frankness, had advised Ross to postpone his departure to muster some strength. Under his guidance, Ross started taking steroids to reduce the swellings and give relief. The benefit might be short-lived but should enable him, the doctor said, to get through the dress rehearsals and into previews.

'After?' Ross had asked.

'Can't say,' the doctor had replied.

Given the intensity of the work during the past six weeks, enforced bed-rest was a necessity and yet a trial. Ross found he slept little but was appallingly tired. In the beginning, awake or asleep, he dreamt.

There were no frontiers between the two states. He had no wish to inspect his life but couldn't avoid it. The genre of the images that flashed through his mind were, he noted, pain dependent. Low pain produced romantic comedy: *in the lobby when they told him the review in the Times for* The Three Musketeers *was a rave; making love to Dee; standing by the window in his study, the view from high up in the old Connecticut house; outside, a glorious spring day, ten-year-old Chloe reading curled up in a sun-lounger, Chrissy playing tag with a friend, Mary-Anne clipping the border; making love to Dee.*

When the pain was bad, he overdosed on the drugs, sniffed coke and dreamt film noir: *George, walking stick raised in fury, outside the Music Box; his mother's face, bruised and blue, after her suicide attempt;*

the hate on Eve's face as she said goodbye for the last time; Chloe, sick and in trouble; running, running down Broadway in the pitch dark . . .

Later, calmer, mostly lucid, he lay in his bed reviewing the work, the tunes in his head, madly going round and round in an endless loop. Despite the set-backs, by the end of the sixth week, as he had hoped, a style had developed; a synthesis of the real and the broadly comic. The actors had found a way to switch from one mode to the other without jarring. With some pride, he felt he had accomplished the almost impossible and made a real entertainment out of the story of Galileo and his struggles against an established, rigid view of the world. Transforming Michael's original book *had* worked. This team had finally absorbed the intellectual core into a fast flowing, enjoyable, witty and, he thought, unique show. He allowed himself a little smile.

But, then, in the bad moments, this seemed a chimera; the optimism slipped away; Ross was stranded in a nightmare of doubts and insecurities, a world where lunacy ruled. Where the very idea of an entertainment about Galileo was preposterous; where in 16th-century Florence, Jerry's pop music made no sense; no song stopped the show; no-one laughed at Conrad's jokes. Where Ross, finally humiliated by George Gibson, saw himself running down Broadway towards a theatre of jeering people before finally dying, tragically, on the fire escape.

Reality was banished. Life had become fiction, melodrama fact.

George Gibson accompanied by Gene Landau and Norman Naff had arrived in Washington at the end of the previous week. They installed themselves in the Castle Court Suite Hotel, along the road from the Marriott Hotel, the home for most of the company during their six-week stay in the capital city. Landau liaised with the management of the National, ensuring budgets and schedules were adhered to, Naff closeted himself with the Washington Press representative they had hired, and George sat in his room brooding.

The day before leaving New York, George had had a further meeting with Gino Bernstein in his office.

'What's the position if I bring someone else in to redirect the show but don't fire Ross?'

The lawyer had put his feet up on the desk. 'Gimme some more clues, George. Why would you wanna do that?'

'I'm unhappy with the way the show's turning out. I seen two runs an' Boardman an' Topp, they can't make it work. Not all of it, but bits. Bits is good. Bits are damned good. I saw it again yesterday, last run before they leave the city. I tell the boys, Jerry an' Conrad, I don't talk to the Director, I told 'em, okay a lot's right, but sure as hell a lot's not. They tell me straight, 'cos I have this good relationship with them, Boardman thinks it's okay. They say all he wants to do is cut the best goddamned song in the show! Guy's nuts, right? Cancer's got to his brain. But I don't want to fire him, you gotta be clear about that. I jus' wanna bring someone else in, to help fix it.'

'It's hypothetical, George.' Gino had said. 'If you bring someone else in, Ross is going to walk.'

'Mebbe yes and mebbe no,' George had replied thoughtfully. 'These're not usual conditions, Gino. The guy's seriously sick, right. I've seen his medical records. Don't ask me how. I know he's only got mebbe three months to live. An' if he don't get rest, not as long.' George smiled and winked at his lawyer. 'I been seeing to that.'

'Is this connected with the questions you were asking me, George, in the Tea Room, coupla weeks ago?'

George chose not to answer. 'Already he's not coming to Washington till late into the technical rehearsals. Plus he's got money troubles, right! *Plus* his daughter's in trouble. The guy's plagued with problems. He can't *afford* to walk away from this show. But, there's a big but, okay . . . Doris and I, we'd be crazy to jeopardise our investment without some fallback position. Consider this: Ross sick in bed or hospital unable to finish getting the show on. Likelihood, then, he won't know or care I bring someone else in to finish the show. You got any Havanas, Gino, I'm out?'

'I don't smoke . . . You *are* crazy, George. If the director is unable to attend rehearsals because of illness he can be removed with the blessings of his union. It's in the contract! You'd be within your rights to get rid of him now. In fact you'd be insane not to. You're already jeopardising yours and Doris's investment by not doing this.'

George folded his arms and looked smugly at Gino. 'Sure I know that. But I got my reasons not to.'

'And what does Doris think about this?'

'She's out of this. Flown back to Antibes. Her boyfriend's walked out, her dog's dead, she's talking about building an ashram for dogs in Nice. She don't give a shit. You seen the advance at the National?'

'Nope.'

'$750,000. That stinks. Only fill a week an' a half. Place can take

261

$540,000 a week. I can afford to drop a million and a half in Washington, but that's it. Anything more an' I'm down the tubes.'

'So what are you saying, George? What's this gotta do with Ross?'

'You gotta let me finish.'

Gino sighed.

'I took a second full page in the Times two weeks ago, pre-selling New York,' George continued. 'We only got $956,000 in the bank ten weeks into selling the show! Okay so it'll hot up as we get nearer to the opening but Gene an' I estimate at the moment that we're gonna open to about $1.2 million. Think that *Miss Saigon* opened to $40 million an' you can see I gotta lotta problems.'

'Sure. But if the word's good out of Washington . . . then Rich likes it . . .?'

'Yeah, yeah,' George dismissed this with an irritated wave. 'I can tell you already the people, they don't *smell* a hit. I lose a million in Washington, an' I've only a nebbishy million in the bank in New York, the figures don't add up. Even a good review in the Times might not save us. We'd have to close too quick.'

'So, what's this gotta do with hiring some guy to replace Ross?'

'You keep missing my point, Gino. I'm not aiming to *replace* him. In fact I wanna *make* sure he goes with me all the way he can.' George spoke confidentially. 'See I've got a strategy to make this show into a hit. It's a plan that's gotta have Ross stay as director but needs someone else to make the show work, because sure as hell he can't.'

Gino smiled and shook his head in wonder at the way George's mind worked. 'Okay,' he said. 'I'll tell you what you want me to tell you. There's nothing says you can't hire two, three or a fucking football team of directors. But if you wanna keep Ross too, then you better make sure he doesn't find out.'

In his Washington hotel, on the Sunday afternoon, as the company was arriving, George was alone, lying on his bed, smoking, looking through a list of directors Betty had culled from the computer. In the next room a ballgame blasted from a TV, making it hard to concentrate. He hated hotels, travelling, being on the road. Alone. 'East or West, Home is Best,' someone had once crocheted on a pillow for him. Much treasured, it sat on his office chair and he sat on it.

'. . . Grounder to Ripken . . .! He flicks it to second . . . One out . . .! He shoots it to first . . . Out number two! . . . A double PLAY!'

Every word from the TV next door reverberated through his

room. *Gotta come up with someone* . . . His stubby finger ran down the names on the paper. Anthony Pyles, Constantine Quertz, Martin Rice . . .

Marty Rice . . .! *There's a talented guy! Choreographer and director. Two for the price of one* . . .

He laid down the list and began to think about Dee. *At least she's not with that asshole in New York* . . . *Saw her twice in a corner palsy-walsy with Ziggy. Mebbe she's cooling off one and* . . . An irresistible urge to clean his teeth and freshen his mouth overcame him. He swung himself off the bed and padded to the bathroom. *After, mebbe, I'll watch that game* . . .

The rest of the afternoon and evening stretched before him and Spectravision only started its adult films after 9.00 p.m. . . .

Without Julie, Lewis felt lost.

She had dissuaded him from chucking the book and returning to London with her. 'Don't be silly,' she had said. 'You're doing ever so well. Now the Indie has accepted your piece on the rehearsal they're bound to ask for a follow up. Clive hasn't stolen all your thunder. Anyway it'll help you find a publisher for your book.'

Eminently sensible advice, Lewis thought at the time. But thinking it through as he unpacked, he knew why he wanted to go home.

He *had* changed. He *was* a new man.

There was plenty of evidence. Watching the run-throughs in New York he had found himself mechanically taking notes; at night, attempting to whip up enthusiasm to type, he'd only complete half a page; he didn't *spill* drinks down himself so much.

It was in the middle of a conversation with Julie, walking through Central Park the day before she left, he suddenly felt able to express what a few months ago would have been inexpressable.

'The bizarre thing is that I've come to the conclusion that musicals are completely idiotic and shouldn't be taken seriously. That being the case,' he said kicking his way through the fall leaves, 'the obsession I had with them was symptomatic of my previous state of mind. I worshipped the people that created those wonderful shows. They were my gods, people like Ross Boardman and George Gibson. The icons have fallen. Maybe, like Galileo, I've learnt to see the world as it is . . . and . . .'

He paused. They were on a replica of a country bridge that passed over not a bubbling stream, but another footpath.

'. . . And it's thanks to you. Well, you and Florence. But particularly you,' he added rather lamely.

She glanced sideways at him. 'That sounds a back-handed compliment.'

'Oh, God, I didn't mean it like that. You see, I feel opened up, alive. Being alive in a new world. Thing is, I'd rather like to live in that world with you.'

Julie laughed. 'Is that a proposal? Sounds about as phony as this bridge! And pretty corny! You think you can live in the real world and come up with lines like that! Do me a favour! I hope your book is better than that!'

She had walked on.

Julie wasn't like any girl he had ever known. She wandered through life amused, detached, controlled, emotionless; taking on anyone and *anything*. Taking life as she found it.

Reflecting on this as he unpacked underwear in the Washington hotel, he realised he wasn't *hurt* by her response. Yes, he thought, a good sign. A sign of maturation. His suitcase was empty and he threw it into the bottom of the cupboard. He stood motionless on the carpet, happy to be freed from the claustrophobia of the New York apartment. *Later, I might wander over to the theatre and watch the set going up. Wonder what Florence is doing tonight? Why did she want a room of her own? I should care!*

Since Julie had left, Florence and he had drifted apart again. She continued to 'unblock' Ziggy and it was yet another revelation to realise that he could cope with that too. He wasn't madly jealous, suicidal.

He was coping.

That was important.

44

Ross arrived at the National Theater in Washington DC in time to
see the last hour of the technical rehearsal and ready to watch the
first full dress in the evening. The steroids had worked, and,
although painfully thin, he appeared re-invigorated with some
colour in his cheeks. He stood at the back of the auditorium
unnoticed by almost everyone and absorbed the atmosphere of a
theatre at work.

Fly, surrounded by Sam Lee and his team of lighting experts,
was running the rehearsal from a table precariously balanced over
the seats in the stalls. Calmly issuing instructions through a
microphone, he talked the actors and the technical teams through
what Ross guessed was the last scene change. Even from so far
back the set was awe-inspiring, the three giant globes revolving
into a new position as he watched.

'Vat do you sink, Ross?' A quiet voice he didn't recognise.

'Magnificent,' he replied, staring at the stage, almost tearful with
the emotion of the moment.

'Danke.'

Ross turned to see Karl-Heinz standing next to him, nodding
appreciatively. There was enough light to see that the designer was
dressed in denims and sneakers.

'You're speaking!' Ross exclaimed.

The German nodded. 'Ya. I'm through with that stupid stuff.
I'm now living in love with a new friend, ya?'

'Oh,' Ross said, turning back towards the stage.

'That French guy. Designer. Paul Etienne. Used to be a friend
of Doris, ya!'

He laughed uproariously, drawing the attention of other
members of the team. Seeing Ross, Fly called a ten-minute break.
His team welcomed him to Washington.

'Hi, Stan!' Ross said. 'How's the orchestra?'

'It's good,' Stan said, delighted to see his old friend, on his feet, with more energy than he'd exhibited in weeks. 'You'll see tonight.'

Jerry and Conrad hugged the director in a genuine display of affection. Others shook his hand heartily. The actors on the stage, blinded by the light and unable to see what was happening, wandered back to their dressing rooms.

'Dee's been goin' crazy to see you, Ross,' Fly said, arriving last. 'I'll go tell her you're here.'

It was a joyful reunion made more so when, out in the last of the daylight, she saw the improvement in him. In the hour they had between the end of the technical and the beginning of the dress rehearsal, they strolled through the chilly December evening, up past the White House.

Dee was shy. 'It's only been a week and we've talked every day but I feel we've got to somehow start again.'

Ross smiled. He was a little breathless from the exertion. 'No, we haven't. It's the same me only better.'

'You're looking much better!'

'The steroids make me feel okay but they say it's temporary. Nevertheless it's a gift.' He wanted to change the subject. 'The technical run looked good. At least the end did.'

'Right. Fly's been bustin' ass. Jerry's been growling around chewing Hershey bars. He hasn't liked this and he hasn't liked that. I think he's been driving Fly wild. Fly can't handle him as well as you. He's been missing Debbie too. He hasn't heard from her for weeks. Me neither. We three used to be thick as thieves but this show's kinda screwed all that up.' She was lost in thought for a moment. 'What else? Oh yeah, Myra's pig's been tellin' Fly what it thinks of the costumes, which is apparently not much.'

'She's a pain in the butt.'

Dee laughed. 'She's a character!'

'Move into the Castle Court with me. Tonight?' he said as they neared the theatre again. His breathing was heavy. He was sweating despite the chill. 'The suite's sizeable.'

'Isn't that where George is? I don't know if I can handle that yet.'

The evening dress rehearsal stopped and started more than Ross would have liked. He let Fly run the show, familiarising himself with the technical details he had planned but hadn't seen executed. George arrived just as the house lights dimmed for the start of the overture. He sat well away from the production table, ignoring Ross.

Ross tried to watch the show with fresh eyes. Prepared for the worst, he was, in fact, pleasantly surprised. It wasn't as funny as he'd hoped but this was, he conceded to himself, only a first dress. Everyone was still nervous working on the ravishing, but difficult, set.

'How're you, Ross? Glad you're well enough to come down.' The run over, to Ross's surprise and the team's pleasure, George had approached the production table, smiling broadly. 'Great run! The show's comin' on just great! Just great! I'm gonna go backstage and tell 'em they're doing fine. Great band, Stan . . .!'

Stan was still in the pit giving notes to the musicians. The team beamed. Everyone except Ross.

'When George talks to me in exclamation marks,' Ross said, 'I gotta watch out.'

That night Dee moved out of the Marriott Hotel into the Castle Court Hotel.

45

The cream of Washington society turned out for the opening night of *Stars in His Eyes*. There were Senators, Congressmen, and a collection of Ambassadors. The Italian Cultural Attaché was very much in evidence dashing between a dozen local schoolgirls he had dressed up as Sicilian peasants. They handed out brochures of Florence, Pisa and Rome to the first-nighters. The local theatre élite, including some of Ross's old friends from his days at the Arena Stage, milled around the lobby. There were even unfounded rumours that the President and First Lady might attend.

They had had three previews. The first and third had gone well, the second badly. Ross had told Lewis that odd numbered previews go well, even badly. The first night, he said, should be after an even numbered preview. In the event the first night, the fourth performance, went as well as could be expected. There were no technical hitches (one of the globes *had* been malfunctioning, but Karl-Heinz, in overalls, armed with an array of spanners, had cured the problem in time). The cast rose to the occasion and gave their best performance. Ziggy and Tara were loved, and the audience gave a standing ovation to Sir Harry Whitney.

But there could be no disguising that something, somewhere was wrong.

Following the performance, Ross, the writers and the production team held a post-mortem in the restaurant of an adjacent hotel. In the ballroom of the same hotel, George Gibson was hosting a First Night buffet party attended by most of the glitterati. His guests were respectful but no-one raved.

Both Ross and George got the same message: first act's okay, second's a problem. Everyone had theories. Jerry blamed it on the choreography. Tam Topp, who had already sensed he was to be the victim if things turned sour, went on the defensive. He blamed the problems on a set that was, he claimed, impossible to work on. Karl-Heinz shrugged that off, 'Sheisse script, sheisse show'.

Conrad was outraged at that. If Harry Whitney spoke the lines as he'd written them, he claimed, the script would work great.

Ross intervened. 'Nothing's changed. There has always been a problem in Act One. They just don't buy the set-up. Galileo and his young self don't seem like the same guy.'

'Yeah,' Jerry said. 'You got a Brit playing one an' a New Yorker playing the other. I knew we shouldn't have cast Whitney, for Chrissakes . . .!'

'Well we have,' Ross said. 'But the problem's in the structure not in the playing. Then, on a detail, my old argument, Jerry. "Play for Love". It stops the show, but not the way we want it to. You gotta have felt it tonight?'

'But they loved it!' Jerry said, clinging to the wreckage. 'I heard that applause, man! You all did. It got the best reaction of the evening.'

'Sure, it did, Jerry,' Tam said. 'But then they got restless and they didn't come back to us for ten minutes.'

'I couldn't tell from the pit,' Stan said. 'What d'you feel, Con?'

'I got to reluctantly agree,' Conrad said, nervously adjusting his yamulka. 'It does seem like it's from a different show. Sorry, Jerry.'

'Well even if we did cut it, whad'ya want?' Jerry said, weakening. 'Another number or cut it and move on?'

'Cut it and move on,' Ross said seizing on the opening that Jerry had given. 'Why don't you guys see if you can cut and stitch. Now let's address the fundamental problem in the first act.'

Half-an-hour later the team, having completed their note session, went upstairs to join the first-night party. Ross only went to find Dee and take her home. He surveyed the room from the door. Nearby, George Gibson huddled with Tara. She was trying to look interested. '. . . An' he didn't turn the damned TV off till 4.00 a.m.! Can you believe that? So they're moving me tonight to another suite . . . You wanna pop up later for a drink?'

'I don't think so, George . . .,' Tara said. 'When I'm in the mood for sexual harassment, you'll be the first to know.'

As Ross moved into the room looking for Dee, they pounced. The theatre establishment in Washington revered him. He had directed some of his best work in the city, lent his name to fund-raising efforts, was the local boy made good on a wider stage. Now they lined up to pay their respects.

Rosie Lafontaine was the last in the line. She was the present Artistic Director of the Folger, a theatre constructed in an old library. Now in her mid-sixties, Rosie, round, larger than life, with an infectious laugh, was of the same generation as Ross, but, unlike him, had carved her career in Washington, never having been

269

tempted by commercialism or Broadway's bright lights. Due to retire next year, she was a highly respected Shakespearian director and scholar. Ross loved her. Whenever he was in town they lunched. Because she was the last in the line, she had him to herself.

'Okay, Rosie,' he said. 'Gimme it straight.'

She put her arm through his and steered him away from the crowd to a quiet table.

'Straight, huh?' She picked some skin off her index finger thoughtfully. 'It's not there, but it's curable. And you know I wouldn't say that to you if I didn't believe it. There seem to be two conflicting styles. One's kinda jokey, vaudeville and the other's kinda serious and sentimental. It's as if you don't trust your material and haven't quite decided which way you want to go. It's hesitant. Go for one or the other. Trust your instincts.'

Ross smiled. 'You got it in one. We changed direction and you've detected something I thought we'd cured. The two Galileos bother you? I mean one being English the other . . .'

Rosie interrupted. 'Absolutely not. Doesn't matter at all . . . But you got a hard time convincing us a dancing, singing Galileo isn't like *Springtime for Hitler* – a huge joke.'

'He sees himself as a kinda vaudevillian figure.'

'Galileo sees himself as a vaudevillian? Gee that's pretty tough to swallow. I see what you're getting at but if you want us to buy it you must find a way of telling us what to expect right at the top. I think you've got the same problem as they had on *Funny Thing Happened on the Way to the Forum*. Steve Sondheim had to write "Comedy Tonight" to let the audience in. You gotta do the same, Ross.'

Ross beamed at her. 'You haven't lost your touch, Rosie. Still as smart as ever, huh!' He gave her as big a hug as he could manage.

She said, 'You're all skin and bones, you old fool! How're you feeling?'

Ross shrugged. He didn't want to talk about it. She didn't press it, she knew anyway. Everybody did.

'Okay, but I gotta tell you something disturbing,' she said. 'I bumped into Marty Rice in the interval . . .'

'Not one of nature's treasures . . .'

'No. I asked him what he was doing here. He looked cagey, evil. Like Jack Nicholson in *Witches of Eastwick*. I got it out of him in the end. He said Gibson brought him down to look'n see. Maybe work with you on the show. Can you believe that?'

She anxiously watched Ross's reaction. If he was hurt he didn't show it.

'Thank you for telling me, Rosie. It's no surprise. Fact is, George

270

spoke to me three days ago. I figured something was up.'

'But Rice for Chrissakes! That . . . kid! How could Gibson expect you to work with him. You seen any of his ballets? Or that pathetic musical version of *Twelfth Night!* It's an insult. What are you going to do?'

Ross smiled. 'Nothing. Play wait and see. When Gibson brings him in, I'll quit.'

Soon after this, Dee managed to extract him from the party. She was in a black mood after an unpleasant encounter with George.

'What did he say?' Ross asked her in the cab.

'We traded insults,' she said. 'I don't want to talk about it.' She only brightened up after a glass of chilled champagne in the suite.

One hour later George Gibson arrived back at the Castle Court. Welcoming him, the girl on the desk gave him his new key card. 'Hope this room'll be quieter, Mr Gibson. Should be. We put you by your director. In fact your doors are right next to each other! So I guess you can shout at him all you want if he keeps you awake!' It saddened the clerk to see her pleasantry produce a grim scowl. She watched her guest disappear into the elevator.

Clutching an empty ice-bucket needing a refill from the machine down the corridor, Dee, with appalling timing, opened the door of her suite at the same moment George opened his. Only inches apart, their eyes briefly met, before he went in slamming his door. The shock of the encounter momentarily stunned her. She was breathless. Her heart thumped. Then, trying to control her shaking, she went in search of the ice-machine.

'He treated you like dirt, Dee. He's a piece of shit. You need never feel guilt,' Ross said after she'd returned and told him the news. Through the thin wall they could hear him angrily banging around his room. 'I've an idea that'll give him something to think about. Drink a little more champagne . . .'

Twenty minutes later, having completed his nightly ablutions, George lay on his bed in his underwear and flicked mute through his free five minutes of Pay TV's adult films. He thought about Tara. *Why didn't that bitch come up an' see me? Am I getting too old to pull these girls? Mebbe that Florence could give me another mouth job . . . What's this . . .?*

George began to be aware that the sounds of lovemaking he was listening to were not emanating from the TV.

What the hell's this?

Then it dawned.

Jesus H. Christ, they're doing it against the wall. Our wall!

The wall was a perfect transmitter. He lay on his bed, holding his breath, not daring to move. Every moan, every gasp, every

271

vibration was audible. Worse, it became amplified in his imagination as he pictured the scene.

A rhythm was established, a drumming on the wall, a naked buttock beating out an ancient tune.

As the tempo and volume increased, George tried stuffing his fingers in his ears to shut out the repulsive noise. But there was no escaping the abomination that seemed never ending. No way could he shut out the image of the woman he'd lived with all those years, *yes*, his wife, eyes shut in perfect ecstasy, pressed against the wall, arms clasped around the thin torso of the man he hated . . .

He's coming inside her . . .

Oh, my Christ . . .

Over and over again . . .

46

Three weeks into the Washington run, at 2.30 p.m. on the third day after Christmas, Ross collapsed whilst rehearsing. He was rushed to the George Washington University Hospital. Dee and John Lewis went with him in the ambulance, holding his hand, stroking his brow. He had been rehearsing the principals, Dee, Tara, Ziggy and Harry Whitney when suddenly, perching on the edge of his chair, he went pale, held his side and collapsed on to the floor, semi-conscious. Lewis stayed with him in Intensive Care whilst Dee went back to the theatre for the evening performance.

The pressure on Ross since the opening had been intolerable. Jerry and Conrad had worked prodigiously, rewriting. The changes restored confidence after the hammering the show received from most of the press. The best, the influential Washington Post, was lukewarm but having, as Ross put it, the wit to see beyond the present to what the show could be and now *was* becoming.

A crucial change had been made to the opening. They now had a new number sufficiently comic to get the show off to a bright start and introduce the principal characters in an amusing fashion. To their relief, the audiences responded positively.

George was in a meeting with Landau and Naff in the New York office, when Charlie Brodsky called.

'He's in hospital,' George said to the two men as he put the phone down.

Landau whistled. 'This is it, huh?'

'Yeah,' George said. 'At last. Here's what we gotta do. Gene, you call the hospital, find out how long they think he's got . . .'

'They're not gonna tell me that . . .'

'Find out! I don't want no excuses! We gotta know *exactly*. Go do it now! From out there!' He pointed to the door and the General Manager went out.

Naff smiled as the door closed. 'Going according to plan, right?'

'No,' George said abruptly. 'Not if he dies now. It's too soon.

273

We still got six weeks before we open here. We gotta get it, exactly right . . . right to the day.'

'You want me to release this to the papers?'

George looked at his Press Representative in amazement. *He is so stupid! I have to explain everything!*

'No, Norman,' George explained tersely. 'This bit we have to keep *out* of the papers. We gotta keep this quiet. BETTY! Get the car! I'm gonna catch the shuttle.'

George liked baths and flying. They cocooned him from the world, comforted him, allowed him time to think. The plane banked sharply as it rose from La Guardia and George peered out of the window watching the ground slipping away. He always enjoyed seeing the cars and the people reduced to insignificance. Just like ants, he thought to himself. *Ants.* George hadn't been in Washington for three weeks. He'd left the morning of the third day after the show opened. Charlie's reports faxed to New York every morning painted a picture of the show's steadily improving fortunes. Now, on the plane, George wondered how optimistic this was. He closed his eyes and cast his mind back to the opening night and the morning after. *Jesus, some twelve hours! Those assholes! Doing it against my wall!*

George hadn't slept much the night of the Washington opening. Every creak startled him. Were they at it *again?* The man was supposed to be dying, for Chrissakes! At 6.30 a.m., giving up any more ideas of sleep, he telephoned downstairs for the papers. The reviews confirmed his fears, the show stank. The time had come to add Marty Rice. At 7.00 a.m. George called him and 20 minutes later they breakfasted together in his suite. Sombre and preoccupied, still unnerved by the events of the previous night, George conducted the interview in a whisper. He listened to Rice's comments and suggestions. Rice was full of ideas, talked loud, fast and expressively, waving his hands about as he explained each choreographic idea.

'Yeah, yeah,' George said. 'Keep your voice down, will ya! This dump's got thin walls. You wanna work with Boardman fixing this show?'

'It's okay by me. I prefer to work on my own but I think you got potential here. Rothstein's written a good book. But what about Ross and Topp? They don't know about this, huh? What's Ross gonna say?'

'I'll fire Topp an' put it to Ross in a way he can't refuse.'

'Yeah, but he will. He's gonna walk off the show, right? Then, what? You want me to do it with the team on my own?'

'Well that's not gonna happen, Marty. See he's sick. He's gonna be incapable. He needs the dough. You two gotta work on it *together*.'

'Why are we whispering, George. No-one can hear us.'

'Well you can't be too careful, okay,' George whispered bleakly. 'You could work with him, right?'

'As I say, yeah, I could. Bigger question is whether he can work with me. An' I gotta tell you frankly, I doubt it.'

'Yeah, well there's a couple of options. I'm either gonna put you on the job tomorrow after I've fixed it with Boardman. Or I'm gonna send you back to New York an' put you on stand-by. Okay?'

'Sure,' said Rice as George ushered him to the door. 'You're the boss.'

Then, in the corridor, to Marty's surprise, George bidding him goodbye, enunciating loudly and clearly, said, 'Thank you for coming to see me, Marty Rice, and offering your help.'

But Ross and Dee, curled up in each other's arms, were fast asleep and heard nothing.

Ross had watched the second performance from the back of the stalls. As the curtain fell at the end of the first act he noted that the audience reaction was markedly less warm than the night before. Clearly they had read the morning reviews. He listened to the chatter as they drifted past.

'This is *terrible*. Did you read the Post . . .?'

'. . . No chance on Broadway.'

'Of course they should have stuck to Brecht. I remember seeing . . . .'

Ross was depressed but he'd been here before. He was confident that the changes planned would turn the show round. They needed patience and hard work.

'Iss not going so well, huh?' Paul Etienne and Karl-Heinz had joined Ross who was supporting himself heavily on the back row.

'Sheisse script, sheisse show. I say that vonce, I say that again. Ve have done wery vonderful vork on show but much to fix ja, Ross?'

Ross smiled wearily. 'If I have the stamina to do it.'

'Ja, sure you have. You vill have much energy, then you go poof and you die. All creative people it's like this.'

'You're a great comfort, Karl-Heinz!'

'Vell no point in bush beating. I too vould like to go out in my prime but now I luff Paul and ve go through ze life together, huh?'

He laughed loudly.

Paul came round to the other side of Ross. 'I speak wiz Doris a short while ago in Antibes, an' she sends you lots of 'er love. She say she sure you gonna crack this show . . . whatever . . . well whatever 'appens.'

'Yeah? That kinda nice remark doesn't sound like Doris?'

Paul grinned and poked Ross in the ribs. He winced. 'You're goddamned right. But she is not ze same woman! No, since Roget die, an' since she know Florence, she's changed beaucoup. She is sinking about opening wis Florence an hopital for sick animals.'

'Oh,' said Ross. 'I thought she was starting an ashram.'

'Zat was last week,' Paul said and turned towards the stage. The orchestra had started the entr'acte.

Half way through the second act, Ross became aware of heavy breathing and the smell of stale cigars. George was beside him, whispering hoarsely into his ear.

'Wanna meet afterwards for a talk. The bar at the Willard.'

Ross nodded, then added softly, 'Hope we didn't keep you awake last night, George?' It was too dark to see his reaction.

After the performance, George had gone straight to the Willard and found a table in a quiet corner. The piano player, whose repertoire consisted mainly of Lloyd Webber, smiled at him. Backstage, Ross gave notes to a gloomy company, before slowly walking the block to the hotel and George.

'What'll you have?' George asked with a fixed smile as he sat down.

'Nothing. I'm tired. I wanna go home to bed.'

'Yeah, well you shouldn't keep late nights. Not a man in your condition. You're driving yourself too hard,' George said mockingly.

'What d'you want to talk about, George? We got little to say to each other.'

George eyed him thoughtfully. 'What's up with you Ross? Why you so goddamn spikey, huh? Why d'you wanna hurt me? What have I ever done to you?'

Ross grimly watched the piano player and said nothing.

'I took this show, a show no-one else wanted to touch. You think I didn't know you an' Kershon hawked it round Merrick an' Mackintosh before you came to me? Sure I knew. But I backed *you*. I *trusted* you . . .'

'Trust? You don't know the meaning of that word . . .'

'An' what do you do to me? You abuse me, humiliate me an' steal my wife . . .'

'She's not your wife, George . . .'

'In name only.'

'And I didn't steal her. She came to me. Why did you do it, George?' Ross asked. 'Why did you treat her so shabbily?'

George shifted uncomfortably in his seat. 'She was very young. You know what these young girls are like, Ross. You fuck 'em then they want to marry you to get your money. Well I knew *that* game! So to avoid any complications later, I took the opportunity to get out fast. I mean I hardly *knew* her. How was I to know she was gonna make a beautiful wife? A hundred times since I would have married her again, properly, an' had some kinda marriage contract drawn up, like Trump or Turner. But I didn't have the guts to tell her, can you understand that?'

'Sure, George,' Ross said. 'I know you too well.'

'Now it's too late. What's gonna happen after you die, Ross? To Dee? Think she'll come back to me?'

'You're a fool, George,' Ross said. 'You operate on the "me first" principle . . . When someone else operates on the same principle you can't stand it. We aren't like bagels in your deli, George. We won't be manipulated and consumed to suit your whims. We fight back.'

'Okay, okay, let's leave the personals outa this conversation.' George had become irritated. This was not going to plan. 'We gotta talk a bit about the show or we gonna find the time an' money we spent going down the tubes. There's an usher I talk to who's no dope. He's just Mr Average even if he does wanna be a dancer. He's put his finger on the problem. You know what he said? He said, the problem with the show, Mr Gibson, is who gives a shit about telescopes, the motion of the planets, whether the earth's round or flat! When's the next fucking number? That's what we wanna know. Now that's pretty damned *smart* . . .'

George nodded sagely then aggressively stabbed at Ross with his finger.

'. . . You gotta get rid of the jokes that don't work, I mean cut the book right down and beef up the choreography! We promise a song and dance show but we don't deliver!'

'Don't poke me, George . . .'

'I pay you, I'll poke you . . .' George said irrationally, growing red.

'Then I'll poke you back,' Ross said and did, jamming his finger forcefully and painfully into George's chest.

George angrily swung his fist at Ross, catching him on the shoulder. Ross, more shocked than hurt, cried out. The pianist, who was in the middle of 'Memories' stopped playing as the fight broke out. The barman, looking anxious, came out from behind the bar.

'Have you quite finished?' Ross shouted at George as the barman arrived to quieten them down. The bar was filling up and the customers stared inquisitively.

'Can I get you gentlemen anything?' the barman said, adding quietly, 'We don't want me to have to call the manager do we, gentlemen? Or the cops?'

'No, s'okay. Hey, Ross, you wanna drink anything?' George was breathing heavily, but the anger was draining away.

Ross rubbed at his shoulder. With little flesh to cover his bones, the blow hurt like hell. He turned to George. 'You want Marty Rice, right? Have him. I quit.'

The barman waited. The piano player gaily returned to work and launched into an up-tempo version of 'Don't Cry for Me Argentina'.

'Gimme another scotch on the rocks,' George said evenly. Then to Ross: 'You sure you don't want anything?'

But Ross was getting up to leave. George half rose and put his arm out to stop him. 'Hey, Ross, come on! I was just bein' affectionate for Chrissakes! I'm sorry I poked you! Anyway, who said anything about Marty Rice! Did I say anything about Marty Rice?' George asked the bemused barman.

'Keep it down gentlemen,' the barman said quietly before leaving, 'or I'm gonna have to throw you both out, okay?'

'Who's Marty Rice anyway!' George said as he pulled Ross back into his seat. 'You wanna cigar? They're Havanas . . . Oh yeah, you got cancer, right. I forgot. I'm trying to speak frankly with you, Ross, an' you throw Marty Rice at me!'

'George, Rice was at the show last night. You paid his fare down. You breakfasted with him. This is because you *like* him? Okay, you have him. Tam and I will leave in the morning *after* I've told the company . . .'

'For Chrissakes will you calm down! Who said anything about . . . Okay, okay so Rice *is* here! I'm not meshuggah or senile yet, Ross, an' if you put yourself in my shoes what would you do, huh? I've got a director who's dying. I've a director who may, at any minute, *not be here,* for Chrissakes! I've a show not working as it should . . . what would you have me do? I just want someone to work with you on the show. That's all I'm asking! I don't want you *off* the show, is that clear? I'd like you to listen to Rice's ideas. They're good! Let him re-choreograph a coupla the numbers then everything'll be fine. I'll fire Topp an' you'll be able to rest up.'

George smiled benignly at Ross. For a moment, Ross pondered how he could best kill George on the spot. *Hold his head under a tub of scotch till his breath stops. Strangulation with the table napkin. Break a chair over his head.* Instead he said, 'George, you're such an asshole, such a shit, it's breathtaking. Let me set it out for you as clearly as I can. I figure it'll take three weeks to get the show right. Your choice is simple. You go back to New York for three weeks and let me finish the job with my team, my way. Or I'm out.'

'You mean,' George said incredulously, 'that you'd dump your fees and royalties rather than work with Marty.'

'Yup. That's your choice, George . . .'

The waiter returned with George's scotch.

'Still the tough guy, huh?' George said, smiling, patting Ross's arm. 'I always said you're the best. Okay! Here's what we do. I go away, you fix the show. But I'm gonna delay opening the show in New York. We'll play extra previews but we don't open till we gotta show working 100%.'

George studied Ross over his scotch. *You gonna buy that, Mr Fixit-in-three weeks? It'll kill you.*

'No!' Ross said sharply. 'That's completely unacceptable! I may not have those weeks, George! We'll have the show right in three weeks from now, and that's going to be the show you'll open on Broadway end of February. Take it or leave it!'

'That's fighting talk, Ross. You do it!' George said happily.

Both men got up. Ross felt unbearably weary. The confrontation had exhausted him.

'Good luck,' George said, offering his hand. 'See you in three weeks. Go in health.'

Ross ignored the outstretched hand. A hoarse 'Goodbye,' was all he could muster before he left the bar and took a cab back to the hotel.

George sat down, delighted. The pressure was *on! And* he had Marty waiting in the wings. Before he left the bar of the Willard, George slipped the surprised piano player a ten–dollar bill.

'You know who I socked?' George asked.

The piano player shook his head.

'One of Broadway's greatest directors,' George said. 'How the mighty are fallen, right?'

The shuttle, shuddering and banking over Georgetown before landing, brought George back to the present. Washington was a carpet of white elegance below. Somewhere down there Ross lay in intensive care. *How the mighty are fallen . . .* He smiled to himself.

Betty had fixed a sedan and he reached the theatre as Stan was beginning the overture. Business had improved. Charlie's reports had not been exaggerated. The theatre was full. Ten minutes later George was convinced a show had emerged. The transformation wrought at the expense of Ross's health was colossal; there could be no mistaking the audience's enjoyment. He was very satisfied. After the show, highly elated but trying not to show it, he addressed a depressed and tearful company in the empty auditorium.

'Ladies and gentlemen, I won't keep you long. I know this has been a deeply disturbing day. I have just been told his condition is stable, thank God. But I can tell you, he would have been as proud as I am for the show you gave tonight.'

He looked around for Dee. She wasn't there. She had been driven back to the hospital as soon as the curtain had fallen.

Sir Harry Whitney spoke for the company. 'Well, George, thank you for coming so speedily to be with us. *Of course* we're deeply shocked about what has happened here today. Ross, as I'm sure you know was . . . is . . . held by us in high regard. It reminds me of another similar occasion in the days when I used to perform live plays on television in England. In the first 15 minutes of one performance, live in front of 5 million viewers, just off camera, one of my fellow actors dropped dead of a heart attack. Well you can imagine the consternation! But we carried on as if nothing happened. We improvised around the gaps in the script and finished the play. The show went on. And so it will for us because this is what Ross would want. Indeed he even told me this very thing after a drink the . . .'

Ziggy interrupted. 'Please can I make an announcement? Florence and I are gonna hold a short prayer meeting for Ross and we'd be real happy to see any of you there. You too, Mr Gibson. It'll take place in Dressing Room Ten.'

Florence nodded and kept a firm grip on Ziggy's hand. Two weeks before Florence had seen the light whilst watching a preacher on cable TV. She had become a member of The Church of the Christian Martyr. Ziggy had taken the faith too. It was the final straw for Lewis.

'One last word, ladies and gentlemen, please,' George said. 'We start our previews in New York in four weeks! Ross and I agreed that we'd only open when we were sure everything is 100%. Well we're 60%. We have work still to do! Goodnight.'

The actors dispersed and George spoke to the production team.

'I want to be honest with you,' he began. 'It's no secret I got Marty Rice on stand-by. What's happened is not so unexpected, right? But, after what I seen here tonight I think *you're* right on the money. Fly, you're doin' a terrific job! We're gonna be a hit an' the quality of the show will be a memorial to Ross . . .'

'Ze guy iss not dead yet, Mr Producer,' Karl-Heinz interrupted.

'Yeah,' George said sourly, casting a disdainful look at the German. 'Anyway, I'm standing Rice down.'

There were murmurs of approval and thanks from the team.

'Now, I want to hear in detail what you guys are planning to do. You gotta fax me details of everything, every day. I'm gonna fly down an' see every third performance an' I don't want any surprises, is that clear?'

He glared at them challengingly. Fly nodded, no-one else moved a muscle. To do so would be to take sides.

'Okay. An' another thing, we're gonna put back "Play for Love" as soon as possible. I want that damn number back before we get to New York. Let's go do it!'

47

At the end of the first week in February, *Stars in His Eyes* started previewing on Broadway. The company quickly settled into their new surroundings in the Metropolitan Grand, happy to be back in their city, at home.

The news from the George Washington Hospital wasn't good. Ross Boardman was conscious but slowly sinking. Dee had been in a great dilemma wanting to stay but pressed by Ross to go. In the end he had won. As she left for New York, he comforted her. 'I'm not afraid. I've directed too many death scenes. As long as there's no pain . . .'

As it happened, after the company left, Ross had a flurry of visitors. Ellen paid an unexpected visit and brought with her Chloe, recently returned from London. His daughter was distraught at his appearance. In bed was a shrivelled and weak old man, incapable of turning over on his own, sustained only by the drips in his arm. The last time she had seen him, he was her vigorous, invincible, champagne-drinking father. She sat beside his bed, held his thin hand and said nothing about her predicament in London. Ross asked if the money had arrived. She nodded and kissed his brow. The kiss spoke plenty. Ross looked at her. She'd changed. She looked older, wiser – a woman. Then they talked, holding hands, crying for the times they had wasted. Ross begged her to keep her sister and half-sisters away. 'Let them remember me as I was,' he pleaded. 'I don't want them here reminding me what a lousy father I was.' Painfully slowly, whilst they watched, he wrote individual letters to each of his children and his ex-wives. 'Distribute them when it's all over,' he instructed Chloe.

Ellen sat against a wall feeling left out. He had eyes only for Chloe. She watched them together and wished that she too had had a child . . . After two hours she accompanied Ross's daughter back to New York.

Rosie Lafontaine paid brief visits, chatting whilst he lay with eyes closed. She was preparing *The Winter's Tale* for her theatre and was full of gossip. He looked forward to her visits. One afternoon, towards the end of the third week in February, Rosie told him about a news item in the New York Times. The Times reported that despite two weeks of previews in New York *and* six weeks out-of-town, George Gibson was delaying inviting the critics to *Stars*. He had postponed the opening night twice for different reasons: there were technical problems with the set, somebody had lost their voice, Ross Boardman was unwell and they were waiting for him to improve.

'What's he up to?' Ross muttered. 'We had a deal, Rosie. I said to him, I'll fix the show in three weeks, you open third week in February. We should have opened today or was it tomorrow? I got no sense of time any more.'

'It was yesterday,' Rosie said gently.

'Get Fly on the phone, will you, Rosie.'

Rosie left a message at the Production Office in the Metropolitan Grand and an hour later Fly called back. He couldn't answer Ross's question. He said nobody knew anything. The show had been going swell, the actors' performances were growing stronger and more confident. A week ago they were playing to full houses, but now, with the postponement of the opening night, the houses were beginning to drop away. Nobody could figure out what George was up to. After each performance he gave Fly notes which he passed on to the company. 'Most of the notes he gives me,' Fly said sotto voce, 'I know get given to him by the barman in the upstairs bar. George gives a lot of credence to his opinions. But they're details. Just the odd line interpretation, an inflection, or a tempo correction. Nothing that would give an excuse to postpone *once* let alone over and over again. Yet George keeps on repeating we're not yet ready to be reviewed. Maybe he figures he can recoup without ever having to open. It wouldn't be the first time. Search me what it's all about. You speak to Dee?'

'No,' said Ross weakly. 'I won't talk to her any more. It upsets us both too much.'

Rosie had gone, and the nurse had given him an injection. The chemical separated his mind from his body. There was no more pain, no more body. He existed solely in his mind, pure thought, dreams, floating in space . . . drifting . . .

Can't figure it out, Fly had said . . . the opening postponed . . . not ready for the reviewers . . . waiting for Ross Boardman to improve. But Ross Boardman wasn't going to get better. What did all this mean? Why had George broken his promise made in the Willard. There was something . . . something obvious . . .

That morning in New York, John Lewis had telephoned Betty at the office to ask her to arrange a meeting with George. She consulted the diary and suggested 5.00 that afternoon. 'I'll be there,' Lewis had said and hung up.

Sitting by Betty's desk in the outer office, waiting for George to see him, Lewis tried to read Variety. Betty all a-dither, muttered to herself as she searched for a lost file. He couldn't concentrate. Instead he found himself thinking back ten months, was it only *ten months*, it seemed a life-time, to a very different John Lewis who had waited, in this same place, to meet the producer for the first time. Nothing in the office had changed. Nothing except him.

George escorted Norman Naff out of his office and ushered Lewis in. The producer seemed in high spirits. 'BETTY! Why the hell didn't you give Jaahn a drink! Whad'ya want Jaahn? GET HIM A DIET SPRITE, BETTY! Now what can I do for you?'

Lewis settled into a chair still warm from Naff's backside. 'I want to go home, Mr Gibson. I want to go back to London, but I can't until the show opens and nobody seems to know when that is. Can you enlighten me?'

George picked up Variety and tossed it across the desk. 'Look at what we grossed last week. See! $457,000! The nut's just over four hundred thousand bucks. We're making nearly $50,000 a week. That's pretty damned good for a show that hasn't opened! The publicity about why I'm not opening's getting people interested. They're intrigued, so I can keep going like this for a bit longer. Then, when we finally open, we're gonna open BIG!'

He banged the desk with the flat of his hand. Pencils scattered.

'Biggest opening this town's seen in years! Bigger than *Saigon!* I'm gonna get front-page space in every paper around the world! Every network will carry it! Watch my lips! You ain't seen nothing yet!'

His face was red with excitement as he pounded the table with his fist. Lewis got the point. He marvelled, yet again, at the 75-year-old Producer's energy.

'That's great George, but I just want to know when that's going to be. Thing is I've nearly finished the first draft of the book . . .'

George interrupted. 'Yeah! Can I get a look? Howd'I come out?'

'Fine. I've got all the background I need except for one thing . . . .'

'What's that?' George asked.

Lewis was suddenly shy. 'Well I'm still pretty unclear about your background. I mean, where you were born? Who your mother was? It's just the story you told me last year about being born and brought up in Cleveland doesn't seem to be the only story. I've heard, for example, that you were born in Lodz, son of a tailor, you worked your passage to New York, apprenticed in a sweat shop, saving enough to bring over your family . . . Real name: George Gibbowitz. Or were you born on the East Side here? I thought maybe you could clear that one up for me . . .?'

George stared at Lewis goggle-eyed, mouth open. Then, beginning with what sounded like a throat tickle, he erupted into a hideous spasm of chest convulsions, hacking, coughing catarrh until he accumulated enough to warrant spitting it into a Kleenex he pulled from a plastic dispenser on the desk. He examined the contents before pitching it across the desk towards a basket next to Lewis's chair. It landed short. The paroxysm successfully deflected Lewis's probing questions.

'Well, never mind,' Lewis said, averting his eyes from the green, gelatinous phlegm, sunnyside-up, beside his left foot. 'Maybe another time. My paper has been accepting regular articles from me, and they want me back as a Deputy Features Editor which is promotion. And there's a girl back home . . . So if you could just give me a little help with the date . . .?'

George cleared his throat and thought for a moment. 'Nope. Can't help at all. It's in the lap of the Gods. But, when the Gods decide, you can be sure you'll know.' He laughed at this obscurity and terminated the interview in a friendly, backslapping fashion.

Wandering up 7th Avenue with little intention except to kill some time, Lewis pondered about the interview. Why did he feel irritated? George's smugness? He held their fate in his hands and he was having a ball playing God . . . Finding himself at the stage door of the Metropolitan Grand, Lewis thought he might as well potter up to the stage, see what was going on. There was little point in going back to the apartment and sitting alone. The place wasn't the same since Florence had moved in with Ziggy.

The stage doorman stopped him as he was about to go up the stairs. 'Urgent message for you, Mr Lewis.'

Lewis unfolded the paper and read: PLEASE PHONE ME RE ROSS BOARDMAN'S HEALTH SOONEST FROM PRIVATE PHONE. G.W. HOSP. 202 994 1000 EXT 2245. SIGNED: ROSIE LAFONTAINE.

Lewis bounded up the stairs and found Fly and Charlie kibbitzing in the production office. 'Sorry, chaps,' he said breathlessly. 'Would you mind awfully if I make a private call from in here? It *is* important and it's not to England, Charlie! It's to

285

Washington. I hope to God it's not bad news.'

They left him to it. Five minutes later Fly and Charlie saw Lewis rush out. 'Is he okay?' they shouted as he disappeared down the corridor.

'I'm flying up to Washington,' Lewis shouted over his shoulder. 'It doesn't sound good. I'll let you know . . . I'll keep in touch.'

And he was gone.

11.00 a.m. the next morning Betty received a collect call from John Lewis in Washington. He was highly agitated. 'Betty, for God's sake put me through to George immediately!'

'Gee, I'm sorry, John, George isn't here right now. If you leave your number I'll have him call you as soon as he gets in.'

'No, it's impossible. I'm at the hospital. Ross is fading. They doubt he'll last more than 48 hours. You got that? He's in great pain and we're going to move him to some place, a private hospice I think. They say it's a beautiful place. They'll make his last hours comfortable. Please tell George!'

Betty became panicked. 'Wait up, Jaahn! Gimme a number where Mr Gibson can call you . . .'

'Yes! Soon as possible, okay. I've got to go, Betty. I'll phone soon. Please find George! Thanks. Bye.'

Betty tracked down George at the Landau offices. Unable to disguise the panic in her voice, she told him the news.

'Phone Lewis back at the hospital!' He shouted down the phone. 'You gotta find out where they're taking him! I wanna be able to get up-to-the second medical bulletins. Get Lewis to phone in a health report every two hours as well, okay? Got that? Tell Lewis on no account is he to tell *any* member of the New York company. Tell him, *coincidentally*, I'd decided to open in the next day or two an' naturally I don't want the company upset. It could destroy the opening an' everything we've . . . no . . . everything Ross has worked for. Say that's what Ross would want. You got that exactly, Betty? Sure? Okay, tell it me back . . .'

She'd made notes and had it exactly.

'You got it . . . Phone Lewis NOW!'

George put the phone down. He beamed at Gene Landau who was sitting at his desk checking through figures.

'One of the opening's we booked was for day after tomorrow, right. Sure was lucky! This is *it*, Gene.' George clenched his fist and smiled. 'I *got* him!'

Landau took off his bifocals and studied the producer. In a rare moment of disloyalty he imagined himself saying: 'You know, George, you're an asshole.' But instead he said, 'Now what do we do?'

'Get the critics in tonight an' tomorrow. I'm gonna phone Naff, you phone Fly. We gotta get to work . . .!'

48

Please God, let this be it! Let me have got the timing right!
It was 1.00 a.m. in the morning; the morning of the New York
opening night. The phone had just rung in George Gibson's
Dakota apartment, waking him up. The omens had been good
throughout the previous day. Lewis had, at frequent intervals,
reported the worsening of Ross's condition. Each time George
insisted he have no contact with Fly or any members of the
company. In particular, he said, 'Dee must not be told. It would
definitely jeopardise her performance.' Better, he said, to break the
news *gently* after the opening night.

Lewis had agreed.

George picked up the phone and heard Lewis's sombre voice.
'I'm sorry to wake you, George. Bad news, I'm afraid. Ross passed
away half-an-hour ago. It was very peaceful.'

'Ahh, Jesus,' Gibson said softly, sadly. 'That's terrible news.
Was anyone with him when he went?'

'Rosie and I, George . . . And the Mother Superior.'

'Did . . . did . . . he say anything?'

'Not really. He was semi-conscious most of the time. He did
keep repeating something about . . . well you, George. But we
couldn't follow what he was saying. I don't think it was "I love
you" though.' Lewis laughed sorrowfully.

'No, well he wouldn't.'

Lewis heard George sniffing. Was he crying?

'It's been pretty tough . . . for both of us, I guess . . .' George
said and loudly blew his nose.

'What are we going to do about telling the company, George?'
Lewis asked, his voice rising. 'I mean if the papers get a whiff of
this . . . The nuns who run this place are asking what we want to
do about a funeral. We must tell Ellen, his daughters . . .'

George sat up in bed, speaking fast. 'Listen carefully, Jaahn, first
you gotta calm down. You're in shock. Now this is very important.

288

You gotta get them to keep him there till *after* tonight's opening, okay! Under no circumstance must anyone getta smell of what's happened. It could kill us if they did. Yeah, well *kill* may be an unfortunate . . . er . . . Jaahn, listen to me! Whatever happens you gotta keep this quiet from the press, from the company, from his family, *everyone!*'

Lewis thought a while. 'Okay. I'll tell them we want to delay making any decisions till tomorrow. I'm going to catch the first shuttle back to Manhattan in the morn . . .'

'No! You gotta stay there with him! I'm gonna pay you $2000 to stay up there for the day . . . You're the only guy I trust . . .'

'Oh, George. I want to see the first night!'

'So see the second night! The first night's not so important . . .'

'But I've been looking forward to it for the last year . . .'

'I'm gonna give you a First Class flight back to England . . . Concorde . . . Anything! But please do me this one favour . . . Think what I done for you, huh? I paid you to write your goddamned book, fed you, *loved* you . . .'

In Washington, Lewis thought before replying. 'My book's going to make you immortal, George . . .'

'Yeah? Great . . . Now what d'you say?'

'Concorde? Okay, George . . . I'll stay 24 hours.'

'Now why don't you give me the name of that what d'you call it – hospice – you're at so I can call about covering expenses . . .'

'Look, I'm calling from the office and the Mother Superior's just walked in. Hold on . . . She wants to talk to you. Mother Superior, this is George Gibson.'

George listened as the phone was passed from Lewis to the nun.

'Mr Gibson?' Her voice was Irish; soft and gentle, like a spring shower. 'Such sad, sad news. But he was taken from us peacefully, in his sleep. He suffered no pain, thanks be to God. And now he's restin' in the arms of Jesus.'

'Thank you, Mother Superior. He was a fine man . . .'

'Yes, he was. He was blessed. We knew him little and late. But we can tell, Mr Gibson, oh yes!'

'Mother Superior, as Mr Lewis has or will explain, it's *very* important that you keep Mr Boardman's passing from the press *and* his friends. Okay? We gotta open a show on Broadway tonight an' we don't wanna upset everyone, do we . . .?'

'We must inform his next o'kin, Mr Gibson . . .'

'No! Please! Not for 24 hours. You gotta fund I can contribute to? He woulda wanted it, trust me.'

'It goes against the grain, Mr Gibson . . . but I guess we can make an exception jus' once. And we do have a little fund . . .,' the Mother Superior said cautiously.

'No *press*, okay?'

'We pride ourselves on our devotion *and* our discretion. The double D, Mr Gibson, the double D!'

'Well thank you,' George said, much relieved. 'You can expect my cheque. Can you pass me back to Mr Lewis an' thank you again!'

Lewis came back on the phone.

'She sure sounds a character,' George said drily.

'She's wonderful,' Lewis replied with enormous sincerity.

'You get some sleep, Jaahn. You sound exhausted. We'll talk tomorrow . . . I'll tell you how the show goes . . .'

'Sure, George. And thank you for being so understanding and generous. 'Night.'

' 'Night, Jaahn.'

George hung up and dialled Norman Naff.

The company had been called for a rehearsal at 10.00 a.m. – an unheard of event on the day of an opening night.

'Tell 'em it's for their own good!' George had said when Fly had reported the company unhappy at being called. 'They wanna hit, they gotta work for it! I'm not *happy*! Not happy with the bows, an' you an' Topp gotta get it right. Then we make this opening night like no other in Broadway's history. Okay?'

Fly had left the office with deep misgivings.

By 10.05 a.m., the actors were sitting sullenly in their dressing rooms. Five minutes later Charlie summoned them to the auditorium.

'Mr Gibson wants us to work on a special curtain call for this evening,' Fly explained. The actors stared back at him blankly. 'It's not going to be easy . . . Stan's gonna teach you a reprise of "Play for Love", then Tam's gonna move it, okay?'

There was some muttering amongst the actors. Tam and Stan looked at each other apprehensively. The atmosphere was tense with deep resentment. They were not going to be co-operative. One chorus member shouted out. 'What's all this about, Fly? We been futzing around ready to open for weeks. Now, at the last minute, you wanna throw *new* stuff at us? On opening night? It's totally crazy, man!!'

Another joined in. 'Yeah! Why don't we have a vote *not* to do this . . .'

But Fly was firm. 'No, guys, hear me out. Mr Gibson wants to make tonight real special. Give it pzzazz. Make it glitzy. Grab headlines. That's what he wants, guys.'

'What does Ross think about this?' Dee shouted from the back.

'We're only lookin' at the curtain call, Deedee,' Jerry said defensively, from several seats away.

'I haven't told Ross,' Fly said, somewhat uncomfortably. 'George is calling the shots. You know what he says – if the show's a smash – it's a pension . . .'

'Yeah, for him . . . not for us!' someone said and they all laughed.

'Let's start, for heavensakes!' Tam Topp said.

The ice was broken and they went to work.

Two hours later they took a coffee break. The stage management brought trays of coffee, bagels, cream cheese and pickles into the auditorium. 'Present from Mr Gibson, guys!' Charlie announced. 'Help yourselves! An' there's more for lunch.'

'Givin' away his pension!' someone shouted to general amusement.

'No,' Charlie said. 'Just no-one's to leave the building.'

It took a moment for the implication of this to sink in. Then it provoked uproar. Everyone was shouting at once.

'Are we being kept prisoner?' Ziggy asked on behalf of the company. Florence sat beside him firmly holding his hand.

Before Charlie could reply, Tara came into the auditorium from the dressing rooms saying: 'Hey, Charlie, what's going on? The phones are dead!'

'This is really too much,' Harry Whitney said. 'I'm expecting a call from my agent who's in town and coming to . . .'

Fly held his hand up for silence. 'Gene Landau is coming over to explain what's going on. Seems that the . . .'

That moment Gene Landau, the General Manager, strode purposefully in from the wings, interrupting Fly. He was flushed and seemed harassed.

'Right on cue, Mr Landau,' Fly said.

The actors, still snacking and grumbling, found places to sit and listen. Landau sat on the edge of the stage to address them.

'George asked me to come down. He'd'a come himself but, as you can imagine, he's gotta lot going on. But you're owed an explanation.'

'We sure are . . .,' someone from the chorus shouted.

'Hey guys, come on,' Jerry interrupted. 'I dunno what's cookin' but I agree with Fly, if it's George, it's gonna be good an' we gotta go along with it. Gene?'

Gene Landau spoke passionately. 'The media is out to get us. It's

291

as simple as that. What you have to understand is that there are guys out there who bear us ill will, an' I mean elements of the gutter press. They're out to kill us. They wanna ruin George an' the show. They've got their teeth into *something* and they're running with it. They been trying all morning to get through to the theatre, to my office, to George. They're besieging the stage door.'

Landau paused for breath and to judge how his words were going down.

'Why?' Florence asked. 'What've they got?'

Landau sighed. He seemed reluctant to go into any detail. 'Nothing specific. They're just running with a rumour. An' we wanna make sure they don't hassle you guys. You have enough to worry about. That's why we got you in quarantine. Plus, I gotta tell you, it does no harm to create a little mystery. The fact we've got you locked up has got the pack sniffing *even* more. Wait till you see the reaction tonight! It's gonna be something else.'

'Yeah, well I don't trust any of this,' Dee said. 'George is up to something an' I don't like it. One of us should try talk to Ross.'

'You do it, Dee,' Harry said.

'I can't . . .,' Dee said unhappily. 'But someone should . . . Fly?'

'No,' Gene Landau interjected quickly. 'That's not a good idea. George has been keeping him informed. He thinks Ross needs as much rest as that hospital can give him . . .'

'Oh yeah,' Dee said quickly. 'Well that's pretty damned ironic. Truth is, it's George who put him there in the first place.'

Everyone shifted uneasily in their seats. There were some things better left unsaid.

'Oh come on, Dee . . .,' Jerry said.

'It's the truth, Jerry! An' you know it! Those three weeks in Washington were hell. Hell for us an' hell for Ross. They almost killed him.'

'He drove *himself*, Dee,' Conrad said. 'He wanted to get the show right more than any of us.'

'It was a war, Con,' Dee shouted as the company listened rapt. 'George won and Ross lost. George drove Ross until he collapsed exhausted. George had no intention of hiring Marty Rice. He was just a stick he could use to beat Ross with. He consistently undermined him. You know I'm right. All of you.'

Her appeal to the company for support just left them embarrassed.

'You should give both of them more credit,' Conrad said quietly. 'This is our opening night, Dee, let bygones be bygones. Tonight should be a celebration.'

'Think who's leaking this stuff to the press,' Dee said, determined to have the last word. 'Norman and George! They play innocent but it's always Norman and George.'

'Give us a break, Dee,' Jerry said.

'Let's get back to work,' Fly said. 'Thanks for coming down, Gene.'

'Break over,' Charlie shouted. And under the tutelage of Tam and Stan, locked in and isolated from the outside world, the company went back to creating the new curtain call.

In the outside world, much was happening, wars were fought, old dogmas faded away, people starved and died. But New York was more interested in what was happening within the Metropolitan Grand Theater. It made the lunchtime news headlines.

Norman Naff had been on the phone non-stop to the TV, to the press. The word was out: George Gibson, Master Showman, had planned a spectacular opening for *Stars in His Eyes*. And more. Something was going to happen during the curtain call, Norman whispered down the phone. Something big, headline grabbing big. *Better be there!* The media tried calling the stage door for more information but the phone company intercepted and said no calls were being accepted. The box office phone lines were jammed with journalists wanting information. It was no good trying Gibson's office either. There, too, the lines were constantly busy, the door was locked.

During the early afternoon, a small group of inquisitive citizenry gathered. By 5.30 p.m. the crowds had grown so big, the theatre was cordoned off and protected by mounted police.

Naff enjoyed every minute. At 3.30 he had scheduled a press conference in a ballroom of the Metropolitan Grand Hotel. Before he went to it, George, who was personally conducting the campaign from Naff's office, rehearsed him carefully.

'We've made this into such a big deal, now we gotta deliver. C'mon, Norman, we gotta go over it one more time . . .'

Norman obediently repeated his speech. 'Ladies and gentlemen of the press, tonight is George Gibson's last Broadway opening. Broadway has been his home for over 50 years. In 1940 he opened his first show an' took Manhattan by storm. Five decades later he's presenting his last, *greatest* show . . .'

'Emphasise *greatest* even more . . .'

'Okay. GREATEST show . . .!' Norman waved his right hand to add further weight to the word. 'How's that?'

'Better . . .,' George said thoughtfully. 'Go on!'

'*Stars in His Eyes* is a characterful musical comedy. It's about people. About Galileo, a historical figure who *cared*. Cared like George Gibson cares.' Norman cleared his throat before continuing. 'Shows are made by the people for the people. They are a monument to toil. Like the building of the pyramids. Sometimes the stories behind the scenes, the personal stories, must be told. This show is one such. Therefore, ladies and gentlemen of the media, Mr Gibson invites you to attend the last five minutes of *Stars in His Eyes*. You will witness, he promises, an unforgettable moment in Broadway history. Watch out for George after the curtain calls!'

Norman was pleased. It felt good.

George was happy. 'That'll get 'em. Yeah the bit about the pyramids is a nice touch, Norman. S'good. Okay, go to it!' And he sent his press agent on his way.

Forty-five minutes before Stan Warburg raised his baton to begin the overture to *Stars in His Eyes* the tension, both sides of the curtain, was palpable. Out front, touts were selling first-night tickets for $250, a mark-up of $190. The ticket office was overwhelmed with angry people demanding seats they claimed had been reserved. But too many tickets had been promised to too many people.

The Front-of-House Manager was yelling down the phone to George, still holed up in Naff's office. 'What the hell d'you want me to do, Mr Gibson? It's a madhouse down here!'

'Keep stalling 'em!' George shouted back. 'Norman's getting the TV crews round to you NOW. I wann'as much chaos as possible, you understand? The lobby's gotta look like they're fighting to get in . . .'

'They *are* fighting to get in, Mr Gibson! As soon as the TV crews are gone, I'm gonna have to release the 100 seats, okay?'

'Sure,' said George, 'that's the idea . . .'

Meanwhile backstage, there was a frenzy of activity. The preparations for the performance went ahead as usual. The stage management checked the set ensuring the globes revolved smoothly, the floor was glazed and clean, the props were correctly positioned. Dressers raced between the wardrobe and the dressing rooms, hunting for lost belts, buttons, jewelry, fixing fallen hems. Charlie distributed first-night presents: flowers, telegrams, and cards. Fly, Tam, Stan and Karl-Heinz went from dressing room to dressing room offering best wishes and soothing words.

'Have you spoken to Ross?' Dee was sitting at the mirror, carefully applying her make-up. Her dressing room, pink and newly decorated, was overflowing with flowers. In a corner, her dresser sat, holding her Act One wig.

'No,' Fly said. 'I called the hospital yesterday and they told me he was no longer there . . .'

'What?' Dee said alarmed.

'He'd been moved to some special place coupla days ago. A clinic or something. They didn't know or wouldn't give me the number.'

'Did they say he was okay?' She looked at Fly in the mirror.

'They didn't say one way or another.'

'How about speaking to Lewis, or Rosie?'

'I tried Lewis's hotel, he'd checked out an' I only got Rosie's machine. She hasn't called back. It doesn't sound good, Dee.'

Dee was silent. 'D'you think they're trying to keep the bad news from us?' She watched Fly carefully to see if he knew more than he was telling.

'I honestly don't know,' he said and she believed him. 'Break a leg!'

'Sure,' she said summoning her wig.

49

It was a poor performance, one of the worst the cast had given in nine weeks of playing. The pre-show tension had not dissipated and no-one relaxed. Throughout the first act, for both the cast and audience, anticipation was high but little connected with the show. No-one could put their finger on it. They couldn't see, of course, they were mere pawns in a serious game. A game played for high stakes.

During the interval, rumours flew round the dressing rooms. One concerned the massive array of TV cameras at the back of the auditorium. George, they had been told, was going to make a speech after the new curtain call. The guess was that he was going to announce his retirement from show business. Was this so newsworthy? There was much heated discussion. Another buzz circulating backstage was of a positive review in the New York Times. Not a rave, but maybe just good enough to sell tickets. No-one knew where these reports originated, but they were recounted as fact. The rumours gave a lift to the company as they began the second half.

It was Florence who first whispered to Dee that Ross had been spotted sitting half way back in the stalls. The set had just transformed itself to the Piazza in Padua and the chorus, now playing townsfolk, strolled in front of a giant slide of the Basilica de Santo. Tara was about to sing 'Play for Love'. Dee's heart fluttered.

'I don't believe it . . .,' she whispered to Florence, who was playing a flower seller. 'Where?'

'Seven or eight rows back . . .,' Florence whispered. 'Il flore! Il flore!'

Dee who had nothing to say in the scene and was hidden in a crowd, anxiously peered into the darkened auditorium. *Could it be? Had he wanted to surprise them? Her? Was he in remission?* Dimly, she could see faces. But none that resembled his. *Wait a minute . . . Was this a joke?*

'I can't see him . . .,' she whispered to Florence as the movement of the crowd brought her close again.

'I haven't exactly seen him myself. But someone told Ziggy they thought someone had seen him,' Florence whispered back as Tara started to sing 'Play for Love'. She nodded towards the singer, 'This is where we lose the audience, right? Crap from here on.'

'Bitch!' Dee whispered, hurt to the core. As angry at herself for believing the impossible as she was at Florence for her insensitivity.

They were half-an-hour from the end.

The curtain fell. The show was over.

The audience responded politely; cheering and standing. But it was, and felt, forced. As the cast assembled in the wings for the new curtain call, George Gibson appeared, for the first time that night, mouthing thanks. Standing next to Charlie at the Stage Manager's desk, he muttered to himself, nervously folding and unfolding his hands, watching the newly rehearsed bows. The curtain fell again, this time, to increased, and warmer, applause.

'That's it! Thank God!' Sir Harry said out loud, setting off for his dressing room and a bottle or two of iced champagne. But he, and the cast were arrested by a commanding voice from beside Charlie.

'Do it again! All of it!'

'What?' Ziggy shouted.

'Go on! Go on!' George shouted, his voice rising above the dying applause. 'Do it again, that call! Charlie get the curtain up!'

'The applause is dying, Mr Gibson!'

'Do as I say!' George said sharply.

Charlie had no choice but to obey. He shouted to Stan over the intercom: 'Play! We're goin' again!' And Stan, equally having no choice, dutifully obliged. The orchestra picked up their instruments. The company, although embarrassed, gamely launched into the routine one more time.

The curtain fell again to small applause, and, as it fell, George strode purposefully on to the stage and asked the company to remain in position.

Charlie raised the curtain.

'Ladies and gentlemen, may I have your attention please,' George said, holding up his hands for silence. From his pocket he drew a white card. The audience, some of whom were already on their feet and heading for the exits, quickly settled and quietened down to listen. 'I hope you agree what you've seen tonight is a triumph!' He paused for the applause he wanted and was given. 'And for this triumph a number of people must be mentioned. Of course the whole company . . .' George led the applause. 'But also the designers of this fabulous set . . .' More applause. '. . . The brilliant Jerry Trimlock who wrote the wonderful lyrics and score . . . where are you Jerry? Come on up . . .'

Jerry, resplendent in a black silk suit, white tie, emerged from the auditorium and climbed on to the stage to take his bow. A huge round of applause greeted the black composer for whom this, his Broadway début night, had been a singular success. He acknowledged the applause before joining the line of cheering actors. Dee took his hand, squeezing it in friendship. They felt close again. The first time in months.

'And of course,' George went on, reading from the card in his hand, 'without a book writer there is no show. This is sometimes a forgotten figure, but not tonight. Ladies and gentlemen, Conrad Rothstein! Come up, Conrad . . .! Conrad came to the show late but made a valuable contribution . . . Come up, Tam Topp, choreographer . . .!'

Conrad and Tam arrived together. They took their applause then joined the line, shaking the hands of the leading actors, kissing the girls.

'. . . The great Stan Warburg and the wonderful orchestra, ladies and gentlemen!'

More acclaim.

Now George paused. His rhythm broken, deliberately and effectively. Then, in no more than a whisper, he said:

'Ladies and gentlemen, we must speak of one person who could not be with us here this evening . . .'

The audience became still. Behind him the cast waited expectantly.

'. . . A man with whom I have worked twice before and who I hold close to my heart. A very *special* person and a very, very dear *friend* of mine . . .'

Everyone in the Metropolitan Grand that night knew George was referring to Ross. Everyone knew Ross lay sick in a Washington hospital.

Dee's heart leapt. *He is here! George has pulled a wonderful surprise!*

'I mean, of course, that dazzling Broadway legend, Ross Boardman.'

There was thunderous applause. The whole theatre had erupted into a spontaneous show of affection; audience and actors alike. George held up his hand for silence.

Christ, he thought, *you have to be dead before they love you. Here's the zinger, you assholes . . .*

'Ladies and gentlemen, it is my sad duty to tell you that, at a very early hour of this morning, Ross Boardman died of incurable cancer in a Washington hospital!'

The whole theatre, it seemed, took a sharp intake of breath.

'Focus on Dee Gibson for Chrissakes!' Norman Naff shouted at the TV News crews ranged along the back of the auditorium. 'Get her reaction!'

At first she felt numb, plunged again into despair. Tonight she was on a roller coaster of high emotion. *Ross dead? No . . .! It's not possible! It's another of their jokes . . .?* It was only last night she had dreamt of him. He was holding her . . . making love . . . alive . . . real.

Then the hysteria began.

Jerry took her into his arms. The months of stress and turmoil had taken their toll. Too much had been suppressed. Now, recorded by the TV cameras from every network in the US, her emotion was cruelly exposed, expressed in the sobs and spasms that wracked her small frame. George, and with him the world, turned to look at Dee. She was three feet from him. *You gave me this idea, Dee. You'll turn it to your advantage, you said. Yeah, right! Well I have! See those cameras, Dee. They got it all. Every one of those tears you're spilling for that dead sonofabitch. Your blubbering in every home in America. If this doesn't send the box office through the roof . . .*

But the moment of triumph had gone, George wanted to finish. He turned front and held his arms up for silence. 'Thank you and goodnight!' *My night, my masterpiece!* He signalled Charlie to bring in the curtain.

Then the unexpected happened. The unplanned.

'You asshole! You dirty, rotten bastard!!' As Charlie reached for the button, Dee, recovering her composure, had angrily pushed Jerry away and taken a step towards George. The sound operator turned up her radio microphone enabling the audience to savour the moment. 'You killed him! Then you pull this stunt! You're despicable!'

And then Dee began to punch and kick. George protected himself as best as he could from the ferocious attack. The audience watched stunned. Was this planned? Was this rehearsed? Part of the entertainment? After watching for some moments, frozen in horror, several members of the company came to George's aid and hauled Dee away from him. Charlie pulled himself together, pushed the button and the curtain began to descend. Stan, who had impassively watched the scene from the pit as if this kind of thing was a regular occurrence, incongruously lifted his baton and the band started the jolly playout music.

'Charlie! Raise the curtain! Quick!' John Lewis had suddenly appeared at Charlie's side.

'What?' Charlie stared at the Englishman. *What now?*

'Do as I say! *Quickly!*' Lewis shouted in his ear.

Charlie was beyond rational thought. He would now do anything anyone said. He took the curtain back up. Stan taken by surprise stopped conducting and the orchestra fell silent. The audience who were up and noisily on their way out turned to look back at the stage. The TV cameras rolled again.

For a moment there was silence.

The cast stared at the audience, the audience stared back. No-one moved, no-one knew what was happening. George Gibson stood centre stage, rubbing his shin, badly bruised from one of Dee's kicks.

Then, in the silence, a sound from the wings. Softly, softly, then growing in volume . . .

Squeak, squeak, squeak.

George forgot his pain for a moment as he and the cast peered into the darkened wings trying to see the source of the sound effect.

Squeak, squeak, squeak.

A wheelchair appeared out of the gloom.

Slowly pushed by John Lewis and Rosie Lafontaine, it contained, wrapped in a blanket, a sick and jaundiced but very much alive, Ross Boardman.

The theatre went wild. The audience gasped, cheered, shouted. The cast cried out trying to make sense of what was happening. Dee rushed to Ross's side, tears of happiness streaming down her face. The sick man in the wheelchair received rapturous applause from everywhere. He managed a slight smile and wave.

John Lewis found himself next to George Gibson. The producer was rooted to his spot on the stage staring in disbelief.

'You planned *this*?' he said to Lewis.

'Ross planned it, George,' Lewis said. 'Rosie and I were mere stage managers. Well, apart from Rosie's brilliant performance as the Mother Superior on the phone . . . Remember?'

George remembered.

'We moved, him, you see, to Rosie's house in Georgetown . . . She looked after him, with a nurse.'

George watched Ross acknowledging the plaudits that echoed round and round the theatre. The audience were loving it. Yes, surely this *was* rehearsed, they thought. It was too good, too neat. Comedy and joy snatched from tragedy. A wonderful night!

Then George Gibson began to smile. '*He* planned it. Well, well, well. A coup de théâtre. A brilliant masterstroke. I should have expected nothing less . . .'

The smile turned into a laugh. A laugh of sheer joy.

Oh boy! Was this going to make headlines . . .!

This was pure musical comedy.

Everything was perfect.

METROPOLITAN GRAND THEATRE

Under the direction of
Hermann Gorelocke, Marvin Tyler

GEORGE GIBSON   DORIS STEIN
present

HAROLD WHITNEY

ZIGGY BRONOWSKY   TARA MARTIN

in

Stars in his Eyes

with **DEE BRUNEL**

ELIZABETH STROMAN   THOMAS PAUL

LEYDON JOHNSTONE   KEN IRVING

and **ADRIENNE FEUER**

Music and Lyrics by **JERRY TRIMLOCK**
Book by **CONRAD ROTHSTEIN**

Set and costume design	Lighting design by
KARL-HEINZ ZEISS	**SAM MOLE**

Musical Direction by	Orchestration and Dance Arrangements by
STAN WARBURG	**PETER LOMBARDY**

Sound design by	Press Representative	General Manager
SAM LEE	**NORMAN NAFF**	**GENE LANDAU**

Assistant Director	Casting	Production Stage Manager
FLY GOLD	**CATHY NEWMAN**	**CHARLIE BRODSKY**

Choreography by
TAM TOPP

Directed by

ROSS BOARDMAN